LETTERS
FROM
BERLIN

Also by Tania Blanchard

The Girl from Munich
Suitcase of Dreams
Echoes of War

LETTERS FROM BERLIN

**SIMON &
SCHUSTER**

London · New York · Sydney · Toronto · New Delhi

LETTERS FROM BERLIN
First published in Australia in 2020 by
Simon & Schuster (Australia) Pty Limited
Suite 19A, Level 1, Building C, 450 Miller Street, Cammeray, NSW 2062
This edition published in 2021

10 9 8 7 6 5 4 3 2

Sydney New York London Toronto New Delhi
Visit our website at www.simonandschuster.com.au

© Tania Blanchard 2020

 A catalogue record for this
book is available from the
National Library of Australia

ISBN: 9781760859831

Cover design: Christa Moffitt
Illustration: © Everett Collection/Shutterstock
Typeset by Midland Typesetters, Australia
Printed and bound in Australia by Griffin Press

 The paper this book is printed on is certified against the
Forest Stewardship Council® Standards. Griffin Press holds
chain of custody certification SGSHK-COC-005088. FSC®
promotes environmentally responsible, socially beneficial
and economically viable management of the world's forests

To my family. They are my everything.

'For one human being to love another; that is perhaps the most difficult of all our tasks, the ultimate, the last test and proof, the work for which all other work is but preparation.'
Letters to a Young Poet
Rainer Maria Rilke

Prologue

Sydney
June, 2019

The yellow envelope sat on Ingrid's lap like a lead weight.

'There's something I want to tell you.' The words left her mouth before she could recall them, and her daughter paused momentarily before she replaced the guitar on its stand. The words hung between them for a second.

'Is everything okay?' Natalie was a classically trained guitarist, but even the soothing strains of her playing hadn't eased Ingrid's taut nerves today.

Natalie joined her on the couch and the flash of concern across her face caused a wave of uncertainty to roll over Ingrid. Natalie was heavily pregnant with her first child. Maybe now wasn't the time to break the news, but her heart was pounding and she had to continue.

'I've received some news from Germany. From Berlin, to be exact.' Natalie's dark eyes darted to the thick envelope on Ingrid's lap. 'It's regarding the deceased estate of my mother . . . My biological mother. She died two years ago.'

'What?' The stunned expression on Natalie's face was hard to bear. 'Your biological mother? I don't understand.'

'I was adopted by Oma and Opa as a baby. I didn't find out until I was about twelve.' Ingrid quickly reached out to hold Natalie's hand. 'They didn't tell me much, except that they couldn't have children and were overjoyed when they got me. In the early fifties, when I was small, they decided to leave Germany for a better life in Australia. They never talked about the war and their life in Germany, not even to me.'

Natalie gripped her mother's hand tight and stared at her, glassy-eyed. 'Did . . . did Oma ever tell you anything about your birth mother?'

'She helped me look for her when I was twenty-one, but we found nothing. The adoption laws in East Germany didn't allow access to information about natural parents. And by the time the Berlin Wall came down I was married, and I had you. It didn't seem to matter anymore . . . so I gave up the search.'

'Why didn't you tell me?' Natalie let go of Ingrid's hand and sagged against the lounge, her face white and pasty.

'I'm sorry, but there was nothing to tell. It seemed kinder to everyone to just let it go. You had your grandparents, and they loved you so much.'

'But this changes everything.' Tears spilled from Natalie's eyes and she dashed them away with the back of her hand. 'I loved Oma and Opa but I've always yearned for extended family and neither you nor Dad could tell me much about my heritage. This might be our only chance to find out more. I want my child to know who she is . . .'

Ingrid felt her chest squeeze like a vice. She remembered when her mother had told her about the adoption – the bewilderment, confusion, betrayal – and the questions that came after. That single moment had shattered who she thought she was and it took years for her to put the pieces back together. Now she understood how her mother had felt telling her the truth and she wished she didn't have to put her own daughter through the same turbulent emotions, but maybe the parcel would offer some answers and together they could make sense of their heritage.

Ingrid leaned forward, reaching for her daughter's hand again. 'I know it's a shock, but I didn't want to keep it from you anymore. Especially with the baby coming.'

Natalie squeezed her hand and gave her a wobbly smile, making Ingrid sigh with relief.

'Do you want to know about your grandmother? The package is full of letters from her, maybe twenty or thirty.'

Ingrid wasn't even sure she wanted to open the letters. She had no idea what they contained – and she knew there would be no going back after reading them. She watched Natalie's face, a faraway expression in her dark eyes, an inheritance from an unknown ancestor. She had to do it for Natalie and her grandchild, if not for herself.

'I don't know how I feel, Mum,' Natalie said softly. 'I can only imagine what she went through to give you up, but she must have wanted you to know about her, writing all those letters.' She rubbed a protective hand over her swollen belly.

'It will never change how I love or remember Oma and Opa, but I think we owe it to her. I want to know our family story before the time comes to tell my own little one.'

Ingrid blinked away her own tears. 'I was hoping you'd say that. We'll do it together, one letter at a time.' With shaky hands she pulled out the papers inside the envelope. A diamond ring, worn with age, spilled out with the letters. She held it in her hand for a moment before placing it on the side table. Natalie leaned across and kissed her cheek and Ingrid swallowed hard. 'The solicitor has suggested we read her last letter first. I'll translate as I go.' Picking up the single sheet, she inspected the delicate, spidery script. This was her mother's handwriting. The breath caught in her throat as she experienced an immediate and physical connection, like a touch reaching out to her through time. It was unnerving and comforting at the same time.

'Twelfth of May, 2017,' she read.

To my dearest daughter,

My name is Susanna Christina Louise Göttmann. I am your birth mother. If you're reading this, then my years of searching are over. I've been looking for you for many years and now at ninety-three years of age, with time growing so short for me, I've appointed others to help find you.

I only ever saw you the once, when you were born. You were adopted not long after, by a good family, and I prayed they'd love you as much as I did. I tried to find you, but under the Soviet occupation, and later, when we became East Germany, no rights were granted to parents who had given their children up for adoption, no matter the circumstance. After the reunification, I hoped for another chance to find you but the new laws were just as restrictive. Still, I never stopped hoping that one day I would see you again.

I'd love nothing more than to look at you and hold you in my arms again, one last time before I die, but if it's not possible, I want you to know that I've never stopped loving you and thinking about you every day of my life. All I can do is tell you my story and hope you learn a little about me. And I wanted you to have something from me . . . this precious ring.

Ingrid put the letter down with trembling hands and picked up the ring, glancing up at Natalie, who was staring at her, wide-eyed.

'She kept searching for you all those years.'

Ingrid nodded, feeling dazed. She had always wondered whether she'd been unwanted and abandoned; it had left her feeling that perhaps she had never been good enough, despite the love her adoptive parents had lavished on her. She curled her fingers around the ring in her hand, her mother's ring. It was warm to the touch, as though her mother had slipped it off her own hand and placed it in hers. Ingrid didn't know much about her mother except that she'd never stopped searching and that proved she was determined, persistent and tenacious and that she loved her.

Natalie hugged her tight. 'She loved you and she wanted you. That must feel good to know.'

'It does,' Ingrid whispered. Relief coursed through her, and more tears sprang to her eyes, but there was something else too – excitement tingled in her blood. Ingrid wanted to know more. They had to keep reading.

She wiped her eyes and turned the page over. 'From the age of seven I grew up on a large estate outside Berlin, belonging to my godparents Georg and Elya Hecker,' Ingrid continued, her voice shaking.

Gut Birkenhof was three hundred hectares, about seven hundred and fifty acres, and named for the ancient birch trees rooted into the hillside near the manor house that many locals believed had guarded the estate for hundreds of years. It was beautiful, straight out of a fairy tale, nestled between the forest and the Dahme River, and a magical childhood home. After my parents, Walter Gottfried and Anna Christina, and my ten-year-old brother Friedrich were killed in an automobile accident in 1931 I went to live with Onkel Georg and Tante Elya there. Elya and my mother had been best friends since school, and she and Onkel Georg treated me like the daughter they'd never had. Their son Leo, who was the same age as Friedrich, took me under his wing and was kind to me, teaching me about the farm, how to milk a cow and look after the horses; practical skills that kept me busy and distracted me from my grief and made me feel part of the family.

Like my parents, Onkel Georg was from ancient landed nobility, a 'Junker', and a very successful timber merchant, but the estate also had a substantial dairy operation, providing milk and cheese for Berlin. It also produced crops like wheat and barley. It was the largest and most productive estate in the area and the main source of work for locals.

Those were carefree days. Then I learnt about Hitler in school and how the Jewish people were considered unclean, corrupt and enemies of our great nation. The Nuremberg Laws of 1935 decreed that those with four Jewish grandparents were considered full Jews and no longer eligible for German citizenship, and those with two Jewish grandparents were 'mischlinge', mixed race. It came as a great shock to me – my beloved Tante Elya was a Jew, originally from Russia, and this meant Leo was of mixed blood. One day, Onkel Georg brought Leo home from school after a terrible racial attack and our innocent childhood days were over.

The pogroms of Kristallnacht erupted three years later and war was waged on Germany's Jewish citizens. I realised my beloved homeland was no longer safe for anyone who did not conform to Nazi views and policies. The mood in Germany was dangerous, and dark times were ahead. Trouble was brewing for our family.

1

It was January 1943 and Tante Elya and I were finally alone in the parlour.

'We have to write that guest list if we're going to have your party in April,' she said, pouring a second cup of tea from the teapot, kept hot on top of the samovar. It was a beautiful vase-shaped silver urn, with a central pipe filled with slow burning pine-cones that heated the water used to dilute the tea. The pot was intricately decorated with brilliantly coloured enamel paint, like a delicate jewelled ornament. It had been her mother's and her grandmother's before her, and reminded Tante Elya of her childhood in Russia. Drinking tea in the afternoon was a daily ritual for her, carrying on the tradition from her family. When I was home I always enjoyed it with her, finding a few moments of peace in an otherwise busy day.

'I don't want a big party,' I said, mortified and excited at the same time. I had been away on my national service when

I turned eighteen so Tante Elya had insisted on celebrating my nineteenth birthday in style, despite the news filtering back about our army's terrible losses in Stalingrad on the Eastern Front and talk that the war was not going well for Germany. It was now grinding into its fourth year and all hope of a quick war had been lost. Even the relentless Nazi propaganda machine couldn't paper over the reality of Germans living daily with stiff rationing, continuous bombings, the loss of their menfolk and the bone-deep fear that the war would never end. It didn't feel right to be lavish, and yet it was exciting to be planning my first grown-up party.

'Don't be silly, *myshka*. We have to make the most of what we have and enjoy the company of those we love. None of us knows what tomorrow will bring.' Water flowed into the china cup from the tap on the bottom of the samovar, tempering the strength of the dark brew, and Tante Elya placed a sugar lump on my teaspoon before handing me the delicate cup and saucer. She was indulging me – with Onkel Georg's contacts, we could still get luxuries like tea and sugar, but Elya ensured we used them sparingly.

'Besides, you're the only girl I have and I want to spoil you a little.' She reached across the table and grasped my hand, her skin still warm from the teacup. 'Your mother would've done the same for you.'

My mother. The last memory I had of her was lying in a field of wildflowers – red poppies, and blue cornflowers the colour of her eyes vibrant against her long golden hair. She was laughing at my father chasing after my brother and me as we played hide and seek. Then I was beside her and my father was tickling my cheek with soft stalks of grass. We'd spent much of the summer in East Prussia, at our property in Marienwerder. We lived in Berlin, where my father had a thriving architectural firm, but we travelled to Marienwerder whenever we could. A little while later, I was lulled to sleep by the sound of the car as we travelled back to Berlin that night only to wake to screeching tyres, a loud bang and a feeling of weightlessness. There was nothing after that until I woke up in hospital to learn that my family was dead, taken from me in those few moments after our car had hit a lone deer on the dark road.

At the age of seven, I inherited everything – a more than tidy sum of money and the property that had been in my mother's family for generations. As my mother's parents had died long ago, and her brothers during the Great War, I was all that was left, but for a long time after I'd wished that they'd taken me with them.

'Come, she wouldn't want you to be sad,' whispered Tante Elya, her dark, expressive eyes misty. I knew she missed my mother terribly too – they'd been as close as sisters since Elya had arrived in Berlin as a young girl, having just lost her mother herself. Now she kissed my forehead and smoothed the long blonde hair from my face, her hands soft against my skin. 'Your parents would be so proud of you.'

All I could do was nod, quickly gazing out the large window that overlooked the garden, blanketed in white after the heavy snowfall the day before. The pale rays of afternoon sunshine sparkled on the icy branches of the trees, making me smile. It reminded me that even in the darkest moments, there was joy and hope to find. The death of my parents and brother had brought me my new family, and I loved them fiercely.

Tante Elya pushed a few sheets of writing paper across the table to me with a fountain pen on top. 'Think about who you want on your list while I jot down a few ideas for the menu. Then we can go through them together.'

I stared at the blank page while I sipped my tea through the sugar cube. My best friend Marika was the top of my list and I thought long and hard about which of my school and university friends I wanted to invite. I was in my very first semester at the Friedrich Wilhelm University in Berlin, studying history, languages and literature, and had made friends quickly with other students who lived on campus with me during the week. It was much like boarding school, which I'd attended since I was twelve, but although I enjoyed the excitement and bustle of the city, I was always glad to be home for the weekend. Despite the persistent bombing raids over Berlin, the city had sustained little damage and the rich cultural life of the capital was unchanged. Berliners were resilient and refused to let the war disrupt their daily lives.

But I had seen another side to the war. For six months before starting my studies, I'd served with the Red Cross at the Beelitz Sanatorium just outside of Berlin, nursing horrifically injured soldiers from the front line. I'd never forget the soldier, little more than a boy, who'd lost half his cheek and jaw from a bullet shot. He'd undergone multiple surgeries in an effort to save what was left of his face, but he still couldn't talk afterwards and had to be fed through a tube in his nose. I knew he'd never kiss his mother again. And the signs in Berlin banning Jewish people from cafes, restaurants and parks – from fully enjoying the city and all it had to offer – so common that they had become invisible to most, were constant reminders to me that the Third Reich was also at war with its own people.

When the Nazis came to power in 1933 Berlin had been home to the country's largest Jewish community – 160,000 strong, about a third of Germany's entire Jewish population. After the pogroms of Kristallnacht in 1938, tens of thousands of Jewish people fled Germany, migrating to places like France, the Netherlands, Palestine, England and North and South America. By 1941 over half had left Berlin and we'd heard it was similar right across Germany. Those who remained – including Onkel Tedi, one of Tante Elya's beloved brothers, and his family – were 'resettled' in ghettos in German-occupied Poland to the east: Warsaw, Lodz and Krakau to name a few.

No matter how benign the Nazi government was trying to make such a mass expulsion, it was clear Germany was getting rid of its remaining Jewish population any way it could.

Onkel Tedi had smuggled out letters telling us of the horrible and cramped conditions in Lodz. The ghetto was surrounded by barbed wire and brick walls, the gates and perimeters monitored by armed police. Prominent quarantine signs were meant to isolate them further from the rest of the city but became self-fulfilling prophesies when poor conditions within the ghettos led to outbreaks of disease. They were forced to work long hours in factories making military uniforms or electrical equipment, their only payment small rations of food barely enough to keep them alive. They were being left to die in their ghetto prisons.

At first we sent parcels of food, clothing, blankets and money to him, but when we heard they hadn't arrived, we used an intermediary to smuggle small items into the ghetto

5

from time to time. It was all we could do to help the deplorable situation he and his family were in.

Those few Jewish people who remained in Berlin – only a small fraction, perhaps 10,000 – were protected because of their level of skill and expertise, or, like Tante Elya and Leo, were protected by marriage. But I wondered for how much longer. I had begun to hate being in the city, at the heart of it all, the seat of the Nazi government, and I missed the river, the forests, the open spaces and tranquillity of life on the land, the welcoming smiles of the staff, the warm embraces from Tante Elya, Onkel Georg's updates about the farm, and Leo's dinner-time questions about my studies.

A knock at the door broke my reverie, and I looked up, startled, from the list of names I had begun writing down.

It was Ida, the housemaid. 'Frau Hecker, there's a letter for you.'

'Thank you, Ida,' said Tante Elya, frowning. It was strange to receive a letter so late in the day. 'I'll read it now while I finish my tea.' The maid walked smartly across the timber floor, her steps becoming muffled on the Persian rug under the table. Elya took the letter and dismissed Ida who already had her coat across her arm, ready to go home to the village for the evening.

'Do you want me to leave you in peace?' I asked, noticing Tante Elya's frown deepening as she turned the letter over in her hands.

'No, of course not,' she said as if coming out of a daze. 'Keep working on the guest list while I read this. Then we can get back to planning your big day.' She smiled, but I could see worry lurking in her eyes.

I set back to work as she asked, but my heart wasn't really in it. My gaze darted across to her as she began to read the letter, her steaming cup of tea forgotten on the table. Suddenly she put her hand to her mouth, as if to prevent a gasp escaping.

'Tante Elya, what's wrong?' I put the fountain pen down.

Her eyes were wide with fear as she glanced across to me. 'Susanna, can you tell Ida to find Onkel Georg and ask him to come to the parlour?'

'Ida's gone home, I think,' I said, already pushing my chair back to stand. 'I'll go and find him.'

'Go quickly, I have to speak with him urgently.'

I paused for a moment, hugging her impulsively, her small frame trembling, before I rushed out the door. Whatever was in that letter had shaken her.

Although she was petite, Tante Elya commanded authority wherever she went. She had an inner strength, a core of steel that I suspected she developed when her family had fled Russia after the 1905 pogroms in Kiev when she was the same age I had been when I lost my family. She had told Leo and me stories of being separated from her mother and brothers as they tried to flee after their house was attacked, then looted and vandalised. She was chased down the alleyways of the city by Cossacks on horseback, with the sounds of screams in her ears. She was finally reunited with her father, who had watched, horrified, as a mob destroyed his office, before racing away to warn his family of the impending danger. Only later did she learn that her mother had been crushed, trampled by a soldier's horse in the mayhem, while trying to escape the rioting crowd. Mercifully her brothers were swept away to safety by the sea of terrified people.

The experience had left an indelible mark on Elya. Her father later moved them west to Berlin, a progressive city where they could live in safety and he could set up his legal practice once again. He was determined to embrace German ways and secure a future for his children among educated Christian society where their Jewish heritage could pose no danger to them. Elya was sent to an expensive school where my mother took her under her wing. My mother was fascinated by Elya's Russian background and ancestry and was fiercely protective of her, teaching her to modulate her accent so that she spoke like a Berliner, and introducing her to the world of the German aristocracy. This was how Elya met Onkel Georg, whose family were old friends of my mother's family.

Tante Elya always told us that Gut Birkenhof had felt like home to her – here, she could be herself, a strange mixture of Russian, Jew and German. It was a place where she could raise her own family in safety, surrounded by the close-knit community. She was always the first one to help those in need and stand up for people who had been treated unfairly. The loss of her own mother had made her compassionate and kind, and when my mother died, she made every effort to ensure I didn't suffer alone. But whatever was in the letter had disturbed this strong, indomitable woman.

Onkel Georg was in his study. He didn't utter a word when I told him what had happened, only pressed his lips tightly together, pushed his chair back from the large walnut desk and walked quickly to the parlour, where he closed the door firmly behind him.

I knew better than to ask questions. Although we out-wardly appeared a normal German family, we lived in constant uncertainty, at the whim of changing Nazi sympathies and policy. Onkel Georg's connections and status had kept Tante Elya's name off the register of the Reich Association of Jews, but we were never sure it was enough to keep her safe. He had close connections to powerful Nazis due to his family's noble lineage and business dealings, securing large long-term contracts with the Reichspost, Germany's postal system, and the Reichsbahn, the national railways, for timber, milk and agricultural produce. More importantly, Onkel Georg had trusted contacts in the Ministry of the Interior, which held all registrations and the 1939 census cards on Jewish heritage, and they had kept Tante Elya's details buried there. But we were well aware that the Reich Main Security Office, the RSHA, which oversaw the deportations of Jewish people from Germany with the might of the Gestapo behind it, could retrieve personal information at any time. We also lived with the constant fear that the Reich would invalidate marriages between German citizens and Jewish people.

I pressed my ear to the door. I had to know what was happening.

'This letter just came,' I heard Tante Elya say. 'It's finally happened.' Her voice broke. 'I've been registered.'

'Let me see.' There was silence for a heartbeat or two, then the sound of Onkel Georg pacing around the room. 'After everything we've done . . . It must be Kaltenbrunner, the new chief of the RSHA. He's SS, supported by Himmler, and it's no secret he's a fanatical anti-Semite.' I could hear the grim horror in Onkel Georg's voice. 'If he gets hold of those census documents.'

'There's only so much your contacts can do. Even those highly placed Nazi officials can't help us anymore.' Tante Elya's voice shook.

Onkel Georg had cultivated relationships within the upper ranks of the government and Wehrmacht, the German armed forces. I'd seen him give visiting officials gifts, and Leo had told me he also sent them baskets of luxury items from across Europe, bottles of cognac, or fresh meat, cheese and vegetables from our farm. He'd even taken to leasing out land and holiday cottages along the river to those wanting a more genteel lifestyle. All to remain a friend and asset to those who wielded power.

I had no illusions about what Onkel Georg was doing. Social connections and the power that came with the upper class meant everything to the Nazis and so far he'd been able to keep Tante Elya and Leo safe. Gut Birkenhof ensured the local economy flourished, employing over half the village at one time or another. And the longer the war went on, the more valuable raw materials and food products became. The government couldn't afford to lose such a reliable supply. All this had kept Tante Elya protected and off the official register, even though her Jewish heritage was known to some of Onkel Georg's Nazi associates. It had kept me safe too – we'd heard stories of Aryan children being taken away from adoptive or even step-parents who were found to be Jewish. And it had protected Onkel Georg from the harassment meted out to Aryans married to Jewish people by Nazis and officials as well as local people, but I could only imagine what his efforts had cost him both financially and personally – he hated the Nazis as much as Leo and I did.

'I had a deal with them.' I heard Onkel Georg slam the table in frustration and anger.

'I know, and it's kept us safe this long,' Tante Elya said, 'but it's official now. My worry is for you and Leopold. You'll be reviled as a traitor to Germany, and Leo will be recognised as a . . . *mischling.*' I heard the catch in her voice. It was a terrible word meaning mongrel or half-breed – like an animal.

'But you're both still legally protected. The register will reflect that you're in a lawful mixed marriage. Nothing will change.' Onkel Georg could be stubborn at the best of times, but what if he was wrong?

'Listen to me, Georg. Everything's changed. My identity card will be stamped with a "J" and I can't go out now without wearing the Star of David. Everyone will know what I am.' Her voice was shaky. 'And what that now makes you and Leopold.'

'Not in the village. Everyone knows and loves us. We're family.'

'People already talk about why I have certain privileges, why I haven't been deported, even why you haven't divorced me. When it becomes public knowledge there'll be no mercy from them.'

'But they've known you for well over twenty years. You're the heart of this community.' Onkel Georg's outrage told me volumes. He knew what Tante Elya was saying was true.

'It doesn't matter. The resentment's already there. Some of them are sick of seeing Nazis flocking to our door and spending extravagant weekends on the river. It makes them nervous. With the Gestapo breathing down their necks, now I'll have no freedom. If I put a foot wrong, they'll make sure I get what they think I deserve.' Tante Elya's voice cracked.

It was no wonder. I knew she still had nightmares about Kristallnacht, when Onkel Tedi's Berlin law practice had been set alight and his son Felix sent to Sachsenhausen, one of the earliest camps set up by the Nazis to hold political prisoners and dissidents.

'They'll come near you over my dead body.' The anguish and aggression in Onkel Georg's voice made my heart clench in fear. I swayed for a moment, clutching at the door frame, then swallowed and brought myself back under control. I had to hear the rest.

'We have to get out while there's still a chance,' said Onkel Georg.

'What chance? Nobody wanted us four years ago when the quotas were tightened. Now emigration's forbidden to Jewish people, we'll never get a visa.'

'I'll try again. There must be a way. I'll go to the American Embassy and speak to your brother in New York. I'll visit all the consulates if I have to. Even the black market. Somebody will take us.'

My body shook at the desperation in his voice.

I was fifteen when they'd tried to sell the estate and leave for America. But Reich officials had denied our request, ironically because of the government contracts that protected our family. Onkel Georg had still been determined to escape somehow, even leaving the estate behind, but the mass exodus of Jewish people out of Germany meant countries like the United States had filled their quotas years in advance and some countries had closed their doors altogether. Tante Elya's youngest brother and his family had managed to emigrate, but we had missed out. There was nowhere for us to go.

Since then, Leo's life had become more restrictive. He had wanted to study agriculture, manage the estate and follow in his father's footsteps but proof of pedigree, including birth and marriage certificates of parents and grandparents, was required for university applications and Leo was denied entry into agricultural college. Acceptance was at the discretion of the university rectors and many did not want *mischlinge* at their institution. Even Onkel Georg's appeals to his Nazi contacts came to nothing.

Like all young men his age, Leo couldn't wait to serve his country and fulfil his duty as a patriotic German, but when he came of age for national labour service and conscription into the Wehrmacht, the law had just been revised to exclude half Jews from the military. When all his friends and our neighbours were called up, and we heard reports of injury on the front lines, the shame he carried only grew. Leo felt useless, but he'd encouraged me to serve with the Red Cross at Beelitz to complete my own Reich Labour Service, a duty all young citizens were obliged to carry out. I couldn't stand by and do nothing, and perhaps it would even help our family by showing I was a patriotic German.

Now everything seemed more precarious and the danger was even closer to home.

I didn't need to hear any more. I stumbled down the corridor, desperate for fresh air, thoughts jumbling in my mind. I felt so helpless, but I couldn't bear the thought of those I loved being persecuted, ripped away to the squalid ghetto prisons.

I found Leo at the stables, silhouetted against the puddle of yellow light from the open door, which cast a cheery glow into the dull and fading afternoon.

'I'll talk to you tomorrow,' I heard him say to a stablehand, his voice muffled by the heaviness in the air. It had begun snowing again, the sky low and leaden, as though threatening to suffocate us.

'Leo,' I called out, the sound falling flat, cocooned by the drifts of powdery white.

'What are you doing out here, Susie? It's too cold. Come on, let's go inside.' He reached my side and threaded his arm through mine. 'Aren't you supposed to be organising your party with Mutti?' I leaned against him, as much for warmth as for support. In my haste I'd forgotten my coat and gloves and my hands were nearly numb with cold.

'We were,' I murmured. 'But then . . .' I began to shiver, with cold and fear.

'Tell me inside.' He propelled me forward, along the path back to the house, and refused to listen to a word until he had me rugged up in a blanket at the kitchen table, the rare indulgence of a hot chocolate in my hands.

The staff had retired for the evening and it was Frau Kraus's night off. She was the cook and head of the household staff. She had been with Onkel Georg and Tante Elya for decades, but rather than live on the estate after the Great War when she was widowed, she'd insisted on remaining in her own home in the village. After finding love again and remarrying, she now shared her home with Hans, our head forester. She'd left dinner gently simmering on the stove and the blast of warmth and smells of meaty broth and onions made me feel a little safer, like being wrapped in a mother's comforting embrace.

I glanced at Leo sitting across from me, waiting for me to tell him what was wrong. He was only a few years older than me, but it still came as a shock to realise how he'd changed in the last few years. The last vestiges of childhood had left him and he was a man now, although his dark wavy hair still fell into his eyes as it had always done. He was straight-backed, tall and athletic like his father, and strong from the work on the estate – felling trees, chopping wood, baling hay, fixing machinery or carting milk. We'd lost some workers over the last year to old age, infirmity and the Wehrmacht, so Leo was determined to make himself as useful as possible. His frustration at not being eligible for national service or the army made him work harder than ever.

'So are you going to tell me what's bothering you? I have all night,' he said, folding his arms and leaning back in his chair.

I took a deep breath and told him everything I'd heard.

'I'm scared, Leo,' I whispered when I had finished. 'If anything happened to your mother or you . . .' I realised I was still cradling the warm cup, half full, in my hands and I put it on the table, unable to finish.

'Don't worry, Susie. Vati will do everything to keep Mutti safe, and I'm in no danger.' He reached across the table and squeezed my hand. 'The law still protects her while she's married to Vati. I'm sure it's all just a formality and life will go on the same as it always has.'

I nodded. I felt relieved that I'd shared my concerns with him but I could see the worry in his eyes even as he tried to reassure me. Onkel Georg would see to their protection as he always had, and Leo would make sure his father's plans were carried out, but this was serious. Our world had shifted abruptly on its axis with the arrival of that letter. But at least we had each other to lean on, just as we had through all the previous crises our family had endured. 'I should get dinner. It's the last thing your mother will feel like doing right now.' I stood from the table and turned towards the stove. Leo's chair scraped across the floor as I ladled soup into a waiting tureen.

'They'll need us both tonight,' he said. 'Here, let me help.'

I nodded, feeling tears well in my eyes.

'It will be fine.' Leo put his arms around me and kissed the top of my head. He smelled of wood chips and the clean sweat of hard work and I hugged him fiercely, as though it would keep him safe forever. I wondered if he could still read my thoughts as he had when we were younger. He stroked my cheek then drew away gently, and heat flushed my cheeks. 'I'll take the soup up for you, it's heavy,' he said, unable to look me in the eye.

'I'll be there in a minute,' I muttered, thrusting the tureen into his hands.

'Don't be long,' he called over his shoulder as he left the kitchen.

I stared after him for a moment and realised that I was shaking. The events of the afternoon had been a terrible shock. The future was unpredictable and uncertain, but a future without Leo was unthinkable.

Leo meant everything to me. He was the love of my life.

2

After what had been a sombre evening, I was glad to be alone in my bedroom that night. Tante Elya and Onkel Georg had sat pale-faced and quiet over dinner and we'd barely touched our food. Little had been mentioned about the registration. I understood that it was still too much of a shock to talk about just yet, but nobody really knew what to say to ease the tension in the room. Only Leo thought to play his mother's favourite songs on the balalaika after dinner, bringing a smile to her face.

Still humming a Russian folk tune, I sat at my dressing table and stared into the mirror as I brushed my long fair hair to a gleam before bed. I didn't want to think about the implications of Tante Elya's letter, it was too frightening. I touched my cheek where Leo's hand had stroked me in the kitchen, even now it tingled with the memory. There was something between us that couldn't be denied, and yet he kept pushing me away.

In the beginning, it was Leo who made the pain of losing my family bearable. Despite the love that Tante Elya lavished upon me and the kind words from Onkel Georg, some days I still felt so alone in the world.

I'd been crying one day, a few months after arriving at Gut Birkenhof. I missed my mother so much, her arms encircling me when I snuggled on her soft lap, the way she'd whisper *Susielein* to me, her cheek warm against my face, the smell of roses, her favourite perfume. I'd slipped away after luncheon, barely eating anything, and wandered aimlessly around the garden and farm sheds. Eventually I'd curled up next to a stack of hay in the barn, the breeze and warm sunshine drying the tears on my face and lulling me into an exhausted doze.

'Susie.' I'd roused at the sound of my name. Friedrich and Leo were the only ones who called me that. I'd half expected Friedrich to be there, grinning at some mischief he'd just created and ready to involve me in his elaborate plan, but it was Leo, his arm outstretched towards me. 'I made something for you,' he'd said shyly.

I reached up and took the object from his hand, staring at it for a moment.

'It's a horse. I carved it from wood . . . I thought it might cheer you up.'

I nodded, touched by his gift and unable to speak. I wondered if he knew I loved horses, just like my mother had. I stroked the small wooden figure, smooth from careful sanding. I'd seen him practising his carving and I knew how much effort he'd gone to for me.

'Do you like strawberries?'

I nodded again, still staring at the carving.

'There's a meadow where the best strawberries grow. Come on, I'll take you there. They're sweet and ripe. You can fill your belly.'

I looked up at him, expecting to see the concern and sympathy that was on everyone else's face, but I saw only hope that I'd join him in his adventure. 'All right,' I whispered.

'Don't tell Mutti,' he said seriously. 'She'll skin both of us if she thinks we won't eat our dinner.' Then he'd smiled cheekily and held out his hand.

His fingers around mine were warm and reassuring. 'Thank you for the horse. It's beautiful.' His face had lit up, making me smile. 'I like horses.'

'Well, I'll show you how to brush them and feed them if you like, and when you're ready, I'll teach you to ride.' The eagerness on his thin ten-year-old face, dark wavy hair falling across his eyes, had made me wonder if he was lonely too.

I'd nodded, overcome with gratitude. 'I'd like that.' Maybe I wasn't so alone after all.

I kept that carved horse with me for months, often in a pocket where I could touch its smooth surface when I was feeling sad. It followed me to boarding school and Beelitz. And the strawberry patch was just the start. Leo showed me all the special places on the estate. During the summers we ran wild, splashing about in the shallow bend of the river where the sandy beach beckoned us to lie and sun ourselves. As I got older, we swam in the deeper waters and took the little boat out fishing, gliding across the smooth surface of the river for hours. While we were young, we hiked the cool, dark depths of the forest with Onkel Georg and his good friend Onkel Julius. He was part of the family and a regular visitor to Gut Birkenhof, after spending much of his childhood on the estate with Onkel Georg. When we knew the forest trails like the back of our hand, we'd go out on our own for hours with bread, cheese and meat packed in bags on our backs. Some days we came home with our bags full of plump brown pine mushrooms. Leo taught me to hunt – hare and pheasant at first and then deer – and he always impressed on me the importance of a clean, quick kill and respect for the animal.

But it was the tiny wooden cabin in the forest that meant the most to us.

The first time Leo showed it to me I was eleven years old. 'This is my special place,' he'd said on the edge of the clearing, pine forest surrounding us in all directions. 'It's where I come when everything gets too much.'

'Can I come here too?' I'd asked anxiously.

'Does everything get too much for you sometimes, Nightingale?' he'd asked, his big brown eyes soft with compassion. He'd given me the pet name the first time he'd taken me birdwatching, when I'd been enthralled by the exquisite song of the small brown bird.

I'd nodded solemnly. 'Sometimes I still have bad dreams about Mutti, Vati and Friedrich.'

Leo had crouched down beside me on the carpet of pine needles. 'It can be your special place too. It will be our secret.' I'd smiled at that.

Later that year, it became a place of refuge. One day Onkel Georg had brought Leo home from boarding school and he'd disappeared into the forest. I knew where he'd be.

'Leo!' I'd yelled outside the cabin. There'd been no reply, just the wind whistling through the trees. I opened the door slowly and peered into the gloom, but found nothing. Then I heard the sound of muffled crying. Pulling the torch out of my pocket, I trained the beam of light to the corner of the cabin. There was Leo curled up into a ball.

I knelt beside him and shook him gently. 'Leo, what's the matter? What's happened?'

'Go away,' he whispered in an anguished voice. 'Leave me here. I want to die.' I stared at him, shocked. Then I wrapped my arms about him.

'You're not going to die,' I said. 'I won't let you.'

He lifted his head after a while and struggled upright so we were sitting side by side on the dusty wooden floor.

'Tell me what happened.'

'I couldn't stand it anymore. My new teacher was explaining the differences between the Jewish race and the Aryans, as if anyone can really tell. Jewish people are banned from the school now, but one of my best friends, Fritz, pointed to me and said that I looked like a Jew. I told him that my mother was Jewish, and so was I and proud of it, but the teacher said that I was *mischling*, only half Jew. After class, Fritz called me a mongrel and wiped his hands on his pants in disgust because he'd touched me. My other friends told me to stay away and called me names that I won't repeat. It was my fault. I threw the first punch . . . but they're my best friends.' His face crumpled then and he sobbed until he was spent.

'You don't need them, Leo,' I'd whispered, taking hold of his cold hand. 'I still love you, and I always will.' He'd kissed the top of my head and we'd sat there until the sun sank behind the trees.

Now, my face flushed at the memory of what had happened at the cabin eighteen months earlier, the last summer I'd spent at home. Leo and I had been hunting and were caught unexpectedly in a storm moving quickly across the mountain range. Rather than push on toward home in the driving rain and high winds, we'd decided to wait it out in the cabin, but the wild weather continued to rage into the night.

'Your parents will be worried,' I said, after laying our belongings and outer clothing out to dry. I shivered in my wet underwear, pulling the blanket from the small camp bed further around my shoulders.

'There's nothing we can do about it.' Leo's chest was bare, his skin glowing in the light of the fire, chest hairs ruddy against the flames and shoulders broader than I'd realised. The muscles of his upper arm bulged as he turned the makeshift spit. I couldn't look away. I'd been feeling things change between us over the summer and this was confirmation that I was attracted to him. 'It's stupidity to travel back in the dark with the risk of trees coming down . . . They'll know it's safer if we take shelter until morning.'

Outside the wind was howling and heavy rain pelted the cabin without break. The temperature was dropping quickly, but the fire was roaring and the smell of roasting hare was comforting.

My stomach grumbled loudly. It had been a long time since we'd eaten.

'You're hungry,' said Leo. He cut away a chunk of meat with his knife and presented it to me on the tip of his blade. 'Careful, it's hot.'

The blanket slipped to my waist as I reached for the meat. It burned my fingers, but I didn't care. It smelt too good. Juice dribbled down my fingers and my chin as I crammed the succulent morsel in my mouth. 'It's delicious.'

'You're messy, Nightingale,' he said softly. He wiped the juice from my chin with his thumb and I watched in fascination as he sucked it clean. Suddenly I was no longer hungry. Leo was looking back at me with the same intensity that I was feeling and my stomach lurched. I didn't know what to do. All I knew was that I didn't want the moment to end.

He reached across and caressed my arm as he picked up the edge of my blanket. 'Aren't you cold?'

I shook my head. His dark eyes were fixed on my mouth and he was so close. I held my breath as I waited for him to kiss me. I had never wanted anything more.

He leaned in and his lips touched mine, soft and warm. My hands rested against his broad chest and slid around his neck as the kiss deepened. I was hardly aware that my blanket had slipped to the floor. He gathered me into his arms, pulling me against the hard planes of his body.

He kissed me again with such passion I thought I'd explode, but then he broke away. 'We can't,' he said, his face contorted with terrible conflict.

I shook my head, not wanting to stop. I reached for him again but he took me by the shoulders, holding me at arm's length.

'The law forbids us to be together: a *mischling* and an Aryan. If we take this any further, I can't guarantee that either of us will be able to stop. One day our feelings will betray us and we'll be discovered.'

'We can be careful,' I said desperately. I knew the laws as well as he did but I didn't want to believe that they applied to us, especially on the estate where we were surrounded by people who would support us.

He lifted the blanket gently around my shoulders. 'It takes only one slip and one person to report us.'

'But you're all that I want.'

Leo took my hand and brought it to his lips. 'I won't deny my feelings for you, Susie, but I can't place you in harm's way.'

I shook my head again in irritation, even though my heart flipped to hear those words. 'But there must be some way.'

'We'd be placing Mutti at greater risk, after everything Vati's done to keep her safe.'

It was a chilling thought and I pulled the blanket around me tighter. 'I'd never forgive myself if anything happened to her or to you.'

'While the Nazis are in power, it's not possible for us. In another time or place, I'd be a happy man, but as it is . . .' His eyes were misty.

I threw my arms around him and hugged him tight. 'Nothing's impossible. One day we'll be together, I know it.'

'There's always hope.' He drew away. 'I'd better get this off before it burns,' he said, glancing at the meat on the fire.

Holding the blanket firmly at my throat once more, I watched him lift the roasted hare from the flames and carefully slice the meat with his knife, but his gaze kept slipping back to me. Whenever our eyes met, I could see the yearning there and knew that what we both were feeling was real. But it didn't change the fact that we had to deny it all for the sake of our family. It was a bitter pill to swallow. We passed the rest of the night pretending that nothing had changed.

But everything changed that night. Leo had kept his distance from me ever since, but it hadn't stopped my feelings for him from growing stronger. And from the way he'd looked at me in the kitchen, I knew that his had too. We loved each other and were meant to be together. I knew why Leo stayed away, but I wasn't going to have the Nazis tell me who I could and couldn't love.

After a week of exams in early March, Marika and I were walking through the university with some of the other girls from the dormitory where we all stayed during the week. We heard the rumble of army trucks along the Unter den Linden, the main avenue that ran east to west through Berlin.

'It's the last of the Jews,' whispered one of the other girls. 'Anyone with a Star of David is being picked up and transported across Berlin to collection points and transferred to trains, heading east most likely.'

I shot Marika a worried look. We had known each other since boarding school and she knew what had happened to Onkel Tedi. It made her furious when the Nazi propaganda machine whitewashed the removal of thousands of Jewish people from Berlin as 'deportation and resettlement'. It was no secret that the Führer wanted all Jewish people out of Germany, but we'd heard whispers over the past months that Jewish people were being deported directly to new eastern camps like Auschwitz rather than the eastern ghettos. It didn't take much imagination to know that conditions in those camps would be far worse than the ghettos.

In his most recent letter to Tante Elya, Onkel Tedi had said thousands of Jewish people from the Lodz ghetto were 'resettled' even further east, but, alarmingly, only days after their departure these people's belongings were strangely returned. The news was hard to believe, especially for people like Marika whose German ancestry kept them far removed from the dark side of the Nazi regime. But, like me, she had to wonder about the truth when Tedi wrote that he believed the Jewish people in Lodz had been sent to a nearby camp at Chelmno and killed. Nazi propaganda had been telling German citizens for years that the Jewish people deserved to be eliminated, but for the regime to actually kill thousands of innocent people was a horrifying thought. If it was true, the Nazis had descended to new depths of evil. What would I do if Tante Elya was sent away?

'I've heard that some have been taken to the Jewish Welfare Centre,' the girl continued, 'supposedly for investigation. They're being held there and nobody knows why.'

'Why have they been separated?' asked Marika, frowning.

'Apparently they're the ones married to Aryans – and *mischlinge* too,' the girl said, dropping her voice even further. The breath caught in my throat at that. 'It's not legal to detain them and yet . . .' She placed her hand on Marika's shoulder and began to whisper confidentially. 'But I've heard the most fantastical thing. Apparently families are gathering outside the building in Rosenstrasse in silent protest. Women with their children, asking why their husbands are being held. Even the bombing the other night didn't deter them.

I've never heard anything like it before. I don't know if they're foolhardy or courageous.' She shook her head in wonder. 'I don't think it will end well.'

'I have to find out what's going on,' I said, starting to walk ahead, hardly able to get the words out of my mouth.

'No,' said Marika as she caught up with me and drew me away from the others, 'stay here. It's too dangerous.' Marika knew me better than anyone, except perhaps for Leo and Tante Elya.

'What if they come for my aunt and Leo next?'

'They're safe at Gut Birkenhof.'

I shook my head. 'They're safe now but they might not be for much longer. I have to know what's happening.'

'Please don't, Susie. It's too risky.'

I couldn't ignore the plea in her green eyes, and I allowed her to take my arm and lead me back to our room to study for our final exam the following day.

But I couldn't sleep that night, thinking about the families incarcerated at Rosenstrasse. I didn't know what was keeping Tante Elya and Leo safe for now – the fact they were outside of Berlin? Onkel Georg's carefully nurtured relationships? I kept imagining how I'd feel if they were the ones who'd been taken away. The thought tortured me, making me toss and turn until the early hours of the morning. An exam felt trivial compared to the plight of those people who'd been taken. Without waking Marika, I shrugged into my thick woollen overcoat, left the dormitory and made my way out into the bitter cold of the early morning.

I was shocked at the scene on Rosenstrasse. Hundreds of women in overcoats, hats and gloves were gathered outside the Jewish Community Centre, standing defiantly shoulder to shoulder. Berlin's police waited warily on the periphery of the crowd for any signs of trouble. Outside the entrance and along the street were the menacing figures of grim SS guards with their deadly weapons.

The women near me smiled a greeting as I joined their ranks. I searched for familiar faces – they were all strangers to me and yet I felt welcomed, embraced by the warmth of their common goal. Despite the fear that crawled at the base of my spine at the sight of so many armed men ready to suppress us, I couldn't help but feel solidarity with these women attempting to protect their own, and a wave of defiance rushed through me. Stamping my feet against the frozen ground, I overheard snippets of conversation spoken quietly by those around me. The detainees were mostly the Jewish husbands of Aryan Germans and sons of such marriages. My stomach twisted in knots, Leo's face never leaving my mind. I couldn't go. It could be my family in there next time.

From time to time the guards stepped forward to shout at us.

'Go home,' yelled one of the men, pointing his gun threateningly at the sea of defenceless and peaceful women. I glanced at those around me. Fear was etched into their faces but nobody moved.

'Disperse now or suffer the consequences,' shouted another SS soldier. The crowd watched him dispassionately, although I felt sure every person present wondered how long they could resist – and how long until the shooting would start.

At midday I saw Marika's copper head push through the crowd. 'Susie! I knew I'd find you here,' she said breathlessly when she reached my side.

'I didn't want to worry you,' I said with a grimace, feeling guilty now for leaving without telling her.

'I know what you're like. When I woke and you were gone, I suspected as much.' She thrust a thermos and a small string bag into my hands. 'I guess you haven't eaten?' I shook my head. 'Well, you need to keep up your strength if you're going to stand here all day.'

I poured a little of the hot liquid into the cup, thawing my numb fingers, and sipped slowly, the rising steam warming my face. 'Oh, that's bliss,' I said. Then I opened the package in the bag – she'd brought bread and hunks of cheese. I tore off a piece of bread and crumbled the cheese onto it and handed it to the woman next to me. 'Here, you must be famished.' She nodded and quickly took the bread and cheese, murmuring her thanks. We stood in companionable silence waiting for something to happen as we shared the food and the hot tea between us.

The guards began to move, mounting machine guns on the street in front of their posts. I could feel a hum of tension rush through the crowd like a shock of electricity. Our food and thermos were forgotten. My mouth felt dry.

'Go, Marika. It's not safe for you to be here.'

'It's not for you, either. I know how much this means to you. If you're staying, then I will too.' I clasped her hand in thanks, glad of her support, but in truth I was frightened of the consequences for everyone present.

Then a car horn blared and a vehicle raced along Rosenstrasse, its occupants, evidently SS, screaming at us to return to our homes. Fear rippled through the crowd and I held Marika's hand tighter. I surveyed the sea of anxious faces around me, but everybody stood their ground. The car headed straight for us and it wasn't slowing down. As it hurtled closer, the crowd surged and Marika and I were ripped apart.

'Marika!' I screamed as women scrambled towards the protection of alleyways and courtyards. I ran for shelter too, looking for Marika's vivid auburn hair amongst the sea of grey and brown hats, but she was gone.

My heart thumping in my chest, I watched as the guards chased women away from the front of the building, but slowly small groups trickled back to their positions. Then I saw Marika among them, unhurt and undeterred. I made my way to her side and took her arm in mine.

'Do you want to leave?' I whispered to her.

'I couldn't go now,' she said grimly, the fire burning brightly in her eyes. 'We're in this together.'

'Thank you,' I said. She understood. I couldn't stand by and watch as others were going through the very thing I feared the most. With Tante Elya's registration, something in me had shifted. I had to find a way to fight back.

It felt empowering standing up for what was right. I could feel the swell of solidarity within the crowd. It was intoxicating. We weren't going anywhere until we'd heard about the fate of the men inside.

To my astonishment, many men were released that day. Tears poured down my cheeks as women ran to their exhausted and dishevelled husbands, sons and loved ones and hugged them fiercely. With the army's recent defeat at Stalingrad, it seemed that the Nazi regime was beginning to lose control. But I didn't know if that made them less or more dangerous.

*

A few days later, I returned home from university. Life continued just the same on the estate but the events on Rosenstrasse barely left my mind. With Tante Elya and Leo still safe, the optimism I felt at the end of the protest began to take root within me. But it was short-lived when Tante Elya told us of the letter she had received from one of her Onkel Levi's friends in Lemberg, a Polish city. Onkel Levi had been writing regularly, even after he had been moved to the ghetto. He and his family lived in constant fear of reprisals by the SS, but they had endured until now.

Luncheon lay on the table as Tante Elya spoke, the meat stew glistening with fat and a bowl of fluffy mashed potato sitting alongside it. Despite the ever-increasing quotas of meat, milk and vegetables owed to the Ministry of Agriculture and Food, we could always find a little extra for ourselves and the local families who needed it most.

'What happened?' Leo asked softly while I pushed the small grey chunks around my plate unenthusiastically. Tante Elya's eyes were puffy from crying, but she looked up at Leo.

'He and his family were shot outside the town. About two months ago. Thousands slaughtered in cold blood. Even the elders in charge of the ghetto.' She looked stunned, unable to believe the words she spoke.

'All his family?' I whispered.

'Two grandsons were spared,' said Onkel Georg grimly. 'They're still there along with whoever's left, but the ghetto's been transformed into a labour camp. They're imprisoned with the fear of death hanging over their heads . . .'

'The Nazis are getting more and more brazen,' said Leo, slamming his fork on the table. 'Onkel Tedi's told us what he's heard in Lodz. They've been transporting thousands from the ghetto in Warsaw, but the Jewish people won't go quietly anymore. Everybody's heard the rumours about these concentration camps. People disappear there. The Nazis can't hide it, hundreds have seen it happen. Why isn't the world sitting up and taking notice? They want to exterminate anyone with Jewish blood!'

The low leaden clouds visible through the long rectangular windows threatened further snowfalls and added to the gloom that had fallen upon us. Not even the sight of snow bells pushing their way through the frozen ground to announce the coming of spring could lift my mood.

'What can we do?' I asked in a small whisper. It was barely conceivable that thousands of people were being sent to their deaths, and yet it could be the future my family was facing.

'There's nothing we can do but sit tight,' said Tante Elya with a hollow voice.

'What about emigration?' I asked hastily.

Onkel Georg shook his head. 'There's nowhere to go.'

Leo just stared into space and I couldn't tell if his expression was one of desperation or anger. Onkel Georg's connections had come to nothing. My family was trapped.

'We carry on as normal.' Onkel Georg's face gave nothing away as he stabbed a cube of meat with his fork.

'We'll be fine, *myshka*.' Tante Elya tried to smile, but she seemed brittle, as though she could shatter any minute.

Leo and I locked eyes and I could see that he wasn't about to accept the situation. Neither was I.

I followed him to the barn after luncheon.

'I'm worried about your mother,' I said, closing the heavy door behind me. It was quiet and peaceful here. 'We can't just do nothing and submit to our fate. I know you agree.'

'Mutti hasn't been wearing the Star of David,' said Leo softly, 'but if she stays close by, on the farm or in the village, she'll be safe. Vati still has some power. The estate and its contracts will protect us all. Nothing's really changed.'

My eyes adjusted to the gloom and I noticed Shushki, my favourite cat, in the hay, steadily licking her brand-new kittens. *Life carries on regardless,* I thought, but it didn't mean we had to accept what was happening around us.

'But the danger to you both is getting closer,' I said anxiously, grasping his cold hands in mine. 'It could be you and your mother at Lemberg, in Warsaw ... I hope they prevail in Warsaw as we did on Rosenstrasse.'

'You went to Rosenstrasse?' His look of incredulity made me bristle, but I didn't react.

I nodded. 'I can't lose you or your mother. I've already lost one family. I can't sit back and allow things to happen to us.' My throat constricted and tears rolled down my cheeks. 'I feel so guilty that you're being persecuted while I have all the freedoms and rights of an Aryan under the guardianship of your father. It's not fair. But I can make a difference somehow. Stand up to the appalling injustices of the Reich.'

'That's crazy talk, Susie!' Leo pulled his hands away. 'You'll get yourself killed even talking like that.'

I wiped my wet cheeks with my sleeve. 'But you know I'm right.'

He stared at me. 'You're too young to be involved in this fight.'

'I'm not a child, Leo,' I said hotly. 'I've seen what this war can do – I served at the hospital, remember? And I'm eighteen; nineteen next month. A woman.'

He looked away. 'I forget how much you've changed. I don't know how to treat you anymore. I just want to protect you.'

'But I don't need your protection. You've always treated me as an equal. I don't want that to change now.'

He nodded a grudging acceptance.

'You should have seen it, Leo. The crowd of women, defying the SS and soldiers. It was incredible. And most of the people detained were released either that day or over the next week.'

'You were never one to step away from a challenge,' he said, shaking his head in amazement. 'I remember that from when I was teaching you to hunt. You're so determined.' He reached out and touched my cheek.

'Well, that's something at least,' I whispered, my cheek ablaze. He was standing so close, I couldn't help but reach up on my toes to kiss him, but he turned his head so I grazed my lips on his short stubble instead. I stepped away as he moved to touch my arm, apology and regret flashing across his expressive face.

'You're turning blue,' he said. 'We can't stay out here.' The temperature was dropping quickly as the sun nudged closer to the horizon. 'Let's show Mutti the new kittens. It will cheer her up.'

All I wanted was for him to take me in his arms. When would he realise that my life was inextricably linked to his whether he liked it or not?

3

The day before my nineteenth birthday I arrived home from university to an air of bustling industriousness.

I couldn't believe the amount of trouble everyone had gone to just for me. It gave me a thrill of excitement despite my reservations about the party. The garden was immaculate with neat hedges lining the driveway, overhung by boughs of delicate cherry blossoms and drifts of bright daffodils sweeping the green expanses of lawn. The manor house looked revitalised too. The white lime-washed walls gleamed against the sandstone borders, embellished by the columns and rich decorations around the doors and semi-circular upper windows. The impressive staircase led the eye to the front door where two welcoming cherubs rested in pride of place above. I could see why so many locals referred to it as the castle.

I knocked and poked my head through the door to the study. 'I'm here!'

'We've been waiting for you, *schätzchen*,' said Onkel Georg, smiling. I walked across to him and kissed his cheek.

'Is it that late already?' Tante Elya's face was tight, her brows creased. She stood in a hurry, eyes wide with alarm. 'Hello, *myshka*.' She hugged me tight. 'I'm glad you're home. I need you for the final preparations.' I knew Tante Elya would have a to-do list as long as her arm and I felt guilty that I'd been away all week.

'Is everything all right?' I looked searchingly at them both.

'Fine, fine,' said Onkel Georg a little too quickly, brushing his thick sand-coloured moustache with his hand, while Tante Elya turned a shade paler.

'Are you sure?'

'Of course.' Tante Elya took my arm. 'Come then. There's so much still to do for tomorrow and I want everything ready so you can enjoy your day.'

Later that afternoon, I ran into Leo in the hallway.

'What's going on?' I asked, grabbing his arm so he wouldn't slip away.

'What're you talking about?' He wrenched his arm free.

'When I arrived, your parents were in the study, behaving very strangely.'

'It's nothing.'

'Don't tell me that,' I snapped. 'Equals, remember?'

He stared at me and shrugged helplessly. 'They don't want to ruin your birthday. Let it go.'

'You know I can't do that.' I touched his arm. Please tell me what's going on.'

'Not here.'

'Your mother's room. We won't be disturbed there.'

Leo followed me to the bedroom where I shut the door firmly.

'Tell me.'

'Our contracts with the Reichsbahn and Reichspost have been cancelled.'

I stared at him, horrified. 'Everything?'

He nodded and the tough exterior that he showed to the world cracked and crumbled away. Tears were in his eyes. 'All the orders, milk to Berlin, timber – everything.'

'After all these years . . . I can't believe it.'

'Not only that – our coupons for seed and fuel are invalid.'

I froze, thinking through the implications.

'There's still a small amount of seed we can sow, but without the fuel it will be near impossible to farm.' He raked a shaking hand through his hair. 'Then there's everyone who relies on the estate for their livelihood or produce . . . We can't let them down.'

I shook my head in horror. 'This is because of your mother and the register? And you'll be noted too . . .'

He nodded, his shoulders slumping.

'Can't your father do anything about it?'

'He's done everything he can. Now that Mutti's status is official, it's difficult for his contacts to step away from the party line.'

I paced around the room. 'I wish I could do something.'

'Smile and be nice to our contacts at your party,' he said bitterly. 'Vati has to stay friendly with them for all our sakes. Just don't tell my parents that you know. They want your birthday to be perfect.'

My gaze fell on the white embroidered pillowcases on the bed and I remembered the many times that Tante Elya had tucked me in next to her, murmuring words of comfort and singing Russian lullabies after I'd woken in terror from the continuous nightmares of the car accident. By the time I was ten, the dreams grew less frequent and I learnt to muffle my sobs so as not to wake her. But Leo, in the next room, often woke and came into my room to comfort me, his arms encircling me to stop my shaking. The warm weight of him against me and the rhythmic rise and fall of his breath always lulled me to sleep.

I nodded, understanding what I had to do. Still shaken, Leo stared at me a moment, his face pale. Before I could offer him comfort, he turned abruptly and walked away.

The rest of the afternoon passed in a blur. Tante Elya kept me busy, but all I could think about was what Leo had told me. It was bittersweet to think that Tante Elya and Onkel Georg loved me so much that they didn't want to spoil my birthday with such devastating news. And yet it felt so wrong to be having this party, but I'd promised not to utter a word. Somehow I found myself down at the kitchen.

'They've been trying to hide it, but Frau Hecker's status is common knowledge in the village.' I stopped short at the kitchen door and stepped back into the shadow.

'People are beginning to feel resentful,' the female voice continued. 'Young Leo lives in the lap of luxury, safe and sound at home while our sons are fighting and dying on the Eastern Front. His mother comes and goes as she pleases like the Queen of Sheba, but I don't see any yellow star on her clothing. It's as if they're untouchable.' I held my breath, astonished. It wasn't a voice I was familiar with, perhaps a casual kitchen hand come to help over the weekend.

'If it wasn't for the work they provide the village, I don't think many would come tomorrow night. People are feeling nervous about being associated with them, especially with all those Nazis hanging around on the weekends.' I pressed my hot cheek against the smooth plaster wall, my chest tight with fear.

'How can you say such things? Gut Birkenhof has always provided for this community, no matter the cost to the Hecker family. They've always been good to us.' A warm glow flowed through me, easing the tension. There was nobody like Frau Kraus. When I'd arrived as an orphan, she'd lavished care and love on me. She was ferocious in her defence of those she loved. 'Frau Hecker can't help who her parents were. You know Herr Hecker's a good man and a hard worker. They don't deserve what's happened to them. Wouldn't you do anything in your power to protect your family? It's time we support them in return.'

'We have to abide by the laws whether we like it or not,' said the other woman. 'Why should they be any different?'

'You haven't been in this village long enough to know how much this family has done for us,' said Ida, our longstanding housemaid. 'Herr Hecker has always brought jobs and money into the district. Good teachers come to teach at the school, our elderly and ill are well looked after and we all share in the good fortune of the estate. We can't just abandon them when they have their own troubles.'

'That's right,' said Frau Kraus. 'Now I don't want to hear any more about this nonsense. We have too much work to do and I want everything just right for Fräulein Susanna's day.'

The banging of pots and pans followed and when I felt sure that the conversation was over I walked into the kitchen.

'Ah, you're home!' Frau Kraus smiled broadly and wiped her floury hands on the tea towel over her shoulder. Suddenly I was enfolded in her warm embrace, the comforting smells of cinnamon and spice wafting from the apron that only just covered her ample frame. I felt like I was a little girl again, safe in her cosy domain.

She drew back and frowned. 'What's wrong?'

I swallowed the lump in my throat. 'Nothing. It's just been a long week.' I glanced at the new kitchenhand, washing pots on the other side of the room, her back to me.

Ida stopped on her way out the door. 'Fräulein Susie, your dress for tomorrow is ready and hanging in your room.'

'Thank you, Ida,' I said, feeling suddenly exhausted. The last thing I wanted to think about was how all this expense was for me.

'Is that all?' Frau Kraus peered into my face.

'Well, to be honest, I'm a bit overwhelmed by all this.' I gestured to the baking in progress. 'I didn't want any fuss.'

Frau Kraus took me by the shoulders. 'Now listen to me, *herzchen*. I know there's a lot going on, but it's Elya's way of showing you how much she loves you. Let her do it. Forget all your troubles for one day and enjoy yourself. That's what she wants to see. That's what we all want to see.'

'I don't know if I can.'

'Of course you can. Take the moments of joy whenever you can get them. They'll sustain you through the difficult times that are a part of life.' She kissed me on the forehead. 'We'll all enjoy tomorrow's celebrations because who knows what the next day will bring with this war. Promise me you'll do the same.'

'I promise.' She was right. And it would give Tante Elya so much joy to see me carefree and happy.

'Sit down at the table and I'll bring you a few of the biscuits you like. You look like you're fading away.' She winked at me and I grinned. In Frau Kraus's kitchen, the world always looked like a better place.

The morning of my birthday dawned bright and sunny. There was no time to think about anything but the day ahead. Onkel Georg and Leo split their time between the farm work and party duties while Tante Elya revelled in the final preparations. It made me realise how much she enjoyed having a daughter. Together we sampled the various morsels from the kitchen, ensured the glassware sparkled, the flowers were positioned perfectly and that we had ample food and drink – wine, champagne and cognac especially. Then she turned her attention to me. Before I knew it, I was standing before my full-length mirror ready for the evening's festivities.

'You look beautiful,' said Tante Elya, standing behind me.

I stared at my reflection. The blue gown we'd picked together suited my willowy height. The soft pleats of the bodice that gathered above my waist accentuated my bust and fell again below my waist in a flowing long skirt, and the belt cinched at my waist flattered my figure further. My fair hair was left long, curled and styled to a gleaming sheen. The whole effect was of simple elegance, like one of my favourite actresses, Ingrid Bergman.

'You're just like your mother,' she said, squeezing my hand. 'I remember standing with her like this on her nine-teenth birthday. It was the night Georg proposed to me . . .' She raised the diamond engagement ring on her hand to the mirror and smiled at the memory. 'Your mother knew he was going to ask me. Although we came from such different back-grounds, we felt like we'd known each other forever . . . that we were meant to be together.' I shivered at those words – *just like Leo and I.* 'Luckily, my father gave us his blessing and we married. I was never more thankful that my family stayed behind in Germany rather than follow my aunts and uncles across the world to America.' She glanced around the room. 'Your mother and I stood together like this again on my wedding day and she reminded me to put my engagement ring on the opposite hand so Georg could place the wedding band on my finger. It's never been off my hand since. Now Gut Birkenhof has been my home for nearly twenty-five years, we've raised two beautiful children and I love him more than ever,' she said.

She kissed my hand, grasped in hers. 'I wish you the happi-ness I've had and I hope one day to stand here with you on your wedding day and see you as blessed as I've been. To love that special person is like nothing else in the world. The heart wants what the heart wants and nobody can change that . . . but I think you already know that.' I looked at her in surprise, sure she was alluding to Leo and me. Then she gathered me in her arms and hugged me tight. 'Your mother would be proud of the determined, steadfast young woman you've become.'

'I'm blessed to have you as my mother,' I whispered, blinking away the tears that threatened to ruin my make-up.

'Thank you for today. I'll never forget it.' Elya understood me – how I felt about Leo, and that even the Nazis couldn't stop me from loving him. If only I could make him understand too.

'Come on,' she said, patting her own eyes with her handkerchief. 'It's time to meet your guests.'

Despite Tante Elya's new status, everyone turned up to the party: all our friends and locals from the village, and many of the farm workers too. I thought of Frau Kraus's advice from the night before and was determined to follow it. The champagne flowed and I found myself feeling light and free, giggling at inane jokes and dancing with my friends to the popular swing music the band played.

But then I saw Onkel Georg's Nazi associates drinking and laughing and I remembered why they were here. These men with power to either destroy our family or help us survive. I struggled to remain courteous whenever they approached me and made small talk, wishing me a happy birthday and complimenting me on my dress.

'Happy birthday, Susanna,' said an older balding man, kissing my hand. He wore his Nazi Party badge on the lapel of his jacket, but his arrogant manner made it clear that he was a senior official. 'When your uncle told me it was your birthday, I had to come to wish you all the best.' His gaze was so intense that I felt the colour rise to my face. His eyes wandered down to the neckline of my gown making me decidedly uncomfortable. 'And I have to say I wasn't disappointed to meet you,' he said. 'You're beautiful – the image of the perfect German woman.' His fingers trailed along my arm and lingered a moment. 'Nineteen is a wonderful age.

Ready to experience the joys of adulthood.' He drew closer, his hand resting on my back lower than it should and he whispered into my ear, the heavy smell of cognac on his breath. 'And ready to learn from someone experienced.'

I looked desperately around the terrace for help. To my relief, I caught the eye of Onkel Julius. I hadn't seen him in years but he had been a fixture in my childhood, a welcome distraction from chores and schoolwork, until he'd taken up a government post in Poland early in the war.

Suddenly he was at my side. 'Susie, happy birthday!' he said warmly, turning me expertly out of the reach of the official and linking his arm with mine. 'And Kreisleiter Mueller, I thought it was you. What a pleasant surprise.'

I started at the name. Mueller was the county leader in charge of Berlin's municipal government. He was a powerful man who held high rank within the Nazi Party. Not a man to upset.

The kreisleiter's face filled with annoyance. 'And who are you?'

'Julius Siebenborn, Ministry of Transport, at your service,' he said with a small bow.

'And what are you doing here?' Mueller asked, his face darkening.

Julius's smile tightened. 'What business is that of yours?'

'Anything that goes on in my district is my business.' He looked around him haughtily, like a king surveying his kingdom. 'This estate is in my jurisdiction.'

I could feel the vibration of anger ripple through Onkel Julius. 'I'm a guest, just as you are, and have every right to be here,' Julius said tersely. 'You have no say about what happens on this estate.' I could see that he was trying to remain contained, his face carefully blank but the muscles of his forearm and hand were taut, as if he was ready for a fight.

'I wouldn't be so sure if I were you,' said Mueller smugly, his eyes drifting across to where Tante Elya stood talking with Frau Kraus in the distance, next to the table of cakes and sweets. Then his eyes slid back to me and he grinned lasciviously. A shiver crawled down my spine.

Julius pushed me behind him and rose to his full height, towering over Mueller. 'You'll never have control of Gut Birkenhof or anyone under Georg's protection as long as we both draw breath. You're out of your league.' I squeezed his arm and he glanced quickly at me. The look of horror on my face stopped him and he immediately drew back, the flash of anger gone. 'Now you must excuse us,' he said affably. 'Frau Hecker has asked to see her goddaughter.' He took hold of my arm and smoothly propelled me away from Mueller, who was red-faced with fury.

'I'm sorry you had to witness that, especially on your birthday,' Julius whispered apologetically as we moved through the crowd. 'But men like him think they can do what they like and he went too far.'

'I'm only grateful that you came when you did,' I said, holding his arm tight in relief and bewilderment.

'Don't worry.' He patted my hand reassuringly. 'Now he's been put in his place, he won't come near you again.' The power play between the two men had shocked me. I had never seen Onkel Julius so angry, but it was evident that Mueller was dangerous and that Julius was prepared to stand up to those who threatened our family.

I nodded, still shaking a little, but determined not to ruin my birthday and to put our troubles to one side for the night. 'I didn't know you were coming tonight. Tante Elya said you were still in Krakau.' I knew the government that oversaw the German-occupied regions in the east was based in Krakau.

'I'm back now, just in time for your birthday,' he said, smiling. He was a little older than when I'd last seen him, the lines around his eyes deeper, the grey noticeable at his temples and flecked through his dark blond hair.

Maybe it was because Julius was nearly ten years younger than Onkel Georg and a generation closer to Leo and me that he'd always been a favourite visitor, often bringing gifts, playing games with us when we were young and talking to us as equals as we got older. Then he'd joined the Ministry of Transport and his work had taken him all across Europe.

'How long's it been?' he continued. 'You were still in plaits and only up to my chest when I last saw you.' He grinned. It had been our joke – Onkel Julius had reminded me how I'd grown each time he saw me by measuring my height against him.

'About five years,' I said. 'I've grown a bit since then.' I didn't want to tell him that he'd changed a bit too. He must have been nearing forty now.

'Well,' he said, looking down, his blue eyes filled with mischief. 'I think you've reached the perfect height. I don't have to bend down anymore to kiss the top of your head.'

I laughed. We were on the edge of the terrace now, safely surrounded by other guests, and I leaned against the balustrade, the small white columns solid at my back and the soft evening air refreshing against my face. I sighed as the dreadful incident with Mueller began to fade.

'I must go,' he said. 'You'll be fine now, but promise me you'll keep away from drunken old men, especially Mueller.' I nodded, feeling embarrassed. 'I'd better find Georg,' he said. 'We have things to discuss before I head back tonight.'

'You're not staying?'

He shook his head regretfully. 'No, I can't, but since I'm back in Berlin, I'm sure we'll see more of each other. It will be just like old times.' He lifted my hand to his lips. 'Have a wonderful night,' he murmured and then turned away. I watched him make his way through the throngs of guests, a man sure of his place in the world.

Later, after dancing with Onkel Georg, I wandered down the staircase and along the path that wound its way through the garden. A little light-headed from the champagne I'd drunk, and feeling somewhat dissociated from the uneasiness that refused to leave me, I didn't see the figure on the path in front of me until it was too late, and ran straight into Leo. Even with his black bow tie loose and draped around his neck and the top buttons of his shirt undone, he looked magnificent. His dark locks had rebelled against the restraint of his slick hairstyle and a riot of curls tumbled across his forehead. I couldn't help reaching up to brush a stray curl out of his eyes.

'Susie! What're you doing out here all alone?' he asked in surprise. I just stared at him. 'Come on. Let's get you back to the party.' He threaded his arm through mine.

'No, wait a moment. I just want some quiet, to take this night in.' I began to shiver.

'Are you cold?' He frowned. 'Here, take my jacket.' He took off his jacket and placed it over my shoulders, the lingering warmth from his body seeping into mine. 'Have you had a good night?'

'Yes, it's been lovely. . .' I leaned against him, feeling safe again. 'Apart from an old Nazi official making lewd suggestions to me. I didn't know what to do,' I blurted, glad I could tell him anything. Immediately I felt the burden lift.

'What?' Leo was livid. 'Did he hurt you?'

'No, it was only talk and Onkel Julius intervened, but the whole situation left me feeling out of sorts.' I didn't want to delve into the threats that had been made or my apprehension, not now. Perhaps in the light of day it would seem less disturbing.

Leo swore, and looked at my face, something unreadable in his eyes. Then he was wrapping his arms around me as if he could protect me with his body. I melted against him, and time seemed to stop, the two of us alone beneath the cherry trees, the lanterns casting a soft glow across the garden.

I looked up and into his eyes again, recalling Frau Kraus's advice about taking joy where we found it, and I kissed him on the lips as if it was the most natural thing in the world.

His lips were soft, his mouth was warm and he responded readily, then he was pulling me closer, his arms tightening around me. I sighed with happiness. The kiss deepened and I lost myself in him; his closeness, his spicy scent, the way the muscles of his back rippled as his hand caressed my waist, the slightly abrasive feel of his chin stubble and the restrained power of the arms holding me.

Then it was over. Leo pushed me away and held me at arm's length. 'We shouldn't be doing this,' he said roughly. 'I'm sorry.'

'No, Leo, I've been waiting to kiss you again, ever since that night in the cabin.' I pulled his hands away and put my arms around his neck. 'I know you want it too.' I kissed him again and felt his need, knew he felt the same. This was the best birthday present I could ever ask for. His arm slid lower and all I wanted was to be as close to him as I could. In this moment I knew I'd do anything for him.

'Susie, we can't. Not here,' he said, a little breathless, stepping back, eyes darting about to ensure we hadn't been seen. 'It's your birthday and everyone will be wondering where you are.'

'Why do you keep avoiding this situation?' I whispered in anguish. 'There's something between us, admit it.'

He took my hand and led me deeper into the garden and under the weeping cherry tree. The boughs laden with pink blossoms hung heavy towards the ground like curtains, screening us from the world outside. He turned to me and took me in his arms. 'I keep avoiding it because I love you and I can't do anything about it.' His voice was husky, filled with frustration and despair. 'You look beautiful tonight.' His hand trailed along the sleeve of my gown. 'So alive and radiant . . . and now that you're here with me, I don't know if I can keep my hands off you.'

My heart was racing but my body softened in his arms. Nobody had told me such things before. It was everything I'd dreamed of hearing from him. It felt powerful and wonderful to be wanted, and loved. He dipped his head to kiss me and pulled me closer.

Then my hands were inside his shirt, against the wiry hair and fevered skin of his chest, exploring his body. I gasped as his palms grazed my nipples, taut through the fabric of my dress, and then his hands were everywhere like a fiery caress, making me burn with desire. He moved lower, kissing my throat and my breasts reverently, until my body arched towards him, wanting more. His hand moved up the inside of my gown, stroking my thigh and brushing over the sensitive tissue between my legs with a light, feathery touch that made my body ignite. I clung to him as his hand grew bolder, firmer. The world fell away and there was nothing but the growing spark within me that intensified until the fire erupted and I fell limp in his arms.

'I can't tell you how many times I've imagined this moment, but this is so much more,' he murmured against my cheek, 'but we should stop before it's too late.'

I shook my head. 'We can't stop now. We belong together.' I loosened his trousers, surprised at the firmness underneath and marvelled at the exquisite softness of the skin, soft as silk.

Leo groaned and took my hands, kissing them. 'We shouldn't.'

'We should.' I reached up and kissed him again.

'You're better off without me,' he whispered, breaking off the kiss and fastening his trousers once more.

'No, that's not true.' I took both his hands, hoping the physical connection would remind him that our bond was stronger than words.

He shook his head. 'I'm nothing but trouble for you.' He pulled his hands free. 'The day may soon come when it's dangerous for you to be associated with our family.'

'I'd never abandon you,' I said fiercely. 'All I want is to be with you.'

'That's what I want too, Nightingale.' He reached for me and held my face in his hands, the longing clear in his voice. 'But the risk is too high. The most important thing for us and our family now is survival. And that means I'll have to love you from afar.'

My heart skipped a beat and dropped at the same time.

'We'll both have to love from afar until we can find a way to be together,' I whispered, thinking about what Tante Elya had said to me. 'Because there'll never be anybody else for me.'

'Susie, where are you?' I heard Marika call from the path. Leo and I pulled apart in an instant, and I turned to the sound of her voice. When I looked back to Leo, he was gone and I was alone in our magical hideaway. I touched my lips, bruised with kisses, and knew that he loved me. I parted the fragrant curtain and stepped back into reality. But I knew Leo and I belonged to each other and I would cherish this moment under the weeping cherry until the day we could join as one.

4

A few weeks later, Marika sat next to me on my lumpy bed in the university dormitory and put her arm around me.

'You can't lose hope,' she said as she passed her handkerchief to me. I was a miserable sight, my nose running and my eyes red and streaming with tears. We should have been working on our conversational English and French, but I could only think of Leo.

'I know he loves me but it still hurts to be apart from him like this.' I blew my nose hard.

Leo had pointedly avoided all contact with me at home, absenting himself from meals and spending all his time on the property. Tante Elya and Onkel Georg made no comment about Leo's disappearances but I noticed the meaningful looks between them and wondered what they knew.

'He's trying to protect you,' Marika said. 'It's difficult and dangerous enough without the way you both feel.' I'd told her about Onkel Levi's death in Lemberg. 'Anyone who knows the both of you can see that you're meant to be together.'

'What makes you so sure?' I asked heatedly.

'Because one day I want someone to look at me the way Leo looks at you,' she said softly.

I nodded, chastened. Marika had spent many weekends and holidays with me on the estate and knew my family well. She hadn't been surprised to hear my news about Leo – she'd told me she thought he'd loved me for as long as I'd loved him.

After that conversation with her, I tried to bury my head in my studies but I was soon horrified by the news that the Warsaw uprising had been quashed and the ghetto burned to the ground. Thousands of Jewish resisters, and the Polish rebels who had aided them, had died while the remaining inhabitants were sent away to camps. I felt numb to the bone. Naively, I had been filled with hope that the protest would succeed and the people would survive the Nazi oppression. But this was not the world we were living in. Now I was sure those people would never be seen again.

I had to do something or I would fall into a state of despair. A few days later, I attended a Red Cross meeting at the university. One of the senior nurses I had worked with at Beelitz was there, recruiting nurses to work on the front and at home. We spoke after the meeting.

'The number of wounded soldiers has risen dramatically since Stalingrad,' she said, packing up her books and pamphlets. 'Those men returning from the Eastern Front have some terrible stories to tell.'

'I thought you would have seen and heard it all,' I said, rolling up a poster for her.

'So had I, but . . .' She shuddered. 'They saw men freezing and starving to death. Their uniforms weren't warm enough and they were reduced to living on meagre rations and horseflesh, or rats when they could get them.'

I thought of those who had died in Warsaw, their fate still heavy on my heart. So many dead, and for what? 'Nobody deserves to live and die like that,' I murmured.

'I agree,' she said grimly. 'But don't say that too loudly. All we can do is help the ones who come back. Why don't you come back to nursing? Your training at Beelitz will be enough to pass the exam. We could use more like you.'

I nodded, feeling a sense of relief. I couldn't help those suffering in the ghettos and camps, but I could work part-time as a nurse and at least do something useful.

That weekend, Tante Elya and I were walking through the village after visiting our housemaid Ida's elderly mother. She'd been ill with pneumonia and was still bedridden. We'd brought milk and broth and flowers to brighten her room and kept her company until one of her other daughters arrived.

'It feels good to be out of the house,' said Tante Elya, lifting her head to the morning sun. It was a crisp spring day, but perfect weather for a walk. 'I've been cooped up for weeks now. It's beginning to drive me crazy. I need to be out talking to people and part of the community.'

Elya had often visited the elderly and sick, offering assistance where she could, but these days she waited until Leo or I could accompany her because the mood in the village was beginning to change.

Just then a group of women walked towards us.

'*Guten morgen*, Frau Hamm,' said Tante Elya smiling brightly at one of the women.

Instead of acknowledging Elya, the women simply glared. It was only after they had passed us that we heard their reply.

'Who does she think she is? Bloodsucking Jew.'

'Where's her Jewish identity now? Not good enough for her to wear? She should be tagged and sent away like the rest of them.'

Tante Elya stopped walking, rigid with shock.

'Don't turn around,' I said urgently. 'There's no point responding to insults like that. They're just ignorant.' I put my arm around her and propelled her forward. I could feel her shaking.

'I helped look after their babies and children,' she whispered. 'I've known them for years.'

It felt like all eyes on the street were on us, waiting for our reaction, waiting for Tante Elya to crumble. I wanted to scream and shout in these people's faces and remind them of Elya's generosity.

Instead I bit my tongue. 'They're just afraid, Tante Elya.'

'They hate me.' She was stricken by the realisation, her face waxy against the pain in her dark eyes.

'No, they're only reacting to what they've been told,' I said. 'They don't know any better. Come on, let's go home.' It no longer felt like a nice day for a walk.

Back at the estate, Tante Elya shut herself in her bedroom. Onkel Georg and Leo were away in Berlin trying to restore the government contracts, so I went down to the kitchen to talk to Frau Kraus. Thankfully she was alone and I could tell her what had happened.

'There's no excuse for behaviour like that. Everyone knows what she's done for the community,' said Frau Kraus, stirring the soup on the stove.

'But what if it goes beyond talk, Frau Kraus? What if someone calls the Gestapo because she's not wearing the yellow star? I don't think even Onkel Georg's connections could stop them from taking her away anymore. Maybe I should leave university and stay home to make sure she's safe.'

There were more and more stories of people disappearing – and not just Jewish people. Sometimes people accused of wrongdoing and those the Reich disapproved of just vanished. I lived with the terror that Tante Elya or Leo would be taken away. Every piece of post, or every knock on the door, was handled with trepidation now. At university, when the phone rang for me my stomach knotted in fear. There were whispers that even some people classified as *mischlinge* had been taken by mistake and had never come back. The Jewish prohibition signs around the city were coming down, too – there was no need for them any longer with barely any Jewish people left in Berlin.

Frau Kraus banged the wooden spoon on the edge of the pot and turned to me. 'You'll do no such thing! And I know they'll never agree. We're all so proud of you, *schätzchen*. Most of us could never even dream of the opportunities you have. Not even your mother or Elya had the chance to go to university. Show them all what you're capable of. The opportunities you take will give you the power to make a difference. Make something of yourself so you don't end up a pawn in this war, or just some man's wife.'

'But I don't know if that's realistic anymore, Frau Kraus.' I pushed a shaking hand through my hair.

I'd started university with dreams of working at one of the embassies when I was finished my degree, or teaching at the university and maybe becoming a professor one day. I wanted to make a difference, contribute somehow to making the world a better place, where tolerance and peace were fostered rather than hatred and war. I wanted to be amongst people and use my skills and knowledge to help others.

Women in academia were still discouraged, as were women in male-dominated professions. I knew it would be years before we'd break through that barrier but I could dream. Hanna Reitsch was one of the great aviators in Germany and a woman I admired. She had won countless gliding titles, set world records and was the first woman to fly a helicopter. She now worked as a test pilot for the Luftwaffe. But perhaps my dreams were naïve and childish. The safety of my family was more important than university.

'The world's turning upside down. If something happens to Tante Elya and I did nothing to prevent it, I'll never forgive myself.'

'The best way you can help is by being educated,' Frau Kraus said. 'She won't be alone in the village. We'll make sure of that.' She left the stove and came to sit beside me squeezing my hand. 'She's a woman that you can't hold down for long. I'll find things for her to do and a project that will occupy her. She'll soon be back to thinking of those who are worse off than herself. And you'll be home each weekend to keep her company and make her smile.'

I kissed Frau Kraus on the cheek. The relief that I could talk to someone who understood me and could help make sense of the world was enormous. She was always there with a solution or a plan.

Frau Kraus had found some boxes of old clothes that Leo and I had worn as children. Tante Elya sorted the clothing and packaged it for children she knew would benefit in the village, and we agreed I would deliver it to the families most in need. Many were thankful and asked after Tante Elya, but others took the clothes reluctantly and some were even resentful that we had clothes to spare when there were so many who had nothing. I was determined to talk to Onkel Georg about the villagers' change in mood as soon as he got home.

I was walking back home along the edge of the river, thinking about the fickleness of humanity, when a figure emerged from the yard of one of the holiday cottages that Onkel Georg rented out.

'Hello, Susanna.' I turned to find the balding Nazi official from my party leaning against the gate post, dressed casually in trousers and an open-collared shirt which strained across his belly.

'Ah, hello, Kreisleiter Mueller. What are you doing here?' I asked nervously.

'I'm having a few days of rest and recreation, thanks to your uncle,' he said, walking towards me with a sly smile. 'Where are you going?'

'Home,' I said quickly. 'Tante Elya's expecting me.'

'I see. Well, let me walk you home then.'

'I'm sure you have better things to do.' I couldn't help the fine tremor in my voice. I wanted to be as far away from him as possible.

'Not at all. What could be better than walking with a beautiful young lady such as you?' He took my arm firmly in his, and steered me towards the copse of trees by the riverbank. 'How is your aunt anyway?' he asked mildly. 'I hear her status has changed. It must cause some consternation not just within your family, but also in the village. One never knows what will happen next, to someone like her.'

'She's a good woman, and she hasn't done anything wrong,' I said.

'Oh, I know, but still there is that matter of her lineage. You must have heard what happens to those who carry Jewish blood? It's getting harder to protect your aunt from her fate, even though she's married to such an upstanding and patriotic German as your uncle.' He shrugged.

I couldn't bear to hear any more. 'I really need to be getting home,' I said desperately. 'They'll be missing me.'

'Soon, soon,' he said, his eyes flat and hard. 'But there might be something I can do to help. Why don't you join me in my cottage and we can discuss it?'

'I can't do that.' I tried to disengage, but he held my arm tight.

'Nobody has to know. You might even find you like it. Then whenever I'm here, you can keep me company for a few hours. Nothing like a little secret, eh?'

I shook my head, bile rising in my throat. 'No, stop, please.'

'I'd imagine that your aunt and Leopold will be especially unpopular around here once it's common knowledge that your uncle's lost contracts because of them. Soon there'll be nobody left to protect you. I bet you'll come running to me then.' He pushed me up against the trunk of a tree. The night with Leo under the cherry tree flashed through my mind incongruously.

'Let me go!' I shoved him with all my might, but he thrust me back hard against the tree.

'You may as well bow to the inevitable, my dear,' he said, sliding his free hand down my throat to my chest and roughly squeezing my breast. 'I'll have you one way or the other.'

'Hermann, leave the girl alone,' interrupted a male voice from the cottage. 'If you touch her, we'll have to find somewhere else to stay, and we'll have better sport with the girls from the village.'

The kreisleiter's face darkened. 'Why do you have to spoil my fun?' he shouted, shoving me away. 'You'd better have one ready for me who can last all night.' He cast his furious gaze at me. 'And you might not be so lucky next time.'

Breathing heavily, I stepped back, took one look at the man standing near the cottage, and turned and ran.

Back home in the safety of the garden, I vomited until there was nothing but bile and then slipped sweaty and shaky up to my bedroom. Onkel Georg and Leo were finally home from Berlin, but I couldn't face them just yet. I couldn't get the hard reality of what could have happened to me out of my head. There was nothing anyone could do to soothe my fears. Curling up under my eiderdown, I imagined Leo's strong arms around me, telling me he would keep me safe from harm, that he would never leave my side.

Somehow I slept and when I awoke there was a tray of cold food on the table next to my bed. Then I remembered what had happened and shuddered. I had to speak to Onkel Georg about Kreisleiter Mueller, about his threat to Tante Elya and about his advances on me. As much as I felt ashamed and dirty at what he'd done, there was no doubt in my mind that he was a dangerous man and Onkel Georg had to know everything to understand the type of threat this man posed to our family.

He was in his study, as was his custom after dinner, but I hadn't expected him to have company.

'Onkel Julius! I didn't know you were here.'

'He came back with us,' said Onkel Georg from behind his desk. 'He's been an invaluable help yet again.' Onkel Georg was smiling but I could see the smudges of exhaustion under his eyes. Onkel Julius wore a small frown between his brows, as if he was trying to hide his concern.

Clearly the business trip hadn't gone well. If there were no new contracts, there would be no choice but to put off workers. My heart went out to Onkel Georg. He'd worked so hard to avoid this situation, yet here we were all the same.

'We missed you at dinner,' said Onkel Julius, standing from the armchair. 'Ida said you were sleeping. Are you well?'

'Yes, just a headache,' I said, waving my hand in dismissal. 'I'm fine now. I'm sorry to disturb you, Onkel Georg, but when you have a moment I'd like to talk to you.'

'You can talk to me now,' he said, eyebrows raised in worry. 'What's happened?' Julius took a couple of steps towards the door. 'No, Julius, stay. You're involved in this now. Sit down, both of you,' he said, nodding at the leather armchairs.

I sat, clutching the seat of the chair, and told him what had happened with Tante Elya in the village. 'And I know about the contracts. I want to leave university for a while and stay home with her. Maybe the money from the lease on my family's Marienwerder property could help with paying the workers for a while instead of going towards my tuition.' It was all I had to offer. I couldn't access my inheritance for another two years.

I watched Onkel Georg's watery blue eyes, waiting for his reaction. He looked haggard after his trip, his face more lined than usual and I noticed how grey his fair hair had become.

'No,' he said firmly. 'We want you to stay at university. Your parents wanted you educated. We'll manage until I find new contracts. And your aunt will be fine – I'll make sure she's always chaperoned when she goes to the village.'

'But what if they come for her on some trumped-up charge from a resentful villager?'

He grasped my hand across the mahogany desk. 'They won't,' he said darkly. 'Your aunt's been through enough persecution in her life and she's the only one left of her family here in Germany. Our family and home mean everything to her and I won't have that taken away from her.' I wanted to believe him, but he looked wretched, haunted by the reality of our situation. It felt like a stone had settled in my belly.

'Your uncle still provides a service to many of the Nazi officials,' said Onkel Julius quietly. 'They've become accustomed to their comfortable, gentrified lives. They won't sacrifice that for one woman who causes them no trouble.'

I thought of the kreisleiter and shook my head. 'I'm not so sure about that,' I said slowly. My cheeks burning with embarrassment, I told them everything that had happened with Mueller.

Onkel Georg turned pale at my words. 'You could've been raped,' he whispered. An appalled look passed between him and Julius.

'I thought I put a stop to his threats and delusions of grandeur but apparently it wasn't enough,' said Julius, his fingers gripping the arms of the chair so that his knuckles were white.

'Conniving piece of filth,' Onkel Georg growled, beginning to shake with fury. He thumped the table with his fist. 'The vultures are circling now that we've become vulnerable but we will not be preyed upon by the likes of him.' Whatever else he was going to say died on his lips when he saw my stricken face and he took a deep breath to compose himself. 'There's no need to worry about Elya. Everything will be fine. But no more visits to the village on your own,' he said tightly.

Relieved, I stood and kissed his cheek, hugging him tight. The smell of cigars was familiar and soothing. 'I'm sorry if I've caused you more trouble.' As much as I would normally resent the restriction to my freedom, the incidents with Mueller had shaken me and I was reassured by the protective gesture.

'It's not your fault,' he said, patting my hand affectionately. 'Now go back to university and make us all proud.' He sat up straight, ready to take on the world once again. 'Make sure you see Elya. She was worried about you tonight, but didn't want to disturb you. Tell her I'll be a while, I still have matters to discuss with Julius.'

I left the room, and headed for the kitchen hoping to find Frau Kraus and Tante Elya there, but it was silent and only the warmth from the smouldering fire in the stove offered any comfort.

Every word that Mueller had said to me about Tante Elya came back to me and I was hit by the gravity of our situation. We couldn't emigrate and we couldn't run a successful business. We were at the mercy of the Nazi leadership and, at a moment's whim, they could decide to destroy our family.

I slumped to the cold stone floor by the stove and, overwhelmed by my fears, I allowed myself to weep. The dark, silent night seemed to swallow me up and I wished for oblivion.

The creak of the kitchen door opening and the click of the wall switch, flooding the room with light, startled me out of my morose musings.

It was Onkel Julius. I sat up, mortified, wiping the tears furiously away. 'What are you doing down here?'

'I came to make some tea. I don't sleep well at night.' He closed the door and dropped to his haunches beside me. 'What's wrong?' He touched my arm. 'Is it about what happened with Mueller?' I looked into his face and saw the earnest sincerity in his blue eyes. His brows were knitted with concern.

My bottom lip began to tremble and I nodded.

'Georg and I will make sure he'll never touch you again.' His face was tight with anger.

I sighed with relief. 'But what about Tante Elya?' I whispered.

'She might be registered now, but she's still protected by law.'

'But losing the contracts is a crushing blow to the estate. I know it's what kept her safe. How's Onkel Georg going to keep valuable relationships with his associates in high places without everything the estate offers?'

'Leave that to me,' he said, sitting on the floor beside me. 'The truth is, we can't get those contracts back because of the abundance of agricultural produce coming out of the occupied territories in the east, which costs the government nothing. But with my ministry connections I was able to help have the estate's orders for seed and fuel reinstated.'

I leant across and kissed his cheek. 'We're so lucky to have you.'

He shook his head. 'No, I owe so much to Georg. And Gut Birkenhof's important not just to you and me, but to the entire district. It does nobody any good for it to cease operations now. The orders should be enough to keep the estate running, and together we'll find new contracts to keep it afloat and keep Georg's associates happy.'

'But the Nazis think they have Onkel Georg where they want him.'

'You mean Mueller?'

I nodded, beginning to shake. Onkel Julius put his arm around my shoulder. I leaned against his chest and began to sob.

'Shh, it's over. You're safe now,' he crooned, kissing the top of my head. 'And as long as the law stands, Elya can't be forced from her home, but you need someone with influence to protect her.' He paused, looking thoughtful. 'I have an idea.' He stood and offered me his hand to help me up. 'I'll tell you my plan when I've made sure it will work. It has to be water-tight.'

I stood staring at him a long minute, it seemed unbelievable that he could find a way through this mess. 'You can help us?'

'Of course. Georg's like a brother to me.' He glanced around the kitchen fondly. 'I remember spending many holidays here

65

when I was a child, with him – and your mother too.' He smiled at the astonishment on my face. 'Our parents were good friends.' He stared into the dying embers of the fire. 'I'll do whatever I can to help. But don't say anything to them yet. Let me work out the details first.'

'Of course.' I threw my arms around him. 'Thank you.'

The stone that had been sitting on my chest lifted. I could start to breathe again.

5

'How are you?' Leo asked as we drove along the quiet country road. He'd just picked me up from the bus I caught home every week from Berlin. 'I haven't seen much of you since your party.'

I looked at him in astonishment. He'd been avoiding me for weeks.

'I'm all right, I suppose,' I said, turning my gaze abruptly to the green forest that surrounded us. 'I've been worried that I might have ruined things between us.'

He shook his head. 'No, but I shouldn't have allowed what happened at your birthday to happen,' he said. 'It was confusing for you and only complicated matters.'

'Well, I'm not sorry,' I said hotly. 'I wanted it to happen. It was my choice, not something that you allowed. And I was not confused.' I pulled my hand away. 'Neither were you.'

'No.' He paused, smiling tightly. 'But you understand why it's not possible for us to pursue our feelings?'

'Of course I understand, but –'

'Susie, there's too much going on,' he broke in. 'With Mutti's registration and Vati's contracts . . .' He shook his head sharply. 'It's obvious we're being watched and I won't take any risk. It would only make things worse. Surely you see that?'

'What I don't see is why you just accept our fate?' I said, the frustration of the past weeks coming to a head. He didn't know about the kreisleiter or about Onkel Julius agreeing that we needed a plan to keep our family safe. 'Why you don't try to fight for us?'

'I *am* fighting for us, for all of us. There are more important things at stake,' he said, slamming his hand against the seat beside me. 'The way I feel about you makes no difference if there's no future for any of us.'

'What are you talking about?' Had something happened that I didn't know about?

'Do you know how close we are to financial ruin? We're selling whatever we can on the black market. It's the only way we're getting by.'

I stared at him, incredulous. 'That's what you've been doing?'

'Vati doesn't need my help renegotiating contracts when he's got Onkel Julius,' he said bitterly. 'He relies on Onkel Julius's friendship and position, but we're the ones in trouble, not him.'

'He's only trying to help.'

Leo shook his head with irritation and barely contained anger. 'There's only so much he can do. I needed to take matters into my own hands.'

'So you've been meeting black market contacts,' I said, making sense of his absences.

He nodded. 'It's incredible what people will pay for what we used to think were basic necessities. We'll keep helping people in the village, but we have to make money to pay our bills, pay the workers and pay for Vati's inducements to the Nazis.'

'What does your father think about this?'

He stared straight ahead, his eyes on the road, while his face mirrored the frustration he was feeling.

'He refused to consider the idea at first, but since he hasn't been able to acquire enough contracts to make up our loss, he's warmed to it.'

'He's desperate, Leo.'

His shoulders sagged. 'I know. He's going to lease more land and build more cottages along the lake, too. He'll encourage his wealthy friends in Berlin to get away from the bombings and chaos of the city. It'll help, but it won't be enough.'

I was shocked at how serious our financial trouble was. 'Please don't leave me out in future, I can take the truth.'

'I know. I just haven't had the chance to tell you.'

I nodded, not entirely convinced. 'But the risk of being caught, Leo . . . Let me help. I want to be involved. You can't carry the burden of this by yourself.'

He looked at me and smiled sadly. 'I know you'll always have my back, just as I have yours.' He reached out and touched my face. 'I love you, Susie, with all my being. In another time or place where being Jewish didn't matter, maybe we'd have a chance, but I'm a pariah, a mongrel, and you'll only get hurt if you're associated with me. You should forget about your feelings for me.' The look of absolute despair on his face made me move towards him, but he flinched, shaking his head. 'We can't. We just have to focus on surviving.'

I hated seeing him in so much pain so I nodded. 'As long as I have you by my side, the rest can wait,' I whispered.

'There's my girl,' he whispered back to me.

Leo kept most of his black market dealings from his father, I learned. It was his way of protecting both his parents.

'Vati knows what we're sending, but he can't afford to run into any trouble if something goes wrong,' he told me the next morning as we loaded boxes into the truck. There were vegetables – crisp cauliflowers and white cabbages, bulbous turnips and sweet carrots, jars of honey, pitchers of milk, tubs of cream, rounds of cheese, fresh young veal, and flour milled from our wheat and rye. Timber products were harder to hide, but Leo found a way to sell them when he could. Produce from Gut Birkenhof always sold for a premium because of our reputation of providing top quality goods.

'Let me come with you,' I said, lifting the last box into place. 'Someone should know who all the contacts are besides you.'

He shook his head. 'Not today. I'm meeting a new buyer, a Berlin restaurateur. I don't want you there if something goes wrong.' I huffed in annoyance but Leo didn't seem to notice. 'Besides, it's better if you're here with Onkel Julius. He'll ask questions if we're both gone and I don't want him knowing what we're up to.' He pulled the tarpaulin over the back of the truck.

'I can't believe you're so distrustful. He's known you since you were born,' I said, shaking my head as I tied one corner of the tarpaulin to the truck.

'He's a Nazi, Susie. We haven't seen him in years and now he's returned to a promotion within the Ministry of Transport. He's highly placed and powerful in the Reich. Who knows what his true allegiances are anymore?' He tugged at the opposite corner, tying the cover down tightly.

Onkel Julius had become a more regular visitor to the estate, often in and out in the same day, talking at length with Onkel Georg or returning late at night with him from visits to Berlin. I felt sure that Leo resented the time his father spent with Julius – talking, working, discussing the estate, meeting with buyers and drinking like they had in their youth.

'Just be careful,' I said. 'Don't take any unnecessary risks.'

'It will be fine.' He smiled and climbed into the driver's seat. 'I'll see you later.'

That afternoon, Onkel Julius offered to drive me back to Berlin. 'I don't like having a driver,' he said as we drove through the countryside in his two-seater Mercedes Benz, the canvas roof folded back to make the most of the sunny June day. Like me, he came from substantial money and an old family. 'I drive whenever I can.'

'What do you actually do anyway?' Leo's comments had sparked my curiosity and I wanted to know why Julius thought he could protect my family.

'I work in Operational Management and Construction. I've just been promoted, that's why I'm back in Berlin,' he said with a flourish of his free hand, the other remaining solidly on the leather steering wheel.

'Congratulations,' I said, putting the information together. 'It must be an important role if you have a driver. But those positions require Nazi membership, don't they?'

'Yes, I had to become a member of the Nazi Party, if that's what you're asking. I could never have landed a decent engineering job, especially one within government. But not all Nazis are like that pig Mueller. Many of us are civil servants who just want to keep Germany running as efficiently as possible during this war.'

'So can you really help Tante Elya?'

The expression on his face became serious. He slowed down and pulled off the quiet country road and onto the lush grass growing on the edge of the verdant forest, turning off the engine before he answered me.

'I've been thinking about what we discussed that night in the kitchen.' He took a deep breath, focusing all his attention on me. 'I promised you I would have a plan, and I do. We would have to work together for it to be successful.' He touched my hand, the leather of his driving glove soft on my skin. 'Please hear what I have to say before you say anything.'

I nodded. Since our conversation that night, I'd been beginning to doubt that he had meant what he'd said. Despite his frequent visits to Gut Birkenhof over the past couple of weeks, nothing had been discussed and my conversations with Leo had made me wonder.

'I'm doing all I can to help Georg find buyers and investors, powerful men in Berlin, industrialists, officers in the Wehrmacht and those in government. But the real problem is that Elya's status is now common knowledge. Half Jews like

Leo are safe for the moment, but I'm sure it won't be long before they're under the spotlight of the Security Office too.'

'If there's anything I can do to keep them safe, I'll do it,' I said. 'They're all I have.'

'I know. They've been my family too for as long as I care to remember.' He patted my arm in sympathy, but his blue eyes were clouded with pain.

'Why do you want to help us? What happened to you?'

Julius sagged in his seat. 'You have every right to ask. Only a handful of people know this about me ... Georg, Elya and your mother among them.' He stared into the forest, gathering his thoughts. 'When I was about five years old, my older brother and I came to live with Georg and his family. My father gambled the family fortune on bad business ventures across Europe. Georg's father intervened and saved our family from bankruptcy. My father's reputation was in tatters and my mother committed suicide. Vati turned to the bottle and was unable to look after my brother and me. That's when we came to Gut Birkenhof. We both stayed until we left school and I never went home again.'

I frowned, not expecting this story. 'I'm so sorry,' I said, not knowing what else to say. His vulnerability touched me, a far cry from the self-contained man I had always known.

'My father died during my last years at school, a drunkard. The shame was almost too much for my brother and me. My brother inherited the estate. He went to manage what was left of our family legacy and I went to university to become an engineer. Georg's father loaned us money to get us on our feet.'

'You owe it all to Georg's father,' I whispered.

'Yes, he gave us the chance to find respectability again.' He shook his head. 'But despite his best attempts, my brother struggled to run the estate and by the time I joined the Ministry of Transport he was dead and the property gone.'

'I had no idea,' I said quietly.

'It was a long time ago,' he said, sighing softly, 'but you can see why Georg is like a brother to me. I owe so much to him and his family. They gave us sanctuary; a home and a family. I'll do anything for him.' I realised then how much we had in common. I'd been given sanctuary at Gut Birkenhof too. It was my home and the Heckers were my family now. I, too, would do anything for them.

'We are your family,' I said, understanding why Julius always came back to Gut Birkenhof. Family was our bedrock, the source of our nourishment and our strength. 'Just tell me how I can help.'

'Do you mean it, that you would do anything? Because it won't be easy.'

I nodded, my head heavy. 'I don't care about myself. I have to do something.'

'In normal circumstances I'd never entertain such an idea, but these are desperate times ... It will mean pretending – lying even – and Georg and Elya might not understand.'

I frowned, feeling uneasy. 'What do you mean?'

'I have the support of powerful men within the administration. If I continue to work with them and support their agendas, I can keep your family safe.' He paused for a moment. 'But there's always the risk of putting such delicate tasks in the hands of others, who you can't completely trust.'

'So what else can we do?'

'There's only one other way. Family members of high-ranking Nazis are looked after and protected, including those with Jewish connections.'

'Nazis protecting their own. That doesn't surprise me,' I said bitterly. 'But how does that help us?'

'Even the families of those rising within the government ministries, like me, can be safeguarded.' He paused, pushing the dark blond hair from his forehead. 'But although I could say that Georg and I are family, it's not enough. We need a closer tie.'

I stared at him dumbly.

'You and I would have to pretend to be courting.'

The blood drained from my face.

'I know it's a lot to ask,' Julius said quickly. 'But in reality you would only have to be seen attending a few social and government events with me.' This couldn't be what he meant. 'I know this isn't what you expected, but the situation with Elya and Leo is delicate and it calls for an unusual solution.'

'But we can't. It's crazy, like some kind of pantomime.' The ridiculousness of it struck me and I laughed out loud, willing him to show me the mischievous grin I knew so well, but he just shook his head, the light between the tall beech and oak trees falling across his face.

'Look, Susie, your parents belonged to the same social set as Georg and me. Your family credentials are impeccable; you're cultured and educated. You can discuss matters of philosophy and literature and speak four languages. You'll dazzle them all and, by my side, you'll be accepted into powerful circles in a heartbeat.' I frowned at this generous assessment of my abilities. 'Men like Mueller wouldn't dare touch or threaten you.

And if any trouble develops with Elya and Leo, once it's understood that they're the family who raised you, any problems will be averted, especially with Georg's lineage and assistance to the Reich.'

I grasped his arm, desperate to believe him, especially if it kept opportunistic men like Mueller away. 'How can you be so sure? How much power do you really have?'

Julius grinned. 'I'm the new Ministerialrat for Operational Management and Construction.'

'The assistant secretary?' He nodded. It was only the third position down from the Minister of Transport himself. Maybe his credentials *were* enough to pull this off successfully.

'It gives me access not only to the minister, but others at senior government levels across the ministries. I'm making contacts in very useful places. I can keep you all safe,' he said with conviction.

My brief relief that this might be a solution dissolved as I thought through the implications. I'd have to rub shoulders with Nazis, those who believed that Jewish people deserved to be treated worse than animals. Then my face fell. 'We'd have to lie to my family?'

Julius shrugged apologetically. 'It can't be helped. We'd have to be seen as serious, our relationship leading towards marriage.'

'Marriage?' I sucked in a sharp breath. There was only one person I ever wanted to talk about marriage with.

'Yes. It'll be a pretence – but it has to be believable to everyone. It's the only thing that will keep them safe.'

I nodded, trying to find an even keel. The idea was outrageous, but so was the precarious situation Tante Elya and

Leo were in. I knew that traditional values, especially in respect to courtship and marriage, were still held in the highest regard by the Nazi regime.

I breathed deeply, the scent of pine grounding and invigorating me at the same time. 'I don't know that we can make it appear real. We don't love each other.'

He nodded knowingly, as though anticipating my opposition. 'Well, how many matches are made from love? For a lot of people in the Reich it's a matter of practical agreement and convenience, usually arranged by the families. It won't seem so strange.'

'But both Tante Elya and my mother married for love. She won't accept it.'

'I've thought about that, too. After the incident with Mueller, Georg asked me if I could look in on you in Berlin, to make sure you're happy and safe . . .' He acknowledged my raised eyebrows with a sigh. 'He worries about you, Susie. If we give it enough time, he won't object because he knows I'll look after you and treat you with respect. And I won't ask anything of you other than for you to look elegant and beautiful on my arm and grace those around you with your wit, intelligence and charm.'

'Leo will know.' And I knew how Leo felt about Julius.

'Leo has no reason to argue when his own situation puts you in harm's way, in the path of men like Mueller. I'm family. Who's better placed to protect you?'

The weight of the potential betrayal sat heavily on my heart, but there was something else too, a powerful, growing sense of relief – of averting the crushing powerlessness – that was almost overwhelming. I would be betraying Leo and his parents, but I would be protecting them too. It would hurt Leo deeply, but it would be worth it if he was safe until a time when we could be together. If we were to have a future, he'd have to survive and, this way, I could help him.

Looking out at the trees, I tried to think it through. The forest was a familiar and comforting sight and I imagined walking through its cool depths, weaving between the dark trunks, scattered shafts of sunlight finding a way through the green canopy and illuminating small patches of bright colour like secret treasures. A sense of calm descended over me. Onkel Julius was offering me a lifeline. I had to trust him.

'How do we do this?' I asked, looking him directly in the eye.

He smiled. 'First of all, call me Julius. Onkel makes me feel old.'

A week later, I walked through the majestic entrance of the Hotel Kaiserhof, arguably the most luxurious hotel in Berlin. It had been a favourite of well-heeled guests for the past seventy or so years and it was here that Julius Siebenborn kept a suite on the third floor. The lobby was buzzing with activity, guests coming and going, the tinkling of laughter emanating from tables where fashionably dressed men and women sat, sipping coffee and nibbling on cakes and delicacies.

I frowned as my eye caught the swastika armbands clumped together at tables and dotted across the foyer. Hotel Kaiserhof had always been one of the premier meeting places in the city, but situated opposite the Reich Chancellery and within walking distance of many of the ministry buildings, including the Ministry of Transport, the elegant space was now taken over by high-ranking Nazi officials, ministry personnel and the green–grey of the Wehrmacht. The carmine stripes displayed on trouser legs denoted high-ranking officers, particularly of the General Staff. There were a few who still wore finely cut suits with their Nazi membership pin on their jacket lapel, and some were even in traditional evening wear.

Some were surely family friends of Onkel Georg, like Julius, others were likely business associates of his, and although there were still some good men among their ranks, I knew that most were corrupt or at least complicit in enforcing laws that had forced the Jewish people from Germany. And now I would have to pretend I was their friend.

'Ministerialrat Siebenborn is expecting me,' I said to the waiter. He nodded and escorted me to a free table. I felt the eyes of men nearby follow me across the lobby, appraising who I was, who I was meeting and what I was doing there. Women, too. It took all of my self-control not to smooth my dress, a simple black velvet bodice with an ivory satin skirt, demure yet elegant.

Julius was taking me to see the Berlin Philharmonic Orchestra – our first outing together. His secretary Hedy had contacted me about the arrangements for the evening and made sure I had everything I needed for the occasion. I murmured my thanks to the waiter as I sat. I didn't know how to feel: excited to be out on my own as a woman, thrilled to play the game of pretence as Julius's girlfriend, or guilty for hiding what I was doing from my family. More than anything I didn't want to embarrass myself or Julius. My greatest fear was that he'd tell me that this was a terrible mistake and that he couldn't help Tante Elya and Leo after all.

Julius didn't make me wait. He was by my side before I could take in my surroundings any further, handsome and impeccable in his tuxedo, hair perfectly in place and freshly shaven.

'Susanna,' he said formally, lifting my hand to his lips.

'Hello, Julius,' I said, smiling. 'Thank you for not making me wait. I'm not sure how much longer I'd survive all these curious glances.'

'Well, my dear, you'd better get used to them. You're a glittering star in the inky night sky.'

'That's very poetic,' I said, feeling heat rise to my face.

'You're the most beautiful girl in the room,' he whispered, sitting across from me.

'You're not wasting any time playing your role,' I whispered back.

'Who said I'm acting?' he replied, winking as he smiled widely.

I frowned and shook my head. Clearly Julius was enjoying himself, but all I felt was embarrassment.

'Let's order a drink before we go,' he said, easing the tension.

The concert was wonderful, a breathtaking performance of Beethoven's Fourth and Fifth symphonies, and, partly thanks to the champagne, I began to feel a little less nervous. As I was introduced to many of Berlin's social elite, I forced myself to relax on Julius's arm.

'Did you enjoy the concert?' asked a lady with a tiara in her grey hair. Frau Stahl, I remembered. We were standing in small groups as people milled about the foyer with drinks in hand.

'Yes, very much,' I said, smiling. 'Beethoven is one of my favourite composers.'

'You're Georg Hecker's goddaughter, aren't you?'

I nodded, taking a large sip of champagne, not sure where this conversation was going.

'We used to see him in Berlin from time to time.' It seemed that everyone knew Onkel Georg, and it struck me that he had been part of this social circle from childhood, before Tante Elya's Jewish background became a problem. 'How is he, and his family?'

'They're well, thank you,' I said.

It was clear she wasn't going to ask after Tante Elya and I felt outraged on her behalf.

'Are you here with Julius?' She looked at me speculatively.

'He's looking out for me as a favour to Onkel Georg. He thought that I could use a little more culture in my life,' I said, smiling despite my outrage. Julius had told me this would be the perfect way to start the gossip that we were close.

'Did I hear Julius say that you're at university?'

I nodded. 'I'm studying history, literature and philosophy.'

'Well, that's wonderful. Girls these days are doing so much more,' she said, sipping her champagne.

'But what's the purpose?' asked a pinched faced woman. 'You don't need an education to be married well, just good breeding.'

'I want to work afterwards,' I said a little taken aback.

'That'll change when the war ends, and the men return to their jobs.'

'Susanna speaks four languages,' said Julius, smoothly interrupting the conversation. 'She learnt English and French at school and her godmother is Russian.'

'Very accomplished,' said Frau Stahl, nodding in approval.

Julius introduced me to Herr Stahl and some of the other older men and we engaged in small talk and discussed literature, history and the ancient philosophers I was studying at university – Plato, Aristotle and Socrates. Some even found what I had to say interesting. It felt like the old days, an evening with Onkel Georg and Tante Elya's friends at one of the many parties I had attended when I was younger. It was something I could manage, despite the undercurrent of anger that hummed through my body that these people could continue to live normally while so many others suffered.

Julius drove me home after and walked me to the dormitory door.

'I think that went very well,' he said. 'I hope the dry old folk didn't bore you too much?'

I smiled. 'Of course not. They're really no different to Onkel Georg's associates and their old friends from Berlin.'

'You're very poised for someone so young.'

I shrugged. 'I've had to be. There's no point losing my composure in company like that. They'd never understand anyway.'

He nodded in agreement.

'I really enjoyed the concert. Thank you.' Despite my nervousness at the beginning of the evening, I felt more confident now that our subterfuge might really work.

'Well, good night, Susie.' He kissed my gloved hand. 'I'd better let you get to bed. I'm sure you have lectures in the morning.' He waited patiently for me to close the door behind me.

Just like an uncle, I thought, *safely delivering me home.* I kicked off my heels and, with aching feet, tiptoed to my room, feeling strangely flat.

6

'You're heading out again?' asked Marika, a week later.

Although she was my best friend, I couldn't tell her what I was doing. I could barely justify it to myself.

'It's just dinner with a family friend,' I said lightly, as I began coiling my hair into a chignon. 'I haven't seen him for a few years.' Julius had decided that a quiet meal was a good chance for us to relax and learn more about each other's daily life.

'It's a fancy dinner if you're dressing like that.' She plonked herself on my bed, waiting for my answer. 'How would Leo feel about it?' A stab of guilt pierced my belly.

In the last week, there'd been moments when I'd wanted to confide in Leo, but I knew he would never understand. This was my way of fighting back, of doing something that neither he nor Onkel Georg could do for our family.

'It doesn't matter,' I said dully. 'We can't be together and neither of us has the right to say what the other does.'

'You may have to wait until this war is over to have a life with him, but never give up.'

'The only chance we'll have is if we lose the war and the Nazis fall from power,' I said bitterly. The speeches given by Ministers Speer and Goebbels at the Sportspalast, assuring German victory now that our armament production had increased and the difficulties of Stalingrad had been overcome, had been received enthusiastically by a massive crowd. It was also widely reported in the newspapers that the stirring words of Goebbels only galvanised the survivors of the recent devastating bombings of the Rhineland to continue the battle against the Allied enemy. Support for the Nazis was as strong as ever.

'Don't say things like that, even here in private,' she hissed, glancing at the closed door warily.

'I'm sorry. Sometimes it all seems too difficult.'

Marika hugged me tight. 'The truth is that I'm jealous that you've found "the one" while I still have no idea what I really want.' She drew back and patted my hair into place. 'Now, finish getting dressed and go and have some fun. Maybe this family friend is a good distraction for you at the moment.'

'Maybe he is,' I echoed, but my heart felt like it was breaking.

The club was understated, but busy, almost every table full, and I knew immediately that this was a popular haunt of people in the know. Julius took my arm as we threaded our way through the room to our table. He was smiling and nodding to other patrons – the Nazi elite, but also ordinary Berliners who could still afford to eat out or had come for a drink and to listen to the music. I'd never been anywhere like this in my life.

'This place feels so alive,' I said, leaning across the table to make myself heard as the band began to play across the dancefloor. 'I love it.'

Julius grinned. 'Wait until the band really warms up and the singing starts. Shall we start with some champagne?'

The champagne went to my head while we listened to the music and waited for our meals to arrive. Julius had ordered for both of us.

'It's veal with a French sauce,' he told me.

'How's that possible?' I was salivating already. I hadn't had veal or a creamy French sauce in so long, even though we sold such produce from the estate.

'It's from the Ukraine,' he told me in an undertone. 'We should enjoy it while it's available.' I nodded, but couldn't help feeling uneasy, wondering what people in the Ukraine were eating. Most of Eastern Europe – Poland, the Baltic states, even previously held Soviet provinces like Ukraine as well as parts of the western Soviet Union – were now under German occupation. This eastern expansionism was fuelled by the Nazi policy of *Lebensraum*, 'living space', displacing locals and settling Germans in the vast agricultural holdings and in control of resources and industry in the east. This was also where the majority of the ghettos and concentration camps existed, far from the gaze and conscious awareness of German citizens. Out of sight and out of mind.

And yet, despite my uneasiness, more than once I found myself tapping my foot to the music while telling Julius about my week at university, and about Marika and the antics she'd instigate to lighten up our periods of study in the dormitory. The lamp on our table cast a soft light across Julius's features, interested and enquiring one minute and laughing at my stories the next. His attention was focused solely on me. It left me feeling giddy and light-headed.

We were halfway through our meal before I had a chance to ask him more about himself. I was eating slowly, savouring every delicious morsel – there were even fresh carrots and beans, a far cry from the usual meagre cabbage and potato or thin stew that was served around the city. I wondered if the owner could be Leo's restaurateur.

'What about you? How's your week been?'

'Busy. I've been involved with coordinating train services across the Reich. Between getting soldiers to the front and military equipment to where it needs to go, ensuring coal trains leave the collieries regularly and keeping the normal passenger trains on time and German passengers happy, it's been a bit of a nightmare.'

'It sounds like it.' It also sounded very tedious to me. 'Is that what you were doing in Krakau?'

'No, I was overseeing the planning and building of new railways lines and stations in the east to make sure there's a smooth and efficient flow back and forward to Germany.' He put his fork and knife down. 'Without an efficient transport system, particularly in times of war, the economy would be seriously affected.' I could see his face light up and I began to understand what made him tick. 'Every part of life revolves around our economy, and the rail system is an integral part of Germany continuing to function as efficiently as possible.'

I pointed my fork at him in a most unladylike manner. 'That's why you love being in government, isn't it? It's not just a career path for you. It's something you're passionate about.'

'All I want is for Germany to be standing strong at the end of this war,' he said. 'I'm just an engineer who understands economics.' He shrugged his shoulders. 'Besides, where would we be without order? War creates chaos, but with good infrastructure, we can at least maintain a level of stability within Germany . . .' He picked up his wineglass and drank before continuing. 'With chaos, we all lose our jobs.' He smiled broadly. 'And I for one don't want to lose my job.'

'I don't want you to lose your job either.' I wondered what would happen if Julius no longer had the influence he currently enjoyed.

He laughed. 'That's two of us at least!'

'All you want is the best for Germany. I think that's admirable.' I reached across the table, took his hand and squeezed it gently, noticing the surprise cross his face briefly.

Julius nodded. 'But I promised you a good night, not boring talk about government and economics. Come, let's dance.' He led me to the dancefloor just as a tall willowy singer resplendent in a long sequined gown took the microphone and began to sing in sweet, sultry tones.

Julius was a good dancer, leading me effortlessly around the floor, his hand on my back holding me close. I was aware of every plane and curve of his body against me, the pressure of his hand in mine and his arm around my waist. Then the music became lively and, with the impish grin I remembered as a child, he stepped up the pace, dipping and spinning me around, making me laugh.

'I have to work tomorrow,' said Julius finally, 'and you probably have some fascinating dissertation on philosophy in the morning.'

'Yes, I suppose we'd better go,' I said reluctantly. I could have danced all night.

A couple of weeks later I found an unexpected moment of stillness after helping Onkel Georg with the milking. I'd followed the cows back to their night paddock while he washed down the dairy floor. Closing the gate behind the last stragglers, I looked up into the fading sky and for a moment enjoyed the peacefulness that had descended with the twilight. Although I enjoyed returning to the familiar routines of daily life on the farm, I hadn't been able to stop worrying about keeping my secret from everyone. In this moment of grace, everything fell away but the slowing of the day.

'I hear Julius is keeping an eye on you in Berlin.'

I turned to find Onkel Georg walking towards me, an empty bucket in his hand, and I gathered myself to face the questions I'd known would come sooner or later.

'Yes, he's taken me to dinner and to the philharmonic,' I said calmly although my heart began beating faster with the fear that we'd been found out. How could I ever explain myself?

He nodded, looking thoughtful. 'Tante Elya and I would take you if we could, but as you know I'm too busy now we've had to let workers go, and Tante Elya can't leave the village.'

'I know,' I said softly.

'We're lucky to have Julius.' He stood beside me and, leaning on the gate, stared across the enclosure. 'He's a good friend and he'll look after you any way he can.'

'He's doing it for you and Tante Elya – he just wants to help.'

'I trust Julius to look after you and keep you safe, especially from men like Mueller. He never had any children and you're like a daughter to him.' He laid his hand on my shoulder. 'Enjoy it, Susanna. He can give you the good life that we can't any longer. He's well liked and will introduce you to some lovely young people. We can't do that for you either now.' He glanced across to me, my face tight with mortification. 'I'm sorry to bring this up, and you might not want to hear it, but we want to see you happy and well married, safe from the situation we find ourselves in, despite where your feelings might lie.' My cheeks reddened and I wondered what he knew about Leo, but he continued talking. 'If Julius can help, Tante Elya and I are grateful.'

I didn't know what to say. 'You, Tante Elya and Leo are all I want,' I said, my voice wobbling. Tears sprang to my eyes.

'Maybe now, but soon it may be too dangerous for you here. Mueller is only the tip of the iceberg.'

I turned and hugged him tight, the collar of his wool coat scratchy against my cheek. His admission scared me. He was always so solid and dependable, with a ready solution to any problem, but now there were things he could no longer do, situations out of his control.

He kissed the top of my head and continued on to the barn with the bucket still in his hand. I waited until he'd gone, and then I cried like a small child. His kindness made my deception feel twice as terrible.

Onkel Georg must have said something to Leo about Julius and me. Washing down the equipment in the dairy the next afternoon, absorbed by the serenity of solitude and the repetitive scrubbing and washing, I didn't hear Leo come towards me.

'Having fun in Berlin, are you?'

I started and turned, shocked by his tone.

'What are you talking about?' The water was still running and Leo stepped forward to turn it off.

'Out about town with none other than Onkel Julius?'

'Leo, he's taken me out twice as a favour to your father.'

'Mingling with Nazis?' His face was filled with contempt.

'He's not like that,' I said quickly. I didn't want to have this conversation.

'And how do you know that? Is he taking a little more interest in you than is proper?'

Rage surged through me. I knew he'd be hurt when he heard about Julius but I was doing this for him. And, besides, he'd made it clear I should forget what was between us. I slapped his face. 'How dare you! He's a gentleman and your father's oldest friend. He would never take advantage of me. He's using his influence to help us. It's not his fault the contracts are gone.'

Leo's dark eyes blazed with fury and he grabbed hold of my hands, as much to restrain me as to restrain himself, I was sure. 'I don't like him spending all this time with Vati. I don't like him spending time with you,' he growled. 'I don't trust him.'

'He's done nothing wrong. You have no right to tell me what to do.' His grip on my arms tightened and I glared at him, breathing hard, daring him to tell me otherwise.

He stared at me, the conflict clear on his face, and then he pulled me close. I closed my eyes, willing him to kiss me, but when I opened my eyes his face was tight with pain.

'Stay away from Julius, Susie. He's a Nazi, and a cheat and a liar like the rest of them. Don't trust him.'

He turned away abruptly and left the dairy. I sunk to my knees, sobbing.

Back at university, I cried on Marika's shoulder yet again. Every time I closed my eyes I could see the fury on Leo's face.

'They're trying to push me away like I don't belong anymore.' I wiped my eyes furiously with the backs of my hands and sat up on the bed.

Marika shook her head. 'Georg's only trying to protect you, as is Leo. They both love you and want to keep you safe,' she said. 'It's getting more dangerous – look what happened with Mueller. Just give Leo some time and space and, you watch, it will be fine when you next go back home.'

I nodded. One day when Leo and I were together it would all be worth it, but until then I had to do what I could to ensure he and Tante Elya stayed safe. My only consolation for now was that Leo's reaction showed he still loved me.

I couldn't tell Marika how Julius was protecting them; it was too risky. I hadn't seen him since returning to Berlin – I was too busy studying for my end of year exams, and my thoughts were turning to the state nursing exam. Marika had decided to stay in Berlin with me over the summer break to help me prepare for the exam. I loved university, but I was desperate to make a difference, to demonstrate some humanity in the face of Nazi tyranny. The news of the Allied bombing of Hamburg through July only made me work harder. The city had been relentlessly pounded by raids for a week and we'd all felt numb at the news of the firestorms. It had shed a new light on how far the Allies were prepared to go to bring Germany to its knees.

Marika helped me study late into the night until she knew the content almost as well as I did. Finally the day of the exam arrived and Julius telephoned to wish me luck, apologising that he hadn't been able to see me – he'd been overwhelmed at work with the devastation of Hamburg.

'The railway system's in chaos,' he told me. 'We've never seen anything like it. Fire's razed the city almost to the ground and the civilian losses are staggering. If we don't get supplies and emergency services there soon, there'll be many more losses. And now Mussolini's government has been toppled, sending senior Reich leaders into a spin. We won't have much support from them to deal with this emergency.'

Perhaps the loss of the Führer's alliance with Italy was a good thing – it made him more isolated and perhaps vulnerable – but I was stunned at the distress in Julius's voice. It made the destruction of Hamburg more real to me. There was no comfort I could give him; I could only leave him to help get the city on its feet once more.

Later that morning I sat in a large austere examination hall filled with women of all ages. I was nervous about passing the nursing exam, especially after listening to the series of instructions barked out by a Red Cross official, but I became so absorbed in answering the questions that the minutes slipped away until it was time to put down our pens. I'd done all that I could. A few days later I was relieved when the Red Cross informed me I had passed and that I'd soon be needed in Berlin because all the available nurses had been sent to Hamburg to deal with the crisis.

It was only then that I managed to see Julius. As we walked through the parkland at Tiergarten, Julius, looking drawn and tired, told me he had some good news to share.

'I've managed to secure Georg a new contract with the railways.'

I shrieked with excitement and threw my arms around him. 'That's wonderful! Does Onkel Georg know?' I drew back and he took my arm in his as we continued walking.

He nodded. 'Yes, I've told him. It's not as lucrative as the one he's lost, but it's for timber and will help keep the estate running.'

'How did you manage it?'

'I have the ear of one of the ministry's most senior figures, Ganzenmüller, and he agreed to the deal. I gave my assurances to the minister himself that Georg and his family are upstanding Germans. I may have mentioned that I'm shortly to become engaged to Georg's goddaughter and ward.'

'What about Tante Elya?'

'I've told him she's only a paper Jew and they understand that she's not involved with the estate. As long as the deal is beneficial to them, they can overlook her status.'

'There's no risk to you?'

He smiled indulgently. 'Only if word gets out about our arrangement, but as far as anyone knows we're in love and have the blessing of your family to marry.'

I nodded slowly. It was beginning to feel very real. 'If we're going to do this, then we have to be partners. We tell each other everything.' It would never be the partnership

Leo and I had, but I still demanded some respect. He nodded. 'I mean it, Julius. Don't treat me like a child. I want to know everything.'

'You might not like what I have to tell you sometimes,' he said quietly.

'I can handle it. I'm stronger than I look.'

'Good. Equal partners. Should we shake on that?'

I held out my gloved hand.

He took it and we shook. 'In that case, there's something you should know.'

'What's that?' Julius's expression was serious, and it worried me.

He led me across the soft grass and we sank into a seat under a large oak tree. 'Keep this between us.' I nodded, and Julius lowered his voice. 'Mussolini's fall has been a great shock and our leadership is nervous that the Reich might be perceived as weakened, especially after Stalingrad. The Soviets have penetrated German lines. We're on the back foot and I think there'll be difficult times ahead.'

'Are we losing the war?' I asked softly. Maybe there was hope that the Third Reich would fall.

'No, but there may be repercussions at home, and after the firebombing of Hamburg . . .' He let the thought hang in the air between us. Nobody had foreseen the terrible aftermath – the city unrecognisable, countless homes destroyed by fire, families without roofs over their heads, thousands of dead civilians and many more injured.

'There may be evacuations here in the capital, causing chaos and mass panic. But my real worry,' he continued in a low voice, 'is that there'll be another round of deportations to take the attention away from what's happening on the front and provide a scapegoat to ease people's fears.'

'But who's left?' I said, my eyes darting across the gardens. Virtually all of the Jewish people of Berlin were gone now, under constant guard in the eastern ghettos or, worse still, incarcerated in concentration camps with the fear of death over their heads. How much longer would they survive with the Nazis bent on their destruction?

'Not many,' he said grimly, 'but those who are still here will be under scrutiny.' My skin chilled with apprehension. 'Only protected people like Elya will remain, and even then, I don't know how much longer they'll be safe ... I think it's time to speed up our courtship.'

When the matron I'd worked with during my national service heard that I'd passed my nursing exam, she asked for me back at the Beelitz military hospital. It was a large complex of buildings fifty kilometres south-west of Berlin that had begun life as a sanatorium for tuberculosis patients and then become a military hospital during the Great War. The Führer had been treated here during that time, a story we heard with each new influx of nurses and doctors. The wide cloisters and verandahs with curved fascia and columns were graceful examples of the grand Wilhelminian style of architecture, but the wounded soldiers saw little more than their ward and a small patch of ground near their building before they were sent back to the front or home to their loved ones.

Luckily I knew my way around because I was thrown into the deep end as soon as I arrived in August. They were short-staffed and new patients had come in from the Russian front after the Red Army offensives on the Ukrainian city of Kharkov and the Russian city of Belgorod just to the north. The mood was sombre after the defeat of the Wehrmacht and the retaking of both cities by the Russians. They had been particularly bloody battles and the casualties were staggering, in their thousands.

I followed the senior sister around the long orderly ward, standing at the end of every neatly made bed with a group of nurses, listening intently and scribbling notes as she allocated patients to each of us and briefed us on their condition.

The ward was full and the soldier in front of us had been thrashing about and moaning throughout our rounds, but now lay quietly, his waxen face the same colour as the white linen.

'Private Schmitt presented a week ago with gunshot wounds to his abdomen and right thigh,' intoned the sister as she checked his chart. 'His right femur was fractured and although the field hospital completed fixation of the bone, he also sustained damage to the femoral artery. Consequently, he has severely compromised blood supply to his right leg and he will undergo surgery for an above-knee amputation. The gunshot wounds are healing slowly. Further debridement may be necessary, but the risk of peritoneal infection is high. This is our first priority. If he develops peritonitis the trauma of an amputation may be for nothing.' She put the chart down smartly on the end of his bed. 'Any questions?'

The truth was that we were dead on our feet. The shifts were long, attending to the terrible wounds of battle and listening to the stories of the soldiers, consoling and comforting them in their pain, both physical and emotional, before forcing ourselves to eat something and then collapsing into bed until the next shift. But I didn't want to be anywhere else.

After a month, I pulled all the strings I had with the matron and the Red Cross so Marika could join me at Beelitz as a nurse's assistant until she had the required experience to sit the nursing exam herself. Like me, she wanted to do something useful and by September we'd both decided not to go back to university. Neither of us felt like we could abandon our patients and the overworked staff. Our work had real meaning compared to the dry book learning of university; we were helping injured soldiers return to health and it felt good to be doing something useful among the daily tragedy that surrounded us. Like Leo with the black market, I had to take action otherwise the helplessness of our situation would eventually overwhelm me.

It took some work for me to convince Onkel Georg and Tante Elya to allow me to quit my studies. Women who weren't at university were now being placed into active war service, not just as secretaries and telephonists, but as flak helpers and artillery auxiliaries. The idea of being sent to a combat zone or being responsible for shooting down enemy planes from flak towers across Germany was frightening. But nursing at Beelitz satisfied our service requirements and kept us both close to home and out of danger. Finally our families relented and we moved our belongings into a room at the Beelitz nurses' quarters.

Julius and I began to see each other whenever we could. We often spent time on our own, getting to know each other better. We had to weather the scrutiny of his peers and keep everyone satisfied that our courtship was real. Julius had insisted on secrecy and, as much as it pained me, I couldn't tell Marika what we were really doing. When I reminded her that Julius was simply looking after me as a favour to Onkel Georg she looked sceptical, with an arched eyebrow and a steely green stare. Then she'd soften, hand me one of her lipsticks, kiss me on the cheek and tell me to have a good time. I knew I couldn't keep the truth from her forever.

Julius bought me a little car so we could see more of each other. Initially I felt quite uncomfortable with his gesture. It was one thing to be taken out to restaurants and performances, even to accept small gifts of jewellery, but this was something else.

'It's too much,' I'd said, staring at the shiny green Opel Olympia.

'I can afford it, and it'll make life easier for both of us,' he'd said, handing me the keys. 'People have to believe we're a happy, committed couple.' I'd taken the keys, nodding dubiously. On the estate, I had driven the truck and tractor for years, but I'd never tackled the busy city roads. With a few lessons from Julius, however, I was navigating the roads between Beelitz and Berlin without any trouble at all. It didn't take long before I was very grateful for the little car. Depending on our work schedules, Julius and I walked and picnicked in the parks and forests near the hospital, making the most of the crisp autumn days, or sometimes we met for lunches and dinners at small restaurants and clubs in the city.

I tried my hardest not to think of Leo – these were the things I'd wanted to do with him – but I discovered Julius was good company. Slowly my childhood adulation of him began to be tempered by the beginnings of adult friendship, although I still felt in awe of him. He was a powerful man who had been all over the world and had accomplished so much already. I was only beginning my journey.

'Fräulein Susanna,' called one of Julius's junior associates. We were at one of the most exclusive restaurants in Berlin, but wherever we went, we couldn't help but run into someone that Julius knew. He'd convinced me that we couldn't let the fear of air raids stop us from enjoying the pleasures of the city.

'Hello, Tomas,' I said, smiling. He was the son of a senior Nazi official, but was known for his wild living. He was generous and funny, which was what attracted most people to him, but underneath the brash exterior, he was kind and sensitive.

'Come, join us,' he said, gesturing to the table.

'Just for a moment,' Julius said.

'Susanna, you must sit next to me,' Tomas said, smiling broadly. I shuffled across the velvet seat. 'Champagne,' he shouted, clicking his fingers to the waiter, 'and lobster, oysters and caviar.'

'Tomas, we already have a table booked,' I said, laughing. I couldn't help but enjoy Julius's lavish lifestyle and it was easy to get caught up in the glittering social life. At times I had to remind myself why I was doing it and, in quiet moments, I recognised the pangs of discomfort I felt as guilt. I couldn't forget the squalor and fear that Onkel Tedi and so many others like him were enduring.

'I know you two lovebirds want some privacy,' Tomas continued, 'but I haven't seen you both in so long.'

'Just one drink,' said Julius, grinning at me.

'Herr Siebenborn,' said the man across the table. He wore a Nazi armband. 'Otto Haffner.'

'Otto works for Kreisleiter Mueller,' said Tomas genially. I sat with a brittle smile at the sound of his name. I still worried that one day I'd come face to face with him again.

'A pleasure to meet you,' said Julius graciously without missing a beat.

The champagne was poured and Tomas clinked glasses with me, sharing a cheeky wink.

'I hear you're a rising star within the transport ministry,' said Otto without preamble.

'I wouldn't say that,' said Julius evenly. 'I just do my job well. I'm there to serve the minister and the government.'

'As do we all,' said Tomas. 'Can you believe that Italy's declared war on us when we still hold Rome? Preposterous!'

I smiled. Tomas was an expert at navigating conversation away from difficult waters.

'We'll force the Allies out before they ever come in range of Rome,' said Otto confidently. The Allies had invaded Sicily and were fighting the Wehrmacht in southern Italy. It was a reminder that the war was no longer moving away from us, but advancing ominously towards our homeland on two fronts, the south and the east. 'The Italians will thank us for keeping the Allied wolf from their door.'

'Tell me, beautiful Susanna, how's university life?' asked Tomas, turning the subject again like a masterful conductor.

'I'm taking a break and nursing at Beelitz at the moment.'

'Because of the evacuations causing such chaos?'

'No,' I said, shaking my head. 'I want to do something practical to help the war effort.'

'She's a wonderful example of patriotism and sacrifice for the Fatherland,' said Julius, smiling with approval.

'An admirable act, my dear Susanna, a shining light to the rest of us,' said Tomas, patting my hand.

'You'd think that with all those leaving the city, we'd be rid of the last of the Jews, fleeing from danger like the cowards they are, but we're not Jew-free yet, despite the public declarations,' stated Otto in a flat voice. 'It's time for us to finally rid this city of them all.' I glanced at Julius in alarm; his expression was stony. 'At least you haven't been brainwashed by them at the university,' Otto said to me as if it was the most natural comment in the world.

'I'm caring for our military men now, Herr Haffner, those injured in battle fighting for our Fatherland.'

'Of course. Your caring nature is the very essence of womanhood. We need more women like you, willing to roll up their sleeves and look after our soldiers.'

I nodded stiffly, my fingers digging into the plush upholstery. Comments such as these were commonplace and I couldn't react to them, no matter how furious they made me. What was more difficult to ignore were the comments about taking further action against the Jewish people. At least now that Julius and I were viewed as a couple, it kept my family safe to some degree.

'Ah,' said Tomas loudly, clapping his hands. 'The seafood has arrived.'

7

It was early October before I made it home to Gut Birkenhof.

'I've missed you,' Tante Elya said, hugging me tight as we waved goodbye to her few remaining friends who had come to visit from the village.

We'd had a lovely time, drinking tea with women who remained steadfast in their friendship to our family, despite our troubles. In fact, it had felt like old times and Tante Elya's dry humour and vivacity had returned along with the colour in her cheeks. The rhythmic crunch of our feet on the driveway as we walked back to the house reminded me of childhood visits to the village where there was laughter, good food and wonderful company. And yet, although the visit had gone well and we still had stalwart allies, the overall mood in the village was more hostile. I wondered if it could ever be like it had been.

'It's good to be home,' I replied, comforted by her words and warm embrace. I looked out across the river, the afternoon sun casting a golden glow across the forest and green farmland on the opposite bank and making the water sparkle. Gut Birkenhof was the only place I could really be myself.

'I know why you stay away but it's not the same when you're not here.' With Onkel Georg and Leo busier than ever on the estate with fewer workers, the isolation had hit her hard.

'What have you been doing?' I asked as we walked arm in arm.

'I've been helping Onkel Georg as much as I can around the farm. There's so much to do and he's spread so thin, trying to keep everything going.' She sighed. 'I wish I could do more, but there are things I can't help him with, you know, operating heavy machinery with the harvest, supervising the logging and reworking the planning schedules for the year and, of course, managing the finances.' I'd noticed that Onkel Georg looked tired, worn down by the worry. When he wasn't rushing about the estate, he was cooped up in his study, no doubt going over the figures yet again. 'Sometimes both he and Leopold take the black market goods into Berlin and are away one or two days. Lately they've been spending more time away.' She stared off into the distance and I followed her gaze. The garden had not been planted out over summer and the hedges were overgrown. It was the last thing on anyone's mind, but at least there was still colour, as cheery white daisies and the autumn roses had appeared.

'Finding more black market customers?'

Tante Elya shook her head and took my hand. 'I have nobody else I can tell and you should know, despite all their secrecy. They've joined the underground resistance.'

'They've what?' I stopped walking abruptly.

'Leopold made the first contact through his black market connections. He couldn't sit on his hands a minute longer. He didn't tell his father straight away, but when he did, Georg quickly joined him. Leopold's very involved now,' she said calmly. 'Georg's more in the background at Leopold's insistence. If anything happens to Georg, we're lost.' She shrugged helplessly.

A warm glow of pride settled in my chest. It was just like Leo to think about how his father had to remain beyond reproach. 'How does it work? What do they do?' I whispered.

'It's only been a few months. All I know is that they meet in Berlin and are putting plans in place to help enemies of the Reich in any way they can. Although it's forbidden, we listen to the BBC broadcasts on the radio at night when the staff have gone home, so we're getting real news of the war and the Allied position, not Nazi lies and propaganda. Georg tells me that with the fall of Mussolini in Italy, there's new hope that the Nazi regime can be toppled too.'

'Onkel Georg told you?' I felt a stab of pain that Leo hadn't told me what they were doing.

She nodded. 'Leopold says nothing, but Georg and I have always told each other everything.' She rubbed her diamond ring absently. 'He didn't want to worry me, but . . .' She stood very tall, as if she was defying the world. 'He's doing all he can to protect this family, but each time he thinks he can relax a little, he finds that he's really helpless to do anything to stop them coming after us.'

'I know that feeling,' I said softly.

She nodded, tears in her eyes. 'He has to do something and so does Leopold. And after what happened to Onkel Levi in

Lemberg . . . we heard that the Nazis burned down the ghetto there recently. I don't know what happened to his grandsons . . .' She blinked away the tears. 'If Leopold and Georg can't protect their own, they'll become broken, shells of men. I'll never let that happen and so I'll support them,' she said.

'It feels good to do something,' I whispered, unable to tell her what I really wanted to.

'We each have a way of surviving, a way of keeping our soul intact. We need hope to live.' It was true of all of us and I turned my misty gaze to the neglected roses with their large pink blooms and fragrant scent. Hope could survive despite the greatest adversity and we would all do what we could to keep it alive. And I harboured the hope that, despite everything, Leo and I would one day be together.

I nodded thoughtfully. 'And that's why I think we have to be involved with the resistance too.' My nursing was no longer enough. I couldn't stop thinking about Otto Haffner's comments that more Jewish people needed to disappear. Onkel Tedi's letters from Lodz and the violent end of the Warsaw ghetto had made it abundantly clear that the Nazis wouldn't stop until all Jewish people were penned up like animals ready for the slaughter. Images of the damaged and broken soldiers I nursed – generations of our men destroyed by the Reich's endless war – were burned into my mind too. I wasn't going to sit on my hands. Doing nothing to resist was as bad as condoning their actions.

A smile widened under Elya's raised eyebrows. 'I think you might be right.'

'It's time for us to talk as a family,' Tante Elya said that night. The staff had all left for the evening and Onkel Georg and Leo had joined us in the parlour after dinner. The thick black curtains were drawn, keeping the light hidden against the dark night and from the enemy aircraft that everyone was fearful of after the destruction of Hamburg. It felt like the place for secrets to be shared, silent plans to be made.

Both men looked up warily, Onkel Georg from packing his pipe with tobacco and Leo from tuning the radio. Leo's dark hair fell across his eyes and the urge to brush the hair from his face and trace my fingers down the curve of his cheek was as strong as ever. I had hoped that months of staying away from him would diminish my feelings but nothing had changed. When our eyes met I knew he felt the same. We were still drawn to each other. Elya's sympathetic glances throughout the evening did nothing to help my agitation.

'Susanna and I want to know about your involvement with the resistance in Berlin. You can't keep it from us any longer,' she said, staring down Onkel Georg and Leo. I leaned forward on the lounge expectantly.

'I have to do something, Elya.' Onkel Georg bristled immediately, banging the arm of his chair. 'I can't sit back and watch our lives being torn to shreds, helpless to do anything about the constant threat to your life.'

'We can't continue to allow thugs and murderers to define who we are and what we become,' said Leo defiantly.

'I can't play their game any longer,' Onkel Georg growled. 'And nothing's going to happen to either of us. I've learnt a thing or two from the last war and we won't take unnecessary risks.'

'We understand why you're involved,' said Tante Elya, flushed with pride. 'But if you think we're both going to sit

107

back and let you do it all on your own while we wait help-lessly, then you're wrong.'

'You don't want us to stop?' asked Onkel Georg.

'No, *milaya*. I wouldn't ask that of you,' said Tante Elya.

'It's too dangerous to involve you both,' said Leo belliger-ently, glowering at us as he returned to his armchair. Onkel Georg just stared as though deep in thought.

Tante Elya shook her head. 'This situation involves us all, whether you like it or not. Susanna and I can't sit in the shadows waiting for something to happen to either of you.' She grasped my hand and smiled. 'We'll both go crazy otherwise. We can help you if you tell us what you're doing in more detail.'

'We're in this together,' I said, squeezing her hand.

'Your mother's right,' said Onkel Georg finally.

'What if something goes wrong?' demanded Leo, his eyes flashing with anger.

'We're all in a precarious position,' said his mother calmly. 'And what about the hundreds of thousands of Jewish people who are worse off than us? Surely we have a responsibility to stand up for them?'

'I have to do this,' I said. 'I can't be a passive bystander anymore.'

Leo and his father exchanged glances and Leo nodded slowly.

'All right,' said Onkel Georg after a moment. The creases of his face were set in stubborn determination and his blue eyes were bright with resolve. 'We work together then.'

'Tell us about the resistance,' said Tante Elya, settling back to continue knitting the jumper she had started for one of the newly fatherless children in the village. The mother refused to take charity from a Jew, but Frau Kraus or Ida hoped to pass on the jumper when it was finished.

'We're with an organisation called Free Germany,' said Onkel Georg, puffing away on his pipe. 'It's a national movement of all those who are opposed to the Nazi regime; people from all walks of life, all affiliations and beliefs.'

'We've had news from resistance contacts in Sachsenhausen,' said Leo, bowing to the inevitability of this discussion. 'They remember Felix.' I thought of Onkel Tedi's son, with dark eyes like Tante Elya and Leo and his mischievous grin. I'd always wondered if he'd managed to survive Sachsenhausen after being sent there after Kristallnacht.

Tante Elya pressed her hand to her mouth, tears in her eyes. 'We'll have to let Tedi know,' she whispered. They still managed to correspond, using friends to smuggle letters in and out of the Lodz ghetto.

'He acted as an interpreter for the Soviet officers and soldiers at the camp until he was transported out late last year,' Leo continued. 'We think he's in Auschwitz now.'

I put my arm around Tante Elya. 'If he survived all that time in Sachsenhausen, he has a good chance of surviving in Auschwitz.'

She nodded, wiping her eyes with her handkerchief.

'From what we understand most of the Jewish people in the camp have been transported east,' said Leo. 'Thousands of captured Soviet soldiers were forced to march from the Eastern Front in the dead of winter early in the war. Now it's primarily a camp for political prisoners, mainly the communists.' I couldn't imagine the conditions they'd endured across

Russia and Poland to make it all the way to Sachsenhausen, so close to Berlin.

'Franz Jacob, one of the founding members of the organisation, has spent time in Sachsenhausen and his contacts have confirmed Felix's reports. It's bad for the Soviet prisoners,' said Onkel Georg, shaking his head. 'Especially the officers. They're considered the leaders of a subhuman communist threat and treated worse than animals.'

'The Jewish and Russians,' whispered Tante Elya, horrified. 'They're our people. If only we could do something to help them.'

I nodded, not knowing what to say. We knew what the Nazi racial policy involved only too well. I felt ashamed to be German.

'We can't do anything to directly help the Jewish people now,' said Onkel Georg. 'We wanted to try, but it's not possible with the resources the resistance has and their primary focus now is on disrupting the regime. The sooner the Third Reich falls, the sooner the Jewish people are freed.'

'The resistance gets information from foreign newspapers and radio outside Germany and makes it available to ordinary people within the Reich,' said Leo. 'It's hard to fathom, but reports about the murder of thousands of Jewish people rarely make the news across the world, not the newspapers or even the BBC. Nobody believes it.'

'What hope do we have when nobody believes what's happening?' I said.

'It's a lot worse than we first thought,' said Georg softly. 'The SS conduct medical experiments on the men in Sachsenhausen which amounts to torture. Their barbarism falls to depths previously unknown.' He shuddered in repulsion. 'And they've been trying various methods of mass execution since the early days of the war, like gassing groups of prisoners in specially devised vans.'

We stared at him in horror, all of us thinking the same thing – if that was happening in Germany, what was going on in the other camps further east? Torture and mass extermination of inmates suddenly seemed well within the realms of probability.

'We have to do something,' I whispered.

'Surely we can do more,' said Tante Elya, shaking her head in dismay.

'We can help the Russians in Sachsenhausen,' said Leo quietly.

Tante Elya's face lit up. 'How?'

'The Soviets will support us,' said Onkel Georg.

'The organisation has strong ties to Moscow. Many of the leading members are communists,' said Leo. I nodded, thinking about the whispers of communist dissidents at university. 'They promote the overthrow of the Nazi regime through the organisation's pamphlets, magazines and radio broadcasts and they want to end this war as much as we do, but we want to do something more concrete.' He was grinning from ear to ear now, like a small boy, itching to tell his secret.

'With the help of the resistance, we've been actively recruiting people to our cause and we're finally putting a network in place from Sachsenhausen to Berlin and beyond. We're helping Russian prisoners of war escape.' The look of pride on his face made my heart soar. This was the man

Tania Blanchard

I loved, a man of action who refused to be downtrodden. 'We'll hide them on the estate until they can be moved on.'

'That's where you both can help,' said Onkel Georg.

For a brief moment, I was overwhelmed with worry for them. They were as deeply involved as they could be. If they were caught, they'd be executed. But I also remembered the hopelessness I had felt before and I knew that none of us could go back now.

Tante Elya and I looked at each other. The determined set of her face and the fire in her eyes mirrored my own feelings. *The enemy of my enemy is my friend.*

'Of course we can,' I said.

A little while later, Julius and I were stretched out on a blanket after our picnic in a hillside meadow near the Beelitz forest. It was a glorious sunny day and we had made the most of it before the icy reach of winter would descend upon us.

'I received another report the other day regarding Elya,' Julius said, flicking away an ant that had come too close to the remnants of our meal.

'What's happened?' I asked, my stomach clenching with fear.

'Complaints from the village again. This time it was about Elya not wearing the yellow star, last time about her entering a shop forbidden to Jews and the time before that about Frau Kraus. Jews aren't allowed to have Aryan servants.'

'Frau Kraus isn't a servant. She works for us and is a dearly loved family friend who's refused to leave us when so many others have abandoned us.'

'I know, Susie. I'm just telling you what's been reported.'

'They resent Tante Elya even being there,' I said bitterly, pushing the sliced apple away from me. 'I know what they say. "She lives a lavish life up in the manor house with servants and luxuries, with her husband and her son safely by her side . . ." But they forget everything she's done for them over the years, and now she's suffering her loss of freedom, and watching Onkel Georg struggle to keep the estate running. But worst of all is the uncertainty and fear she lives with every day.'

'Mueller's behind some of it too, possibly even stirring discontent in the village when he's there.'

Gooseflesh stippled my bare arms. 'Why is he doing this?'

'He's a man with a massive ego, who wants what he's never had and jealous of those who have it. Despite rising through the ranks of the Nazi Party and acquiring great power, he still doesn't have the status he craves. He's unable to break into the social circle of the elite without the family connections or lineage we have.'

'But why us?' I asked, desperate to understand why my family was being targeted.

'Deep down he knows he'll never be one of us, so he uses whatever situation he can to manipulate and exert his power to get what he wants – he's an opportunist and a predator.' I nodded slowly, making sense of what he said. 'With your family destabilised, I'm sure he's aiming to coerce you into doing what he wants, and even getting his grubby fingers on Gut Birkenhof. It's his ticket into the private club he so desires to be part of.'

I had no illusions about Mueller being an egocentric opportunist but I couldn't believe he was set on taking

Gut Birkenhof. I remembered the night of my party and the charged conversation between him and Julius, like two bucks fighting for territory. Now that I knew more about Julius's childhood, I understood his fierce protection of the estate, but I wondered if what was happening in the village was Mueller's revenge for Julius's personal attack on him that night, a salve for his wounded pride. Regardless, there was no doubt that Mueller was a threat, not just to Tante Elya and my family, but also to me. I was grateful to have Julius's protection.

'The locals have no love for the Nazi officials who come to Onkel Georg's cottages,' I said, 'especially someone like Mueller who throws his weight around.'

Julius shook his head, pulling up a stalk of wild grass. 'But they're nervous, too, and fear reprisal for being associated with Elya. Their way of distancing themselves from her is by doing what's expected and reporting her.'

'Even though many of them have known her for most of their lives?'

'Fear is greater than anything else when it comes down to survival.'

'Except for love,' I whispered, thinking of Leo. 'Should we be worried about what they're saying?' I was light-headed with anxiety. 'They're deportable offences.'

He reached for my hand and brought it to his lips. 'No, I've taken care of it. All reports regarding your family come to me before they're processed and nobody asks questions when they're dropped.'

I touched his cheek. 'Thank you. We're lucky to have you, Julius,' I said. 'But how can you do it without question?'

'Ganzenmüller has the organisational control for the department and together we work with many powerful men who can ensure these reports disappear.'

'People can't help but want to do things for you. No wonder you're a rising star within the ministry.' The woollen blanket I had borrowed from the hospital was scratchy against my hands as I shuffled next to him, stretching my stockinged legs to get more comfortable.

'I don't do it for the sake of naked ambition, you know. I really want to make a difference creating policy that's beneficial for Germany. If I were the minister I could do so much . . .' Julius broke off small sections of the stalk and threw them into the grass.

He had always been a mystery to me growing up, but there was so much more to him than I'd realised and now I was beginning to see what a complex man he really was. I couldn't work out why he wasn't already married with a family, because from what I knew he was kind, considerate, thoughtful and funny: a good man who would make some lucky woman very happy. He was handsome for someone his age, too, with a strong, chiselled jaw and an aquiline nose, balanced by a soft, full mouth. He kept himself in good condition, his stocky body strong and powerful, his dark honey blond hair kept short and neat, and he was always dressed immaculately, even now in an open-collared shirt and casual trousers. He had an easy manner that made people around him comfortable and he was well liked. The more I learnt about him the more I felt he was like a mature wine or cheese: mellow and full of flavour, with a lingering intensity. I enjoyed his company more each time we saw each other.

'There's nothing like doing something you're passionate about, where you're really making a difference,' I said, picking the fluffy tops of the wild grass within reach. 'I love watching our patients leave the hospital on discharge, hopefully as whole men again, but usually better than when they arrived, especially considering the challenges that come with the injuries we see. No matter where we're from and what we believe, we're all the same where it really matters. We all love our families, want to live happy lives and be useful citizens. That's what nursing shows me every single day. I live for the day that people remember that.'

'You know that could be seen as dangerous talk, Susie,' said Julius quietly. 'Some would even say treasonous.'

'But you know better than that.' I sat up tall, crossing my legs under me and matched Julius's gaze.

Julius leaned across and took my hand. 'You have to be careful,' he said urgently. 'Only in the most private places can you talk like that. If anyone heard and took offence, you, your family and even I could expect a visit from the Gestapo.'

I looked at him defiantly. 'Don't tell me you'd rather be part of a government controlled by Nazi policy and rhetoric? A minister kept in line by party heavyweights isn't a man who can make a difference.' I squeezed his hand. 'You and I are the same. That's why we're together, doing what we're doing.'

He kissed me suddenly on the lips, quite a chaste kiss, but the shock of his soft lips on my skin took my breath away. 'Stop talking,' he murmured. 'I agree with you, but never speak those sentiments out loud again. If I have to stop you with a kiss, then so be it.' His face was close to mine and I was aware of the stubble on his cheeks, despite his clean-shaven appearance.

His eyes were large and mesmerising and I couldn't stop looking at his mouth.

'I ...' He kissed me again, this time with a little more feeling, and I couldn't help but kiss him back.

'I said stop talking,' he said in all seriousness when he broke away. 'Promise me you'll be careful. You can't take what we're doing lightly.'

'I know. I promise I'll watch what I say ... But now you know what I think – and I know how you really feel.' I pressed my fingers lightly against my lips, trying to make sense of what had just happened and the confusion of emotions it had provoked.

His fingers trailed across my cheek, making me catch my breath. My heart beat faster. I was aware of his nearness, the warmth radiating from his body and the tingling in my sensitive lips. 'We're kindred spirits, Susie,' he said softly, 'but you're so young. I've seen and heard things that would make you weep with despair. I don't mean to scare you, but sometimes I lie awake, the images of what I've seen etched into my mind and I think I'll go crazy. I know what can happen to those who speak out, those who are defiant.'

I stared at him a moment, taking in the vulnerability behind what he'd said. 'Things you saw when you were in Krakau?'

I knew the Poles had been brutally treated. And I knew Julius well enough to know how confronting that would have been to him. Like me, he believed that all people deserved to be treated with respect and humanity.

He nodded, a haunted expression crossing his features. 'I try not to think about it, but when I'm alone in the dead of night . . .' He looked at me with such anguish. I put my arms around him and held him tight, as if I could protect him from the pain he obviously carried.

'I was at Rosenstrasse when the women protested against the incarceration of their husbands and sons,' I said. 'It could have been my family there. I have a good idea where those men were going. I might be young, but I've seen and heard things too. Those women never gave up fighting for their men and I felt their collective strength. I knew then that we could beat oppression. That's why I speak the way I do.'

Julius pulled away in surprise. 'You were really there?' I nodded. 'You could have been hurt – shot or killed.'

'But I wasn't,' I said, frowning and feeling a little deflated. 'It was just a crowd of peaceful women, wives and mothers.'

He took me by the shoulders, his expression stern and eyebrows knitted with worry. 'No more dangerous activities. Ensuring your family's safety is a constant fine balancing act with the right word in the right ear at the right time. You can't do anything to endanger that goal.' I thought about telling him about the resistance, but Leo had sworn me to secrecy and I couldn't ask Julius to risk any more.

He must have seen the anxious expression on my face because he gathered me to his side and kissed the top of my head. 'You're young and passionate, and that's something I love about you.'

One morning in early November, the first Russian prisoner of war arrived on the estate. We'd waited, nervous and impatient, since the previous day when his carefully planned escape had taken place. Anything could go wrong, and we were ready for the arrival of the Gestapo at any minute.

Although a number of strategies had been considered, a simple but daring plan had been decided on for the first attempt, to minimise the risk. With the help of the resistance, Onkel Georg had acquired an SS uniform and the forged pass and documents of a prison guard. They had been left at an appointed place within the Sachsenhausen complex, allowing the Russian to simply walk out the camp gates to a rendezvous point where Leo was waiting to take him south to Berlin. The Russian stayed at a safe house overnight before continuing further south with Onkel Georg to Gut Birkenhof. I knew that he was to stay with us a few days before it was safe enough for him to travel, but I didn't know the route he was taking back to Russia. It was safer that way, compartmentalising each stage of his trip, although I suspected that Leo and Onkel Georg knew the entire plan.

Hans and Frau Kraus were the only two on the estate who knew our plans and we trusted them implicitly. Hans and Leo often worked together, finishing up a busy day over a relaxing beer. Hans was exempt from military duty because of an injury sustained during the Great War and because, like Onkel Georg, he was involved in the production of essential services and his skill in the timber industry was highly regarded. After Hans had seen the Russian to the cabin in the forest, Tante Elya and I headed out with some blankets and an eiderdown, some warm stew, fresh bread and a thermos of hot chamomile tea from Frau Kraus.

I led Tante Elya along the barely discernible path through the heavily wooded forest. When the tiny timber cabin thrust into sight, nestled in a small clearing deep in the heart of the forest, I recalled the day I'd found Leo curled up in distress all those years ago.

I wondered what I'd find inside this time.

The man was gaunt, skin and bones. His clothes hung pathetically from his frame, like an absurd imitation of a child playing dress-ups. Tante Elya began to converse with him in Russian, trying to soothe him with her tone. There was a camp bed along one wall where I placed the extra bedding we'd brought, a bucket in the corner and a small fireplace which was empty. It was too dangerous to light a fire. We gathered around the little table, the Russian greedily eyeing the food Tante Elya was unpacking.

'This is his first proper meal in nearly two years,' she whispered to me as she put the food in front of him and poured a cup of tea.

'You've been at Sachsenhausen for that long?' I asked him in Russian. He nodded sadly, taking the cup and drinking the warm tea, closing his eyes in bliss.

He began talking as he shovelled food into his mouth.

'I came with many other prisoners of war in late 1941. We were forced to walk back to Germany from the front line, but given barely enough food to keep us alive, let alone survive the march. Our coats and boots were taken from us and we were left to dig holes in the ground for shelter with our bare hands when we slept. Many of us perished along the way. Those who didn't wish they had.' He stared at us bleakly, his sunken eyes blank.

'At Sachsenhausen we were treated worse than animals. We were left starving, our rations cut to less than the other prisoners. We were given no warm clothes, so we froze in winter, and were beaten for no reason. Our political commissars and any they discovered were active Bolsheviks were singled out for the worst treatment. Many were executed, shot with a single bullet to the head while digging trenches for their own graves.' His voice broke and he looked away, wiping his eyes. Then he gathered himself and continued, determined to bear witness. 'Others were given drug cocktails, making them descend into insanity, turning them into monsters so they even forgot they were human, and some died of gassing as the SS tried more efficient execution methods. But maybe it was better than the experiments . . .' He shivered at the ghastly memories and Tante Elya gently placed her hand over his, tears in her eyes. His hazel eyes were glassy, but he smiled at her with gratitude. He ate the stew more slowly now, and I realised that he was unable to eat much after having had so little for so long.

'How did you survive?' I was horrified by the brutality of what he described, although it confirmed what Onkel Georg and Leo had told us.

'I kept my head down and my mouth shut and somehow I survived. I was interned with Yakov Dzhugashvili, Stalin's son. He was shot dead during the evening walk. Not even the highly valued prisoners are safe.' I raised my eyebrows in astonishment, but I shouldn't have been surprised. There was no telling what the Nazis would do.

Tante Elya poured more tea and he sipped the hot liquid carefully. 'Thank you for helping me,' he said.

'It's the least we can do. I'm ashamed of what my adopted home is doing to my compatriots.'

On our walk back, Tante Elya seemed different, happier somehow, as though having some contact with her own people and culture had reminded her of her strength. And perhaps helping thwart the Nazis also gave her some purpose and allowed her to channel her anger and defiance. The Russian was gone in a few days, moved on to the next safe location on his perilous journey home. I prayed that he made it. If his escape was successful, more would be planned, but it also depended on the constantly fluctuating state of German control over its territories as battles were won and lost on the front lines. It was a fine line between risk and daring, with many lives held in the balance. I was so very proud of Leo and Onkel Georg being involved in making those final calls, but I didn't envy their position.

At Beelitz, injured men had been flooding into the hospital from the Eastern Front around Kiev for the past few weeks. It was hard to believe that the romantic old city of Tante Elya's childhood was now being reduced to rubble, destroyed by both the German and Soviet armies as they struggled to take control of the city.

'How many more can we take?' whispered Marika as the new arrivals were crowded into the ward we were working in. 'It's not like we can discharge those that are already here, some require nursing for weeks or months yet.'

'We'll manage,' I said quietly as we moved to another bed. I glanced back at the new patients down the ward. Most were waxen faced, exhausted with pain and lack of sleep, while others were sweating and hardly lucid, mostly in the grips of fever. I could only imagine what they'd endured, many travelling for days in cattle cars by rail, or by road in the backs of trucks.

Screams of agony rent the ward as one of the men was moved onto a bed.

'God almighty!' said Marika as she jumped with fright.

I put a soothing hand on her shoulder. 'This is the worst time. Once the new arrivals are settled, it won't be so bad.'

Marika nodded, her face pale against her auburn hair, and followed me resolutely through the ward.

We have a battleground of our own, I thought. There were the usual front line injuries from gunshot, shrapnel and explosions. Many of the injuries we saw were horrific, especially the multiple blast injuries from explosions that left the victim with head trauma, ruptured eardrums and eyes, internal injuries and haemorrhages to the lungs and abdomen that were often hard to assess, as well as the broken bones, lacerations, and widespread burns that were more visible. I found the burns particularly hard to look at. They were incredibly painful for the patient, difficult to treat and the resulting scars often left them maimed. The many amputations the doctors had to perform were also difficult for the men to face. The prospect of learning to function without a limb was daunting for most and many had lost more than one limb. But at least these men survived where many had not.

It was hard to learn of the state many soldiers had been reduced to – men who were fighting for our country. We'd been told about the necrotic frostbite injures of the last two winters when we first arrived and that alone was enough to take in. It wasn't unusual to find one of us quivering in the bathrooms retching uncontrollably, or in the corridors of the nurses' quarters, sobbing with relief, exhaustion or despair. There were so many men and so many whose lives would never be the same again. Then there were those who, after everything they'd suffered, died at this point, so close to home.

One man reached out and grasped me on the arm. 'They're coming, you know. The Red Army. And when they do, there'll be no mercy.' I pulled away, shocked.

'Are you all right?' Marika was by my side in an instant.

'I'm fine. He's just ranting, probably crazy with pain.'

We both looked at the soldier. His eyes were wide and desperate, as though he was watching a terrible scene over and over again.

'We've held Kiev for two years and with this new battle we're receiving so many casualties,' she whispered. 'Maybe the Russians are taking it back.'

'Trauma,' I said, with as much authority as I could muster. 'I've seen it before. I'll give him something to help him sleep.'

I shivered. Clearly the soldier believed what he was telling us. Was he some kind of prophetic angel? Would the Soviets save us from Hitler – or merely take over where he'd left off? I remembered Tante Elya's stories of the Russian pogroms from her childhood. I shook my head in irritation. I was exhausted and not thinking straight.

8

By the time the leaves were falling from the trees like coloured confetti, whispers of a new round of deportations had begun. Those who remained in Berlin – so-called privileged Jews by virtue of their connections or skill – were being placed in 'protective custody' before being transported to the eastern labour camps.

'My father's accountant was escorted by the Gestapo from his home in the early hours of the morning,' Tomas had confided to Julius and me earlier over coffee and cake. 'It's been a week and nobody will tell us where he is. He's the only one who understands our books and Vati's furious, but it makes no difference. I don't think we'll see him again.' He shook his head sadly. 'He's a good man and he doesn't deserve this treatment.' My horror had welled at his words but I'd only shared a glance with Julius, desperate to leave poor Tomas and find out what Julius knew.

'Is it true? Have you heard anything?' I asked Julius, unable to appreciate the beauty as we walked through Tiergarten. The sound of traffic along the tree-lined avenues that led to the Victory Column was muted. Except for the brief glimpses of the golden statue glinting through the trees, we could have been in the middle of the countryside.

'I'm afraid so,' he said, tucking my hand into the crook of his arm. 'Jews married to Germans and their children are the only ones still protected by law, but I don't know for how much longer. There are no other Jews to deport.'

'What are we going to do?'

'There's only one thing to do. Announce our engagement.'

'Whatever we have to do,' I said quickly. I couldn't have Elya and Leo any closer to danger.

'It should ensure Elya and Leo's safety, but this is serious and I'm afraid you'll have to mingle with more Nazis.'

'I know the stakes, Julius,' I said, gritting my teeth, 'I'll be discreet and charming.' But the thought made me sick. I'd have to hide my disgust and become the epitome of social graciousness and glittering conversation.

'I'll have a ring made for you.'

'A ring?' A wave of dizziness washed over me. It was becoming too real.

'Of course. It has to look legitimate. There's a government gala I want you to attend with me next week. Let's announce it then.'

My stomach swirled with apprehension at the thought of telling my family. There would be no going back after this.

*

A few days later, I was on the bus heading to Gut Birkenhof. Julius and I were having dinner at the estate but he was running late, stuck in a meeting, and would follow me when he could. I was counting on his support to tell my family of our engagement. I didn't know how I was going to face Leo. How could he possibly understand?

Tante Elya had insisted that we would have rabbit, no doubt one of the dwindling numbers that Onkel Georg and Leo captured in traps across the estate. There was going to be a proper sauce, the precious cream scraped from the top of our milk, and flavoured no doubt with the mushrooms I had helped Frau Kraus thread onto long loops of string and left to dry in the cellar months ago. I felt touched by the thoughtfulness of the meal, Tante Elya using valuable ingredients to welcome me home. I wondered if she and Onkel Georg were expecting our news, whether word had got back to them about how much time Julius and I had been spending together. Either way, I loved her for the effort she made.

We had to eat without him in the end. Tante Elya put a plate together and left it on the stove for when he arrived. I was surprised when Leo sat at the table with us. I hadn't seen him when I'd come in. Although conversation was stilted at first between Leo and me, soon it seemed like old times, he and Onkel Georg talking about the farm and the decisions they would need to make about crops and livestock, Tante Elya adding her opinion on the matter. Agriculture was a family affair, one I had grown up with, and so I understood the technical points and the business considerations involved. The conversation had invariably turned to my life at school or university, what I was studying, and a lively philosophical, cultural or historical debate always resulted, but now I told them about my nursing and how I was learning new procedures to accommodate the horrific battle injuries that we were confronted with. But the empty seat next to me and Leo's presence across the table was almost enough to drive me to distraction.

I could barely look at him, afraid that my guilt was plain as day. But I could feel him watching me and I couldn't help but glance at him from time to time, my eyes drawn to his mouth as he spoke, wishing those lips were against mine and his expressive hands were caressing my skin. As always, when our eyes locked I knew that the attraction between us was as strong as ever.

'What have you been doing with Julius in Berlin?' asked Leo casually as he put down his glass.

I felt the heat rise from my throat into my cheeks. 'He's been teaching me to drive,' I said, smiling brightly, glad I hadn't brought the Opel. I hadn't wanted to answer questions about such an extravagant gift before I announced my news.

'Oh, very good,' said Onkel Georg, nodding with approval.

'So you've been spending a lot of time with him then,' said Leo. His body was coiled like a tight spring.

'A bit, I suppose,' I said, guardedly. 'He's taken me to a couple of concerts and a few dinners, to broaden my horizons, and introduced me to a few people.'

'So you're making new friends then?' said Onkel Georg, looking hopeful.

I nodded, sipping my beer so I didn't have to answer.

'Perhaps life in Berlin suits you,' said Tante Elya, but I could see the shrewd look in her eyes.

'I'd rather be here at home with you,' I blurted out.

Her face fell and she quickly hid her wobbling smile behind her serviette.

'Nonsense,' said Onkel Georg. 'A young girl like you should be the centre of a glittering social scene. You're right where you should be.'

I could hear the telephone ring across the hall. Footsteps clicked across the timber floor and Ida knocked and entered, then whispered into Onkel Georg's ear.

'It seems that Julius is delayed,' he said. 'Problems with the railways again. He apologises to you all, but he won't be able to make it tonight.'

I paused, fork and knife in mid-air. The gala was in a few days and I was needed at the hospital every other hour. Tonight was our one and only chance to break the news.

'Onkel Georg, can I speak to you in your study after dinner?' I asked calmly.

'Of course.' Suddenly I was fascinated with the contents of my plate, but I could feel Leo's burning stare on my skin.

It seemed like an eternity until everyone had left the table. I watched nervously as Onkel Georg retired to his study, but a burst of irritation flamed through me as Leo accompanied him without apology or a backward glance at me.

I kept Tante Elya company as she embroidered in the parlour, telling her about the staff and life at the hospital while listening to her favourite piano concerto by Tchaikovsky on the gramophone. The grand, emotive music spoke volumes to me. It reminded me of the highs and lows of love, the passion and pain involved in tapping into its true nature.

'Do what makes you happy,' said Tante Elya softly behind me when I finally heard the study door open and close and

I slipped from the lounge, 'and don't give up hope. We never know when we'll get what we want most.'

I turned and saw the sadness on her face. I was sure she knew what was coming. I hated the idea of causing her any concern and wanted nothing more than to tell her what I was doing – what I really felt about Leo – but it wouldn't do any good. Everyone had to believe that my engagement to Julius was genuine. Love would have to wait. I only nodded instead.

'What is it, *liebchen*?' Onkel Georg asked as I sat down on the worn leather seat opposite his desk.

I clenched my hands in my lap to stop the terrible shaking that had overcome me. My heart was hammering through my chest, but I had to do this. I swallowed hard.

'As you know, Julius has been looking after me in Berlin.' He nodded, slowly sipping the tea Tante Elya had sent in for him, but I noticed the frown that quickly crossed his brow at my omission of 'Onkel'. 'He's kindly taken me to more restaurants and concerts than he's had to and introduced me to many of his friends and associates.'

'So he's found you a match then?' He put his cup down on the saucer and gave me a frank look, his blue eyes clear and bright.

There was no point beating around the bush. 'Julius has asked me to marry him and I've said yes.'

Surprise bloomed on his face, quickly followed by relief. His shoulders visibly relaxed and I realised that it hadn't been totally unexpected. 'Is this what you want?' he said, his eyes searching mine.

'Yes. He's been kind to me and I know how much you wanted a good match for me.'

He sighed and smoothed down his bushy moustache. 'Elya told me she suspected as much, but . . .'

I took hold of his hand, rough with callouses. 'Isn't this what you wanted? He's your oldest friend after all.'

'But you're my daughter.' He kissed the top of my head. 'I've known Julius most of my life. He can be fickle with women, but he couldn't have chosen any better than you. If he's made you this promise he will protect you with his life. But he's much older than you, old enough to be your father . . .' A warm glow rushed through me at his concern.

'We plan to make it official at the government gala.'

'Well then, it sounds like it's serious. He'll make a good husband and he's an ambitious man but, remember, he's a Nazi. You must understand that a marriage to him places you within the circle of powerful men who have put this family in danger.'

'But, Onkel, it could also protect our family. Julius loves you and your friendship is of the utmost importance to him.'

He pulled his hand free, his face a mask of concern. 'Susie, please tell me you're not doing this for the wrong reasons.' I wondered if he'd seen through me. 'Do you have any feeling for him at all?'

'We love each other,' I said. It wasn't a complete lie. I did love Julius in my own way, adoring him since childhood, but he would never be the great love of my life. He'd never be Leo. 'Something just clicked between us these last months in Berlin.'

His eyes narrowed at my words. 'I know he's always been fond of you since you were a child and I've always trusted him, but please tell me he's only ever been a gentleman.'

'Of course!' I jerked back, offended. 'He would never disrespect me. He's serious about the responsibility you gave him to look after me. He told me that he meant to court me in a respectable manner.'

'You're sure about this?' His expression was ferocious and I knew all he wanted was to protect me. I almost broke down and blurted the truth.

'I am. He wanted to be here to tell you himself and ask for your blessing.'

He sat silent for a moment while I held my breath, then he nodded. 'If it's what you want, you have my blessing, but remember that we're always here for you.'

'Thank you, Onkel Georg.' I hugged him tight. He only wanted me safe and happy. Exactly what I wanted for him, Elya and Leo.

When I returned to the parlour, the light was still on. Tante Elya was waiting for me, the embroidery on her lap.

'Come and tell me, *myshka*. What news do you have?'

I sank into the lounge by her side. 'Julius asked me to marry him.'

'And what was your answer?'

'I said yes.'

'Oh, Susanna.' She put her hand on my arm. 'I know he's been helping us and we're in his debt, but is this what you really want?'

I turned my head, my eyes squeezed tight, holding in the tears that threatened to overflow. 'It seems that I can't have what I really want,' I said, my voice shaking. I took a deep breath and turned to face her. 'Julius is good to me, he makes me smile, and I know that Onkel Georg wanted a good match for me with someone who could take care of me.'

'I see.' Her face was filled with compassion, but her dark eyes were sad. 'Can you learn to love him?'

'Many matches have started with less . . . I think so, with time.'

'I'm so sorry, *milaya*, but maybe it's for the best. He's in a position to keep you safe from uncertainty and for that at least I'm grateful.' She put her arms around me and held me. 'Never forget how much we love you.' She kissed my forehead and we stayed like that for some time, relishing the quiet moments together.

That night I didn't sleep well.

I dreamed I was in the back seat of the car again, wrapped safely in the darkness as the gentle movement and soft drone of the engine lulled me to sleep. A sudden screech of tyres jolted me awake and I pushed myself upright as a sickening thud forced our car off the road. I heard my mother's scream as our car took flight, felt the terror welling inside me as I groped for something to hang on to, anything to anchor myself to the ground with. And then the moment of impact when everything went black. Then I was running through a tall maze of green hedges, crying. I thought my family were all dead, but then I could see them, all my family, past and present, at the end of the maze. But when I got there, I was consumed by horror. Emaciated, lifeless bodies were lying in a pile like rag dolls – their unseeing eyes staring up at me.

I woke up with a start in the early dawn. I felt exhausted and rattled. My dreams always seemed so real, the raw emotions lingering for hours after, setting me on edge, but this one stiffened my resolve. No matter how bad it was going to be, I had to tell Leo of my engagement.

But in the end it wasn't me who broke the news.

'Susanna's getting married,' said Tante Elya at breakfast after the milking. I sat rigid, waiting for his reply.

'Are you being funny?' said Leo. He looked dishevelled and was dark under the eyes as though he'd had a bad night as well.

'Your mother's serious,' said Onkel Georg. 'Julius asked her to marry him and she has agreed.' The look of complete shock and hurt on his face was almost my undoing.

'That's the most ridiculous thing I've ever heard,' he said stony faced, refusing to look at me. 'I've got better things to do than hear about Susie's social life.' He pushed his chair back, threw his napkin on the table in disgust and stalked out of the room.

'It's a shock to him, not something he expected,' said Onkel Georg, wiping his mouth. 'But he'll calm down soon enough and congratulate you properly then.' Tante Elya remained silent, but I saw the pain in her eyes and knew it wasn't just for me.

I nodded and stared at my plate. How was he ever going to forgive me?

It didn't take long for him to confront me. I was coming out of the barn after feeding hay to the older calves when Leo grabbed me by the arm and towed me back into the shed.

'Let go of me,' I snapped. 'What are you doing?'

'What am I doing?' he roared. 'What are *you* doing? After I warned you about him!' His eyes blazed with fury.

'He's been helping this family, if you remember. Anyway, I don't have to listen to you,' I yelled back, wrenching my arm free. 'Your father wanted me to marry someone who can look after me.'

'Someone with money and power,' he said with contempt. 'A filthy Nazi who's only helping us because it suits his purpose. But what happens when he falls from grace or, God forbid, we lose this war? What happens to you then?'

'It's not your problem,' I spat back. 'I'm doing my duty as a good daughter. Your father's happy with the match.'

'And you?' He was watching me warily now, unsure of how I'd answer.

'I'm happy enough.' I noticed the flash of satisfaction before his face darkened.

'If he hurts you, I'll break his neck.' He was shaking with rage, but I couldn't allow myself to feel guilty for his hurt pride. I'd chosen my path.

'Oh, Leo, spare me the heroics. Just be civil to him.' I touched his arm, wanting him to somehow understand. 'I don't want to see you hurt either. If we can both survive the war, who knows what will happen after?'

'What are you talking about? You'll be a married woman with his mewling brats at foot.'

I slapped him hard across the face. 'Don't *ever* speak to me like that again. I have my own reasons for entering into this marriage, but don't presume to know what I will or won't do.'

He grabbed me by the shoulders. 'I can't bear the idea of his hands on you.' His breath was ragged on my neck.

'He hasn't touched me.'

'Oh, but he will, the first chance he gets. As soon as you're officially claimed, his paws will be all over you. You're just a girl, but you'll end up a ruined woman if he leaves you.'

'Leo, don't do this!' I pushed him away. I couldn't tell him that my relationship with Julius was strictly platonic. If he knew about the arrangement, he would try to prevent our engagement. It would ruin everything.

He pulled me to him. 'You can't do this, Nightingale.' His breath stirred the loose hairs curling around the back of my neck and face. 'I'm yours and you're mine. You told me we were meant to be together.'

My heart clenched. He was as close to despair as I was. Tears filled my eyes, and my voice broke with emotion. 'There are things out of our control, Leo. This is one of them, but it doesn't mean that my feelings for you have changed.'

'Then I can't let you do this. Surely you won't go through with it, just to please my father.'

'I've made my choice. Being aligned with the right people is beneficial for all of us right now.' I pulled away, wiping the tears from my cheeks and looking into his face, willing him to understand.

He swore under his breath and turned away, but then he was back, gathering me in his arms and kissing me hard. I held him tight and kissed him as if it was the last time we would ever be like this. In my heart I knew it had to be for now.

'I love you and you love me,' he murmured at last as we broke off the kiss. I just stared into the rich depths of those expressive brown eyes.

'Yes, but now I have to say goodbye.' I stepped out of his embrace and walked out of the barn without looking back. It was the hardest thing I'd ever had to do.

I made my way to the kitchen to see Frau Kraus. I had to do something – stir soup, chop onions, peel potatoes – or I'd go crazy with everything going round and round in my head.

She could see how upset I was and handed me a bowl of dough. 'Knead,' she said.

Pounding and working the dough helped me work out my frustrations and calm down. 'I'm getting married to Julius Siebenborn,' I said when the dough was done. I put it near the warm stove to rise.

'Are you now?' said Frau Kraus, sniffing the contents of the huge pot on the stove. 'I know that Georg is doing everything to keep you at arm's length from the dangers faced by the family but is this what you want?'

I sank into the chair at the table. 'All I want is to help them.'

She grunted. 'Julius has money, power and influence.' She looked at me shrewdly as she threw the chopped up vegetables into the pot. 'I suppose Leo's not happy about it.'

My shoulders slumped. 'No, but it's not his decision. It's mine.'

'That's right. It's yours. Men think they own us, but they don't.' She smiled and patted me on the shoulder. 'We all do things we wouldn't normally do in times like these and, sometimes, despite our best intentions, we even enjoy them. But we should never allow it to change who we are and never forget why we're doing them. That's how we retain our power.' I frowned. There was no doubt that I enjoyed Julius's company and there were elements of my life with him that I unexpectedly appreciated – the champagne, the fine clothes and soirees – and times when the guilt rose like a serpent and I had to remind myself that there was a purpose to my life with him. The conflict within me was becoming harder to ignore. 'You get what you want out of Julius because I guarantee he thinks you'll do whatever he wants you to do. One of these days the war will be over and things will improve. Just you wait and see.'

I got up and kissed her on the cheek. 'You always know what to say to make me feel better.'

'Do I, *schatz*?' She looked surprised, but flushed with pleasure.

Julius and I met at the Hotel Kaiserhof for coffee and cake in between my shifts at the hospital. Most tables were full, and although we had a table in the corner, it was still noisy.

'It was inexcusable making you tell Georg on your own, but it couldn't be helped,' he said apologetically. He looked pale and drawn, as if he'd had little sleep. 'It's crazy on the Eastern Front with the latest offensive, and keeping the trains on schedule with the extra troop movements, and some of the lines damaged, is a nightmare. At least Georg and Elya took the news well. I told you it would be fine. In fact Georg telephoned me last night and gave me his blessing.'

'It was difficult, Julius,' I said, trembling at the memory of Leo's reaction and trying to hold onto my composure. 'It's not something I should've had to do alone.'

'Let me make it up to you.' He put his hand in his pocket and pulled out a small box. 'Open it.' He looked hopeful, his anticipation betrayed by the slight tapping of his fingers.

I opened the lid, and gaped. 'It . . . it's gorgeous,' I said, staring at the engagement ring. It was magnificent: a platinum band set with a large glittering centrepiece diamond, flanked by two smaller, baguette-cut diamonds on either side.

'Try it on,' said Julius, smiling. 'I want to make sure it fits.' I felt overwhelmed by the extravagance and the expense but remembered Frau Kraus's words about doing what was necessary to get what I wanted.

He lifted it out of the box and, even in the dull afternoon light, it sparkled brilliantly. He took my hand and slipped it on my finger. For better or worse, my fate was now tied with Julius's.

I turned my hand to view the ring from different angles but I didn't know what to say. I felt like all eyes were upon us and the weight was oppressive.

He reached across and kissed my hand. 'Hedy's booked a day of pampering at the salon so you'll look your best for the gala. I have a new gown for you to wear, but it's a surprise. It'll be delivered to you in time for you to dress.'

'Julius, you didn't have to.'

He stood and pulled me to my feet. 'I want this to be the most glorious night of your life. Everyone will tell me that I'm the luckiest man alive to have you on my arm.'

I wrapped my arms around him, his warmth and strength giving me the comfort and reassurance I needed. I reached up to kiss him on the mouth for the benefit of all the prying eyes and I heard applause break out around us. This wasn't a private moment after all. We were making a public statement, proclaiming that we were now betrothed.

9

'**Y**ou did what?'

Marika stared at the ring on my finger. She'd come to stay with me at the Adlon Hotel where Julius had booked me a room while I was in Berlin for the gala. It was just as famous as the Kaiserhof and only a few blocks away, but, more importantly, it was the centre of the social hub of Berlin.

I nodded sheepishly. 'It's true.' She took hold of my hand and inspected the ring, her eyes wide at the size of the diamond.

'And you didn't think to tell me.' She dropped to the bed aghast.

'I know, I'm sorry. It all happened so fast. Before I knew it really,' I said lamely, sitting beside her. I hung my head in shame. But there was no way I could have told her before. It was too complicated.

'I should have guessed, I suppose,' she mused. 'The extravagant gifts, the clothes and that car . . .' She fixed me with

140

those scrutinising green eyes. 'What about Leo? I thought he was the love of your life.'

'He is,' I said softly.

Marika shook her head, exasperated. 'I don't understand.' How could she when I couldn't tell her that I was doing this to ensure Tante Elya and Leo's safety, to keep them out of the camps? She didn't know about the conditions the Soviet prisoners were subjected to in Sachsenhausen, the experiments. The Nazis kept this dark underbelly of their operations well hidden from the German people.

'I don't expect you to.' I sighed. 'It's hard to explain.' I didn't know whether to scream or hide my head in my hands and cry. 'Onkel Georg wants me married to someone who can protect me.'

She jumped up from the bed. 'But Julius? It's one thing to have a little romance with him, quite another to marry him. Besides, like you'd go and accept your fate just like that, married off to someone you don't love. He didn't even come to Gut Birkenhof with you to announce your engagement.' Marika wasn't buying my story – she knew me too well – but I had to try to convince her.

'Please just be happy for me.'

'Of course.' She frowned and sat next to me, taking my hand in hers. 'I just never expected this . . . but if you're happy I'd better congratulate you.' I noticed the look of concern cross her face before she smiled broadly and embraced me. 'You can always count on me,' she whispered into my hair, and I nodded and squeezed her tight.

*

The gala was held at the Hotel Kaiserhof. The foyer thronged with well-dressed men and women and I wondered how I was ever going to find Julius. But I needn't have worried. He was waiting for me by the entrance looking dashing in a well-cut evening suit.

'You're breathtaking,' he whispered into my ear as he took my arm. My hair was curled and twisted up off my nape, accentuating my long neck, and the floor-length, long-sleeved gown in slinky white satin, although demurely cut, showed off my slim silhouette. The large diamond on my finger was hard to miss, sparkling in the light.

'Thank you,' I said. 'I enjoyed today and I love the gown.' The day of pampering had been everything I could possibly have wanted to look and feel beautiful for the gala.

'You look perfect,' he said, smiling.

We made our way into the ballroom and I scanned the room as we waited to be shown to our table. It was hard to miss the displays of Nazi power everywhere in the city, banners hanging in the streets and in public buildings, but I'd never seen anything like this. The massive swastika banners draped against the magnificent, classical arches and columns were juxtaposed against the luxurious furnishings, but the grand, imperial space perfectly reflected the designs of the Nazi Party. The message was clear: this was Germany's new royalty, a new order in an ever-expanding empire that was determined to remain in the hearts and minds of all people for many years to come, much like the ancient Romans.

Men in various military dress uniforms stood tall and proud, outshining those in civilian evening dress, but not Julius. Most men here were leaders within the party, men with the power of life and death, and knowing what I already did about the decisions they made with such impunity regarding the lives of ordinary people, causing misery to thousands, I could only turn away in disgust. Instead I gave my attention to the ladies, all dressed in the finest evening wear, and I was thankful for Julius's choice of gown for me.

'Julius.' A balding, portly man walking past stopped next to us.

'Herr Direktor, I see you've made it.'

'Yes, the meeting with the minister went late, but we got here.' He glanced across to me and I could see the look of appreciation on his face. 'Are you going to introduce this enchanting creature on your arm? She looks like an angel.'

'Herr Direktor, this is my fiancée Fräulein Susanna Göttmann.'

'Lovely to meet you, Fräulein,' said the direktor, smiling benevolently. 'I've heard so much about you. Congratulations to you both.' He slapped Julius on the back. 'It's about time you had a wife to keep you respectable, especially if you want to rise further in the ministry. You're a lucky man with someone so beautiful.' My smile remained, but I was angry at being considered nothing more than a pretty yet required accessory. 'I'll send my wife to meet you, my dear. But first I'll find my table. I need a drink,' he said before disappearing back into the crowd.

'Charming man,' I murmured.

'He's important, Susie, as are most of the men in this room. Men like him were raised in a world where women have little say in anything outside the home.' He grinned. 'They wouldn't know what to make of modern women like you.'

'I'll be good tonight then,' I said quietly.

Julius introduced me to his associates and I expected to meet more men like the direktor, but most were courteous, especially those who worked with Julius, even taking an interest in my university studies and nursing work. I found the Minister of Transport, Herr Dorpmüller, to be a man like Julius, an engineer dedicated to keeping Germany's transportation system running efficiently. And I was pleased to finally meet Ganzenmüller, the influential man Julius worked closely with and admired. Later in the evening, I noticed them drinking cognac and in deep conversation. Julius was becoming known in the upper circles of the Reich and powerful associates like Ganzenmüller were what we needed to protect Tante Elya and Leo.

The night passed with many congratulations and small talk, mainly with the women about fashion, luxuries that were difficult to obtain and proud stories of sons on the battlefront told by terrified mothers. Once it became known that I had been studying at university, there was even talk of art, philosophy, history and languages. There were those who espoused that my place was at home, but I quickly put them straight, explaining that I was now a nurse working at a military hospital, helping the war effort, and that gained me a degree of grudging respect. It made me angry, being judged by such hypocrites, many who carried the staunch belief that they were untouchable. But the continuous inconsequential conversation dulled my sense of outrage to a slow and drawn-out exasperation and soon the faces merged into each other and I couldn't remember all the names.

As we said our goodbyes at the end of the night, I noticed Julius with a woman across the room, her mouth close to his ear and her hand on his arm in a rather possessive manner. I turned to wish goodnight to the couple sitting at our table and when I looked back, she was gone.

'I want to talk to you about something I found out tonight,' said Julius, as we made our way out of the ballroom. 'But not here. Come upstairs to my suite where I can tell you in private. It's about Elya.'

My heart began to race. 'Is she in danger?' I whispered.

He shook his head. 'Don't worry. I'll explain more when we go up.' He smiled reassuringly as he guided me towards the stairs that led to the upper floors of the hotel. 'Did you enjoy the gala tonight?' he asked, making conversation as we made our way.

I was grateful for the distraction. 'It was quite a night,' I said. Truth be told, I was feeling exhausted and a little light-headed. I wasn't sure how many glasses of champagne I'd had – first to get through the nervousness, then to wet my dry throat from so much talking, and finally to numb the boredom and my simmering anger at the meaningless chatter that occupied so many present.

'You made quite an impression,' he said. 'You were spark-ling.' We were walking along the corridor to the rooms and it was blissfully quiet compared to the ballroom.

I looked up at him. 'Was I really? Did I make you proud?'

His eyes went wide with surprise. 'Of course. You're an incredible young woman. The men you met tonight won't forget you or your accomplishments. Most will want to do anything to keep you smiling and happy. We'll meet the important ones again at the opera and ballet, at dinner, and we'll remind them how as a couple we embody the essence of German ideals.'

I nodded, feeling the heat rise to my face. I couldn't believe I had that effect. It was a lot to take in. 'Who were you talking to before we left?' I asked lightly.

He shrugged. 'I don't remember. I spoke to a lot of people tonight.'

'The woman,' I said pointedly. 'The very attractive brunette.'

'Oh, Collette.' He waved a hand dismissively. 'She's an old friend. I haven't seen her in years.'

'Really? It seemed that she knew you quite well.'

'You're not jealous, are you?' he asked, grinning.

'I know I have no right to be . . . but maybe a little,' I said, too embarrassed to look at him. He had a reputation, but I'd seen no evidence of other women since we'd started our courtship. 'Is there anyone else, Julius?'

He stopped and took my hands in his. 'That part of my life is long over,' he said. 'I have you now.' We stood very close and I wondered what it might be like to be properly kissed by him.

'What do you get out of this engagement?' I whispered feeling flustered.

'You,' he said, his hand at my back steering me to his door. 'You're intelligent, eloquent, accomplished and beautiful.' I didn't know what to say to that. He unlocked the door and escorted me into the suite.

The sitting room was luxuriously appointed and comfortable, a far cry from the nurses' quarters at Beelitz.

'Relax while I get us some champagne,' he said gesturing to the lounge upholstered in expensive silk brocade.

'I don't really need any more,' I said as I sank gratefully against the plump cushions, glad to be taking the weight off my feet.

'Just a small glass,' said Julius, taking the bottle out of the ice bucket on the table beside us and popping the cork. 'We haven't celebrated our engagement and it's been such a successful evening.'

'A small one then,' I said, watching him pour two glasses but wanting nothing more than to shut my eyes for a minute or two.

He handed me a glass and sat beside me. 'To us,' he said, touching his glass against mine.

'To us and our successful endeavour,' I said, smiling. I took a sip. 'There were lots of congratulations tonight, so I think our ruse is working.'

'You were perfect. I told you that you didn't have to worry. Everyone's happy for us. They love you and gladly welcome you into our midst with open arms.'

I nodded, not sure that I wanted to be a part of the Nazi social elite. It meant that I was one of them, with the same warped values and attitudes. It felt wrong in all sorts of ways. I took a large swallow of the champagne. But I had to remember why I was doing this. 'What's happened with Tante Elya?' I asked anxiously. 'I saw you talking to Ganzenmüller for some time. Is everything all right?'

He nodded. 'It is now. I found out today that Elya's been reported for using the black market.'

I froze. Someone had betrayed not just her, but Leo too, if only by implication.

'Why can't they leave us alone? She's no threat to anyone.' I felt sick.

'Black marketeering's a serious offence. When I looked into the complaint I discovered it was about the food parcels

147

that Frau Kraus distributes around the community for Elya.' He raked his hand through his cropped hair and shook his head in disgust. 'Some bright spark from the village, I suspect at Mueller's prompting, realised that Elya could never have supplied that many packages containing rationed items that aren't sourced from the farm – biscuits, sugar and the like – without accessing the black market.' I breathed a sigh of relief and sipped more champagne. Leo's operations hadn't been blown. 'But my concern was that if anyone decided to investigate further, they'd find more.'

'What?'

Julius briefly rested his hand on my leg. 'I know that Leo's been trading goods on the black market.' I stared at him in surprise but not without some guilt. In the beginning, Leo had asked me not to tell him anything about the black market dealings and, although I trusted Julius implicitly, I wanted to keep my word. Besides, there had never been a reason to discuss it with him, even though I'd been tempted to tell him a few times. 'It's no surprise considering the lost contracts and it seems that he's just like his father, resourceful and pragmatic. But any probing would implicate both Elya and Leo, and possibly Georg too, not to mention all those contacts that Leo's made in the business.'

'It would be catastrophic for all of them,' I admitted.

Julius nodded. 'And it could give Mueller the opportunity to take Gut Birkenhof for himself, especially if he's the one behind it all.'

'That can never happen,' I said, shaking with fear and fury.

'I couldn't agree more,' said Julius. 'That's why I had to nip it in the bud. Make no mistake, Mueller's a powerful man with powerful friends but, lucky for us, I also have friends in powerful places. I was able to call in a favour and ensure that that report never sees the light of day. Elya, Leo and Georg are safe and any further complaint in that vein will conclude that supplies in those food parcels came from the pooling of rations from a variety of benevolent individuals to aid those in need across the community.' My body sagged as the tension I'd been holding was released.

'You did that tonight?'

'Yes, it couldn't wait. I didn't want to risk it.'

I placed my hand on his. 'You called in a favour, but what did it cost you?'

'Nothing I haven't already pledged.' He took my hand to his lips. 'Politics is a complicated game but as long as I'm aligned with the right people, I don't expect there to be any problems. We'll stay one step ahead of Mueller and keep your family safe.'

'Julius, I don't know how to thank you for everything you've done. You've helped with the contracts, ensured the seed and fuel orders arrived, kept me safe from Mueller and eliminated every threat against my family.' I shook my head in amazement. 'You've done everything you've promised to protect us and I'm so grateful . . .' Tears welled in my eyes. 'I can't imagine what might have happened without your intervention.'

'Then don't imagine it. As long as I'm by your side, you have nothing to worry about.' I nodded and picked up my glass but it was empty. Julius grinned. 'Talking is thirsty work,' he said, reaching for the champagne bottle.

'No more,' I said, shaking my head. 'I won't be able to stand up otherwise.'

'A last toast,' he said, filling up my glass before raising his. 'To the future and to lasting happiness.' I took another sip, knowing I'd regret it in the morning. All I could hope was that my shift the next day would be quiet. Julius leaned across and kissed my cheek. 'Are you happy?'

'Of course.'

'With our arrangement?'

'I never imagined it would be so easy with you. Sometimes I have to pinch myself to make sure it's real. You've been so good to me, given me so much.'

'It's only what Georg wanted for you: safety and protection from the dangers surrounding your family and a life you deserve.'

'But if he really knew.' I smiled wryly.

'He never has to know if we become a real couple.'

'What?' My head was beginning to feel fuzzy.

'Don't you know how ravishing you look?' he said softly. His hand slid up the side of my thigh.

I grabbed hold of his hand. 'What are you doing?'

'Come on, Susie, let's have a little fun. Don't you want to find out what the fuss is all about?'

The yearning in his eyes made me confused and afraid. 'Don't be silly,' I admonished.

'I'm serious. We trust each other and enjoy each other's company. Why not?'

'Julius, we had a strict arrangement.'

He sighed and caressed my arm instead. 'Susie, we're in this now. Let's make the best of it. I meant all those things I said to you tonight. What I want is you.'

'But we can't.' I tried to move away but I only sank further into the lounge.

'Is there someone else you have feelings for?'

I dropped my gaze. I couldn't tell him how I felt about Leo. Somehow it didn't feel right. Those emotions were intensely personal and my memories of him were what kept me going when I despaired of a future without him at all. 'So there's no reason for us not to try to have a full and meaningful relationship.' He brushed loose hair from my face, securing it behind my ear. 'I know you feel the connection we have and I've seen the way you look at me sometimes. You're too young to know what love is, but I do, and I'm telling you it's what we have.'

I frowned, trying to think through what he'd said, wondering if what I felt for him could be called love. He did make me laugh and I could be myself with him, the woman I was becoming, and there was no doubt that I was attracted to his power and the life he could give me. But it wasn't as powerful as what I felt for Leo. It was nothing like it.

'You really are beautiful and I would never hurt you.' He dipped his head to kiss me and I tasted the lingering traces of the expensive cognac he'd been drinking. He gently pushed me back into the lounge, and his hands slid over my hips gliding over the satin of my gown, firm, steady and experienced. 'Stay with me tonight,' he said, his voice rough with need. 'Do this one thing for me. Let me show you what love is.'

'Julius . . . I,' I said, feeling trapped. The room around me began to spin. He'd done so much for my family and this was all he asked of me in return. But it was the one thing I couldn't give to him. All I could think of was Leo under the cherry tree and how I vowed to wait until we could finish what we'd started that night.

I was feeling so disoriented that when Julius scooped me off the lounge and carried me to his bed, I could hardly resist. The room was still spinning slowly and the bed was so soft. All I wanted to do was shut my eyes but then his hand was inside my gown. I pressed my hands against his. 'Wait, Julius.' He kissed me again, ignoring my protests and his hands caressed my body, not like the sizzling touch of Leo's that ignited my desire, but still depleting my resolve with his insistence. Then his hand was between my legs and I knew it was too late to refuse. I would do what he wanted. He was our protector.

He spread my legs wide and he hovered over me as I felt a firm pressure thrusting against my softness. I clung to him until at last he slid home with a sharp stab of pain. As the pace quickened and the thrusting intensified, he drew into himself and I felt alone and adrift as he plunged himself deeper into me. All I could do was hold on until he collapsed, shuddering on top of me.

'That was incredible,' he said after a moment or so. 'I've wanted this for so long.' He rolled off me and lay on his side looking at me. I pushed my skirt down over my thighs and sighed shakily. 'You're so beautiful,' he whispered, caressing my cheek. 'I'm sorry it was rushed. I couldn't help myself. Next time we'll take our time and explore the delights we each have to offer. I'll show you what pleasure's all about.'

'But we're not married,' I whispered. 'And there won't be a wedding.'

He rested his hand on my belly possessively. 'We're engaged and it's time for our relationship to become something more than a sham. What's more believable than a couple in love who can't keep their hands off each other? This is the modern day, you're a modern woman, but you don't have to worry, we'll be discreet.'

'Am I just another one of your women who you'll use and then discard when our arrangement is over?'

'How can you say that?' He looked genuinely hurt. 'I'll always protect you and look after you, and I promise to give you a good life and treat you right. Just love me as I love you. That's all I ask.' He kissed my cheek gently.

Thoughts of Leo and the love we shared came unbidden into my head. What I'd done with Julius felt nothing like the night with Leo under the cherry tree. I'd responded to Leo with an uncontrollable passion that I didn't experience with Julius. Where I'd felt close to Leo, I'd only felt dissociated from myself with Julius. I couldn't change what had happened but I knew that I'd now stepped into the unknown and that everything was now different for me.

I nodded, feeling hollow and confused. 'I have to go. I have a shift at the hospital tomorrow.' All I wanted now was sleep and oblivion before Marika and I had to drive back to Beelitz.

Perhaps in the cold light of day I could make sense of what had happened.

Marika found me sobbing in the shower the following morning, sitting on the floor, curled in a ball and heedless of the water that was running over me. She turned off the water and wrapped a towel around me.

'Come on. Let's get you out of here.' She helped me up and I followed her out, water dripping onto the tiled floor. Now that I'd stopped crying, I felt numb. She placed another towel on my head, twisted it and tucked the edges in like a turban. 'There, no more drips,' she said.

She took my hand and led me back to our room where I sat perched on the edge of a chair. I couldn't speak. I didn't know what to say. My eyes were raw from crying and my head hurt.

'What's wrong, Susie?' Marika crouched down in front of me, her face creased with worry. I glanced at my gown, still crumpled on a heap on the floor by my bed. 'Did something happen at the gala?' I clasped both hands together tightly across my abdomen. It ached there and between my legs, reminding me of what I'd done. There was no escaping it.

I nodded. 'I let Julius have me. I was waiting for Leo, but now. . .'

Marika dragged the other chair next to me and sat, draping her arm around my shoulders. 'Tell me what happened.'

So I told her, haltingly at first, but then the words came and the emotions with it: anger, guilt, mortification at my stupidity and, finally, desolation. With Marika's arms around me, fresh tears began to fall.

'It's my own fault, but I can't take it back and Julius wants more.' My shoulders slumped with wretchedness. I was so confused by what had happened. I'd always believed I had a strong sense of morality so the guilt at what I'd done seemed like a bottomless lake.

'He took advantage of you. I don't care if he says he loves you.' She was angry too, and that helped, but I should have

154

known better. How could I have been so naïve? 'You have to break your engagement. Your aunt and uncle will understand . . . And Leo will break his neck,' she said darkly.

'I can't.' I shrugged helplessly. Her look of astonishment broke my resolve and I decided I couldn't hide the truth from her any longer. I told her of my arrangement with Julius, how it had all started and the whole story since. 'I'm trapped. He's done so much for our family and I feel obliged to him. My family's safety is worth more than anything.'

'He's no better than Kreisleiter Mueller,' she said through gritted teeth. 'He might be more handsome and charming, but he's just as manipulative.' She was shaking with rage. 'He's using your fear of what's happening to the Jewish people to his advantage.'

I shivered in the wet towel, but it had less to do with being cold than the uneasiness that now crept up my spine at Marika's words. I didn't want to admit that I could have been wrong about Julius, about his motives. He was Onkel Georg's most trusted friend and I'd known him since I was a little girl. I thought that I understood him. We had so much in common, we were both taken in by the Heckers . . . we were kindred spirits. But Marika was right. Julius had manipulated me into sleeping with him. That realisation allowed me to sit a little taller. I knew what I had to do.

'I know he's got what he wants, but I have to stay with him for their sake. He'll do anything for me then.'

Her green eyes were wide. 'How can you be so sure?'

Whatever I told Marika, I knew she wouldn't understand, not really. There wasn't always a right and a wrong. Life was more complicated than that. It was about the shades that lay in between. I was beginning to learn what people were prepared to do to for the right reasons.

'Because he'll be afraid of losing me and the only family he's ever really had.' I straightened in the chair, feeling more resolute now that I'd said it out loud. 'If we're together, he's no longer the lost little boy, but a proper member of our family and a part of Gut Birkenhof, which has always felt like his home.' It all made sense now that I'd articulated it. 'I've learnt something valuable. I'm his weakness and that's my power over him.'

'So you're going to play his game.'

Frau Kraus's words came rushing back to me. Julius had manipulated me into sacrificing something precious, but although my feet were now firmly planted in his world, I could still regain my power. I thought again of how he had made the black market complaint disappear. He had the power to protect my family but I could use what he wanted from me to keep them safe. I would get what I wanted from Julius too.

I gazed into Marika's anxious face. 'I'll give Julius what he wants and be the perfect fiancée if that's what keeps my family safe. But my heart will always belong to Leo.'

10

On the night of the twenty-second of November air-raid sirens woke me. It was late when I'd gone to bed. Utterly drained from a busy night on the ward, I'd fallen asleep straight away, and it seemed only minutes later that the blaring forced me awake. I jumped out of bed, fuzzy-headed.

'Come on,' called Marika, pulling on her coat. I nodded, suddenly alert, and pushed my feet into my shoes and grabbed my coat from behind the door. We rushed down the corridor, now congested with bodies, and towards the air-raid shelter.

The Allies had begun their assault of Berlin four days earlier, forcing us into the hospital bunker for the first time in many months. The drone of aircraft overhead was our only indication of what was happening outside. Nobody knew what to expect, but as we crowded around the radio in the early hours of that first morning, we discovered that the cloud cover over the city had kept the damage to a minimum. We'd smiled and laughed, elated that we'd been spared, some even saying that Berlin couldn't be touched. But they were wrong.

'The government district suffered a direct hit,' one of the nurses said over breakfast that morning. 'Parts of the city are on fire.'

Murmurs of consternation erupted around the room, the same fear on everybody's lips. Berlin had survived a number of air raids earlier in the year with no serious damage, but the dread following the firebombing of Hamburg had been almost suffocating. The evacuations from Berlin had left the city eerily empty and those left behind believed it was only a matter of time before the Allies turned their attention to the capital.

We had no idea of the scale of the disaster that had befallen Berlin until we were all called to a briefing later that morning. A skeleton staff would be left at Beelitz and all remaining medical and nursing staff were being sent to Berlin to assist with the aftermath: basic triage and emergency treatment before patients were shunted off to various hospitals across the city. Marika and I were to join the team.

As we drove into the city, a nightmarish landscape unfolded through the back windows of the van. Roads were closed and the bombing had damaged streets, buildings, tram tracks, electricity lines and water pipes. A massive firestorm had ripped through entire suburbs. Marika and I held each other's hands tightly but spoke barely a word as our van traversed the many detours and back streets. Blackened ruins greeted us, even in the affluent and beautiful suburbs of Tiergarten and Charlottenburg – blasted, gutted buildings and homes with collapsed walls, shattered windows and rubble strewn haphazardly across once beautiful gardens and tree-lined avenues. We saw the blank faces of people in shock. Fires were still raging in the distance, the red hue and black plumes of smoke reminding me of Dante's *Inferno*. It was as though we'd descended into hell.

When we finally stopped, we were immediately directed to a cordoned-off area in a small park. Confusion reigned all around us, the air filled with the moaning and whimpering of unrecognisable creatures: bodies covered in burns; broken bones protruding through skin, pearly white against bloody wounds; other people visibly intact but covered in grime and most likely suffering from head knocks or internal injuries. These were obviously the worst cases and, as I unpacked bandages onto a trestle table that had somehow materialised, the park began filling with dazed residents, their faces blackened, wandering aimlessly. Others arrived, pale and anxious, clearly looking for their loved ones. I wondered whether Julius's building had survived the bombing. Despite what had happened after the gala, I still needed his protection for my family. But there was no time to think about him now.

'These burns are the worst I've ever seen,' murmured Marika as we aided the patients assigned to us. Most of them were either lying or sitting on the ground in shock.

I nodded, trying not to breathe in the smell of burned flesh that enveloped us. Some people's injuries were likely caused by burning, falling debris, others were from the engulfing firestorm, and others were from God knows what ... I bent down to assess a woman in front of me. She was barely conscious with thick, black patches adhered to the skin of her feet and lower legs.

'How did she receive these burns?' I gently asked the young woman crouched by her side, holding her hand.

'She ran onto the road in a panic after the air raid.' Her eyes were huge and filled with terror as she relived the moment. 'There was fire all around us. She started screaming and she couldn't move. The tar on the road had melted and was burning her. She was stuck.' She blinked away the tears in her eyes. 'Soldiers came and rescued her, but she didn't stop screaming, even when she was carried here on a stretcher.' I glanced at Marika, the worry on her face matching the concern I felt.

'We'll look after her now,' said Marika. 'Get something warm to eat and drink. The food van is set up in the middle of the park.' She helped the young woman, who was clearly exhausted and traumatised, to her feet and pointed the way. 'Then go home if it's still standing or go to the shelter and rest until accommodation can be arranged for you.' The woman nodded, but gazed at her friend, reluctant to leave her.

'She'll be in good hands,' I said, cutting the woman's skirt free from the hardened tar on her legs. 'We'll treat the worst of her burns here and get her to the hospital as soon as we can. You can visit her there.' She turned, trying to hide the relief she was obviously feeling, and stumbled away.

Hours later, we had attended to all the serious cases and there were only minor injuries requiring attention. I noticed Marika gazing over at Doctor Stahl who often worked on our ward. I hadn't missed the long glances each had given the other over the last weeks. I wondered who would pluck up the courage to talk first.

'Can you finish up with Doctor Stahl?' I asked, smiling cheekily at her.

'Why, where are you going?' The usually poised Marika had turned a shade of beetroot red.

'To find Julius,' I said. 'If he dies, so does my family's protection.'

A look of repulsion flashed across her face at the mention of his name. 'So you've forgiven him then?'

I shook my head. 'But my family comes first.' I was weary and ached all over, but I wouldn't be able to sleep until I knew whether he was okay.

'Go. I'll make sure we wait for you,' she said, stretching her back after hours of standing and bending. 'There's not much more to do here now.'

I squeezed her hand. 'What would I do without you? I'll be as quick as I can.'

Picking my way through the rubble and around smouldering ruins, it took me some time to reach the Hotel Kaiserhof. We'd been told about multi-storey buildings collapsing, trapping those who had taken refuge in the shelters beneath. Many had died and those who had been pulled free from their tombs suffered terrible injuries. I didn't know what I would do if I found Julius dead or dying.

But nothing prepared me for the visceral shock that hit me when I laid eyes on his damaged hotel. It was like a punch to the gut. Walls had crumbled and collapsed, part of the roof had caved in and debris was scattered across the street. The sign above the grand entry remained, but the life of the imperial darling was gone: the building gutted, blackened and empty, sections of the outside façade standing precariously on their own. I doubted that anyone who had remained inside would have survived.

Panic began to churn inside me. Julius had proven how valuable his protection had been for my family. I didn't know what I would do if he'd been killed in the air raid. I glanced up the street in despair and noticed that the Reich Chancellery had been barely touched. *Why couldn't those bombs have hit there instead and killed the Führer?*

A man I recognised approached me. 'Fräulein Göttmann?'

I nodded, feeling dazed.

He drew me away from the street. 'I'm Herr Eckert, on Ministerialrat Siebenborn's staff –'

'Is he safe?' I interrupted.

The man looked exhausted and was covered in a film of grime. 'He's alive.'

My shoulders slumped with relief.

'I can show you the way to his secretary's apartment.'

'Hedy?'

He nodded. 'Julius was injured and had nowhere else to go.' He gestured to the building behind us. 'His suite's gone.'

'Of course.' My mouth was dry.

'I'll take you to him. The zoo's been hit and it's dangerous. Animals have escaped their enclosures and may be prowling the streets.'

I nodded. It was bizarre to think lions or crocodiles could be around the next corner but I followed Herr Eckert closely.

'He's been asking for you,' Hedy said as we walked down the hallway of her apartment.

'What happened?'

'He was hit on the head by falling debris,' she whispered. 'After we left the air-raid shelter, he noticed a building begin to collapse and shouted for us to get out of the way. One of

162

the men with us seemed dazed and didn't respond. Julius ran to him, pulling him to safety just as the wall fell, but he was hit in the process. Who knows what might have happened if he hadn't been there?'

Julius was sleeping, his face almost as pale as the bandage around his head and the crisp, white sheets of the bed. My heart clenched, taking me by surprise. He seemed so helpless and vulnerable lying there.

'How is he?'

'He'll be fine. According to the doctor, it's a nasty laceration and bump, but he doesn't think his skull is fractured.'

'Thank you for taking him in.'

Hedy's eyebrows rose in surprise. 'Of course. He can stay here until he's well enough if he likes, but knowing him, as soon as he's on his feet, he'll move to his new suite.'

'New suite?'

She nodded. 'He had me arrange one at the Adlon.'

'Susie!' Julius sounded groggy. His eyes were open although a little glazed. He smiled weakly and then winced as he tried to lift his head off the pillow.

'Don't do that,' I said, placing my hand gently on his shoulder, as Hedy left the room. 'You've had a bad knock to the head.'

He touched the bandage gingerly. 'Susie, I'm glad you're here. I want to talk to you about the night of the gala.'

I tried to remain aloof and cool as I sat in the chair by the bed, but in truth, now that I knew he was safe and well enough, a hot rush of resentment and anger gushed through me.

'I know you've been angry with me,' he said quickly, watching my face. 'I never planned for it to end that way . . .'

'How can I believe a thing you say?' I said, fixing him with a glare. My hands were shaking with fury and I clasped them tightly in my lap. 'You took advantage of me.' Hot tears slid down my cheeks in spite of my resolve not to show him any emotion. 'I wanted to wait for the right time,' I whispered miserably, dropping my head into my hands.

'I thought it was what you wanted too.'

Rage reared up inside me and I wanted to slap his face, but I had to acknowledge that I had been attracted to him and to his power.

He was sitting now and, despite being the colour of puce, he remained upright. He reached for me and pulled me to him, holding me tight. I didn't resist. 'I'm so sorry,' he said. 'I've shared things with you that I've never told another human being. I can be myself with you, not all those things I am to the world, just myself. I've enjoyed every minute of our courtship – each time I couldn't wait to see you and talk to you again. You've ruined my playboy reputation but I don't care. It's you I want to be with. If I lose you because of this . . .' he whispered into my ear.

'You say you're sorry,' I said, struggling to find the right words. 'But I want to know that you'll respect me.' The thought of losing him had made me realise how much I needed him. I had to find a way to make our relationship work for the sake of my family.

'Of course I respect you. I'll prove it to you every day we're together, I promise. Just say you'll stay.'

I drew away. The anguish in his eyes told me that his apology was real.

What choice did I have? 'I'll stay,' I said quietly.

*

The bombings continued relentlessly into December. Berlin became a city of strange contradictions, with early snow lightly covering the charred remains and rubble in one part while other parts of the city were burning. And each morning the ruined roads were slick with ice and even more treacherous to citizens who already had enough to deal with.

Julius insisted he was fine and didn't require nursing. He had new rooms at the Adlon Hotel where he conducted his work until he could manage going into the ministry without dizziness and headaches crippling him. Much to my relief, with the extra workload we both carried because of the bombings, we barely had time to see each other. Then the Berlin railway system was hit in mid-December and Julius worked night and day to put the Reich's most important transportation network back on its feet.

Although Beelitz was south-west of the city and hadn't been hit, we spent night after night in the hospital bunkers as the sirens sounded and planes droned overhead. Our soft murmurs were punctuated by the groans of patients upset by the quick evacuation of the wards until careful repositioning by the nurses or extra medication soothed their pain away. I noticed Marika and Johann Stahl often sitting side by side, talking in low voices to each other. It wouldn't be long until romance blossomed between them, I was sure.

Tante Elya pleaded with me to come home and Julius agreed I should go, as much for my own safety as to reassure Tante Elya. I was allotted a week off after the relentless nights and almost daily emergency triage expeditions to the bombed-out areas of the city. Exhausted, I joined the exodus out of Berlin.

As it turned out, the bombings had a silver lining. Many of Onkel Georg's acquaintances sought refuge in the countryside and decided to lease cottages in the most beautiful parts of the estate over the winter. Some even bought plots with the intention of building more permanent homes when the weather allowed.

'How much more can the city stand?' Tante Elya asked the evening I arrived, her embroidery needle suspended above a piece of fabric stretched tight over a circular frame. The continual bombings had caused the electricity to be intermittently disrupted and I didn't know how she continued to do her fine needlework in the light of only a few candles scattered between the lounge chairs. But the dim lighting and the heavy blackout curtains, which kept much of the heat inside the room, made the room cosy, the perfect environment for the sharing and keeping of secrets. Onkel Georg sat with us, smoking his pipe while we waited for the BBC news broadcast and it was my first chance to tell them about the damage and carnage I'd witnessed.

We had been listening to the magnificent tenor voice of Ivan Kozlovsky, Tante Elya's favourite opera singer. He was Russian and Tante Elya was playing his Ukrainian folk songs tonight – stirring and emotional, they were close to her heart, songs of her childhood. She had sung them to me and Leo often at bedtime when we were children. Leo even learnt how to play some of them on the balalaika. It seemed like a lifetime ago now.

'The city will survive,' said Onkel Georg confidently. 'Berlin's spread out with wide avenues, parkland and forests. It won't burn like Hamburg did.'

I hoped he was right. 'There are teams working around the clock to clean up the streets and repair roads and the railways,' I explained. 'It'll take time to restore electricity and water everywhere, but people seem cheerful enough and are managing with what they have.' I settled back into the lounge with my fresh cup of chamomile tea. I was so looking forward to a full night's sleep in my own bed. And in the morning I needed to talk to Leo about how I could help more with the resistance.

'What about those who have lost their homes?' asked Tante Elya, her brow creased with concern.

'They're being accommodated around the city or out in the country.'

'It seems that life goes on,' said Onkel Georg, puffing on his pipe. 'Now, let's see what the English have to report tonight.' He turned on the radio and twisted the knob until a British voice crackled into the room.

'Turn it down, Georg,' whispered Tante Elya, glancing at the closed door and the heavy curtains drawn across the windows. The penalty for listening to foreign radio was imprisonment – and for someone like Tante Elya, it would mean instant deportation to a labour camp.

'Nobody's here, and we still have the record playing,' said Onkel Georg, turning down the volume anyway. We crowded around, listening to the news while I translated the clipped English tones into German. Leo and Onkel Georg knew some English and could convey the meaning to Tante Elya when I wasn't home, but I was glad of my language studies at university which ensured we understood almost everything.

'So the Allies have finally decided to work together against the Nazi threat,' said Onkel Georg after the report, turning the radio back to the nationally run station. Britain, the United States and the Soviets had met for the first time in Tehran a few weeks earlier, announcing their determination to work together to win the war and establish peace.

'The Nazis tell us that they're still winning this war, but it sounds as if the Allies will defeat them,' said Tante Elya, her eyes wide with optimism.

Onkel Georg squeezed Tante Elya's hand. 'I'm sure it won't be long before they begin an offensive on European soil.'

'The sooner, the better. Tedi and all the others in the ghettos and camps need them to hurry before it's too late.' She dabbed her eyes with her handkerchief. After the liberation of Kiev in November, few Jewish people had been found alive. We'd heard from the resistance that some American journalists had been invited by the Soviets to report on the Jewish massacres at Babi Yar and the dismantling of the Syrets concentration camp by the SS. Tante Elya had cried for days, mourning the loss of her city and community.

'The killing has to stop,' I said grimly. 'The men on the battlefield, civilians in the bombings and the Jewish people in the extermination camps.' How many more would perish before it was all over?

Later that night, on my way to the kitchen in the darkened hallway, I nearly screamed with fright as I ran straight into Leo.

'I thought you weren't coming home until tomorrow,' I said, breathing heavily. My heart was pounding wildly, not just from the scare, but from the sheer closeness of him and the need to touch his skin. I wanted only him. But I'd made my choice; the only choice I could make.

'I wasn't, but I'm back now.' He stared back at me with the same longing, tinged with sadness and regret. I hadn't seen him since he'd found out about my engagement. He would beat Julius to a pulp if he knew what had happened at the gala.

'Did it all go well?' He'd been to see Franz Jacob and Anton Saefkow, the leaders of the underground resistance in Berlin.

'It did. Our Russian made it back to Moscow and we've made plans for the next escape.'

His stomach grumbled loudly.

'Are you hungry?' I said.

'Starving!'

'Come down to the kitchen. I'm sure there's some leftover dinner.' I glanced across to the open parlour door. 'There's something I want to talk to you about.' I saw the frown form across his brow. 'Don't worry, I don't want to fight with you.' Before he could say anything, I grabbed his arm and led him down the stairs to the kitchen.

I put fried potatoes, a bowl of sauerkraut, slices of bread and cheese on the kitchen table in front of him while he watched me warily in silence.

'I want to do more for the resistance,' I said, sitting opposite him.

'Helping Mutti with the Russians is enough.' He stabbed some potato with his fork and crammed it into his mouth. I wondered when he'd last eaten.

'I can do more.'

'Have you told Julius?' He kept his eyes on his meal, displaying little emotion.

'No. I want to do this myself. I know you don't approve of our engagement, but can we please put our differences behind us? I'm perfectly placed to help.' I could see the tension in the line of his jaw, the way he clenched his teeth. I knew how hard it was for him to accept.

He closed his eyes briefly as though in pain and then nodded slowly. 'What were you thinking?'

I took a deep breath. 'Julius introduced me to some senior Nazis at a government gala. I can tell you and the resistance any pieces of information that I pick up from his colleagues.'

'You would do that. Use Julius?' His look of incredulity shocked me.

Rage blazed through me, fierce and hot. 'You have no idea what choices I've made,' I said, banging the table. 'If I have to spend time with Nazi swine, pretending to enjoy their company, I may as well have the satisfaction of working against them. How else will I be able to bear their arrogance, their smug smiles and self-righteousness?'

He just stared at me, the food forgotten, taken aback by my vehemence.

I had to make sure he understood that I could do this. I was going to get what I wanted from my relationship with Julius, just as Julius was getting what he wanted. That night's BBC broadcast had fuelled my hope that the Nazis could be defeated. 'This is wartime, Leo. Everybody has a reason for doing what they do. Even one small thing could add to the jigsaw of understanding about what the Nazis are doing and help bring them down.'

A look of dawning comprehension slid across his face. 'You really want to do this, Nightingale?'

'I already am,' I said, lifting my chin in defiance. 'Just tell me what I should be listening out for.'

Leo nodded. 'We have a lot to talk about then.'

11

Julius and I attended the opera at the Unter den Linden in January 1944, about a month after my conversation with Leo. Julius hadn't been able to join us for Christmas at Gut Birkenhof because of work, and the opera was our first public outing since the announcement of our engagement at the gala. He was attentive, his hand on my back as he guided me through the crowded foyer, but the thought of spying for the resistance gave me a thrill. I was nervous and excited.

'You look beautiful,' he whispered into my ear as he handed me a glass of champagne. 'I've missed you.' He'd been trying hard to appease me with thoughtful gifts and kind gestures and I was wearing a fine woollen gown that he'd given me. Although it clung to my figure, it was very elegant and I was aware of the appreciative glances of various men in the crowded room.

Many of Julius's associates and their wives or girlfriends were present, faces I recognised from previous meetings, and small talk about Christmas distracted me from worrying if I'd have the opportunity to hear anything worthwhile to take back to Leo. The men had gravitated to each other, leaving the women together who gossiped about the latest round of seasonal parties. I couldn't believe how they could talk about such inconsequential matters when our cities were being bombed and our soldiers were at war. Boys from the Hitler Youth, some as young as twelve or fourteen, were working as flak helpers, manning the anti-aircraft batteries across the city. Some had even joined our men on the front lines. How many hundreds of thousands of soldiers had died on the battlefields and how many innocent Jewish people had perished because of the Reich? I couldn't wait to take my seat in the darkened concert hall so I could relax the smile plastered to my face.

Miraculously the grand opera house had avoided damage in the recent air raids, but it had taken hits earlier in the war although repairs had returned it to its former glory. As Julius and I were shown through the double doors to our seats on the second level of the curved dress circle, I marvelled at the ornate beauty and opulence of the interior with its domed ceiling and spectacular crystal chandelier suspended from the centre. There was no mistaking where the Nazi elite sat when they attended the opera: a spacious balcony embellished with a large banner emblazoned with a swastika was just in my line of sight below us. I shuddered with disgust, feeling grateful that I didn't have to make conversation with those men tonight.

Then I was transported to another world, ancient Egypt in fact, with the sublime music and the glorious voices of Aida and Radamès. I'd never seen Aida before and was captivated by the performance immediately.

I cast a furtive glance at Julius as the lovers sang. He looked as enthralled as I did, but he'd seen my gaze and leaned across, whispering in my ear, 'Do you like it?'

'It's wonderful,' I whispered back. He smiled, genuinely pleased, and took my hand, interlocking his fingers with mine.

Suddenly the music was rent by the blaring sounds of the air-raid siren.

'Come, we have to go,' said Julius over the noise of voices pitched high with anxiety and bodies shifting en masse from their seats, everybody moving quickly to the doors of the hall. He grasped my hand and held tight. 'Don't let go.' I nodded and followed close behind in the dim light. The press of people around us began to swell. I was more frightened of falling and being trampled than being bombed.

We were led by the air-raid wardens down to the shelter. I was surprised to find members of the orchestra and some of the singers wedged into the room with us.

'All right?' asked Julius in an undertone.

'I'm fine,' I said, my nostrils flaring as I adjusted to the slightly dank smell of the basement. Not even the perfume many were wearing could mask the odour of so many bodies in such a confined space. A low murmur of voices punctuated the silence as people began talking quietly. We'd all been through this enough times now for it to be second nature, but it didn't stop my heart hammering in my chest, wondering if we'd be hit this time. I listened hard for the tell-tale sound of deep engines throbbing over our city and the bone-jarring explosions in their wake, but I couldn't hear anything yet.

The bunker was crammed with patrons, Nazis, performers, musicians and staff. The seating was taken mostly by women, more than a few who had surreptitiously removed shoes not designed for long hours of standing. Julius fell into conversation with some other government officials and it was the perfect opportunity to listen to the conversations around me.

'Have you heard that the Soviets have taken back Kiev?' said one woman, diamonds dripping from jewellery adorning her leathery neck and fleshy forearms. I knew already – Tante Elya had celebrated the victory with a bottle of vodka she'd kept for just the occasion.

'Our troops are being pushed back towards the pre-war Polish–Russian border,' murmured a man with a military badge on his lapel in conversation with Julius. 'We're losing ground we can't afford to lose, not with our losses in North Africa and the Allies trying to get a foothold in Italy.'

'Don't worry, my dear,' said an ageing gentleman with a Nazi armband, patting the woman's arm in reassurance. 'We'll win this war.'

'How can you be so sure?' asked her friend, eager to be involved in the conversation.

The Nazi leaned in towards the women, his arms around both of them. 'We have a secret weapon,' he said in a low voice.

'What?' whispered the friend, moving closer to the ageing official, her eyes wide with anticipation. He moved his hand lower down her back and over her rounded behind, and I grimaced.

'We're building the most powerful airplanes in the world,' he said. 'Soon we'll blow the Allies out of the sky and we'll be untouchable.'

The women laughed, playfully slapping his arm and chest in congratulations. He looked very pleased with himself indeed.

The military officer speaking to Julius moved closer, lowering his voice. 'We're about to move production of the engines south-east to Zittau and out of the Allies bombing range,' he murmured. 'That old fool thinks they're ready to go, but it will be months before we have enough built and the jet engines tested in the Messerschmitt Me262 before they can be delivered to the Luftwaffe.'

My spine tingled with excitement. This sounded like something that could be useful. I couldn't believe my luck. I wondered if all Nazis were so arrogant that they thought they could talk in public places about military and government movements. Suddenly the muffled drone of airplanes overhead filled the air and conversations stopped as everyone listened for the whistling of falling bombs and the explosions that would follow. But this time the engines faded into the distance. We were spared. With the air raid over we were allowed to re-enter the concert hall. Aida and the Egyptian princess returned to the stage and continued as though nothing had happened, and soon I was swept away by the intensity of the music and the dramatic storyline. All my emotion was invested in Aida and Radamès. I blinked away tears as I watched the star-crossed lovers being pulled apart and foiled at every turn. It was as if I was watching Leo and me. I caught myself holding my breath as I willed them to be together with every fibre of my being.

As we applauded the singers and made ready to leave the hall, I wondered with a hollow feeling whether Leo and

I were destined only to find each other in death. My maudlin thoughts were interrupted by someone calling my name.

'Fräulein Göttmann!' People were milling about in the foyer, waiting for those collecting coats and scarves from the cloak room. I turned in the direction of the voice and froze.

'Kreisleiter Mueller,' I said as genially as I could while looking around for Julius. He was deep in conversation with Ganzenmüller and another acquaintance, Ernst von Glaubrecht, who I'd met that evening. There was no escaping the fat, balding man making his way towards me through the crowd.

'My dear Susanna,' he said, 'how lovely to see you.' He grasped my hand and brought it to his lips. 'Have you come with Georg?'

'No,' I said, trying to remove my hand, but he held it fast.

He looked me up and down. 'It looks like you need some company. It's not seemly for a young woman to be alone in public.' He raised an eyebrow in speculation. 'Can I escort you home?' He slid his free hand around my waist and began to propel me forward.

'No, thank you. I'm here with someone.' I looked for Julius again, and found him searching the foyer for me. We made eye contact and when he saw who was with me, he pushed his way through the throng to my side.

'I'll have you remove your hands from her,' said Julius mildly, but his face was explosive.

'What?' Mueller rose to his full height and puffed his chest out like a rooster. 'How dare you speak to me like that. Do you know who I am?' He looked Julius up and down as though assessing the threat to his prize.

The press of people exiting the theatre slowed and stopped around us, watching salaciously as the drama unfolded.

'I've met you before, Herr Mueller, at Susanna's nineteenth birthday, and I'll say it again – take your hands off her.'

I sucked in my breath. Julius hadn't used Mueller's official title as the County Leader of Berlin, which was disrespectful, as his Nazi Party rank was higher than Julius's.

Mueller peered up at him. 'I remember you ... Julius Siebenborn. You're a family friend of Georg Hecker.'

'That's right,' said Julius. 'And Susanna and I are betrothed.'

Mueller looked stunned.

'Yes, we're engaged to be married,' I said, smiling sweetly. I held up my hand to show him my engagement ring and prove Julius's claim.

'Congratulations to you both,' he said stiffly as he let go of me and stepped away.

Julius put his arm round me and pulled me into his side. 'Stay away from her,' he said. 'As I've told you before, she's way above your station.'

The old man could barely contain his humiliation. 'You smug little upstart,' he hissed close to Julius's ear. 'You'll regret you ever crossed paths with me.' Then he took his leave.

Julius swept me out of the foyer and into the street. 'We won't need to worry about him anymore,' he said as we walked the few blocks along Unter den Linden to the Hotel Adlon.

'You don't think he'll cause us more trouble? You didn't have to goad him like that,' I said.

'What can he do now?' he asked, waving a hand in dismissal. 'I've already ensured he can't hurt Elya and I can protect you.'

I nodded and breathed a sigh of relief.

'But I know I'm the luckiest man.' He stopped on the footpath and drew me to him. 'You've agreed to give me a second chance. You're everything I want.' He dipped his head and kissed me.

My car was parked at the Adlon, and I entered the spectacular lobby on Julius's arm, marvelling once again at the large, square marble columns and the curved arches that followed the lines of the vaulted ceilings. The hotel was lavishly decorated in the French style of Louis XVI and it felt like we'd stepped back in time to a more genteel although extravagant era, far from the bombings of Berlin, far from war.

'It's such a beautiful hotel,' I murmured. 'How is your new suite?'

'It's beautiful,' said Julius. 'Would you like to come up?' Then he frowned in concern. 'Only if you'd like to, of course,' he said quickly.

'Just for a drink, then I have to go back to Beelitz.' I didn't want him to think that he could take me or my acquiescence for granted.

He nodded. 'Of course. I'll never presume again.'

Julius's sitting room was similarly styled to the hotel foyer. The lounge suite, complete with winged chairs, was a rich walnut, the backs and legs of the chairs carved with ornate designs and covered in a pastel green jacquard fabric. Double doors covered in heavy curtains led out to a balcony that looked out over the Brandenburg Gate, now hidden in the darkness of the city's blackout restrictions.

'What would you like to drink?' asked Julius as I sat on the plush lounge. 'A little digestif or liqueur?' He searched through bottles in the liquor cabinet, lifting one up, and then another.

'What will you have?' I asked.

'Cognac,' he said, 'but I have champagne too.' I almost smiled at how eager he was to please me.

'I'll have cognac,' I said.

'Are you sure? It's not a drink that women usually enjoy.'

I lifted my eyebrows at him. 'Let me try it.'

He poured and handed me a crystal glass filled with amber liquid.

I took a big gulp of the cognac and spluttered as I inhaled the fumes as well as the potent liquor.

'Slowly,' said Julius, taking my glass as I coughed. 'Do you want some water?' I shook my head and Julius grinned, returning the glass to me before picking up his own. 'Spirits must be sipped slowly to savour the taste and appreciate the aroma. They're a lot stronger than wine, or even champagne.' He sat on the lounge next to me and demonstrated.

I took a smaller sip this time.

'Let it linger on your palate.'

I sipped again. 'It's very different to wine, like drinking liquid silk.'

'We'll make a connoisseur out of you yet.' He smiled.

I leant across to kiss him. There was no point in prolonging the inevitable and this way I controlled how it would happen. If he really wanted me, as he said he did, then sex was a powerful tool for me to get what I wanted too.

'Susie, I don't want you to feel you have to,' he murmured, pulling back.

I tipped the glass to my mouth and then kissed him again. 'I want to,' I said. 'Take me to bed.'

*

Leo was very pleased with the information I'd gathered at the opera.

'You did well, Nightingale,' he said to me a few weeks later at Gut Birkenhof. We were shovelling snow away from the paths and entrance to the kitchen, before Frau Kraus arrived back from the market in the village. She and Ida were the only household staff that remained. The others had left to care for family or because they didn't want to be associated with our family any longer. 'Your report was valuable,' Leo said, 'and Bernhard wants you to continue.'

Leo had passed what I'd heard on to underground members in Berlin who were able to verify the authenticity of my intelligence. Bernhard Bästlein, one of the leaders of the resistance, had sent his personal congratulations to me. He'd escaped from prison and had joined forces with Franz Jacob and Anton Saefkow in Berlin.

'Although German troops are being pushed back into Poland, those fighter planes could still make the difference in the war and turn the tide back in Germany's favour,' said Leo. Our family had been glued to the radio most nights, listening for anything about the Allied offensive. The BBC news was reporting that the Russians had taken back Leningrad, held by the Germans since 1941.

Leo leaned on his shovel, his breath misting the air, and the proud way he looked at me was enough to make me want to burst into tears. But I only smiled and nodded. All I really wanted was for him to see me as I was – no longer the child he'd grown up with, but the woman I had become.

'It feels wrong plotting against our own country,' I said as a wave of guilt washed over me. I thought about the men

I cared for at Beelitz and knew that many more of our soldiers would be injured or killed as a result of any Allied offensive against Germany. 'This isn't how it's supposed to be.'

Leo had handed me a canteen of water and I took it gratefully.

'I know, we're Germans first,' he said.

'It's just so hard seeing injured soldiers every day and wondering if I'm contributing to their loss and injury.' I took a long swallow of the cool water.

'What the Nazis are doing to our nation is wrong, Susie. They have to be stopped.' He smiled. 'Thanks to you, we know where they're building the plane engines. With our network of contacts we can infiltrate the factories and prevent those engines from working properly.'

'You can do that?'

He nodded, grinning at my stunned reaction. 'See what you've done? You've made a difference.'

'No. *We've* made a difference.' I handed him back the water, standing taller and feeling more confident.

It was late March when the air raids finally stopped. After four months of bombings, it was a blessed relief to sleep through the night once again. Although most of Berlin had been affected, the Allied attacks hadn't destroyed the city like they had in Hamburg, nor had they caused the collapse of the government and administrative sector of the capital. Berlin and its people had endured.

When I wasn't working at Beelitz, I was with Julius. Marika's looks of sympathy soon turned to acceptance as she watched me settle into the relationship.

'Are things going well with Julius?' she asked one day when we had a few moments to talk. 'You seem happy.' We still shared a room at the hospital but I wasn't there much and Marika had been spending a lot of time with Johann Stahl, who was supposedly helping her study for her nursing exam, now she had the necessary experience behind her.

I nodded, dropping my starched nurse's cap onto the table and shaking out my newly cut shoulder-length hair, which was so much easier to manage than the long hair I'd had since a child. 'He loves me and he's good to me. He's protecting Elya and Leo, and there's been no more trouble from Mueller. We're both getting what we want.' I shrugged my shoulders but Marika lifted her eyebrows and gave me a look.

I sighed, kicking off my shoes and slumped into a chair. 'All right, the truth is that he's considerate, in and out of the bedroom.' I couldn't suppress a small smile, thinking about it. I'd acquired a supply of condoms from the black market and insisted on using them. A baby was the last thing I needed in this complicated situation. Julius had acquiesced, despite birth control being illegal under the Nazis. Not worrying about pregnancy had allowed us more freedom in the bedroom, something not lost on Julius and something I was beginning to appreciate. 'I'm attracted to him, and part of me might even feel something more for him. He's endearing, even when he's not trying, but . . .'

Marika put down her cup of ersatz coffee and frowned. 'You say it's over with Leo . . . maybe you have to let him go. I had my doubts about Julius at first but you've made your choice and you could do a lot worse than him. I wonder if you could even be happy with him.'

'I know.' Leo and I could never be together but it didn't stop me pining for him and wondering what our life together might have been like had we lived in another time or place.

'Julius loves you,' said Marika. 'That's all most of us ever want: to be loved.' I was lucky to have the love of two good men. Marika was still waiting for Johann to speak those three little words.

'Maybe you're right. Maybe I should give him a chance.'

'The Allies have hit the war industries hard,' Julius said one bright May morning, his sandy head resting against the pillow. 'They're vital to Germany winning this war. We have trains scheduled to take armaments to the Eastern Front, but production is behind and some of the factories have had problems with assembly. Sabotage, I suspect.'

'Really?' I said, almost choking on my coffee. I'd been sending small snippets of information back to Leo, and when I'd gone home for my twentieth birthday a few weeks earlier I'd given him a full report. Some of my information had been useful in helping the resistance create disruption, mainly in the factories around Berlin. 'How bad is it on the Eastern Front?'

'Worse than we feared.' He sat up and swallowed some of his coffee. I didn't know how he could do that. It was scalding hot and I could only sip mine slowly. 'We're losing territory that we've previously gained. We've lost Kiev, Leningrad, Crimea, southern Italy, and we're barely holding Estonia.'

'Why is that?' I asked, looking up from the newspaper. Ironically, I'd been reading an article in *Das Reich* explaining the difficulties in an Allied invasion on European soil, citing the slow progress of the Allied advance through southern Italy as a prime example. It was barely worth reading, mainly propaganda aimed at soothing German citizens' fears of an imminent Allied invasion and proving Germany's dominance in the war.

He turned to look at me and lowered his voice. 'There's talk that the Führer's not listening to his generals or High Command. After Stalingrad, confidence in his decisions has been seriously undermined.' They were treasonous words in the wrong company, but he knew how I felt about the Nazi regime and our Führer.

'What can we do?' The warmth of the coffee cup in my hands seeped into my fingers. Part of me was overwhelmed by the futility of the situation, but with Julius on side, a man with power and influential connections who felt as he did, maybe something could be done.

'Some think that the Führer's overthrow by assassination is the only solution.' He shrugged. 'It's a solution that amounts to suicide. He's too heavily guarded. Nobody can get close to him. The best we can do is fight until the very end and pray to God that we win.' My heart sank. He didn't have the will to do anything serious about his concerns. I wondered who he'd been talking to. Whoever they were, they obviously trusted him to confide such subversive opinions.

'Julius, do you really believe that? He has to go, and the Nazi Party with him.' I itched to tell him about the resistance – and that he could help in so many ways – but I didn't dare after what I'd been doing. He would take it as a personal betrayal.

'We just have to survive this war, win or lose.' He kissed me on the lips. 'Now, let's have breakfast.'

Maybe whoever he had been talking to could convince him to fight for change.

12

It was 6 June 1944 and it was finally happening – the 'unlikely' Allied invasion. Onkel Georg, Tante Elya and I were in the parlour at Gut Birkenhof, crowded around the radio. 'D-Day has come,' the BBC announcer stated. 'Early this morning the Allies began the assault on the north-western face of Hitler's European fortress.'

We stared at each other in astonishment then, slowly, broad grins spread across our faces as we realised the significance of this moment.

'It's the beginning of the end,' said Onkel Georg, tears in his eyes.

'I barely dared to hope,' whispered Tante Elya, grasping our hands and kissing them both in turn.

'The tide has turned,' the announcer continued. 'The free men of the world are marching together to victory.'

'It's really happening,' I said, stunned. I thought of all the men and women who had worked towards this day, all the small and large acts of resistance within our own homeland.

Over the following weeks I came home to the estate whenever I could so I could huddle around the radio with my family. We followed the reports describing the beach landings in Normandy and the Allied attempts to press on inland in the face of heavy German shelling. Our emotions were in constant conflict: sadness and despair warring with joy and hope. Had the Allies been pushed back or had they made it safely from the coast of France?

Soon it was clear: the Allies were coming and Germany was now fighting a war on two fronts. The bloodshed on both sides made it hard to rejoice, but change was in the air and, with it, the promise of salvation from the Nazi regime.

This hope boosted the morale of the resistance movement.

'I'm worried about you after what's happened with Bernhard,' I said to Leo one afternoon in July, as we walked back to the truck. I'd been rostered off for five days after working three weeks straight and had come home for a couple of days. Tante Elya had sent me to pick Leo up from the forester's cottage, where he'd been having a beer with Hans.

Bernhard Bästlein had been arrested in late May and, after spending time at the Reich Security Office, where we all knew he'd been tortured, he was back in Sachsenhausen once again. By now, a handful of Russian POWs had been freed, all of them via Gut Birkenhof, and the resistance was contemplating getting Bästlein out. But he was heavily guarded and it risked exposing the entire operation if the escape failed.

'It's all right,' he said, patting my shoulder. 'I would've been arrested by now if he'd said anything.' It had been a nerve-racking month, expecting the Gestapo to show up at our doors, especially as Julius's protection wouldn't extend this far as he had no idea about our involvement with the resistance.

'Maybe you and your father should lie low for a while.' The danger was beginning to feel very real and I didn't know what I'd do if Leo or even Onkel Georg was arrested.

He shook his head. 'No, we have to keep going. Something big's about to happen. Franz Jacob wasn't sure if it would work out, but it looks like it's going ahead.' The excitement in his voice made me shiver as the carpet of old pine needles crunched underfoot. I loved it here, tucked away in the forest far from the manor house, the estate buildings and sheds.

'What is it?'

Even though we were alone, Leo dropped his voice. 'A member of the Kreisau Circle has made contact. They're a high-ranking resistance group – they want our movement to be involved in a plot to assassinate Hitler.' I thought immediately of Julius and what he'd told me a couple of months earlier. Surely it was connected. 'Vati and I went to a meeting in Berlin a few weeks ago,' Leo continued. 'We discussed ways that we can help the conspiracy.'

'Why didn't you tell me?'

'Vati was against telling you anything. He still doesn't know about you spying on Julius's friends.' He smirked. 'But I didn't want to put you at risk until we knew for sure that it was happening. This time, I think it has a real chance of success and there's a final meeting in Berlin the day after tomorrow.'

I clasped Leo's hands, grinning from ear to ear. 'It's happening?'

He nodded, grinning back. 'I knew you'd want to be involved.'

'How?'

'I want you to know every detail of our plan in case something happens to Vati or me. The Gestapo haven't picked up any of us in the group besides Bästlein, so I think we're safe, but you never can tell. I want you to get word to our contacts in Berlin after the meeting with the final preparations. If we're being watched, you're a safer option.'

'Of course, I'll always have your back,' I said, elated that he was including me. I felt strong and powerful, proud to be involved in crucial resistance work.

The next night I stayed with Julius. I had another couple of days off before I had to return to the hospital. He was in a strange mood, unable to settle.

'What's wrong?' I asked. He was sitting in his chair and I put my arm around his shoulders from behind. He put down the book he'd been trying to read, while staring into space. 'Difficult day?' I moved around to the side of his chair and sat on the edge.

He pulled me into his lap. 'Not now you're here to distract me.' He kissed me.

'Really?' I brushed my hand over his short bristly hair, noticing that it had become increasingly grey of late.

'Do you remember when I spoke to you about the officials who have lost confidence in the Führer?' he asked softly.

'Of course.'

'There's a plot against him, and I've been approached.'

190

'To be involved?'

'Yes – to be involved, or to allow it to happen and become part of the new government afterwards. General Olbricht, Colonel von Stauffenberg and members of the Army High Command are at the centre of the plot.'

'What did you tell them?' My heart was racing. I wanted Julius to step forward and fight for what was right.

He shook his head. 'I can't become involved. I'm part of the current government. As much as I object to what this regime is doing, my duty is to uphold the government. But if their plan is successful, I'll happily join a new government, one that will broker peace and rebuild Germany.'

I drew back, furious with him. 'You can't be serious! You have to do it. It's your opportunity to make a difference, to force the Nazis from power.'

'What if it doesn't go to plan? What if it doesn't end well? I have you to think about – and your family.'

'But it will. It will work. It has to.'

Julius stared at me icily and my stomach dropped. 'Do you know something about this?'

'How could I?' I said, turning away.

'Susie.' He grasped my shoulders, pulling me back. 'What have you been up to? I can't keep your family safe if I don't know where to expect the dangers.'

'I don't know what you're talking about.' All I could think of was the respect that Leo had finally shown me as a woman, the pride and admiration in his eyes. I couldn't give that up.

He gripped my arms hard. 'Are your family involved in this?'

'Julius, you're hurting me.'

'Whatever you're doing you have to stop.' His face was creased with worry.

'Let go of me,' I said, raising my voice. Immediately he let go, realising what he had done, and I stepped away, rubbing my arms and glaring at him.

'How can I keep them safe if you won't tell me?' he whispered. 'We can work out the best thing to do together.'

I stared at him, debating what to do. He was powerful and had access to information that we did not.

'Do you promise we'll do it together?'

'Only if you tell me everything.'

He'd shown himself to be loyal to our family. Hadn't he kept Elya and Leo safe? 'My family and I are part of the resistance.' I dropped my head, unable to look at the disbelief on his face. 'I couldn't tell you,' I muttered. 'I didn't want to compromise you.'

'You didn't want to compromise me? I already am because of you. Whatever they're doing, tell them to stop. It's too dangerous.'

'It's too late.'

'What do you mean?'

I sat opposite him on the lounge and told him haltingly about Onkel Georg and Leo's role in the resistance, about their involvement in the plot to assassinate the Führer and the meeting in Berlin the next day.

'I can't tell them what to do, but I want you to stay away from the whole conspiracy,' said Julius, rubbing a hand over his head in exasperation. 'There are too many ways for things to go wrong, too many people involved. I don't want you caught up in it.'

I jumped to my feet, my face flaming with anger. 'You promised we'd work together. I have to help them. Leo and Onkel Georg are relying on me.'

He stood and grabbed me by the wrist. 'Promise me you won't go anywhere near that meeting or relay messages to resistance contacts.'

'Let go!' I shouted. 'I'm not married to you. I can do what I like.'

'What if they're being watched? One of their leaders has already been arrested. What if the Gestapo are waiting for the right moment to strike?'

'We all have to take risks for what we believe in. At least we're taking action. You tell me you think the Nazis have to go, but they're just words, Julius. You're willing to put up with the way things are until somebody else does something about it. Well, I'm not!' I pulled away from him. 'I'm going.'

Julius's face reddened and his hands clenched by his sides in rage. 'You know *nothing* about the devastating consequences of ill-conceived actions,' he said, barely controlling his voice, 'but I do. Don't make that mistake, Susie.' He strode to the door and turned to me. 'Stay here tonight,' he growled. 'It's too late for you to drive. I'll spend the night at the ministry. I've got plenty of work to do.' He slammed the door as he left.

It took me some time to calm down, furious at his inaction, his inertia. He was becoming more and more like a politician. They played with words all the time, but how many of them stood by their words, took action to make them real? After polishing off the rest of the good bottle of red that he had been waiting to share with me, I realised in a foggy haze that maybe he was worried about me, about my family. There *was* a serious risk of being discovered. Perhaps I wouldn't smash his crystal glasses against the wall or tear the pages of his books and throw them in the fire, after all. Instead, I ran a hot bath and indulged in a few moments to myself, a rare luxury, soaking away the day's tensions until, pink-limbed, I dragged myself from the tub and fell into bed and into a deep sleep.

I woke to persistent knocking at the door early the following morning. It wouldn't stop and, bleary-eyed, I pulled on my silk robe and stumbled to the door, wondering where Julius was. Only when I opened the door to the concierge did I remember our fight and the fact that he had stayed at work all night.

'A message for you, Fräulein Göttmann,' he said, handing me a note. 'I apologise for waking you, but Herr Siebenborn told me it was urgent and that I must hand it directly to you.'

'Thank you,' I murmured, frowning as I closed the door. Padding barefoot across the Turkish rug, I tore open the envelope, ready to curse if it was a hastily written apology.

> *My darling Susie,*
> *Please telephone your uncle and tell him that today's not a good day to visit. Something has come up unexpectedly at work and I have no idea how this day will end. Send him my apologies.*
> *Yours,*
> *Julius*

To anyone else his words would mean nothing, a domestic communication, but I knew Julius would have spent the night putting out his feelers about the plot. He must have heard something. It could only mean that Onkel Georg and Leo were in danger. The paper slipped from my fingers and onto the floor. Wild-eyed, I glanced at the clock on the mantelpiece. I still had time.

I rushed to the telephone and dialled. The telephone was ringing. 'Please answer,' I whispered as I held the earpiece tightly to my ear.

'Ida,' I said urgently when she answered the phone. 'It's Susie. Is Onkel Georg there?'

'Fräulein Susanna, your uncle's already left for Berlin.'

'How long ago? With Leo?'

'Both of them left over an hour ago. Do you want to speak to Frau Hecker?'

'No. I'll talk to her later,' I said, my heart thumping painfully in my chest.

I put the phone down, trying to produce a single coherent thought. In desperation I telephoned Julius, my hand shaking as I dialled the number, thankful that Hedy put me straight through to him.

'Susie, did you get my message?'

'My uncle's already left,' I said, trying to keep my voice steady. Anyone could be listening to our telephone call.

'Wait for him at home. I'm coming.'

'See you soon,' I said, feeling a little dizzy. I hung up the phone. A mixture of relief and worry flowed through me but I couldn't just sit and wait. I had to go and find Onkel Georg and Leo myself.

I changed hastily and scribbled a quick note to Julius to tell him what I was doing. I was in my car before I could talk myself out of it. Driving away from the Adlon, I prayed that he'd understand.

I parked the car a few blocks away from the apartment block where the meeting was to take place. I still couldn't get used to the sight of bombed-out buildings and homes ravaged by fire, alongside those that hadn't been touched with their neat gardens unscathed. As least the roads were repaired and in good working order. Wearing a wide-brimmed hat, I strolled through the neighbourhood with a book in my hand. I looked like anyone out enjoying the summer weather, ready to relax on a sunny park bench or under the shade of a tree. Meanwhile, my eyes darted to and fro, looking for anything or anyone familiar, a car or the faces of Onkel Georg and Leo, but I found nothing. Frustrated, I circled back and walked past the apartment block again, seeing nothing untoward. I frowned in worry as I walked causally across the street and sat in a small park further down the block. I could see the entrance of the apartment block from here. I glanced at my watch. It was twenty minutes until the meeting. Maybe it had been cancelled. But what if the meeting had been moved to another location and I didn't get to them in time?

There was nothing I could do but wait. All my senses were on high alert, but all I heard was the sound of children playing in a yard nearby, laughter punctuating the babbling of childish voices, and the faint, incessant barking of a dog in the distance. Somebody was cooking and my nose wrinkled as I caught the waft of cabbage soup. Perspiration trickled down my back as the sun beat down relentlessly, not even a breath of wind to stir the damp hair at my neck. There was nobody in the park but me and, as I scanned the street and the building opposite, still nothing seemed out of place. But I couldn't shake the feeling that something wasn't right.

Suddenly two figures emerged at the end of the street. Onkel Georg and Leo. I held my breath, frozen in place, not sure what to do. I knew they were in danger but I didn't know where from. Out of the corner of my eye, I saw a couple of men in civilian dress materialise from a nearby doorway. They'd been waiting in the shadows. The hairs on my arms stood on end. I scanned the street again as Onkel Georg and Leo moved closer to the apartment block. Then I saw them – everywhere, men in uniform, hidden from the street in doorways and alleyways, but ready for action and waiting for instructions. Gestapo.

I'd never reach Leo and Onkel Georg before they entered the building. Once inside, they'd be followed and trapped. I had to do something. Jumping to my feet, I began to cross the park, desperate to somehow close the distance between myself and Onkel Georg and Leo. I was too far away for them to hear me shout. Blood pounding in my ears, I ran faster towards the street. Everything seemed to move in slow motion. My whole world was about to implode before my very eyes. They had nearly reached the apartment block.

'Onkel Georg,' I shouted, waving my arm wildly. A brief look of confusion crossed his face as he turned and saw me. He smiled and waved back as he and Leo waited for me to walk quickly towards them. It took all my willpower not to scream a warning across the road.

'I've been waiting to take you to luncheon. You're so late,' I said, kissing him on the cheek. I could see the wariness on his face and how Leo's eyes narrowed as he scanned the street. 'Don't look but you're in danger and we have to get out of here,' I murmured.

'I'm sorry we're so late, *liebling*,' said Onkel Georg without missing a beat. 'We were delayed at the estate with a difficult calving.' He shrugged his shoulders. 'It couldn't be helped.'

'But we're here now and I'm starving,' said Leo, grinning.

I slipped my arms through theirs. 'Let's go then. Julius will wonder what's happened to us.' I turned them away from the men waiting in the shadows and, with all the poise and composure I could muster, walked with them back towards my car, while chatting about the deliciously warm weather we were experiencing. I didn't know if we would be stopped, but I refused to look behind me. Only Onkel Georg and Leo could feel the fine tremor that racked my body as I delivered them from danger.

It was only when we were safely in the car and we had pulled away from the kerb that I sighed with relief.

'What are you doing here?' hissed Onkel Georg in the passenger seat next to me. 'How did you know we were here?'

'I told her, Vati,' said Leo from the back seat. 'In case something went wrong.'

'There's a reason I didn't want Susie involved,' Onkel Georg said crossly. 'It's too dangerous.'

I looked in the rear-vision mirror, relieved there was nobody following us, and saw Leo's own face darken. 'If you haven't noticed, Susie's more than capable of looking after herself and it seems that she's just saved us from trouble.'

'The Gestapo were waiting for you,' I said shakily. 'Julius sent me a message this morning to tell you not to visit today.'

'He knew we were coming?' Onkel Georg asked sharply.

I sighed and slowed the car as we approached an intersection, although every sense within me screamed to keep my foot down and get as far away from that apartment building as possible. 'He told me last night that he's been asked to join the plot against the Führer. I was upset with him because he thinks there are too many risks for it to work. He guessed that I knew something, so I told him. I thought that he could help since he was already involved.'

'You took a big risk, Susie,' said Leo accusingly.

I knew how he felt about Julius but I shook my head in frustration. I had to make them understand. 'I don't know how he found out or what he knows, but when he sent me that message he was risking his job and potentially his life. I telephoned the estate, but you'd already left. Julius wanted me to wait for him, but I couldn't, knowing that you might have been walking into a trap.' I told them what I'd seen. 'Those men were waiting to raid that apartment building. Once you were inside, it would've been too late.'

Leo's face was white as his eyes met mine. 'Julius might have warned you but it was you who took the risk by coming here.'

'I could have lost you both,' I whispered. Tears welled in my eyes and I couldn't see the road properly. I dashed them with my hand, battling to keep the shock of what had happened under control. We weren't safe yet.

'But we're both here because of you and Julius,' said Onkel Georg gravely. 'It seems that I've underestimated you.' He squeezed my shoulder and smiled wryly. 'I should have known better. Thank you for your bravery and courage, *liebling*.'

'Any of us would've done the same,' I said. 'We're family.' The cold fear in the centre of my chest began to melt with the surge of warmth at his words. Everything I'd gone through was worth it to hear him say that.

Leo looked behind us.

'Anything?'

'Nothing . . . We have to get word to the others.'

'We can't, Leo,' said Onkel Georg, his face tight with apprehension. 'Not just yet. It's too risky. We don't know who's been detained and who's being watched.'

'But we'll never get another chance if we're exposed,' Leo said, stricken.

'First we have to make sure you're both safe,' I said. 'I'll take you back to the Adlon and we can decide what to do from there.'

Julius's relief was evident when I opened the door to the suite with Onkel Georg and Leo behind me. 'Thank God you're all safe,' he said, ushering them into the sitting room. 'Are you all right?'

Georg nodded. 'We're fine, thanks to you and Susanna.'

'I can't believe you went out to stop them by yourself,' said Julius, hugging me tight to him. 'Anything could have happened to you. Why didn't you wait for me?'

'I didn't know how long you'd be and it could have been too late by then,' I murmured, beginning to shake now it was over.

'Come and sit,' he said with his arm around me. 'We could all do with a stiff drink.'

I noticed Leo's eyes narrow as Julius guided me to the lounge before following with Onkel Georg. We collapsed onto the chairs, staring at each other in shock while Julius poured us all a whiskey.

'How did you know?' asked Leo as he took the glass from Julius.

Julius sat next to me on the lounge and sighed. 'After Susie told me, I went into the ministry. I made some delicate enquiries using people I trust and I learnt that a Gestapo raid was taking place today at the location of the meeting.' He took a long swallow of liquor.

'I wasn't sure it was the Gestapo until I saw them,' I said, a shiver running through me.

'I couldn't tell you any more than that. I only hoped that you'd understand and alert Georg,' he said.

I nodded, sipping on the potent spirits, nearly gasping. The fiery liquid warmed me from the inside and began to loosen the tension I held in every part of my body.

'We could've been arrested without you both,' said Onkel Georg. 'You put yourselves at risk.' I noticed that the hand holding his glass was shaking.

'I had to do something,' said Julius. 'I believe in what you're doing although I can't be involved myself. We're family, after all. Especially now.' He patted my knee affectionately. 'But it's Susie we have to thank. If it wasn't for her quick thinking, we may not have got you away.'

I stared at him in disbelief. I was expecting a first-class quarrel for not listening to him, not praise.

'She would do anything for her family,' he continued, 'and I admire her for that.' He leaned across and kissed me.

'Of course, Susie's family and we look out for each other,' said Leo, his voice rising. 'But why didn't you come instead of her? What she did put her at risk of being caught.' I glared at Leo for questioning Julius's intentions but he refused to look at me, only staring intently at Julius, who tipped the glass to his mouth before answering.

'I wanted to come myself and told Susie to wait for me here. I couldn't go straight to the meeting place – I was worried I'd be followed after the interest I'd shown in the matter. When I came home and found Susie gone, it was too late for me to do anything except pray that she'd reached you in time.' He raked his hand through his hair. 'I've been worried sick.'

Leo said nothing but I could see that he wasn't impressed and I wondered briefly what would have happened if I hadn't gone myself.

'I would have been just as worried if I'd known, but she's strong-willed like her mother,' said Onkel Georg softly. 'Your parents would have been so proud of you today, Susanna, just as I am.' I smiled, grateful for his acknowledgement and support. He walked over to the heavy sideboard to fill his glass with more whiskey. 'But we'd best keep a low profile for a while.'

'What about the others? How will we know if anyone's been arrested? If our plan's been compromised?' Leo sat up on the edge of his chair.

'I can help with that,' said Julius. 'I can find out if anyone's been arrested and if the conspiracy's still going ahead.'

'You'd do that?' Leo's look of incredulity made me angry. Julius was the reason he was here drinking whiskey, rather than languishing in a prison cell awaiting Gestapo torture.

'I'm a part of this as much as you are,' said Julius, matching his gaze.

'Well, it looks like we're all in this together,' said Onkel Georg. He clinked glasses with Julius. 'Here's to the resistance.'

I stayed the night with Julius, after Onkel Georg and Leo had left to return to the estate.

'We were lucky today,' I said, watching Julius undress for bed. His stocky frame was still powerful, even at his age. His shirt strained across his broad shoulders as he began to unbutton it, revealing a well-muscled torso and thick upper arms. He slid his trousers off, revealing white buttocks against tanned, bulky thighs.

'Two arrests so far, but there may be more. I hope they listen and lie low.' Julius had gone back to the ministry after Onkel Georg and Leo had left and made careful enquiries about the morning's raid.

Two unfortunate men had been caught at the meeting. One was going to be a great loss – the resistance leader Anton Saefkow – while the other, Reichwein, was a member of the Kreisau Circle. Nobody knew what the fallout would be.

'You're not mad at me?'

'I've learnt something about you,' he said softly. 'You can't help but do what you feel. I can't change that, nor would I want to. It's what makes you passionate.' He slipped in between the sheets.

'Thank you for understanding but most of all for discovering the threat to Onkel Georg and Leo, and warning me.' Tears glistened in my eyes. I had come so close to losing them today. I turned on my side to look at him, laying my hand on his chest. I could feel his heartbeat, steady and slow. 'It could have ended in disaster but thanks to you we prevented it.'

'I couldn't let anything happen to them.' He lifted my hand to his lips. 'But don't you know that everything I do is for you? I want a better world, a better Germany, so we can live the life we want, so we can have a future together.'

'What kind of future Julius? ' My heart began to beat faster.

He rolled onto his side to face me and I gazed into his steadfast blue eyes. 'I want to marry you but only when I can offer you a future not filled with fear and uncertainty. I don't want to bring up children in the world we live in now,' he said, resting his hand over my belly.

Julius had proved yet again that he was a man who kept his promises and who I could rely on, a man who loved me. And now he wanted a future with me, a life of security and children. It was time for me to see if I could feel something real for him.

13

'It's happening,' Julius said, bursting through the door, his usual calm and unflappable demeanour gone. It was the evening of the 20th of July and I'd driven across to the Adlon after my morning shift.

'What?' I said, putting down the book I'd been reading.

'The assassination plot.' He took off his jacket and slung it carelessly over the back of the chair. 'The Wolf's Lair with the Führer inside has been bombed and Stauffenberg's using the Replacement Army to take over the government quarter. It's crazy out there. Once they have Berlin, the coup will be successful.' He shook his head with wonder. Stauffenberg was a staff officer of the Replacement Army, which trained new recruits to reinforce front line divisions. I jumped up and took his hands.

'Finally!' I felt giddy and light-headed. Everything was about to change. I couldn't even contemplate what that might look like, what it might mean for me.

Although there had been further arrests in the days following the meeting Leo and Onkel Georg had narrowly missed, somehow the real conspiracy hadn't been jeopardised. My heart had gone out to the courageous men who'd refused to betray their fellow conspirators. There was little hope for them, but their silence ensured that hope continued to burn for us.

'For the first time Germany can really hope again.' He kissed me deeply and I wrapped my arms around him in joy.

'What happens now?' I asked, a little breathless.

'We sit and wait until the Nazi leaders are taken into custody and the government buildings secured. When we have Berlin we can begin to put a new government in place.'

Julius sat on the edge of the lounge, clearly exhausted, and I sat beside him, intrigued by this new turn of events.

'And you? Will you have a position in the new government?'

He shrugged. 'I was offered one, but it remains to be seen whether that eventuates. They were talking about State Secretary or Minister of Transport.'

I kissed his cheek, rough with day-old growth. 'That's wonderful – it's what you've always wanted. You can make a real difference!'

'It'll be a big job putting Germany back on its feet, making sure the infrastructure is in place . . .'

'I know you can do it.' I smiled, filled with excitement and relief.

We decided to have dinner in the suite and wait for news of the Führer's death and the success of the coup. Neither of us could eat too much, we were both nervous about the hours ahead and the news that was coming, but we also knew it would be a busy and tumultuous time for Julius and these few hours of quiet were important for him to gather his thoughts and focus his energies for the days ahead.

'There'll be a reckoning for all the things the Nazi Party's been part of,' Julius said, swirling the contents of his wineglass. 'The new government will have to be accountable, not just to Germany, but in the eyes of the world.'

'It's time for them to pay for their crimes,' I said savagely. 'All the lives they've destroyed, the unspeakable acts of degradation.' How many thousands had already died at the hands of the Nazis? Most of the ghettos had disappeared along with their residents, 'resettled' in one of the many concentration camps where they were forced into hard labour, or sent to death camps like Chelmno, Sobibor, Belzec, Auschwitz, Treblinka, Majdanek and Janowska. As more prisoners escaped these camps, including the Soviet POWs we'd helped liberate, we discovered the depths of depravity the Nazis had sunk to – hundreds of thousands of Jewish men, women and children, exterminated in gas chambers. It beggared belief, but deep down I knew the reports were true. And the longer the war continued, the more soldiers – men and boys – perished in defence of this reprehensible government.

'But where do we draw the line?' Julius asked. 'What about those who were only following orders, doing their jobs? It will be chaos.'

'Someone will have to determine whether acts have been committed voluntarily or were forced.' I stared into my glass, beginning to see the enormity of what was ahead. Who had the impartiality to make such a ruling?

'Everyone, especially in government, has played a role in perpetuating and making Nazi policy real. None of us can get away from that. I know there are things I've regretted, things I'd change if I could go back in time,' he said.

'We all have regrets, Julius. We have to live with them, but now we have to move forward and make Germany a better place. I know you can do that.'

'Let's pray that you're right.'

It was after midnight when the soft music playing on the radio was interrupted by the blaring of an announcement. Julius and I were jolted out of our sleepy haze as we listened intently. This was it. I held his hand tight, ready to celebrate the end of Nazi rule. Suddenly a voice rang out over the airwaves.

The Führer's voice.

'If I speak to you today it is first in order that you should hear my voice and that you should know that I myself am unhurt and well . . .'

Julius and I stared at each other aghast.

'The claim made by the usurpers that I am no longer alive is being contradicted at this very moment now that I am speaking to you.'

The Führer's voice carried on calmly to explain that the plot to overthrow the government had failed and that the main conspirators had been executed. His voice rose only as he made it abundantly clear that the traitors of the Fatherland would be rooted out and punished.

The look of horror on Julius's face made me shiver with fear. 'All for nothing,' I whispered.

'Stauffenberg and other good men have died . . . but the Führer won't rest until he has everyone involved,' he said grimly.

I tried to keep my emotions in check. 'You were approached to form part of the new government. Are you in danger?'

He shook his head. 'No, I didn't agree to anything . . . it was all just talk.' But I could see the fear in his eyes.

'We were so close.' I put my arms around him and rested my head on his chest, tears rolling down my cheeks as the consequences hit me.

'Germany's doomed,' he said, holding me tight.

Life quickly returned to a semblance of normality, but Julius felt distant somehow. He never mentioned the plot again – it was as though something had died in him.

'What do you want me to say, Susie?' he asked when I pushed him on his ambitions of leading the ministry towards a better Germany. 'Everything's changed. It's time to keep our heads down. Nothing's going to plan.'

'What do you mean?' I was beginning to see that the way Julius saw the world was complex. For Leo and Tante Elya, life was black and white because of the constant peril they were in. It came down to survival and instinct – how they believed they could remain safe. But Julius's life wasn't in danger, and that had allowed the line he walked to become less distinct, more shades of grey.

He sighed, putting down the papers he was reading. 'We can't even transport the new engines that the Luftwaffe has been waiting on.'

I put down my tea, anticipation swirling through my belly.

'Why not?'

'They've had problems with the manufacture of the engines and production has slowed down to a trickle. It's almost laughable how inefficient the whole process has been. These new engines were supposed to change the course of the war, making our planes unbeatable in the sky, but with the Allies marching across France, Paris within their sights and the Soviets advancing on Warsaw, we're running out of time.'

I felt sorry for Julius's frustration, but I wanted to shout with glee. These were the engines the resistance had been targeting because of my intelligence. 'If we continue on our losing streak,' he said grimly, 'we'll soon be fighting a war on home soil – fighting for Germany's very existence. We're losing, and that makes the Führer nervous, meaning he's unpredictable and capable of anything. We just have to survive now by staying under the radar.'

Julius believed that the best course of action was to steer Germany through the remainder of the war with as little impact to the economy and governance as possible. I didn't agree. Despite the Führer's new vigilance to opposition, the resistance remained committed to bringing down the Nazis any way they could, even by contributing to Germany's losses in the war. Julius knew I supported their cause but he didn't prevent me from returning to Gut Birkenhof where he suspected I'd be involved in resistance activities. He only kissed me, held me tight and asked me to be careful.

I continued to bring small pieces of information to Leo whenever I could. Although Bästlein, Jacob and Saefkow had been captured, the resistance was more determined than ever to strike a blow to the Nazi heart for the sake of those they'd lost trying. In fact, some of their plans were finally producing rewards and every action that brought the Allies closer gave the resistance something to celebrate, especially each battle won by the Soviets in the east. They would be first to liberate the remaining ghettos and camps of the east, like the Majdanek and Sobibor extermination camps in eastern Poland closest to the front. I knew that Tante Elya would be overjoyed if we were liberated by the Russians, and I began to wonder what life would be like if that happened.

Miraculously, Tante Elya had received a hastily written letter from Onkel Tedi in Lodz and she began to read it as we all sat together in the parlour after dinner one night.

'We were ecstatic to hear about the Allied invasion of Normandy. We have a small radio hidden and from time to time we can listen to what's happening in the world outside of the ghetto,' she read. 'We hear that the Russians are inching closer to Lublin and Warsaw, but I don't know if liberation will come in time for us.' Tears were filling her eyes, making it hard for her to continue reading. The Soviets had already taken Lemberg, but had found no evidence of the Janowska concentration camp, believed to be near the city, and we hadn't heard if any of the Jewish people living there had survived. We already knew that few Jewish people were found alive in Kiev.

'Here,' said Leo. 'Let me read it for you.' He took the page from his mother's unresisting hands. 'The relocations have begun again, sending thousands to an unknown destination, although we believe they've been sent to Chelmno. I don't know why because we're working like dogs to fill the ever-increasing armament quotas.

'There aren't many of us left. I've heard from reliable sources that we're the last operating ghetto in Poland. The hope that we're safe because we're necessary in completing this work is fast fading.' Leo stopped, glancing quickly at his mother.

'Finish it, Leopold,' she said with quiet determination. He nodded, frowning in concern, but he knew not to argue with his mother. Tante Elya grasped my hand and held it tightly. We were all bracing ourselves for what Leo would read next.

'If the letters stop, you'll know why. I only hope that our compatriots reach us in time and that we all survive this war and see each other again. Otherwise we'll meet again in heaven, reunited with Mama and Papa and, I fear, Felix too. Give my love to Leopold, Susanna and Georg. Goodbye my darling Elya – your loving brother, Tedi.'

Tears ran down my cheeks. Leo looked anguished and Tante Elya sat rigid next to me.

'He has to make it,' she said as Onkel Georg came to her side. 'They all have to make it.' There was nothing we could say. 'We have to do something.'

'We're doing everything we can to bring this war to an end as soon as possible. Only with the liberation of the camps can we ensure their safety,' said Onkel Georg, holding her tight.

'I sit here in comfort and safety because of who I married while my brother and uncles and other Jewish people like them are dying or live in constant fear for their lives.'

I knew she was right. And I was even more guilty of living a life of luxury. It didn't feel right, and the longer I immersed myself in that lifestyle with Julius, the more I struggled to keep my perspective. I was doing it to protect my family but I couldn't avoid the harsh reminder that many Jewish people were being treated worse than animals. 'We can only hope that the Red Army reaches them before it's too late. We have to help the Russians if nothing else,' she said. Leo and I shared a glance. If only I had access to information that could help the Jewish people in the east and Onkel Tedi and his family. 'We have to get more prisoners back home.'

'Of course, *liebling*,' said Onkel Georg. 'We can do that.'

All I could think about was what the Nazis would do to the remaining Jewish people in the Reich, like Tante Elya and Leo, when all the Jewish people in the eastern ghettos had been dealt with. My relationship with Julius was now more important than ever.

Back at the hospital, we heard rumours that the Russians were moving closer and closer.

'They've stopped on the Vistula, outside Warsaw,' said one of our patients, while Marika and I were discussing his wound management.

Marika had passed her nursing exam months earlier, but there'd been no time to celebrate as she was rostered on to her new position within hours of her news.

'The Poles have begun an uprising in the city, but the Russians just sit and wait, allowing our troops to get the city under control once more and improve our defences,' continued the soldier.

'Why would the Russians do that?' I thought about Onkel Tedi and bile rose to my throat at his words.

He shook his head. 'I don't know, but it plays right into our hands.'

Hearing these stories of the Red Army halted outside a city fighting for its survival and not lifting a finger to help,

I began to wonder what fate was in store for Germany. I felt afraid.

'Can we hold them back?' asked Marika quietly.

The soldier shrugged. 'A year ago I would never have imagined the Russians coming this far or the Allies advancing on Paris, but the Führer promises we will overcome them.' He grinned, showing gaps where his teeth were missing. 'Don't worry, the war isn't lost yet.'

Wiping the perspiration from my brow, I shared a look with Marika. Part of me didn't want Germany to lose the war because of the devastating effect it would have on our country, on our soldiers and the good people who remained but part of me rejoiced with each advance. I couldn't lose Tante Elya or Leo.

Not long after, I was sitting in Julius's suite with the late summer sun streaming in from the window on my back. It was a peaceful Sunday morning and my day off. I was reading a book on ancient Rome.

Julius came into the room. 'The Allies have liberated Paris,' he said. 'They tell me that the Parisians are celebrating. I wouldn't mind some wild French celebrations,' he said, smiling wistfully. 'We don't have much to celebrate these days.'

'That's wonderful, isn't it?' I asked after watching his frown deepen. 'The sooner the war's over and the Nazis are gone, the sooner Tante Elya is safe.' I squeezed his hand in encouragement.

He nodded, deep in thought. 'I think that soon we'll have to bow to the inevitable and it only makes sense to cut our losses, but with the failed Luftwaffe counterattack on Paris, the Wehrmacht is scrambling for extra troops and openly recruiting boys from outside the Hitler Youth into their ranks now.'

'I can't believe we don't have enough grown men to fight and have to resort to sending children to war. Surely the war can't continue much longer like this?' I said.

'While the Führer continues to tell Germany that we can win this war, our soldiers will fight until the very end.' He put down the paper and stared out towards the Brandenburg Gate. He was drawn, with black circles under his eyes. Long hours at work and a hopeless outlook for Germany's future had seen him become more and more distant. 'So much bloodshed could be avoided, as well as the destruction of Germany's infrastructure and economy. It's going to be a disaster once the war is eventually over.'

'What can we do?' I was worried about him. A man who wanted to change the world and make it a better place was now trapped, fighting a war he no longer believed in.

He smiled weakly. 'There's nothing we can do but continue to do our jobs and wait.'

'There's nothing wrong with you,' said Dr Stahl about six weeks later. My blood tests had arrived, and I was sitting across from him in one of the small consulting rooms at the hospital.

I'd been tired and light-headed and Julius had been worried that I'd been pushing myself too hard at the hospital with back to back shifts. After some prodding from Marika who pointed out that I was pale and that my uniform hung a little loose on me, I'd finally seen Dr Stahl, Johann, now that he was her boyfriend, who agreed that I'd probably picked up something in the hospital. I'd been waiting on the results of blood tests before he'd prescribe me any medicine.

'What do you mean?' I frowned in puzzlement.

'You're pregnant.'

'I'm sorry?' Surely I'd misheard.

'You're pregnant,' he repeated.

I stared at him in disbelief. 'Are you sure? I can't be.'

'The blood test doesn't lie, Susie.'

I thought back desperately – my last period had been in August and it was now October. It wasn't unusual for me to be a little late sometimes, and admittedly I'd lost track of time with the long hours I'd been working, but three weeks late . . . The blood drained from my face and I felt like I couldn't breathe.

'I could be, but . . .' I looked at him in consternation, feeling dislocated from myself.

He covered my hand with his own. 'So, not expected then?'

'No,' I whispered. 'We've been diligent but there must have been an accident.'

'How will Julius take the news?' he asked.

I shrugged. 'I honestly don't know. We've talked about having children one day.' I gazed out the window, out onto the gardens, while Johann put the test results into my file. My first thoughts were for Leo, not Julius. My heart still belonged to Leo, no matter how I tried to push my feelings for him away. A stab of pain seared through my chest with the real-isation that the small but steadfast hope I'd harboured that Leo and I would be together one day was now completely destroyed. There was no future for us. My life was now forever tied to Julius's. Although Julius loved me, and I had come to love him in my own way, I wondered how he'd take the news. Bringing a child into the world at a time of war, under the shadow of the Third Reich, wasn't something I wanted, but here I was . . .

'You and Marika both have news to share.'

My wandering thoughts were jerked back to the present. 'What?' I looked at Johann, uncomprehending.

'I proposed to Marika last night. We're getting married in December!' I was still spinning and struggled to drag myself from my own thoughts but his joy was evident. I forced my own worries to one side and smiled warmly to show him how happy I was for them.

'How wonderful!' Marika had found the love she'd been searching for. 'Congratulations, Johann. You're both lucky to have found each other.' I gave him a brief hug before closing the door behind me.

I'd never been so grateful for the demands of work, which occupied my attention and gave me the time I needed to digest the news, to accept what a pregnancy meant for me. When I should have been sleeping between shifts, I often lay on my bed staring into space, in a haze of disbelief and confusion. My relationship with Julius was complicated and a baby had never been part of the bargain for me. I worried whether he was ready to become a family man, whether he'd accept this pregnancy or reject me. It would scandalise the village if I returned home, unmarried and pregnant, and my family had enough problems without caring for a fallen woman and her illegitimate child.

It was a couple of days before I saw Marika and she shared her exciting announcement. I wept with happiness for her, hugging her tightly. Johann was a good match for her and I listened as she told me about her plans for the future, beginning with her wedding. I couldn't ruin her special moment, but it seemed that soon both of us would be leading different lives: Marika as a married woman and me as a mother. I'd have to get married before I told my family the news. It would drive a permanent wedge between me and Leo. My head ached at the thought. I had a lot to work out but it was time to tell Julius and talk through what to do next.

That night, I had Julius's favourite meal waiting for him – roasted venison in a juniper and red wine sauce, braised red cabbage and spätzle – hot on the table when he arrived back at the suite after a long day at the ministry. There was a special grocer that many in the know used who could be relied on to find those little luxuries that had all but disappeared on ordinary shelves. He was one of Leo's black market contacts, and it made me smile knowing that some of the estate's produce ended up here, the exorbitant prices passed on to those who had forced Onkel Georg into this predicament in the first place.

'Something smells good,' Julius said, walking into the sitting room.

'I've made you dinner.' I smiled to cover my nervousness.

'You've gone to so much trouble,' he said as we sat at the carefully laid table, complete with a single burning candle in the centre and a small vase of miniature white roses. He inhaled. 'It smells divine.' He reached across the table and took my hand. 'Nobody's ever cooked for me like this. Thank you.'

I squeezed his hand, blinking tears from my eyes. Cooking was such a small thing, yet it meant so much to him. I wondered if anyone had lavished love on him since he had left Gut Birkenhof. No wonder he visited us at the estate whenever he could.

'It's delicious,' he said after a few mouthfuls. 'I'm a lucky man to have you.' Thank God Tante Elya and Frau Kraus had taught me well. The meal was cooked to perfection.

'Hopefully our children will like it one day too,' I said, feeling faint. *How did I ever get here?* I took another swallow of the mellow wine to fortify myself.

His eyebrows rose in surprise at my comment about children. It was something he'd talked about but not a topic I'd ever raised. 'Of course they will. They'll be fat, healthy and rosy-cheeked if this is anything to go by.'

'Well, I think we'll find out sooner rather than later,' I said softly, watching his face intently as it dawned on him what I was saying.

'You're pregnant?' He stared at me.

'I'm sorry. I know we didn't plan for this to happen now. The timing is all wrong, but –'

Before I could finish, Julius jumped to his feet with a whoop, pulled me from the table, crushing me to his chest, and kissed me soundly.

'You don't mind?' I asked slowly, still in his arms.

'*Liebling*, I couldn't be happier.' He looked into my face and kissed my forehead, then led me to the lounge and settled me on his lap.

'You've given me reason to hope for a better life, with a family of my own.' He placed his hand protectively over my stomach. 'And you don't have to go back to work. I'll look after you.'

'The baby doesn't arrive for quite a few months yet,' I said, smiling. 'And remember, I'm a modern woman. I love my job.'

Julius nodded. 'Have you told your family?'

I frowned slightly, thinking how to tackle this delicate subject. 'I wanted to talk to you first.' I touched his cheek. 'I wasn't sure how you'd take the news.'

'You're my life, Susie. I'd never abandon you.' I sagged in his arms at those words.

'I can't tell them that I'm pregnant outside of marriage,' I whispered.

He nodded thoughtfully. 'Yes, it does change things. I think we should keep it quiet until we're married. We're surrounded by people with very traditional values who would view your condition as scandalous.' He squeezed my hand in reassurance and smiled. 'Then we can announce the news of your pregnancy.'

'The sooner the better,' I said, glancing down to my still flat stomach. But Julius was right; we had to be seen as the golden couple within his social circle and government ranks. And the marriage would cement Tante Elya and Leo's safety further. My responsibility was to them and this child now – and Julius, too, as my husband.

'Of course, *liebling*.' He kissed me on the head. 'I'll throw the most lavish, most memorable wedding Berlin has ever seen,' he said expansively. 'I want the whole of Berlin to know I'm marrying you, Susanna Göttmann.'

'Don't do that,' I said, laughing. 'Something small and simple will make me just as happy.' The doubts and worries of the past days lifted from my shoulders, with the knowledge that my family's future was secure. I felt light, perhaps even joyful.

'Anything for you,' he said. 'You've just made me the happiest man in the world.' He bent to kiss me once again and I wrapped my arms around him, grateful for this man and determined to try to love him with all of my heart.

Julius and I agreed on a date for the wedding in mid-November and I needed to tell my family the news. I was excited to plan a wedding with Tante Elya, but most of all I wanted to tell her that she was going to be a grandmother. However, that news would have to wait until after we were married. And, of course, I was worried about how Leo would react. Arriving at Gut Birkenhof without calling ahead, I found that Tante Elya wasn't anywhere in the house.

On my way to find her, I turned towards the sound of a voice calling my name. My heart lurched to my throat. 'Kreisleiter Mueller,' I said as politely as I could, my heart beating a little faster. I halted halfway down the stairs to the driveway where he was standing next to his car. 'Are you looking for my uncle? He's not in the house at the moment,' I said tersely. 'He must be around at the milking sheds.'

'Thank you, my dear,' Mueller said, with a smirk. 'It looks like I'll have to come back another time.' I nodded, relieved. 'But since you're here, I do have something to tell you, something I think you'll want to know. I've been waiting for our paths to cross again.'

'I have to go,' I said, feeling clammy.

'It's about your fiancé, Herr Siebenborn.' His face was serious now, his eyes hard as he walked up the stairs towards me. 'I wanted to know what kind of man he was and so I went digging into his past, a past he's put some effort into hiding. Then I discovered why.' He stopped and leaned back casually against the balustrade, but he was watching me closely. 'Julius Siebenborn has a mistress in Berlin, a married French social-ite, Collette Bisset, and another mistress and child that he's discarded and abandoned in Krakau. I hope for your sake that it doesn't become your fate.'

For a few moments all I could hear was roaring in my ears. Then I saw Mueller's smug smile and felt myself fill with fury. 'How dare you make up lies about him,' I said with deathly calm, advancing on him. 'I don't want to hear another word. Get back in your car and leave.'

'Oh, they're not lies. I have proof.' Mueller reached into his pocket and pulled out an envelope, looking triumphant. 'The child's birth certificate,' he spat, tossing it onto the step in front of me. 'I was going to leave it with your godparents, but this is much better.' He turned and strutted back down towards his car. 'I don't like being made a fool of, especially in public. You should heed my warning before he makes a fool out of you, too.' He opened the car door and glanced back at me. 'Goodbye, *chérie*, perhaps I'll see you in Berlin.'

I stood there shaking until the dust had settled down the driveway and I could no longer see his car. Then I slowly bent to pick up the envelope.

14

I stumbled blindly into the house and up to my bedroom. Once I had closed the door, I opened the envelope and pulled out a sheet of paper. My hands were shaking.

It was a copy of a birth certificate – the details of a boy born in Krakau in August 1942 with Julius stated as the father and certified by the General Government, Distrikt Krakau. Julius had worked in Krakau during 1941 and 1942. I scanned the document and found the name of the mother, a woman Julius had never spoken of. There was no denying that the certificate was real. There was something else inside the envelope, and I scrabbled to pull it out, almost dropping it in my haste. It was a photograph of Julius and Collette holding hands – taken at the recently reopened Bar Lebensstern in Berlin, only a few weeks ago.

Wrapping my arms over my belly as if to protect my baby from this blow, I sat down hard on the bed, feeling sick. I remembered Colette, the woman from the government gala:

a tall, willowy, elegant brunette and I now understood the possessive way she'd touched him – the confident sexuality of a woman whose affections were returned. Was he thinking of her when he took me that night?

Although Mueller was an evil old bastard, his words rang through my mind. Would Julius abandon me and the baby as he had done with the woman in Krakau? Did he really plan to marry me if he had another mistress in Berlin all this time?

When I emerged from my room, still unsteady, I heard Leo's voice down the hallway talking to Ida.

'Is your mother home yet?' I asked him outside his bedroom, forgoing any pleasantries.

'No,' he replied, 'Ida said she and Vati won't be back for hours.' He frowned, taking in my appearance. 'Are you all right?'

'No,' I blurted. I hadn't meant to say anything, but I needed to tell someone.

'You look awful. What's happened?'

I closed my eyes, taking in a deep breath to hold myself together.

'You look like you're about to fall down.' He took hold of my arm and pulled me into his room, guiding me to the edge of his bed. 'We won't be disturbed in here,' he said, closing the door. 'Now, what's wrong?' He sat beside me, concern etched across his features.

'Oh, Leo, I've been such a fool,' I whispered. I held out the envelope containing the devastating news.

Leo said nothing while he perused the document and photograph. 'Where did you get these?' he asked darkly when he'd finished.

'Kreisleiter Mueller was just here to see your father and gave them to me.' I looked up at him, the ferocity in his face blurred by the tears in my eyes. 'He was going to give them to Onkel Georg. He told me that Julius still has a mistress here in Berlin.' I gestured to the photograph. 'I've seen her with Julius before, at the gala when we announced our engagement.'

'I knew Julius wasn't to be trusted.' He shook his head with disgust and stared at the photograph for a moment. 'Why would Mueller do this?'

'Julius humiliated him, first at my birthday party and then at the opera.'

'I didn't think Julius would be that stupid,' he said. 'Mueller has an enormous ego. He's not a man to cross lightly.'

'What am I going to do?' I whispered. 'We've just set the wedding date for November. That's why I came home, to let your parents know.'

'A wedding?' Leo was incredulous.

I nodded, feeling wretched, tears sliding down my face. 'And now . . .' I couldn't tell him about the baby now. I felt ashamed and used. I was such a fool. 'Why didn't he tell me about his child?'

'Because he's a coward,' he said through gritted teeth. He jumped up, running his hand through his hair in agitation and began to pace the room until his eyes locked with mine. With a look of apology he was by my side immediately and he put his arm around me. I leaned into his solid warmth like I had when I was a child. It was comforting.

'Don't tell your father,' I said. He jerked beneath me, his chest taut as a drum. 'I'll deal with it myself and tell him when I'm ready.'

'What do you mean you'll deal with it?'

'I have to confront Julius.'

'You'll go back to him?' I could feel the tension humming through his body.

'I have to talk to him. Perhaps there's a reasonable explanation.'

'What possible explanation could he have? There's no disputing this evidence.'

'Oh, I don't know, Leo,' I said miserably. I knew that he'd support me whatever I chose, but things were right or wrong for him, black or white. Even if I could explain, I wasn't sure that he'd understand why I'd made the choices I did and accepted the sacrifices I had for the sake of my family.

I could feel him shuffle beside me, as though he couldn't get comfortable, before taking a deep breath and allowing the words to tumble out. 'Susie, do you love him?'

I knew how hard it was for him to ask but the truthful answer was just as difficult for me to give and I wasn't sure it was something he wanted to hear. How could he understand without knowing all the circumstances? How could I tell him without hurting him? 'I don't know . . . Not like I love you. I'll never love anyone else like I love you . . . But he's been good to me and I suppose a part of me loves him for that.'

'I won't watch you suffer like this. He has to pay for what he's done.'

'No, Leo. I'll deal with Julius. Stay away from him.' I looked into the face I loved more than any other. It was breaking my heart. He wanted to stand up for me, protect me, and I loved him all the more for it. I wanted to tell him about the baby, but I couldn't. 'Promise me you won't do anything rash,' I said.

'I promise,' he said huskily. I could see how much it cost him to say it. 'But just say the word and I'll give him a piece of my mind.'

Leo offered to come back to Berlin with me, but I told him I had to do it on my own. It was enough to know that he was there for me. I returned to the Adlon, put the birth certificate and photograph on the table for Julius to see when he came in and waited nervously. I hoped beyond reason that there was a chance they weren't real.

'What's this?' he said, shrugging off his jacket. He picked up the certificate, a frown deepening across his brow as he realised what it was. Then he picked up the photograph, his voice soft. 'Where did you get these?'

'Kreisleiter Mueller was waiting at the front steps of Gut Birkenhof.'

'He's a troublemaker, Susie.'

'But is it true?'

He just stared at me and I waited, barely daring to breathe. He put the papers back on the table. 'It's complicated.'

I couldn't believe it. It was true. I began to sob. Julius sat beside me on the lounge and put his arm around me. 'Shh. We can work this out.'

'Don't touch me.' I stood abruptly and moved to one of the winged chairs. 'I wanted to give you the benefit of the doubt before I thought the worst of you,' I hiccoughed through my tears. 'Is there a good and logical reason for this?'

'I should have told you,' he said, sighing. 'There were so many times I wanted to . . .' He stood abruptly and walked to the glass French doors, staring out over the Brandenburg Gate. 'When I was in Krakau, I met Margarete. To me it was just a fling, and then she fell pregnant.' I couldn't see his face, but he was still, like a statue. 'She wanted to marry, but I wasn't ready. I barely knew her. So we agreed to wait until after the baby was born.' A sob escaped my lips. He turned to me then, his eyes wide with concern. 'It was different with her. I love you, Susie.'

'Just tell me what happened,' I said with a strangled voice.

He nodded and started to pace the room. 'When our son was born, we were so happy, we planned to marry as soon as we could.' He slumped back onto the edge of the lounge. 'After what my childhood was like, you know how much I want my own family.' His eyes were pleading with me to understand.

I couldn't answer him. I only stared.

'But before we could arrange the ceremony, our little boy died. Not even three months old, lying in his cradle. He was cold and blue.' He looked at me then, the grief etched across his white face. 'Nobody could tell us why.'

'Oh God,' I muttered, my hand moving protectively to my belly. 'Julius, that's awful.'

He nodded, raking a shaking hand through his hair. 'Under the Reich, the penalty for killing your child – even from the time it's in the womb – is death, and I worried I'd lose Margarete as well. We were both questioned, but suspicion fell directly on her and she was accused of smothering her own baby ... But I'd been beside her all night, every night, during his feeds and when she'd put him back to bed. She wasn't capable of that – she adored him.'

'What happened?'

'Eventually she was cleared, but neither of us coped well with his loss and the investigation. We couldn't look at each other without being reminded of what had happened. Then I was offered a promotion back in Berlin and we agreed it was better that we part ways.'

'Why didn't you tell me?' I whispered, my anger and betrayal warring with my compassion for his loss.

'I couldn't.' His voice was choked with emotion. 'Every time I think of him, other images come up to haunt me. His death feels like a punishment for not doing more to prevent what I've seen. You have no idea what that's like . . .' The anguish behind his eyes was heartbreaking, but I didn't know how to feel. 'When I was in Krakau, I was sent by Ganzenmüller to check the railways that were part of the Ostbahn,' he whispered. Then the words seemed to fall out of him, his voice like an automaton. 'One day I was taken to inspect the line that had been built to the camp at Treblinka. A train had arrived early that morning with prisoners. They were Jews. When the doors were opened the stench that poured out was indescribable. Then I understood. The carriages had been packed beyond capacity . . . who knows how long they'd been travelling. Only a small number walked off that train, others were carried – but so many more were already dead, putrid and in a state of decomposition.' He spoke faster now, as if it was a relief to get it out. 'It was the stench of death, Susie. There were men, women and children. I'll never forget one woman clutching the corpse of her dead baby to her chest. She only started screaming when the guards tried to rip the child from her grasp . . .' Tears filled his eyes. 'That dead child and baby Josef are interchangeable in my dreams. There was nothing

I could do but watch on in horror. And the guilt that I didn't do anything at all carries on.'

I realised I was breathing heavily. I shook my head to try and clear the awful vision of Jewish people being transported like animals and enduring horrible deaths, if not through neglect then through extermination. 'But you promised to tell me everything, that we'd be equal – partners. You've kept all of this from me.'

He nodded miserably. 'I'm sorry.'

And then I remembered the French woman. 'What about Collette? I asked you once before about her, the night of the gala, but here's a photo of the two of you taken only recently. How do you explain this? Tell me, is she your mistress?' I bit out.

'No, I promise you. She and I had a relationship before I left Berlin years ago, but it was over long before I met Margarete in Krakau. She wanted to resume our relationship when I came back, but I told her that I'd met you.'

'Julius, you're holding hands in this photo, only weeks ago.' I stared hard into his eyes.

'She's having trouble with her husband and didn't know who to turn to. How could I turn her away? I was only trying to comfort her. We've known each other for such a long time. She was so distressed . . .' He caught my glare. I wasn't convinced. 'I swear to you that nothing's happened between us.'

I sat immovable, somewhere between despair and hope. He left the lounge and dropped to his knees beside me. 'I swear to you, Susie. There's only you. I love you.' He placed his hand on my belly. 'I swear on the life of our child.'

I looked at him for a long moment. 'What happens to us?' I asked. Although he might not have deliberately set out to hurt me, Julius was the kind of person who let things happen around him rather than make a stand. Maybe everything had been pulled out of proportion, designed by Kreisleiter Mueller to cause the most trouble and pain between us. Maybe Julius was right and Mueller wanted me and the glittering prize of Gut Birkenhof. Or maybe it was Julius who was lying to me. But none of it mattered. I had our child to think of.

'Susie, you're the one I want to spend my life with. I won't do anything to jeopardise that.'

'Promise me you'll never see Collette again.'

'Yes, of course.'

'Our wedding goes ahead in November and no more secrets between us.'

'No more secrets,' he said solemnly, reaching up and kissing me gently on the lips.

Back at Beelitz, I knew I had to tell Marika what was happening. I waited in our room for her to come off shift, thinking about the implications of my upcoming marriage.

I was reluctant to relinquish my independence and the purpose and fulfilment nursing gave me but once I'd had the baby I'd be expected to stay at home. I didn't want to become a housewife, even one belonging to the glittering social and political elite. I shook my head with frustration, determined to spend whatever time I could with Marika at Beelitz, helping her plan her own wedding and enjoying the twilight of our girlhood together. We'd been friends for so many years and neither of us knew where life would take us after this.

'All well?' she asked, sitting opposite me with a cup of tea and a couple of biscuits.

I nodded, smiling weakly. 'How's everything going for your wedding?'

'Johann doesn't care if we get married in a tent, so long as we're married. Mutti's arranging the venue and a dressmaker for the gown.' She dunked her biscuit in the tea and popped it into her mouth before it fell into the cup.

'I'm pregnant,' I said quickly before I could take back my words.

'What?' she spluttered, nearly choking on the biscuit.

'About two months.' Tears blurred my vision as I told her about Julius's joyful reaction, the wedding, Kreisleiter Mueller and his revelations and my confrontation with Julius. 'The wedding's in a month, but first I have to tell Onkel Georg and Tante Elya that I'm getting married . . . and Leo,' I said softly.

'What about Leo?'

'He'll be furious when he finds out I've decided to stay with Julius.' I shut my eyes, tears sliding down my face. 'But the baby changes everything,' I said, my hand over my belly. Everyone had their own reasons for doing what they did and a way to convince themselves that their choices were the right ones.

'Oh, Susie,' she said, squeezing my hand sympathetically. 'Just remember that I'm always here for you.'

That weekend, I went back to Gut Birkenhof to announce my wedding plans. I didn't know how I was going to tell Leo, but my worry was cast to one side when Tante Elya announced she'd received a scribbled letter from Onkel Tedi.

I found her standing by the front door, her face stricken. 'It was a miracle he managed to send this. I didn't expect to hear from him again.'

'What does it say?' I asked, dread swirling in my belly.

'They were in the last transport to leave the ghetto. It's empty, everybody's gone.' She stared at me with wide eyes. It was mid-October now, but who knew how long it had taken for us to receive the note.

I took her arm, guiding her to the seat in the entry. 'Did he know where he was going?'

'Not Chelmno, like he thought in his last letter, but probably Auschwitz, further away from the Russian advance. He was happy that maybe he'd see Felix again, have his family all together in one place before he died.' Her hands were shaking and the scrap of paper fluttered to the floor.

'Tante Elya, I'm so sorry,' I whispered, my arms around her.

'The Russians are so close . . . my only hope is that they'll liberate them before anything terrible happens.'

'Mine too.'

But still I wondered why the Red Army was camped outside Warsaw, allowing the Nazis to strengthen their position and dispose of their enemies, including the Poles and the last Jewish people in the ghettos of the east. What was in store for German citizens if the Soviets arrived on German territory and marched into Berlin before the Allies? Would they become new oppressors rather than our liberators? I couldn't believe that was possible. They were Tante Elya's compatriots and we were rescuing Soviet soldiers from the clutches of the Nazis. They were our saviours. And yet the thought refused to leave my mind.

We arranged tea in the parlour, wanting to take Tante Elya's mind off the letter. She seemed so happy to have us all together for the first time in ages, listening to Leo play Russian folk tunes on the balalaika and recounting stories of her youth. She was animated, her dark eyes flashing with joy and her expressive face conveying longing for her simple childhood and her homeland.

Frau Kraus and I made a honey cake, Tante Elya's favourite treat when she was a child. Leo made sure we had all the ingredients we needed from his black market connections. It was a success and her eyes shone with delight and fond memories, then closed in bliss with every forkful she took to her mouth.

'Soon we'll be sitting around the samovar talking about how good life is with the Nazis gone,' she said, sipping her piping hot tea.

'It can't be much longer now,' said Leo, putting down the balalaika. 'The Allies have reached the German border at Aachen and soon they'll be marching their way to Berlin.'

'Yes, but what will happen in the meantime? Himmler's Volkssturm is a disgrace, sending boys and old men to defend the home front,' Onkel Georg said with disgust. 'We've already lost a generation of young men and many of their fathers, and now young girls like Mina in the village are being called up to become flak helpers.'

Mina was our housemaid Ida's granddaughter. I knew Ida had recently left Gut Birkenhof to take care of her as Mina's mother had been arrested for having relations with a foreign worker – it was now prohibited for Germans to fraternise with foreigners, particularly Poles and Slavs.

'Vati, you're getting a little morose,' said Leo, looking pointedly at his mother.

'I'm sorry, *liebchen*. I've been furious ever since I heard the news that the program has been launched. We were a country who prided ourselves on our honour. Where's the honour in sending little children to war?'

'It's time to get the milking done, Vati,' said Leo, standing up hastily.

'Take Susanna to help you. I'm going to sit with your beautiful mother until dinner.' Onkel Georg kissed Tante Elya's cheek.

'There's the gallant gentleman I remember, just as handsome and kind as the day I met him,' said Tante Elya, blushing with pleasure. She fiddled with the diamond engagement ring on her hand.

'And you're still the light of my life. I don't know what I'd ever do without you.' He took her hand, gazing at the ring, and brought it to his lips.

'Go on, the pair of you,' said Tante Elya, smiling radiantly. 'I'll take any time I can get with your father. Maybe we'll take a walk before dinner.'

It made my heart clutch to see the love between them after all these years. I could only hope that Julius and I would be happy together . . . Then I winced. I still had to tell them about the wedding.

'Tedi's letter has shaken them both,' I said to Leo, pulling on my boots in the utility room by the back door. 'Everything's so uncertain.'

'It's the everyday things that become precious, like spending time with those you love,' he said softly, putting on his heavy coat.

'The milking won't wait.' I stood abruptly. I couldn't do this with him. I'd made my choice.

'Susie, tell me what happened with Julius.' He grasped my arm before I could turn away.

'I'm staying with him, Leo.' I sighed, exhausted from the constant pretence and layers of deceit. 'It's complicated.'

He stood stock still in disbelief. 'He lied to you,' he snapped in outrage, 'and I can almost guarantee that he'll continue to be unfaithful to you.' He shook his head and grimaced. 'How can anything he tells you get beyond that fact?'

'It can't.' My shoulders slumped. I was so tired. I wanted it all to stop.

He rubbed his face in exasperation. 'What's the hold he has over you? There's something you're not telling me.' He scowled but the desperation in his voice made my heart break.

'It's nothing.' I tried to pull away, but he only drew me closer.

'Susie,' he beseeched, turning my head so that I would look at him. 'I was wrong. I can't live without you, much as I've struggled against it. I only wanted to protect you but I see that you're a strong woman who refuses to be a victim of circumstance. If anything, you've been the one who's protected me. Vati and I could be dead or in a concentration camp if it wasn't for you that day with the Gestapo.'

'It was Julius who discovered the threat to you, but I'd do anything in my power to make sure my family's safe,' I whispered, laying my hand on his cheek.

Realisation dawned in Leo's eyes. 'That's it. He's promised to protect us if you stay with him.'

'Leo, it's not like that.' I shook my head in frustration.

'Then tell me how it is,' he said brusquely.

'It started as an arrangement.' I couldn't meet his eyes. 'He offered to help after your mother was registered and we lost the government contracts.'

'I bet he did,' he snarled. Our faces were close. 'What was his price? Did he make you sleep with him?'

'No,' I said angrily. I was furious that he was attacking Julius who was protecting our family, furious that he'd made me blurt out the truth, but most of all furious that he'd got to the heart of the matter so quickly.

'Don't lie to me!' he said, shaking me by the shoulders as though he could make the truth fall out of me.

'It was never part of our agreement. He was completely honourable and then we got engaged and . . .' I couldn't do it anymore. 'It was what he wanted. He loves me.' But I was just like Julius, allowing something to happen that I wasn't sure or happy about. I felt like a hypocrite for being critical of him.

'And I pushed you away,' Leo said. I nodded miserably, and he sat heavily on the hard bench.

'It seemed a small price to pay for keeping you safe.' I sat beside him, feeling washed out and empty.

'How could you think that?' He pulled me close and hugged me tight. 'Leave him. He can't protect us any more than we can protect ourselves.'

'But if there's any chance that he can, I can't risk your safety, especially now after Onkel Tedi's letter.'

He shook his head with frustration. 'Come home, and we can be together on the estate until this war's over. Then maybe we can declare our love to the world.'

If only it was that easy. I looked into his dark eyes, wishing that things were different. 'Leo, I love you and you mean the world to me, but I can't. I'm marrying Julius.' Silently I willed him to understand before I said the two words that I knew would destroy him. 'I'm pregnant.'

The look of injury on his face was more than I could bear. He knew that I was lost to him now. I stood and walked to the door and out into the fading light.

15

bout a week later, Julius and I were enjoying a rare lazy morning at the Adlon. We were the picture of happy domesticity, discussing the details of the wedding and our lives together. I refused to dwell on my conversation with Leo because every time I thought of it I wanted to cry. The look of desolation he'd given me was seared into my mind. I had never wanted to hurt him. The tragedy was that he was finally ready to act on his love for me, but it had come too late. My future was now with Julius and our baby and it made no sense to focus on what could never be.

We both had fond memories of our childhood on Gut Birkenhof and spoke briefly about bringing up our child on my family property in Marienwerder. In six months, when I turned twenty-one, I would take legal possession of the estate, but we decided that it would be too far from the seat of the government in Berlin and from family. I wondered what condition the estate would be in by then and if there'd be anything to farm, especially if it lay in the path of the Soviet forces. Although we continued to receive wounded soldiers from the Eastern Front, where the Soviets had now penetrated Lithuania, Latvia and Hungary, the talk was of how the war had finally made its way to German soil with the arrival of the Allies in Aachen, near the German borders with Belgium and the Netherlands.

We were finishing off a light breakfast of toast and marmalade and tea when we heard a knock at the door. I frowned at Julius.

'Who can that be?' Any urgent meeting at the ministry was usually telephoned through and we rarely got visitors this early.

Julius shrugged. 'We'll find out soon enough,' he said as he rose from his chair to answer the door.

'Leo,' I heard him say as the door closed and both men entered the sitting room.

'What a lovely surprise. What are you doing here?' I asked, noting his furious expression.

'I've come to take you home,' he said, his tone icy.

I stood quickly and pushed my chair back from the table. 'Why? What's wrong? Is it your mother?'

'Do you know your fiancé is involved with the murder of thousands of Jewish people?' He was shaking with rage.

'Don't be ridiculous,' said Julius, clearly shocked.

'Leo, you're mistaken.' I touched him on the arm, trying to soothe him, but he was hard as steel. 'Come, sit and have a cup of tea. Tell us what you're talking about.'

'I wouldn't accept a single drop from him. He's been to Treblinka and Auschwitz. He's seen what they do there.' His fists were clenched by his sides, but I could see by the set of his shoulders that he was ready to throw a punch.

'I know, Leo,' I said. 'He was shocked seeing people coming off the trains at Treblinka. He had to inspect the lines there.' I knew Leo despised Julius and wanted to protect me, but this was going too far.

'Not just that.' He shook his head in frustration. 'He's seen the gas chambers where they murder thousands of men, women and children every day. How do you think he was promoted to assistant secretary last year? He performed an important function in Krakau and the promotion was his reward for his service and his silence.'

Julius's face was red with fury. 'How dare you come into my home and accuse me of murder!' he bellowed.

But I felt chilled to the bone. 'Julius? It's not true is it?' I whispered.

'Can't you see what you're doing to Susie?' Julius put his arm around me. 'Of course it's not true, *liebling*, you know how I feel about what's happening,' he said to me, but I could feel every muscle of his body taut against me.

'Lies are the only thing coming out of your mouth, Siebenborn,' said Leo through gritted teeth. 'I paid Mueller a little visit. He doesn't like you very much, does he? He has copies of all sorts of interesting documents.' He stood tall, triumph glowing in his eyes.

'Leo, I asked you not to get involved,' I whispered, sick to the stomach.

'Don't worry, Susie. He's bluffing.' Julius pulled me to him. 'Leo, it's time for you to go. I know you're protective of Susie, but she's my responsibility now, and we'll be married within the month.' He slid his hand down over my belly.

Leo was shaking with contained rage, his eyes transfixed on the possessive hand on my stomach. I pulled away from Julius, not wanting to spark what was becoming an explosive situation.

'Leo –'

'I'm not going anywhere,' Leo barked. 'And I have the evidence right here.' He reached into his pocket and unfolded a document. He held it out to me. 'This is his signature, isn't it?' I couldn't help but glance at the page. It certainly looked like a report from the Ministry of Transport – official stamp and all – with Julius's distinctive signature at the bottom. I felt sick. 'Mueller has the rest.'

'What is this, Julius?' I whispered, stunned. I took the page from Leo and thrust it into his hands.

Julius grimaced. 'I know what it looks like, but I swear to you I didn't know what was happening. I was at Treblinka, inspecting the train lines and stations, like I told you. Then I was given a tour of the camp. I was horrified – shocked – but there was nothing I could do. The same happened at Chelmno and Auschwitz before I was asked by Ganzenmüller to write a report.' Beads of perspiration had formed on his forehead and he was trembling.

'And . . . you just accepted it?' I couldn't believe he'd said nothing and done nothing about something as monstrous as this.

'You know I couldn't have accepted it – and I still can't – but opening my mouth would do nothing but create trouble for us. This is bigger than any of us, than any resistance group. I just thank God it will end when we lose the war.' It was then that I realised the extent of his cowardice; Julius would never do anything that put him truly at risk. 'I couldn't

242

tell you everything, Susie,' Julius interrupted my thoughts. 'I wanted to protect you from the terrible things that were happening.'

The typescript on the document in Julius's hand blurred. He'd known all along what was happening at the camps and had withheld it from me. I was swamped with horror. And then all of a sudden I was tired – so tired of trying to decipher what was the truth and what wasn't.

'*Were* happening?' Leo shouted, glaring at him. 'They're *still* happening! I've seen Ministry of Transport reports of the numbers that have been transported to these camps each month. Mueller showed me. Reports sent on to the Reichsbahn so they can be paid their pound of flesh, literally, for the passenger fares . . . and signed off by you.' He turned to me. 'He's involved with Ganzenmüller in secret meetings across the ministries that plan and organise the next transports of Jewish people for relocation.' He laughed, mirthlessly. 'They call it resettlement, but we all know what it really means. He has to take responsibility for what he's done.'

My eyes widened and I began to tremble with shock, unable to believe there was more, unable to believe that Julius was involved.

'After everything I've done for your family, this is how you repay me.' Julius's face was purple and he stepped towards Leo menacingly. 'If you don't watch yourself, you'll end up in one of those camps. Not even the love I bear for your father or Susie will protect you.'

'Julius! You don't mean that,' I said, horrified.

'Are you threatening me?' Leo rose to his full height, his fists ready.

'I'll make it clear for you so there's no misunderstanding.' They were nose to nose now. 'If you cause any more trouble, or even come anywhere near Susie and I before we're married, I'll send you there myself.'

'Enough!' I screamed. 'Both of you!' My heart pounding in my chest, I yanked Leo by the arm, towards the door.

Leo resisted, his eyes wild. 'You heard him, Susie. He wants to send me there too. He's just like the rest of the Nazi scum.'

'Get out!' bellowed Julius. 'Before I do something I'll regret.'

Leo reached for my hand. 'Come on, Susie, let's go.'

'She's not going anywhere,' hissed Julius. 'She belongs here with me.'

'You? You're no better than a cold-hearted killer. She's coming home with me.' Leo grabbed my arm.

Much to my astonishment, Julius burst out laughing. '*Susie* knows a good thing when she sees it.' He held out his hand to me. 'Come, *liebling*. Leo's leaving.'

I was quivering – surely I was in the middle of a nightmare that I'd wake up from any moment. I shook my head. 'How could you be part of this travesty?'

'You know I'm not a murderer. I want to help stop the senseless killing of people by the Nazis. You know I would do more if I could.'

But Julius was a man I didn't recognise anymore, a man I didn't want to be anywhere near. 'Can't you see? You're a Nazi. You're one of them.' The secrets, his son and mistress, were one thing, but how could I stay with a man who'd not only known about the transporting of thousands of people to the camps in the east and the murder of so many innocents, but had been involved? It was too much. We'd have to find another way to protect Tante Elya and Leo.

There was only one choice for me. 'I can't stay.'

Julius stared at me as though I'd gone mad. 'You can't leave me,' he said. 'You're pregnant with our child.'

The stunned look on his face made me resolute. 'I'm not staying. Not after this.'

'If you leave here, don't come back,' he growled, stepping threateningly towards me. 'I won't be able to guarantee your family's safety.'

'We'll have to take our chances,' said Leo, steadfast by my side.

I squeezed Leo's hand gratefully. 'Take me home to Gut Birkenhof.'

Tante Elya and Onkel Georg were in the study when we arrived home.

'It's over between Julius and me,' I said flatly. 'I know you think I'll have a better life with him but I'm never going back. My place is here with you.' I knew my eyes were red and puffy from crying but even with the looks of concern on their faces, I couldn't bring myself to tell them any more. Leo had promised not to say anything about Julius's involvement with the transport of the Jewish people until I was ready. I couldn't believe Julius could do it while he was also protecting Tante Elya and Leo, but it also made me wonder how much of what he'd told me was real. How much had he really done to ensure my family's safety?

Onkel Georg's gaze shifted to Leo, who shook his head imperceptibly. He frowned and said nothing.

Tante Elya squeezed my hand in sympathy. 'I'm sorry, *myshka*. Maybe it's for the best.'

I nodded, a tear sliding down my face. 'I'm going to my room,' I murmured.

I placed my engagement ring on my dresser and didn't come down to dinner that night, even ignoring Tante Elya's knock on my door. I couldn't face her just yet. My stomach churned every time I thought about what had happened and I always came back to the same conclusion. Julius had betrayed me and the immensity of what he'd done took my breath away. There was no way I could go back to him: even for the sake of Tante Elya and Leo, or for our child. I had no idea how I was going to tell Tante Elya and Onkel Georg that I was pregnant or how I was going to bring up an illegitimate child without a father. The thought made me nauseous with fear. But it was surely better than staying with Julius. I had gone against everything I believed in to be with him – my love for Leo, my hatred of Nazis, putting up with his lies and betrayals. I had allowed myself to be mesmerised by his lifestyle, his power and his charm. Now the blinkers had been ripped from my eyes and I was ashamed of what I'd done. How many times had I drunk champagne and feasted on lobster when I knew Jewish people were suffering in the concentration camps? While Julius knew what was happening there and was signing their transportation orders? I was nothing but a silly, naïve girl. Even as I tried to sleep – my body curled around the baby as if I could protect it from this terrible distress – I relived the morning's confrontation behind closed lids.

It was well into the small hours of the morning before exhaustion took hold and I finally found solace in sleep.

I withdrew into myself and moved through the next couple of days in a stupor. Despite the looks of worry and concern cast my way, everybody respected my privacy and left me to wander aimlessly about the garden or sleep through the afternoon and evening in my room. Night stretched out forever when I only had the silence and my own thoughts to torture me, until I slipped into an uneasy sleep, then woke unrefreshed to the sun already high in the sky, peeking through my curtains.

On this day, it was late morning when I woke, my head heavy and dull. It took a moment to remember why I was home and then the horror of the last few days came back to me. It was as if a dark shadow had attached itself to me and there was nothing I could do to escape it. But with a little distance, it seemed a little easier to bear. I could begin to accept the terrible facts and work out how to tell my family the truth.

As I was dressing, an awful cry broke the silence of the house, followed by sobbing. I stumbled down the stairs to find Tante Elya in the parlour. She was slumped in a chair with Leo standing white as a sheet and dazed beside her, a page in his hand.

'What's happened?' I glanced from one to the other. 'Is it Onkel Tedi?'

She shook her head. 'It's Leopold.'

My heart began to hammer.

'I've received my letter,' he said woodenly. He lifted his hand with the paper. 'My National Labour Service Obligation. I leave in a fortnight. ' I felt light-headed. *Not Leo.*

'It's my fault,' she sobbed. 'If I wasn't a Jew . . .' A stab of pain sliced through me as I remembered Julius's threats. *What have I done?*

'It's not your fault,' I said, hugging her tight. I knew it was Julius, the timing was right, but I couldn't tell her that it was my fault. My eyes met Leo's but I saw no accusation there, only grim acknowledgement.

'Go and find Georg, as quickly as you can,' Tante Elya said, patting my shoulder. 'He'll know what to do.'

Onkel Georg went to see Julius at the ministry that same day. Julius had refused to see him, so he'd waited in the foyer of the Adlon and confronted him there. Onkel Georg said Julius had seemed stricken when he told him he was unable to help Leo, but his regret didn't help us. He denied our engagement was over but Onkel Georg had told him that, as far as I was concerned, we were finished and if he refused to help Leo that their friendship was over too. I wished I'd been there to watch Julius squirm under his fury.

Onkel Georg had failed, but I had to try. I left on the bus to Berlin early the next morning. Tante Elya knew where I was going. Onkel Georg and Leo would have tried to prevent me, told me that it was a pointless exercise. Men had their pride, but I was willing to forgo mine if it secured Leo's freedom.

Arriving at the Adlon, I prayed that Julius hadn't left earlier than usual for the ministry. I let myself in, my heart pounding so much I felt I would faint. I could hear movement in the bedroom.

'Julius?' I called out hesitantly. I wasn't sure of the reaction I'd receive.

He strode into the sitting room, dressed in a shirt and suit trousers, his face a mask of cold indifference.

'You're back,' he said stonily. 'Are you here to beg my forgiveness?'

'Julius, I can't get past what you're a part of, but I don't believe you're a bad man. Only that you're unable to stand up to what's wrong.'

His eyes narrowed. 'I told you, my hands are tied. I don't like it any more than you do. I don't have the luxury to stand up and voice my repugnance for what's going on. I'd likely lose my life and, if not, then certainly my career, and I'd never be able to protect your family. I could never have done both.'

'But Leo . . . you promised to look after them.' Tears were in my eyes. 'What about Leo?'

He put his hand on my shoulder. 'I'm sorry, Susie. He's not the only one. A fresh round of recruitment is underway to boost our war effort, *mischlinge* mainly. As I told Georg, if he's already received his letter then it's too late.'

'I know you can do something about the names on those lists, about who goes or doesn't go on those trains.'

He stepped away and shook his head in irritation. 'It's his service obligation, the same for all citizens of the Reich. He should see it as an honour to be helping our war effort. He's doing something useful for his country, just like the rest of us.'

I looked up at him through my tears, appalled. 'Julius, you know it's not the same. He's being sent to a labour camp – imprisonment.'

249

'It's a work camp, somewhere for recruits from all over the Reich to stay while they work on a project. Nothing more,' he said dismissively.

'Nothing more than Nazi lies and deception, you mean,' I hissed. 'That's exactly how it started with the Jewish people – now it's the *mischlinge*.'

Julius was a politician through and through, hiding behind his words, and that made me afraid. I tried another tack, reaching out to touch his arm. 'Julius, I can't lose him like I lost my parents and Friedrich. You know what it's like to lose your family.'

'Don't you understand?' he said, turning, his eyes blazing. He shook me by the shoulders. 'If I really wanted to see harm come to him, I would've arranged for him to be transported to Auschwitz.'

I gasped, stunned by the truth of what he'd done. But I had to do something, appeal to his sense of family to make him see reason and undo it. 'But we both know what happens now. The chances of him coming home are next to none. Tante Elya and Onkel Georg will never get over it.'

'If he does what he's told and keeps his head down until the war's over, he should be fine. After that, who knows what will happen to any of us.' He sighed, wiping away my tears with the ball of his thumb as I stood there trembling. 'We're a family now. Nobody else matters except you and the baby.' He put his hand on my belly. 'Georg and Elya have so much to look forward to: a wedding and a new baby arriving before too long. Our child should be the focus now.' I stilled at his words. 'Now, if you're staying, I'm willing to put all this unpleasantness behind us.' He smiled, as though he'd just concluded a difficult piece of negotiation in his favour. I felt like a piece of carved marble, cold and lifeless.

It was then that I understood. This was what Julius had always wanted: to be the centre of Onkel Georg's family. He was jealous of Onkel Georg, who had had parents, a wife and people who loved him. Julius felt Georg had been handed wealth, a good name and the family estate on a silver platter. Julius wanted to be the most important, most valued and most loved member of the Hecker family and our marriage and child was the way he would achieve it. Leo had got in the way. Julius had removed him and wasn't going to lift a finger to help him. All the choices I'd made, all the compromises, all my sacrifices: they'd all come to this. I'd helped remove Leo.

I swallowed. *One more try.* 'That depends.' The dangerous glint in his eye made me pause. 'Are you going to help Leo or not?'

Julius frowned, his eyes still dangerous. 'You belong to me. Our child binds you to me forever.' His expression was triumphant. 'You've got nowhere else to go.'

'Please, for the love of God, Julius!' I cried out. I was out of my mind with fear. I had nothing else to lose. 'I'll do anything you want, Julius. Just help Leo.'

His face was against mine. 'Leo? It's always about Leo. But you forget – your allegiance is to me and our child.' He twisted my arm so it was halfway up my back.

'Julius, stop! You're hurting me.'

He released my arm and pushed me away, so I stumbled and broke my fall on the edge of the lounge. 'I think this conversation is over.'

'I hate you!' I screamed, lunging at him. I wanted to scratch his eyes out. 'You're nothing but a coward.'

He hit me across the face, my head snapping back with a searing pain and sending me sprawling to the floor. Stunned, I placed my hand on my cheek, feeling the burning heat rising. Then I lifted my hand and saw blood.

'You bastard! How dare you!'

'How dare I?' He stepped towards me and I shuffled back hastily on the floor. 'How dare *you* place us in this precarious position? We had everything and you're the one who's ruining it.'

I scrambled to my feet, afraid.

'You will stay here and we'll be a family whether you like it or not.'

I edged towards the door, trying to work out if I could get to it before he'd reach me. 'I won't. I regret the day I ever agreed to your arrangement.' I was shaking in fury. 'You think you can play around with people's lives. You're no better than those Nazi thugs,' I spat at him with all the venom I could muster, and then ran for the door.

But he was fast. He grabbed me by the hair and dragged me back across the room. 'You might think that of me now, but I'm the father of your child. If you do anything more to jeopardise our relationship I will come after you with the full force of the law behind me and take our child from you.' He threw me against the wall, the impact jarring my spine and winding me. I slid to the floor, gasping. 'Then you'll really know what I'm capable of. I'm your fiancé and soon I'll be your husband. Don't you forget it.'

He left the room and returned a moment later with his suit jacket and tie. 'I expect you here when I get back.' His look of utter contempt made me shrink further to the floor and then I heard the door slam behind him as he left the suite.

Shaken, I got to my feet, my head aching. I straightened my clothing, cleaned up my bleeding nose and a cut inside my lip and applied makeup over my cheek. I removed the engagement ring from my pocket with trembling hands and placed it on the table. I left without a backwards glance, and yet fragile as glass. I desperately wanted to slip into the little Opel still parked in the garage, but instead walked briskly through the lobby and waited for the doorman to hail me a taxi to the bus station.

As we pulled out onto the Unter den Linden, I allowed myself to breathe but I couldn't cry. Not now.

16

Tante Elya met me at the door. My head was throbbing, my face was sore and my back had begun to hurt on the journey home. I knew I'd have some bad bruises when I dared to look.

'He wouldn't do a thing.' I bent my head. 'I've failed.'

'We knew it was a slim chance.' She took my face in her hands and made me look at her. I winced. 'What happened?' Her expression almost made me break down. 'Julius did this?' I nodded, tears filling my eyes and she hugged me close. 'Oh, *myshka*!'

'It looks a lot worse than it is.'

'He's finally shown his true colours.' She gathered me into her arms. 'Come, let's get you inside. You never have to see that man again.' My tears fell then.

Frau Kraus plied me with salves and ointments for my injuries while Tante Elya made me tea. My body ached when I woke the next morning, and as I slowly stretched I gasped with pain. The events of the previous day came tumbling back like a nightmare. I made my way to the bathroom and stripped, staring into the mirror, appraising my condition. Dark purple bruises rose fresh against my pale skin, vivid reminders of what had occurred. Gently probing with my fingertips, I felt along my cheekbone, the flesh tender and puffy, and then to my sore scalp and the back of my head where a sizeable lump remained. My tongue lightly explored the inside of my cheek and lip and found the slightly silvery taste of the small swollen wound where my teeth had penetrated. I shuddered as I recalled Julius's violent rage, but I had left him and I was essentially intact.

But then the cramping in my belly began. Frau Kraus was the only one I could confide in as the clutching pain continued. Then the blood came.

'Bedrest,' said Frau Kraus. 'If the bleeding stops the baby should be fine.' The shock of Julius's betrayal had prevented me from really considering how I was going to raise a child on my own. And now it seemed I might never get the chance.

Once Frau Kraus had me tucked up in bed, raspberry leaf tea by my bedside, she looked more closely at me, frowning at the bruises blooming on my face and arms.

'Do you think it's why I'm losing the baby?' I hiccoughed, crying again.

'It's all right now, *herzchen*,' she said, patting my hand. 'If Georg ever gets his hands on Julius, heaven help him.' I nodded, wiping my tears away. 'This could be his doing, but you've also suffered a terrible shock with Leo's letter. Early pregnancy can be uncertain like this, even in the most perfect conditions. Rest now.' She kissed my forehead. 'I'll get some more ointments for those bruises.'

I nodded, grateful for her love and devotion, the tears welling once more.

But by the end of the day it was all over. I'd lost the baby.

'Perhaps it was for the best,' said Frau Kraus gently and I could only nod numbly.

The shower was the only place I felt free to release the torrent of emotion inside me. Under the gentle rain of warm water flowing over my head and skin, I sank to the bottom of the bathtub sobbing. My whole world had turned upside down in a short space of time and all the hopeful plans and expectations had come to this – betrayal, loss and heartbreak. It was then that I realised that Julius could never have stopped the Gestapo if they'd decided to go after my family. I'd been naïve to think that he was so powerful. As it turned out, he wouldn't protect Leo, and Tante Elya was still protected by marriage. I felt like a fool. I'd sold my soul for nothing.

The following afternoon after milking, Leo brought up a pot of tea to my room from Frau Kraus. I was up and about, with strict instructions from Frau Kraus to take it easy. I was resting before dinner, watching the sun set from my bedroom window. I had telephoned the hospital to let them know I was unwell, and had managed to organise some leave. By now my face had bloomed to a deep shade of blue and Leo was anxious to make sure I was comfortable and had everything I needed.

'Stay with me,' I said, smiling sadly. 'I've missed you, and I don't want to waste precious moments like these.' We had fallen into our easy manner, like old times, now that Julius was no longer an impediment between us. The knowledge that Leo might be taken from me forever also spurred me on.

He nodded and sat beside me, the sinking sun casting a soft glow across the fields of barley, the birch trees shimmering silver and gold in the light.

'Thank you for what you tried to do for me.' He lightly traced the bruise across my cheekbone. 'I'm sorry for what happened to you. I feel responsible.'

'It wasn't your fault. You only opened my eyes to what Julius is truly like . . . I was such a fool.'

'And the baby?'

I shook my head. 'I lost it, Leo.' Tears welled in my eyes.

He was silent for a moment, then whispered, 'I'm so sorry.' He squeezed my hand. 'I worried when you didn't come down yesterday and Frau Kraus was in and out to you. Are you all right?'

'I'm fine. She made sure of it.'

'He'll pay for what he's done.' He poured the tea, his face creased in anguish.

'I don't want you or your father going anywhere near him. Julius can't hurt me anymore. There's nothing holding me to him now. I'm never going back.' I cupped his face, his skin soft and warm under the rough stubble. It felt natural and effortless to be this close with him, unlike Julius. There was no doubt in my mind that my feelings for Leo were real. They felt right and rang true in a way that my feelings for Julius never had. 'Julius can wait. The more pressing matter is you. What are we going to do?'

'What we must,' he said simply, passing me the cup.

'We have to get you out of Germany,' I said, sipping the fragrant mint tea. 'Everything's in place with the Russian escapes, surely we just have to activate a plan.' Leo was due to leave in two weeks.

'No, Susie. I have to go. I have to honour my obligation. It's the only decision I can make.'

I banged the cup down. 'You don't! You can't just accept this.'

'Think about it. If I don't present myself, what do you think will happen? They'll replace me with somebody else, but even worse than that, they'll come after Mutti and, if they can, after Vati and you. I won't have that.'

'We'll all go,' I said, clutching his arm.

'You know we can't all get away safely, and if we did, what about those we leave behind? Hans, Frau Kraus ... the list goes on. They'll be questioned, tortured even. There are too many lives at stake.'

'But I can't lose you.' I began to tremble at the thought.

His arm was quickly around me. 'It will be all right,' he whispered.

'How can you say that? I won't lose you, I can't.' I broke down and sobbed. 'It was one thing not to be with you or even have you in my life. I could live with that if I knew that you had your freedom.'

'I'll come home once we're liberated.'

I looked into his earnest face. 'But, Leo, you have to survive until then.'

'The Nazis won't kill us while they need us to carry on with the war effort.'

'But what happens when the Nazis know they're beaten? What happens to you then?' I grasped his hand and held it tight. Images of overcrowded cattle cars and people sent to their deaths rushed through my mind. 'We have to get you out of here, it's the only way.'

He brought my hand to his lips and squeezed his eyes closed for a moment. 'It's a work camp, Susie. We have a good underground network in place. I'll let you know where I am. Hard work won't kill me, but running away might kill all of you.'

'Your father's contacts?'

He shook his head. 'We've exhausted all the options. There's no way out. If anyone was going to help, they would already have done it. Don't cry,' he said, wiping my tears. 'The war will be over before long and I'll be home again.' He kissed my wet face and then my mouth.

'Promise,' I said shakily. 'Promise me you'll stay alive and come back to me.'

'I have so much to live for. I promise.'

I couldn't avoid Onkel Georg for long. He joined us in the parlour before dinner and insisted on knowing why my face was battered. He leaned forward in his chair aghast after I told him.

'He's been lying to her from the start,' said Leo, his anger barely contained. He was standing behind me in support, as though to protect me from any further harm. 'He's involved in transporting Jewish people to the eastern ghettos and camps.'

'Is this true?' Onkel Georg's bushy eyebrows rose in astonishment.

I nodded. 'He promised me that he could protect Leo and Tante Elya, but he hasn't, has he?' Bile rose to my throat, hot and bitter. I saw the realisation on Tante Elya's face, as if she had suspicions that were being confirmed. Then I told them all of it – Julius's baby, his mistress, even my miscarriage – and felt an enormous weight lift from my shoulders. I'd been hiding the truth and keeping secrets for so long it had become unbearable.

Onkel Georg looked stricken. 'I've failed you,' he said, pushing a trembling hand through his thinning hair. 'To think that I believed I could trust the Nazis if I befriended them and gave them generous gifts . . . Vipers, all of them! And Julius is the biggest hypocrite of them all. If I'd known this yesterday when I saw him . . .' He slammed the side table with his fist.

'It's all right, Vati,' said Leo, stepping towards his father in alarm.

'No, it is not. Everyone's abandoned us and I can't even protect my own family . . . None of you.'

'Not everyone's abandoned us, Vati,' said Leo. 'We still have all our friends in the resistance. We'll fight on.'

Onkel Georg stood abruptly, walked stiffly to the drinks cabinet and picked up the cognac he'd been saving for my wedding day. 'I have work to do.' We watched in silence as he stiffly left the room.

'I'm sorry, Tante Elya,' I whispered, feeling very small inside.

'He just needs time to digest everything that's happened.' Leo squeezed my shoulder, his face unreadable as he stared after his father.

'I wish they'd take me instead,' Tante Elya muttered, dabbing her moist eyes with her handkerchief. 'It's my fault that you're all in this situation in the first place.'

'No, Mutti. I'm fit and strong, a good worker. I'll manage until this war is over. You and Vati have to look after each other and keep things running here. Susie's promised to come home as often as she can to help while I'm away.'

She grasped his hand across the lounge. 'I'd rather you leave Germany and have a chance. You're young with your whole life in front of you. I've had my time. I'll take your place.'

'No, Mutti. It's not how it works and you know how it would risk everyone else.'

Her shoulders slumped in defeat. 'If Susanna can't persuade you then nobody can.' I'd already told her about our conversation. She nodded, sadly. 'Well, if you're sure and your decision's made, we have much to talk about before you leave.'

I spent the next few days with my family. The Red Cross had approved my request for two weeks leave from the hospital. There was still work to be done around the estate and while Onkel Georg wanted to attend only to the essentials, Leo insisted that they get as much done as they could before his departure. They spent hours out on the farm and Leo later told me that, while they worked, they discussed the resistance and the contacts that might be useful to him wherever he ended up. I helped Frau Kraus and Tante Elya in the kitchen, making butter and cheese and picking the autumn vegetable and fruit harvest, storing carrots and beetroot in the cellar and preserving apples, early pears and white cabbage as sauerkraut. We enjoyed time as a family too, walking in the garden and, as I became stronger, through the forest, picking mushrooms and bagging rabbits with Leo, as we had when we were younger. For the first time in many years Onkel Georg sat with us in the parlour after luncheon and dinner rather than heading back outside or retiring to his study. Leo joined us too, although I felt sure he'd rather be out working than sitting around where he had time to think. Tante Elya would talk about old times, going through photo albums of when we were children and reminiscing. Onkel Georg even shared stories of his childhood in Dortmund and summers spent on the family property, Gut Matildenhof, with his older brother whose sons had perished on the Eastern Front.

I prayed that the safety Leo's status had afforded him wouldn't now be the cause of his demise. He had to survive until the end of the war.

'I'm so worried about him,' said Tante Elya one afternoon when Leo had gone to have a beer with Hans. I'd seen the look on his face. He'd had enough of his parents' constant worry, and probably mine too.

'I've made contact with another network in the resistance,' said Onkel Georg, lighting his pipe. 'As soon as I can find out which project Leopold will be transferred to, I can have my people keep an eye on him. He's safe as long as he's on a work detail. It's not a concentration camp.' We had no doubt about the atrocities that occurred in concentration camps, especially the death camps.

'We can't lose him now. After everything we've done.' Her lips were pressed together in a straight line as she stared down at the darning in her hands.

'We won't, Elya. I won't let that happen.'

She nodded, straightening her back before bending her head to her fine needlework once again. Onkel Georg and I just looked at each other, a silent agreement between us. It was up to us to keep this family together.

Frau Kraus was the only household staff member who remained and, under her watchful eye, I accompanied her to the village store to help carry home necessities we couldn't produce on the estate, like the small rations of flour, sugar and assorted household items.

'Adelina, you're not still shopping for that lot, are you?' a voice called out in the store.

Frau Kraus turned to the scowling face of one of the local women. I was browsing among the near empty shelves and she hadn't seen me.

'What lot is that?' asked Frau Kraus, pulling herself to her full height, which was a somewhat intimidating sight.

'That lot up in their castle at the estate. Not so fancy now, are they?' she sneered. 'I hear that boy's finally got what's coming to him. About time he does his bit. All our men have.'

'How long have the Heckers been good to this village? We've thrived because of Gut Birkenhof,' retorted Frau Kraus. 'They've always been part of this community. Now that times are tough, through no fault of their own, you want to abandon them, stomp on them and grind them further into the mud? You should be ashamed of yourself.' My heart swelled with gratitude.

Most other people would have quailed at this verbal barrage, but the woman stood her ground, her chin defiantly in the air. 'I wouldn't say that too loud around here, Adelina,' she said. 'People don't like that lot and if you don't do the smart thing and jump from the sinking boat, you'll drown with them.' Frau Kraus turned back to the counter, ignoring her comments. 'Jew-loving bitch.'

Frau Kraus rounded on the woman and was beside her in two strides. 'What did you say?'

The woman stepped back. 'You heard me,' she said, moving towards the door. 'I'd hate to see your husband in prison and that lovely home of yours go to some stranger.'

'Get out of my sight.' Frau Kraus advanced on her and the woman scrambled for the door, making a hasty exit.

'Frau Kraus.' I was by her side in an instant. 'It's all right. Come and sit for a minute.'

'No, I'm fine.' She shook her head, but she was pale and her hands were shaking. 'I'm sorry. You shouldn't have had to see that.'

'Don't pay any attention to her, Adelina,' said Herr Wenck, the shopkeeper from behind the counter. 'She just lost her son and grandson this last year and I've not heard a kind word from her mouth since. Loss does that to some people; it makes them bitter and miserable.' It was an inescapable truth that I'd seen for myself. War could bring out the best in people but it could also bring out the worst. Then there were those who accepted the status quo, like Julius. It all came down to survival.

Frau Kraus nodded. 'I know. That's why I didn't say more.'

'Does everyone feel this way?' I asked tentatively. The mood of the village had been one of suspicion for some time, but now it seemed hostile, explosively so.

'Most, but not everyone, Fräulein Susanna. Anyone with a bit of common sense left would know that none of this is their fault,' he said, wrapping a package. 'Frau Hecker's a good woman and Herr Leopold's a hard worker. Both of them were loved and respected before the Nazis arrived.' He handed Frau Kraus the package. 'Here, take this home and enjoy it. It's on me.'

'Thank you, Ernie,' she said. 'I don't know where we'd be without people like you. Say hello to Erma for me.'

'I will. Keep a good eye on them, Adelina. And, Fräulein Susanna, look after your aunt and uncle. They're going to need you when their boy goes.'

'Thank you, Herr Wenck, I will,' I said, grateful for this man's decency. But I was horrified that people who'd known us for most of their lives were now ready to lynch us or anyone else who stood up for our family. I knew it was partly driven by their own fear. They were worried that their previous association with us would mark them as targets.

'I can't believe how bad things have become,' I said to Frau Kraus as we walked back home along the river.

'Don't worry, *herzchen*. There's still plenty of support for your family. Your aunt and uncle aren't alone.'

I squeezed her hand gratefully. The trees along the river were losing their leaves, their branches bare and vulnerable.

'What will you do when Leo leaves?' she asked. I closed my eyes briefly to shut out the pain, as if that was even possible. 'I've seen how the two of you are together. When are you going to have the sense to see what's in front of you?'

I nodded. 'We've loved each other for so long but there's always been something in the way of us being together.

Now with Leo going, I don't think either of us wants to leave things unsaid. We may never get another chance . . . if anything happens to him.' I stopped at the edge of the river and tossed a stone across the water, watching it skip across the top until it disappeared beneath.

Frau Kraus nodded and put her arm around me. 'Come, let's get back. You'll want to spend as much time with him as you can.'

Leo looked around the tiny wooden cabin. 'This has always been our special place. I'm glad you suggested we come here.'

'It's our last night and I wanted to make it special.' I couldn't believe he was leaving the next day. I wished I could drag back the hours and days of the last two weeks, but I was grateful that I'd had the time with Leo. We'd become even closer while I regained my strength, reminiscing about old times during our walks in the forest. There was no denying our deep connection as we exchanged yearning glances and stole kisses whenever we could, our hands lingering. Leo was patient and gentle with me, holding himself back from the electric desire we both felt. But we knew without saying a word what was going to happen when I suggested we visit the cabin together.

The tiny table was laid with a cloth and set with two bowls and cups. A casserole dish sat in the middle next to a lit candle, a chunk of bread and a flask of tea. The fire we'd lit in the fireplace was burning slow and bright and would last all night. It wasn't much, but it was enough for us. We'd spent the evening with Leo's parents but had stolen away after they'd retired, with our little supper and extra quilts and blankets for the camp bed. I was well enough now for us to finish what we'd started three years earlier.

He took my hand in his. The candlelight illuminated his eyes, yet cast shadows across his face. But I didn't need to see him to know how he was feeling. 'I don't know when we'll have time like this again. Just you and me, with nobody else to tell us what we should or shouldn't be doing.'

A rush of emotion washed through me and I shut my eyes for a brief moment to steady myself.

'We've wasted so much time,' I whispered.

'Then let's not waste another minute.'

We undressed each other slowly in the firelight. I wanted to remember every tiny detail. It had been darker under the cherry tree and, despite the intensity of our passion that night, there had been no opportunity for slow, erotic seduction. Tonight, the shadows created by the soft light cloaked the mysteries of his body and then revealed glimpses of the slopes and planes as he moved. I touched him, almost shyly, unbuttoning his shirt and removing it from his broad shoulders and long, sculpted arms. The closeness of him was intoxicating as I pulled away the last of his clothes, my hands skimming his firm buttocks and strong thighs. The brisk air in the cabin caressed my body and made my nipples stiffen as he released my dress and it slid to the floor. When I was finally naked, it was with pride that I stood before him. He may not have been the first, but he was the first and only one I would ever give myself fully to. My heart was bare, but it was filled with joy.

'You're breathtaking,' he murmured, hands following the curve of my hips.

'And you're glorious,' I whispered back. I reached up, resting my hands on his chest, resisting the desire to lean against him so we were skin to skin. I kissed him and he pulled me to him roughly. I wrapped my arms around him. I wanted to be closer still.

Our lovemaking was furious. Both of us had waited so long for this moment that when it happened we couldn't contain ourselves, riding the crest of the surging wave with unbridled ecstasy and sliding into oblivion until we lay replete, tangled in blankets and quilts on the rough wooden floor.

He was so beautiful. His dark wavy hair, now untamed around his head, his chocolate brown eyes that gazed at me with such intensity I thought my heart would burst, the scratchy roughness of the day-old growth on his strong jaw, the high cheekbones that defined his oval face . . . And those full lips that I wanted to kiss forever.

'A pfennig for your thoughts,' I whispered, fingers tracing the line of his collarbone as he held me in his arms.

'I don't think I'm capable of much thought at the moment,' he said, smiling slowly. 'The only thought coming to mind is how wonderful you are.'

'Wonderful?' I echoed.

'Well, I'd go as far as saying magnificent, but I'd like to reserve that statement until I've conducted a little more research.' He grinned. 'It's a long while until morning.' His fingers trailed up my arm then followed the contours of my body until he found the slippery wetness between my legs and the cabin melted from my mind. All that remained was Leo.

We took our time, exploring each other and discovering the way we each liked to be touched. It was almost more intimate than the act itself. I knew the passion between us was something special, and not felt by everyone, but it was more than that. When we came together we were one as I'd sensed we would be. I would never have called my relationship with Julius passionate and our joining had only ever been a physical one. But with Leo it was like a meeting of the spirit, our true selves. We were meant to be together. How was I ever going to be parted from him again?

Lying in each other's arms, we whispered our hopes and fears to each other, revealed our dreams and desires, feeding each other stew and bread, drinking from the flask of tea when we were thirsty. I couldn't think of anything more perfect.

Finally, as the night reluctantly faded to the early light of day, our lovemaking became almost desperate as we tried to sear the memory of each other on our bodies and minds.

'I love you,' whispered Leo, still arched over the top of me. His skin glistened with sweat in the lamplight, and his eyes were fixed to mine, dark pools of love that I could immerse myself in forever. I smiled softly, overcome with joy, but it was bittersweet.

'I love you too.' I pulled him to me, his body hot and slick on mine. 'I want to stay like this forever.'

'We'll be together again. Memories of you naked beneath me will keep me going in the meantime,' he said, smiling slowly. He kissed me, his lips soft and gentle, and then more demanding.

'Don't leave me, Leo.' I wrapped my arms around him and clung to him.

'I'll never leave you. You'll be in my thoughts every day until I come back to you. We'll plan a life together.'

'I can't wait. It means more than I can say.' I kissed him again, tears sliding down my cheeks and mingling with his as we said goodbye the best way we knew how.

17

Leo and the others who had been called up had to present themselves at Anhalter Bahnhof, once one of Berlin's busiest train stations, now running only a fraction of services due to the bombings and damage. Armed SS guards manned the entrance to the terminus but I felt reassured by the trucks and buses parked alongside the station, reminding me that this was simply a call-up for a labour force to support the final push in this war. Desiccated leaves swirled around our feet in the November breeze as we waited nervously outside the station with other families bidding desperate farewells to their loved ones. Refugees from the east, and workers and travellers rushed past, their eyes sliding over our gathering and quickly away. They all knew what this was.

The loudspeaker announced that it was time for registration.

We'd already said our goodbyes but Leo embraced his mother once again. He hadn't wanted her to come, worried about her status, but she'd insisted. She was wearing the yellow

271

Star of David on her coat, and the only thing that prevented her from being carted away were the invisible bonds of her marriage. She was trembling and crying, and Onkel Georg put his arm around her as he had a few final words with his son.

Then Leo turned to me. 'Leo, don't go.' I clutched his arm.

'I'm here,' he said, gathering me to him. I could feel the beat of his heart against my chest, the softness of his freshly shaved cheek against mine, the rasp of his thick woollen coat against my neck and his strong, capable hands on my back holding me upright. All in that single moment.

His hands slid lower over my bottom and he pulled me even closer.

'Leo, your parents,' I stammered nervously.

'I'm sure they already know, but I don't care if they don't.' He dipped his head and kissed me deeply. 'I love you, Nightingale.'

'I love you, Leo.' Tears streamed down my face. 'Come back to me.'

'Look after Mutti and Vati while I'm gone.'

'I will.' We drew apart, but I held his hand, unable to let go yet. 'Stay alive, Leo.'

He nodded and stepped back, our eyes still locked, our link unbroken until my reach had stretched to its limit. It seemed he let go and turned in slow motion, walking away from me and towards an uncertain future. He entered the building and disappeared from view.

Tante Elya, Onkel Georg and I didn't speak a word the whole journey back to the estate. When Onkel Georg and I went out to do the evening milking, Tante Elya accompanied us and Frau Kraus insisted we have a small bite for dinner, though none of us were hungry. But, remembering my promise to Leo, I forced them to eat. It sapped all the energy I possessed and it felt as though I was moving through thick molasses.

Tante Elya stared unseeing at her embroidery until she roused herself and climbed the stairs to Leo's room where she stood in the doorway, unable to step beyond the threshold. I took her arm and led her into the room. She sat heavily on the edge of his bed and, with her head in her hands, she finally allowed herself to cry. I wrapped my arms around her and she collapsed slowly to the bed where we lay together, caught within our own memories of Leo. Gradually she told me about some of her happiest times with him, sitting and reading stories in this room with him as a little boy. Then I told her about the day not long after the car accident when Leo had given me the carved horse to cheer me up and shown me the best strawberry patch. I shared the whole story of our love and our determination to be together. She hugged me tight, and told me how happy she was for me and Leo. I was glad I'd told her. I didn't want to keep any more secrets and the news – and its hope of a bright and happy future together as a family – was something that could buoy all of us through this dark time.

'Stay strong, Leo,' I whispered into the night.

Life went on. I returned to Beelitz a few days later, having taken as much time off as the patience of the Red Cross would allow. There was so much work to do, so many more injured soldiers arriving from an increasingly desperate war. I told Marika everything. She shook with fury when she heard of Julius's violence and cried with me when I told her I'd lost the baby. It was a lot to take in, but she was steadfast in her support.

'I can't believe that the officials have been transporting Jewish people like cattle, and making them pay for the privilege. Where's their shame when they put their signature to the profit sheets and transfer funds from one department to another, like it's an ordinary business transaction? And then you tell me that they're being gassed, slaughtered like animals.' She was pale and trembling, her eyes wide with horror. She stared into the distance for a moment, trying to comprehend the enormity of what I'd told her. 'I'm just sorry I ever encouraged you to make an effort with Julius,' she said finally, shaking her head in disgust. 'He's a manipulator and a coward and as bad as those who set this evil in motion . . . It makes me ashamed to be German. I'm so glad you've left him.' I squeezed her hand in gratitude.

'I can't believe I stayed with him as long as I did. He sucked me into his glittering world, made me doubt myself and my own instincts. But finding out about the Jewish people was the tipping point. And when he hit me, I knew exactly what he was made of.'

She put her arm around me in comfort. 'But you have Leo now. Finally you're together as you should be. Do his parents know and approve?'

I nodded. 'Tante Elya knew all along and Onkel Georg suspected. Tante Elya reminded him of how they'd met and how they knew they were meant to be. Now Leo has to stay alive so he can come back to me.'

'He will. He has you waiting for him.' I wanted to hug her even more.

But it was as if my conversation with Marika had stirred and awoken Julius's spectre. When I finished my shift, he was waiting for me at the entrance of the dining hall. My heart rose to my throat when I saw him, but I couldn't avoid him.

'Hello, Julius,' I said stiffly. He leaned closer to kiss me on the cheek and I flinched. He drew back in consternation.

'Can we go somewhere more private and talk?' he asked.

'You can talk to me in the dining hall or not at all.'

He frowned, a look of hurt in his eyes. 'I want to apologise . . . I love you.'

'Well, you have a funny way of showing it.' I clasped my hands together to stop them from shaking and made my way to a table at the back of the hall where we would be afforded some privacy. I didn't care if he followed or not.

'I'm sorry, Susie,' he whispered, sitting down opposite me. 'I was so afraid of losing you that it made me crazy.' He reached across the table to grasp my hand, but I quickly pulled away, pressing my hands into my lap. 'Please come back to me. I promise I'll never do anything like that again. I swear it on the life of our child.'

'I lost the baby,' I said brusquely, the anger flaring hot and unruly within me. 'It's your fault.'

Horror blossomed on his face at the realisation of what he'd done. I didn't care. I knew how much he wanted a family, but I couldn't find it in my heart to console him. Part of me wanted to punish him, too, for what I'd allowed myself to become when I was with him. I felt ashamed whenever I thought about the luxury we'd lived in, my acceptance of his world and the power of the Nazis as we made deals to supposedly keep my family safe. I'd become like him in some way, blotting out the horror of Onkel Tedi's life and all those persecuted by the Nazis. I'd known all along that it felt wrong.

'Are you all right?' he said, his voice cracking.

'I'm fine now.' I pressed my knuckles to my lips. I didn't want to cry.

'I'm so sorry, Susie, for all of it.' His bright blue eyes were full of remorse. 'I never meant to hurt you. You mean the world to me.' He held out my engagement ring. 'We can still have the wedding and we can try for another baby.'

I stared at him in astonishment.

'I know you're angry with me but let me make it up to you.' He put the ring in front of me.

I pushed the ring back across the bare table. 'I don't want your ring. There's nothing left between us.'

He nodded. 'Let's take it slow. This war will be determined in the next couple of months. The ministry's being moved to the countryside south of Berlin, to Gross Koris, and all the essential staff are going. It's too risky to stay in Berlin with the Allies moving towards us. Our operations can't be disrupted. They're crucial for Germany to continue to function, and for the war. I'll be spending much of my time there. Take the time you need, but don't stay in Berlin. Go home to Gut Birkenhof where I know you're safe. We can start over when the war ends.'

I couldn't believe what he was saying. 'Julius, we're finished. Whatever hold you had over me died when I saw that transport document with your signature on it. Leo's gone, you made sure of that, and Tante Elya has Onkel Georg to protect her, as she always had.' I pushed back my chair and stood. 'Goodbye, Julius.'

He grabbed my wrist as I walked past him. 'We're over when I say we're over,' he said through gritted teeth, his eyes boring into mine. 'I'll give you a couple of months to heal, and then I expect you to wear your ring again.' He pushed the ring hard into my palm. 'You're mine. Make no mistake about it.' I glanced around the room. People were selecting food at the counter and some were sitting at tables eating, reading and talking to colleagues. Julius's gaze followed mine. He knew I could make a fuss.

I pulled my arm free. 'Leave me alone,' I hissed. 'I never want to see you again.'

'We'll see about that.' His eyes were blazing now. Glad we were in public, I put the ring back on the table, made my way out of the dining hall and found my way to the ward where I knew he wouldn't follow me.

Leo's letter arrived on one of my days off back home. Tante Elya read it aloud when we retired to the parlour after dinner.

29th November, 1944

Dear Mutti, Vati and Susie,

I'm writing to let you know that I'm well. I'm working for the Todt Organisation and, as you know, they manage construction projects across the Reich, so I'm lucky to be working not too far from home. Currently our crew are working on reinforcing the runway of an airfield. It's physically demanding work, but not hard and it's something I can manage well after the years of outdoor work on the farm. We're living in a camp nearby and walk the short distance to and from the construction site every day. Because we're voluntary workers, we're allowed to write one letter a week to our family and we're paid for our labour. You don't need to worry about me at all.

I hope you're all well too. I will write again soon.

Your loving son,

Leopold

Tante Elya looked up at Onkel Georg and I, misty-eyed.

Onkel Georg nodded. 'I told you not to worry, he'll be fine.'

'But he doesn't really say much,' I said dubiously. 'And he's not there voluntarily.' I wished that he'd been able to write to me alone. *Maybe next time.*

'He has to maintain the façade. How can he say anything else?' said Onkel Georg. 'His letters will be read and monitored by men within the Todt Organisation. Anything sensitive will be censored or not sent at all but at least we'll have contact with him.' We both must have looked crestfallen. 'Don't worry,' Onkel Georg continued quickly. 'He'll send us a proper letter soon. I have someone within Todt who'll smuggle his letter to me. Then we'll know the real situation.'

After Julius's visit, I asked to be transferred to another hospital around Berlin. Marika was leaving to complete the final preparations for her wedding and it made sense for me to go too – to make a fresh start without the worry of Julius turning up whenever he liked. It was a teary goodbye to the staff and patients at Beelitz, and then a last longing glance over the calm, sprawling gardens and ornate buildings as I left the grounds in the back of a Red Cross transport truck.

The giant monolith of the Tiergarten flak tower rose from the surrounding parkland of the Berlin Zoo, its guns trained on the sky, ready to protect Berlin's government district. Not only did the concrete fortress house the armaments for the rooftop anti-aircraft guns and the personnel to man them, there was also a bunker large enough to fit fifteen thousand Berliners, or so the matron told me as we climbed the spiral staircase to the eighty-five bed military hospital on its third floor. Later, I heard whispers from the other nurses that the second floor housed a climate-controlled room where priceless artefacts from the city's museums and galleries were stored. I could only imagine what exquisite treasures lay under my feet and wondered absently how I could gain access to the room, just to view the many precious and ancient items.

The Tiergarten hospital was a complete contrast to the facilities at Beelitz. Smaller and more compact, it was far more efficient, and easy to get from one ward to the next and to the operating theatres. The patients coming in from the front were mostly acute with terrible injuries that more often than not required surgery.

Some of the animals in the zoo below us had been killed during previous bombings and many had been sent to other zoos within the Reich, but some remained. It was strange to hear the sounds of Africa while we nursed injured soldiers: the roar of the lions and the trumpeting of the lone bull elephant, Siam.

I spent most of my time in theatre where my skills were developed in a new direction, ensuring the appropriate surgical instruments were sterilised, ready and in good working order, and assisting the surgeons during surgery.

'The saws must be placed this way for Herr Bettingen,' explained one of the sisters who'd been there for some time.

Bettingen was one of the most respected surgeons in Berlin. 'And he likes you to report on the patient's condition pre-surgery, and sometimes assist him with the clamps and positioning. It's quite specific, especially for amputations, so make sure you understand what procedure's being performed before you scrub in.'

I thought I'd seen more amputations at Beelitz than was necessary in one lifetime, but apparently not. And, unlike Beelitz, I didn't get to know my patients over a long period of time, as their care was handed over to the post-surgical nursing staff and they were then sent elsewhere to rehabilitate. The work was frantic, but I felt safe within the citadel. I slept and ate in the small nurses' quarters within the building between shifts and on my days off I'd go home to Gut Birkenhof on the bus. We were a close-knit community who kept to ourselves, although there was a friendly rapport with the Luftwaffe soldiers and the flak helpers who manned the guns above us. Best of all, Julius didn't know where I was.

The next time I came home in December, more news from Leo was waiting.

'Leo's sent us a special letter,' said Onkel Georg after dinner, sitting on the lounge chair closest to the corner lamp in the parlour. He put on his reading glasses. We were waiting for the evening BBC news.

Dear Vati,
I'm at Zerbst Airfield, only one hundred kilometres from Berlin.
About five hundred of us arrived the day we were registered.

We live in a camp not far from the airfield. Even though we're supposedly voluntary, we're guarded at all times, particularly when we're marching between the airfield and camp. We're not allowed to leave camp on our days off, nor are we allowed to have visitors. As you probably guessed, our letters are monitored and censored. So please be careful what you write.

My work crew is hardening the runway of the airfield for some new aircraft that will be arriving soon. There's talk that they will change the course of the war. I suspect it has to do with those aircraft engines that have taken so long to be perfected! Let's hope it's too late for them.

Onkel Georg looked up, puzzled at the mention of aircraft engines. I hadn't told him about my intelligence work for the resistance because he would've tried to stop me and there seemed no point in telling him after I'd left Julius. I only shrugged my shoulders and managed to look just as confused. I couldn't believe that our actions had contributed to such an extensive delay in the Nazis' prize project. It gave me a rush of pride, which I knew Leo felt too. We were still doing good work.

We're working ten to twelve hours in the cold, the work is physically demanding and we have only basic rations, but most of us are managing. Some are struggling, though, and they're punished for their low productivity with beatings. We try to help them as much as we can, but we all know that we're expected to work like this until our bodies can't take any more. But all we have to do is make it to the end of the war. Looking out for each other is the key to our survival.

This job is only until the end of the month when they want the airfield ready. Then our crew will be moved on to another project.

Tell Mutti and Susie that I love them.

I'll write again when I have more information.

Your loving son,

Leopold

'He knows what to do,' said Onkel Georg grimly. 'Now we know where he is, the resistance will keep an eye on him. He's tough and smart and he'll make it to the end.' I grasped Tante Elya's hand and nodded. If anyone was going to make it, it would be Leo.

But I had no idea we should've been worried about Tante Elya. Early the next morning, I awoke to pounding on the front door. I cracked open my eyes but it was barely light yet. The hammering continued and I heard hurried steps move past my room and down the stairs. Pulling on a dressing gown, I followed the sound of raised voices, stopping at the top of the stairs. I froze at the scene unfolding in front of me in the pre-dawn.

'We have deportation orders for Frau Elya Hecker,' said the SS officer at the door, handing across some papers. The breath caught in my throat.

'No, that's not possible,' said Onkel Georg in shock. 'She's my wife. The law protects Jewish people married to Germans.' He stared blankly at the pages in his hand.

'The Reich Main Security Office have issued a new edict – all those with Jewish blood are to be deported. We're just following orders. As you can clearly see, the paperwork's all there.'

'There must be some mistake,' said Onkel Georg, his eyes wild. I felt light-headed. This was the moment we'd always dreaded.

'You'll have to sort it out with headquarters but, in the meantime, we have our orders.' The officer pushed past Onkel Georg and into the entry.

My heart thumping in my chest, I raced to Tante Elya's bedroom and closed the door behind me.

'You have to hide,' I whispered urgently.

'There's nowhere to go, Susanna,' she said, dressing quickly. 'I'm not hiding like a rat in the dark. I've done nothing wrong. If the law no longer protects me, then I'll have to go with them.'

'You can't,' I sobbed. 'I won't lose you too.' Visions of the day Leo left rolled across my mind, and then flashes of the old nightmare – of the car accident that killed my family.

She smoothed the hair from my face and gazed at me lovingly. 'We all have to be brave, *myshka*. Even me.'

The bedroom door opened. 'Frau Elya Hecker?' It was one of the officers.

'Yes,' she said, standing tall and defiant.

'Pack a small bag and then I'll escort you downstairs while your husband speaks to our superior about your deportation order.'

'Very well,' she said calmly. 'Susanna, get my overnight bag from the wardrobe please.'

I did as she directed. Her hands shook as she placed items into it. I placed my hands on hers. 'I'll do it,' I said gently. She handed me what she wanted and, numbly, I folded and packed them until she was done. I turned to the SS guard.

'She's just a harmless mother and wife,' I said beseechingly. He stood in the doorway, stony-faced, keeping his eyes on his prisoner. 'How can you be so cold-hearted?'

Tante Elya touched my sleeve in warning. 'Let's see what Georg has managed to find out.'

Carrying her bag, I followed her down the stairs. Onkel Georg was on the telephone in the hallway and he looked up at us, his face grey. A second SS officer waited in the entry.

'Sit here, Frau Hecker,' directed the SS soldier, pointing to the seat next to the telephone.

I sat beside her and took her cold fingers in mine, willing myself to remain calm for Tante Elya's sake, although every sense screamed at me to take her and run. It seemed like hours that we listened to Onkel Georg speak, argue, yell and wait until, finally, in the bright morning light, he handed the receiver to the SS officer.

'Your superior,' said Onkel Georg, his shoulders sagging. He stood beside Tante Elya and placed his hand on her shoulder.

'Very good,' said the SS officer. He placed the receiver down and turned to us. 'There's been a mix-up. Your deportation order has been lifted. Good day to you.' With that both men walked to the door and left.

Onkel Georg hugged us both to him and I felt faint with relief.

'It's over now,' he said. 'The law hasn't been changed. They had no right to come here.' I could feel him tremble and Tante Elya's body shuddering with silent sobs. Julius's protection had been worth more than I knew. We still had the law to protect us, but I wondered for how much longer.

*

Marika's wedding day in December was beautiful. It made me smile to see her so happy with Johann, but I longed for Leo. Would we ever be able to have a day as joyous as theirs?

The deportation incident had shaken everyone at Gut Birkenhof but we were determined to continue with our resistance activities, moving on Russian prisoners of war as we always had, and listening to the BBC, which daily contradicted the Nazi propaganda still fed through Germany's radio and newspaper channels. We weren't going to be cowed into submission through fear. But I was still coming to terms with the cost of leaving Julius.

His telephone calls and letters to me at Gut Birkenhof went unanswered. I was still furious that he'd removed his protection from Tante Elya. At least he had the decency not to come calling, although part of me wished he would. I would have delighted in seeing Frau Kraus, Hans, Onkel Georg and Tante Elya tear strips off him. There wouldn't be much left afterwards.

When I wasn't working at the hospital, I was home on the estate. Leo's letters assured us that he was surviving, but then they stopped. Onkel Georg reached out to his contacts to find out why. Christmas came and went. Soon the year would turn to another: 1945.

Tante Elya and I were in the kitchen one afternoon, putting together a box of fresh supplies for the new Russian who would be arriving after escaping a transfer to another camp. Onkel Georg's frame filled the doorway.

'You're back,' said Tante Elya, folding a blanket. 'We were worried about you.'

'I think you should sit down,' he said, his face grim.

'No, just tell me.' Tante Elya clutched my hand, her eyes wide.

'Leo's been transferred to Buchenwald.'

Tante Elya cried out and stumbled, and I helped her to a chair, my own breath ragged.

Buchenwald was a concentration camp in the German state of Thüringen. We'd heard much about it from the resistance. Many political prisoners were interned there, including a number of prominent communists. It was notorious for its harsh conditions and the starvation inmates had to endure, exacerbated by long hours of forced labour – 'extermination through labour' as it was called. According to our ex-prisoner sources, camps like this had their fair share of executions too, usually shootings and hangings.

The world around me began to swim, the voices distorted and not making sense. I felt like I was underwater and drowning. Strong arms held me and guided me to the kitchen table where I sank onto a chair.

'Susie. He's alive. You can't give up hope yet.' Onkel Georg's words penetrated the shock and brought me back to the excruciating reality. He nodded encouragingly. Tante Elya sat beside me, her face as bloodless as I was sure mine was.

'I think it's my fault,' I whispered.

'How can it be your fault?'

'Julius has tried to make contact, but I've refused to have anything to do with him, and then with the visit from the SS . . .'

Tante Elya shook her head. 'We don't know it was his fault the SS came knocking. I know Julius has always been a jealous man, wanting what Georg has, and I'll never forgive him for what he's done to you, but surely he wouldn't stoop to something like this?' She couldn't believe he was capable of such malignant actions and once I would have agreed. But now I knew better. He was a monster in the guise of a charming, chivalrous man. I wasn't sure what he was truly capable of anymore.

Onkel Georg pulled a chair out from the table and sank onto it. 'I thought I knew him, but he's become a Nazi to the core. Perhaps I should pay him another visit. I want to know if he's had anything to do with this.'

'No, Georg!' Tante Elya put a restraining hand on his arm, her eyes wide with alarm. 'It makes no difference now, and we need you here.'

'Please let it go, Onkel,' I begged. 'After everything that's happened . . . Tante Elya's right.' I felt sick thinking about what Julius could do if he wanted to.

'Shh, I won't go if you don't want me to,' Onkel Georg said, putting his arm around me. 'This family's protection comes first, but he's responsible one way or the other. He started this by refusing to help with Leo's labour service. If I ever set eyes on that bastard again . . . one day he'll get what's coming to him.'

None of us could be sure just how deep Julius's involvement went, but tucked safely into Onkel Georg's side I felt like a small child and this fleeting feeling of safety gave me strength. I wasn't alone. I never was.

'What can we do for Leo?' I asked in a small voice.

'The resistance has contacts within Buchenwald. I've already sent word to the kapo of the construction labour detachment. He's a prisoner functionary and intermediary between the SS and prisoners,' explained Onkel Georg. 'He'll keep an eye out for Leopold and ensure he's placed in a good work detail.'

Tante Elya kissed my forehead. 'See, we have a plan,' she said brightly, 'we'll all be together again, I know it.' But I could see the worry in her eyes.

18

There was no hiding from news of the advancing Soviet line. More soldiers arrived at the Tiergarten hospital with terrible injuries, and those who were able told us the truth of the matter.

'The Russians have taken Krakau and Warsaw,' muttered one solider, barely old enough to shave. I doubted he'd last the week with his horrific wounds. 'We can't beat the Soviets, there's too many of them,' he said despairingly. 'They'll be here in Berlin before long. You should go while you can.'

'We're safe here,' I said soothingly, but spikes of fear stabbed through my gut at the thought of facing a vengeful, victorious army. I'd heard enough now to wonder how we'd be treated by the Russians if they arrived in Berlin before the Americans and the English. I still found it hard to reconcile the heroic, romantic people of Elya's Russian folklore and stories with the cold-hearted avengers marching our way.

'You're not safe,' the soldier said. 'I've seen thousands flee along icy roads and through thick snow before the Red Army. Even the prisoners from the camps in the east are being marched west before the Soviets arrive. I don't know how they walked at all. Most could hardly stand. They were so thin; a gust of wind could knock them over.' His eyes were wild with the sights he'd seen. 'It was as though I'd reached the gates of hell. It won't be long before we're all there.' He shuddered. I touched his forehead, expecting a high fever with his ranting, but he was only warm, not burning up. I frowned, wondering how much of his rambling was true. 'Can I write a letter to my mother?' he asked plaintively. 'I wish I could sit in her lap and hug her as I used to one last time.' He was crying now, pitiful as a child.

'Shh,' I said, smoothing the hair from his brow. 'I'll help you write your letter after you sleep. You'll see your mother soon, when you go home. You won't be going back to the front.' He nodded, sighing deeply as he closed his eyes. The medication was setting in. I checked his file – he was only fifteen and yet he'd seen more than most people had in a lifetime. Generations of men were being wiped out, thousands dying in each new battle.

I began to pay closer attention to the youngest members of our strange community, the flak helpers. I was surprised to find that Ida's granddaughter, Mina, was here. She was only thirteen.

'How long have you been here?' I asked as she hugged me tightly, tears in her eyes.

'Four weeks,' she murmured. 'It's so good to see someone from home. I've missed everyone.' I kissed the top of her dark head, my heart clutching at the cruelty of taking children away from their families and into the face of danger.

Mina explained about her work and introduced me to her new friends at the Zoo Tower, as it was affectionately known. There were boys from the Hitler Youth and girls from the BDM, probably much the same age as my young patient, I thought, but once I began chatting to them, I discovered some were as young as twelve years old. I was appalled that children so young were being made to handle and move munitions, helping man the anti-aircraft guns and learning how to operate them. None of them seemed terribly worried because we'd seen few air raids in the past months, but I wasn't sure how long that would last.

I began bringing fruit and biscuits to them every now and then. Many told stories of older brothers on the front line, some had sadder stories of fathers and brothers who had already perished, and mothers who were barely able to put food on the table. To them, the flak tower seemed like a much better place – here they had warm beds and full stomachs and the camaraderie of their units. But I remembered what the city had been like a year earlier, when much of Berlin had been battered by the bombings. I kept an eye on Mina.

The next day, Tante Elya called me home. They'd received a letter from Leo.

Frau Kraus brought tea and joined us in the parlour as we read it together. Onkel Georg sat straight and tall with the letter in his hands as though preparing himself for a blow.

23rd January, 1945

Dear Vati,

When we finished at Zerbst my unit was transferred to another job, but I was transferred to Buchenwald. I don't know why. I've made the transition well enough, having come from a work camp, but there are other new arrivals who aren't coping with the conditions, the constant hunger.

I squeezed Tante Elya's hand. 'He's all right,' I murmured. But none of us touched our tea, the steaming cups of yellow liquid cooling quickly on the coffee table.

Because of our contacts, I've been accepted by the resistance here. It's a very strong group, a mix of political and non-political prisoners, not just communists, and from a range of countries and backgrounds. We're preparing for Germany's defeat, smuggling weapons into the camp and organising sabotage in the munitions factories. When our overlords become preoccupied with the advancing armies of the Americans or Russians (who knows who will arrive first) and then with their own survival, we'll hit back.

'There's no stopping him,' said Onkel Georg, his eyes shining with pride.

Robert Siewert is a very important man in the leadership of the resistance and uses his position as kapo here to help as many of us as he can. He's been teaching the children bricklaying so they have useful skills, and helps to hide any prisoners at risk and gives them new identities. After the execution of Ernst

Thälmann last year and the speech he gave at his memorial, he's being watched by the camp administration and has to be careful what he does.

'Who's Ernst Thälmann?' I asked.

'He was the leader of the Communist Party of Germany and a candidate for the presidency against von Hindenburg and Hitler in 1932 before the Nazis took power and he was arrested,' said Onkel Georg, looking up from Leo's letter.

I nodded, understanding why he had been murdered – he would have been a rallying point of opposition to the Third Reich, a threat the Nazis could not afford as Germany drew closer to defeat. Sadness washed over me as I wondered how many good people would be left by the end of this war, and how many more the Nazis would murder before they were toppled from power.

But he's been good to me and has made sure I've been placed in a good labour detachment, not in the quarry attached to Buchenwald itself. I'm now at the Ohrdruf work camp, about sixty kilometres away.

Ohrdruf was created a couple of months ago and already there are thousands working here. We spend our days digging tunnels, removing rock and rubble, building roads and a railway line. It's hard to tell what we're working towards, but there's talk of secret underground headquarters and a communications centre for the government. SS guards from Auschwitz have joined our own guards here and that makes me believe that the rumours are true.

The days are long, fourteen hours. I'm used to the hard work, but the conditions are unimaginable. We survive on nothing more than watery soup. Those who fall behind from exhaustion or starvation are severely beaten. Some can't go on any longer and drop dead or are shot dead, but in my crew we are all still fit and strong enough, and we look after each other. We're some of the lucky ones, sleeping in huts. It's cramped because there are so many of us, sleeping on the floor on old straw with nothing more than the clothes we wear for warmth. It's the one advantage of sleeping pressed together like sardines. Those who sleep in the tents are often the first to suffer from exposure or get sick. There's no medicine or extra food for them. I've seen those who are ill or injured on the job just disappear, sent to Bergen-Belsen, so I've heard. I can only guess what happens to them there . . .

There's no thought of refusing to work because any dissent is punished with execution. They make us watch and then carry the dead to a shed where we pile them up and sprinkle the naked corpses with lime. It's sickening; prisoners who have been executed or those who have died from starvation and are so emaciated that they're little more than skeletons. The shed holds about two hundred corpses and when it's full they're taken to a pit about a mile away to be buried in a mass grave. It's horrific, but it only makes me more determined to survive until the Allies liberate us.

Give my love to Mutti and Susie.

Your loving son,

Leopold

'At least you know he's alive and people are watching over him,' said Frau Kraus, turning her head away. But I'd seen the tears welling in her eyes. 'In the meantime, you'd better get busy doing what you do to bring this government to its knees,' she said to Onkel Georg. 'The sooner this war ends, the sooner our loved ones can come home.'

I couldn't agree more. Although Leo had assured us he was coping, I was still worried and I could see that same unspoken concern in the faces around me too. As Germany's inevitable loss in this war moved closer with each passing day, I was concerned about the unpredictability of the Nazis and the SS. Tante Elya's deportation order was testament to that. And I couldn't get the image of Leo out of my head, huddled up on a wooden floor, sleeping cheek by jowl with other strangers, having to witness and do the bidding of depraved camp leaders. It made me sick to think of it, but it fuelled my anger, too, reminding me of the reason that Leo was there in the first place.

Working long hours at the Zoo Tower hospital was a balm to my tortured soul. When I wasn't working, I was at home helping Onkel Georg on the farm or assisting with the escape of the Russian soldiers. We'd already saved over a dozen men, but it consumed him now that Leo was gone. Onkel Georg couldn't do anything for his own son, but, as Tante Elya explained to me, by saving these other men his sense of help-lessness seemed less overwhelming. It was the same for all of us. On a visit to the village I'd told Ida that I was looking after Mina as best I could.

Berlin was in lockdown. The city centre had been bombed by the Allies and now fires raged, destroying whatever the bombs hadn't. Cultural icons and many of the government buildings, including the Reich Chancellery, had been damaged, but still the Führer remained unscathed. Government offices were already closed and had relocated to remote and often secret locations. *Just like the government to run away*, I thought, but work continued the same as ever at the Zoo Tower.

Like other hospitals, we were on standby, ready to accept staff and patients of evacuated hospitals closer to the Allied and Russian lines. Whenever we weren't looking after patients, we were conducting a stocktake of our supplies and finding ways to make what we had last as long as possible. Preparations were made to bring in experienced medical staff and resources into the more fortified positions – places where we could protect our patients and would be able to take the injured once Berlin was under siege. I was overjoyed to learn that Johann and Marika, who'd returned to the Beelitz hospital after she was married, were being transferred to the Zoo Tower. I was excited to see them both and to be working with them again.

'I can't believe you're here,' I said, hugging Marika tight in the middle of the hospital corridor. She looked radiant even in her nurse's uniform. 'Married life's treating you well?'

She nodded. 'We're so happy. We have a little house in Kreuzberg now that we've been transferred. Johann's been promoted to surgical registrar so now he can begin his training to become a surgeon.'

'Well, he'll learn quickly here,' I said. 'The injured are arriving much sooner now that the front line's getting closer.'

'I can't believe it's taken the Soviets so long to cross the Vistula River,' she whispered. 'They've been outside Warsaw for months.'

I pulled her into an empty room. 'I know.' A sense of foreboding had been growing within me as I'd been hearing reports of Soviet retribution as they made their way west towards Germany. 'At least they've finally taken Warsaw and patients have spoken of them liberating Auschwitz.'

'Any news about Tante Elya's family?'

I shook my head sadly. 'Nothing yet. We heard through the resistance that the camp was almost emptied when the Soviets arrived and the Nazis had already marched most of the prisoners back towards Germany. They could be anywhere.' *If they're still alive,* I thought. There were also reports from our patients, of prisoners dying by the side of the road from exhaustion, or being executed by the Germans for lingering in their lines.

'And Leo?'

'He's on work detail near Buchenwald, but he's managing.' Her look of horror relaxed.

'It shouldn't be long.'

I fervently hoped not.

The Allies flew day and night, bombarding Berlin, destroying what was left of the city and forcing thousands to flee. Some lived in derelict buildings with no electricity or water, while others sought refuge in the homes of friends and family, or simply waited in shelters for it all to be over.

The ruined remains of the Kaiser Wilhelm Memorial Church, damaged over a year earlier, rose above the dwindling tree line of the Berlin Zoo and Tiergarten, a constant reminder of what our city had been reduced to. Much of the surrounding woods had already been cut down for firewood during the long winter when no other fuel was available. I remembered the walks Julius and I had taken through those magnificent parklands and couldn't help but mourn the loss of Berlin's famous forest.

High-level Nazi leaders had moved their headquarters here next to a major communications centre, but we rarely saw any of the Nazi Command. Defeat was inevitable now. Either the Zoo Tower would become a target of Allied bombers or – if we survived the bombs – it would be one of the last places to fall in Berlin. Whether that would be to American or Russian forces, no one could be sure.

After each air raid I looked out the hospital window and saw a sea of people slowly leaving the safety of the tower bunker and returning to their homes. Hundreds of mothers settled their babies back into prams that had been left outside the bunker. It amazed me how many people the tower could shelter.

We were all so used to the air raids by now that people filed in and out in a relatively calm manner. We nurses and doctors always stayed with the patients, unless we were seconded to emergency centres set up around the city, providing first aid and emergency care as well as assessing injuries and allocating people to the already crowded hospitals of Berlin.

Back at the tower, the booming sound of the anti-aircraft guns on the platform above us was somewhat unnerving as it announced the arrival of Allied bombers within range, but these guns gave us our greatest protection. My heart went out to the brave souls manning those guns, visible and vulnerable to enemy fire.

I'd told Marika about the young flak helpers and we made sure we saw Mina and her friends whenever we could. One afternoon, Marika and I slipped into the girls' dormitory with contraband: chocolate. The girls were still in uniform, but exhausted after the continuous night-time attacks, some smoking cigarettes to keep them going. Nobody was getting much sleep and nerves were beginning to fray.

'I want to go home,' said Frieda, one of Mina's twelve-year-old friends, her voice wavering. 'I'd rather go to prison than spend another day up on the platform waiting for enemy aircraft. When they come, we work as fast as we can to fetch the ammunition, but I'm so scared. All we can hear is the guns, hoping we've hit them, but what we really do is keep them from flying too low. Then there's the explosion of bombs falling across the city and we're always waiting for a bomb to fall on us.' She burst into tears, and Mina put her arms around her, comforting her as best she could.

'I just want to hug my mother before I die and tell my little brother to be a good boy and look after her.' Frieda dashed the tears away angrily. 'But I don't think I'll ever get the chance.'

'I have no home,' whispered another young girl, still holding her chocolate. 'Our apartment block was bombed and my mother and brother have left the city. I don't know where they've gone. We haven't been granted leave for weeks. None of us can be spared now.'

'We're the ones defending our city,' said a tall, lanky girl, 'but nobody sees us shaking so hard we can't hold our machine guns.' Frieda's words had punctured the tough façade of these young soldiers and they were now voicing their true feelings. 'It's when we're in bed, when nobody's watching, that many of us cry. Some want to go home so badly they're ready to desert.'

Marika and I looked at each other, speechless. Then a loud boom reverberated through the dormitory and a number of girls screamed, quivering.

'Mama!' cried a young girl with large blue eyes, chocolate smeared across her mouth. 'I want my mama.' The others moved quickly to her, hugging her and whispering soft words.

'It's all right, Emilie,' said Mina. 'You're safe here.' I noticed a puddle of urine pool on the floor, beginning to trickle towards us, and then an explosive sob. Marika and I glanced at each other.

'Come,' I said, gently steering the girl towards the bathrooms. 'Let's get you cleaned up.'

Over dinner that night at Marika's new home in Kreuzberg, I was furious about the abuse of these children. 'We have to get them out,' I said angrily. 'Before one of them deserts and gets themselves arrested.' I couldn't do anything about Leo or Tante Elya's precarious situation but I could help these youngsters.

Marika nodded.

'I promised to watch over Mina, but none of them are safe. We might be in a fortress, but those children are terrified. And with the way this war's going, some might never see their families again.'

'What are you thinking?'

'I'll speak to Onkel Georg. We have to put the perfect plan in place. Those children deserve to be home with their families.'

'Count me in,' said Marika with a defiant tilt of her chin.

Mina, Frieda and their two friends were our test run. Marika handled the logistics on the Berlin end, making sure they were escorted out of the city. I met them on the road near the village, and we made our way to the estate where Onkel Georg and Tante Elya hid them for a few days, feeding and clothing them and then arranging their journeys home. Nobody knew what was going to happen over the next few months and time with family was precious. A week later, Frieda was the last to be picked up by her mother, and I hugged her tiny frame to me.

'Goodbye, Frieda, and good luck.'

'Thank you, Susie. I'm going home because of you,' she said, smiling, her breath misting in the cold air.

'Hug your mother, and your brother, too. Be safe and be careful until the war's over.' She nodded. 'Now go. She's waiting for you.'

As the car pulled away and disappeared down the road, gladness filled my heart.

Around this time Onkel Georg received word that Russian officers were being summarily executed at Sachsenhausen – forty-five had been shot dead in one day.

'The Nazis know the war's lost,' he said, sitting behind his desk. 'It's only a matter of time before Germany's completely occupied and Berlin falls. They're killing as many of their enemies as they can before that day comes.'

'Jewish people and communists,' I muttered. In some districts, even protected Jewish people like Tante Elya were being sent to prisons and camps within German borders, despite the law. It seemed very haphazard.

'I've been told that, as the Red Army's advancing, the camps are emptying – mass executions ahead of the long march west by the more able prisoners.' He shook his head in disgust. 'We have to do what we can and move quickly to get as many out of Sachsenhausen as we can. But it's also time to think about getting Leo out.' He spoke grimly.

Dread sat heavy in my belly. 'Count me in.'

19

At the hospital a couple of weeks later, I was told I had a visitor. At first I was fearful, worried it could be Julius. Emilie, one of the remaining young flak helpers, accompanied me into the snow-covered street. I'd promised Mina that I'd look out for her until we could get her home.

'Onkel Georg! What are you doing here?' I hugged him tight, relief coursing through my body.

'I have news.' His face was sombre. He glanced at Emilie, small in her oversized uniform and bulky coat.

'Come on, Emilie. Let's take a walk to the zoo. Maybe they still sell ice-cream.' The look of sheer bliss that came over the girl's sharp features was enough to melt my heart.

'Can we see some of the animals?'

I smiled. 'Why not?' Although there had been substantial damage to the enclosures, repairs had been made and it was possible to view the animals that remained. Berlin wasn't going to be deterred by the Allied attacks: it was business as usual.

Emilie ran ahead, her plaits swinging, as Onkel Georg and I followed. I bought her a small ice-cream cone which she carefully licked, savouring every sweet mouthful while wandering nearby between the enclosures.

'What's happened?' I asked in a low voice. He was pale and his forehead beaded with sweat despite the snow on the ground. Trepidation swirled through my body.

'It's Leopold. I received this letter from my contact here in Berlin.' He pulled the paper out of his pocket with a trembling hand and passed it to me.

We've recently discovered that Isaac Guttenberg, the physicist nominated for the Nobel Prize, and your son Leopold have been placed on the Level 3 listing and are marked for execution. The Nazis are accelerating their attempts to exterminate all Jews in their jurisdiction before they lose this war, even good workers like them. However, now that Auschwitz has been liberated by the Soviets, we fear that we have little time to instigate a plan to ensure their safety. . .

I stared at Onkel Georg, numb with fear. 'We have to get them out of Ohrdruf.'

Onkel Georg nodded, taking off his glasses. 'We're out of time,' he said.

I glanced at where Emilie had last been standing. She was still there, safe and sound. I placed my hand on Onkel Georg's arm. It was tense, coiled tight. 'What can I do?'

'With the help of the resistance, I've been formulating a plan, but we'll have to rethink it so we can implement something sooner.' I could see him already running through scenarios and casting aside options. 'But there are very few I can trust with this. Hans is helping, of course.'

'My shift has finished. Let me come with you. I want to help him as much as you do,' I pleaded.

'I know, *liebling*.' He smoothed my hair from my face as he had done when I was a child. 'That's why I'm here.' He glanced across to Emilie, who was enchanted by the antics of the monkeys. 'Let me arrange a few things and I'll pick you up in a couple of hours.' Pride flamed bright within me. Onkel Georg knew what I was capable of and he knew I'd give everything to help.

'Onkel Georg, if anyone can get them out of there, it's you.' I kissed his icy cold cheek. 'I'll do whatever you need.'

'I just hope we have a watertight plan in time,' he said, rising heavily to his feet.

'So do I,' I whispered. This was the day I had feared the most. I had to put all my emotions to one side for the sake of what we were about to do. Whatever else I'd tried to do to keep my family safe, this was the time to risk it all, the time my actions mattered the most.

'Emilie, it's time to go,' I called. Shyly she slid her hand in mine as we walked through the zoo.

'Thank you for bringing me. I've never been to the zoo before,' she said quietly. I squeezed her hand.

'Well, we'll have to come again,' I said smiling, although all I could think about was Leo. This world meant nothing without him.

*

305

Later that evening, in the forester's cottage at Gut Birkenhof, we ran through the possibilities with Hans, plotting long into the night. The resistance had already supplied officers' uniforms and they could forge documents and a fake pass to gain access to Ohrdruf, but it would take time, and none of us knew how long Leo and Isaac had.

'The truck's the best option,' said Hans, his weathered face creased in concentration.

'I agree,' said Onkel Georg, pouring over the detailed notes and plans of the sub-camp and the surrounding area. 'Trucks are coming and going constantly on a work site like that.'

'How can you tell?' I asked anxiously.

'Between removal of dirt and rock from the tunnels, delivery of steel and timber sleepers for the railway line and gravel for the road, there'll be plenty of activity,' explained Hans, finishing the cold coffee left in his cup. His confidence and knowledge made the knot in my stomach begin to relax. Like Frau Kraus, he was someone we could always rely on.

'That gives us opportunity to go in with one of the resistance's modified trucks,' said Onkel Georg. 'There's a hidden compartment that Leopold and Isaac can stow away in.'

'But we still have to get in without arousing suspicion and somehow get them into the loading area and the truck without anyone noticing. Then get out again and safely away before anyone realises they're missing ... There's a lot that can go wrong.' Panic began deep within me at the thought of it all, but Hans only nodded slowly, his shaggy mane of greying hair falling over his eyes, while Onkel Georg just looked thoughtful.

'That's why we have to make sure every part of our plan is perfectly arranged, timed and organised,' said Hans grimly. 'Georg and I have a lot of experience now and know the pitfalls, but we still have to go over each section of the plan again and again until we've ironed out any potential problems and lowered the risk as much as possible. Leopold has powerful people on his side in the camp and they'll get him and Isaac into position, but we'll only get one attempt.'

'We can't lose him,' I said resolutely.

'Then let's get to work,' said Onkel Georg, determination blazing in his eyes.

Only days later, Tante Elya stood before us in the freezing pre-dawn, wishing us success and refusing to let the tears that welled in her eyes fall.

'Bring my son back to me,' she said in farewell.

Hans had arranged for us to pick up the modified truck from the resistance in Weimar, about three hours south-west, and not far from Ohrdruf.

'Susie, I'm so very proud of you,' said Onkel Georg in the growing dawn, which revealed a pewter-coloured sky, heavy with snow. 'We always wanted a daughter, and when you came along, you were a blessing in our lives. I should never have pushed you towards Julius, but I thought I was doing the right thing to protect you.' He shook his head. 'You're a strong woman, like your own mother, like Elya. I'm so sorry for what happened.'

I touched his hand on the wheel. 'I'm stronger for it, Onkel. It's something none of us could have foreseen.'

'All I want is to see you and Leopold reunited, to marry and have a family of your own.'

'And I'd love nothing more than to see your grandchildren on your knee and watch them with you on the estate,' I said softly. 'They'll adore you just as I do.' I didn't miss the misty-eyed joy on his face at the thought.

He reached for my hand and squeezed. There was no need for any more words.

The trip to Ohrdruf was the longest of my life. After picking up the truck and changing clothes, I moved into the driver's seat and we slipped easily into the line of trucks on the outskirts of Ohrdruf, bound for the work site. We were dressed the same as the other truck drivers, complete with fake passes that the resistance had thankfully been able to supply in time. I was playing the part of a young female apprentice, a normal sight in Germany now that all the men were away at war. There had to be two of us to delay or distract the guards if Leo and Isaac were late to the meeting point or if something went wrong.

My heart thumping, I tried to look nonchalant, bored even, as we entered the gates of the camp, two high fences rimmed with barbed wire between the outside world and the work site. I willed myself to remain calm, focused, detached from my emotions. SS guards could smell fear and even the slightest hint of nervousness could betray us. I'd memorised all the details of the plan until I could recite them in my sleep and I couldn't think of anything except the job in front of us. All the time I'd spent with Julius – the lying and pretending for a greater cause – had surely prepared me for this moment.

I followed the road through the construction site and between the hills on both sides. I'd had enough practice driving the trucks and tractors on the estate so I felt relatively confident in my driving skills, but I was still anxious. The snow-covered ground on either side of the road was flattened and barren and the site sat like a ragged scar on the surrounding landscape. The hills loomed above, but where once they were all heavily wooded, now the forest stopped at the crest of the highest hills. The side closest to the road was desolate and brown, naked limestone cliffs evidence of the butchering of the landscape.

Guards roamed the site while others were stationed outside the tunnels or wherever there was construction activity. I saw only a few work crews, pitiful-looking men dressed in little more than rags, thin and haggard, hacking away at the rock with picks, shovelling dirt into small trucks, and carrying large, heavy boulders of stone and baskets of rubble away from the work site. They were bow-backed and staggering. I searched desperately for Leo's face, but didn't find him. It occurred to me then that the majority of the workers would be inside the tunnels, digging the mountain by hand, spending all day underground, in the dirt, dust and stale air. It took all of my willpower not to cry for these broken-down men, all of my willpower not to imagine Leo among them.

We had to wait in line as the loader filled each truck with debris, rock and dirt.

'How long will this take?' I whispered, staring at the truck in front of us as we rolled forward.

'About half an hour to fill each truck. There are two still in front of us,' said Onkel Georg calmly.

'Leo and Isaac know what to do, when to come?'

He nodded. 'As long as all goes to plan with our diversion, they'll slip under the truck while it's being loaded. Until then we just wait.'

The minutes seemed to last for hours.

'This really is hell on earth,' I whispered. 'How can any humans have such disregard for life?"

'It's human nature, the very worst of it.'

'We're no better than animals,' I said bitterly.

'We're worse than animals,' said Onkel Georg fiercely. 'Animals don't turn on their own like this, animals don't foul their own nests. I don't know how God can look upon us as his creation. I don't know how there can be a God who allows these atrocities to occur.'

I reached across and put my hand on his arm. It was all I could do with unfriendly eyes upon us.

Finally the truck in front of us lurched forward and my breath caught in my throat. It was our turn to be loaded.

'Not a word,' said Onkel Georg, as we inched forward. 'Let me do the talking.'

I nodded, swallowing hard. He reached across me to show our passes to the guard on duty, who peered through the window at me.

'What's the world come to when they let women learn how to drive trucks?' scoffed the guard.

'I agree. Women don't belong in construction, but with all the men at war,' Onkel Georg said, shrugging. 'This one's not bad, but she still has a lot to learn.'

'Better you than me, I say.' He handed back the passes to Onkel Georg before gesturing to the loader to begin filling the truck.

Suddenly there was a shout as the truck in front began losing its load from its open tailgate. Rubble poured onto the road and the truck stopped as SS guards shouted and gestured to the driver. Along with the loader operator, they rushed to the back of the truck to see what had happened, arguing about whose fault it was.

Onkel Georg kept his gaze forward. 'Keep your eyes open now.'

'Where is he?' I murmured. I couldn't see Leo lurking in the shadows anywhere. 'Have you seen him?'

'No. Perhaps he's well hidden. We have help on the inside, remember, and they managed the tailgate accident perfectly. They'll make sure he gets to us.'

'God, I hope so,' I breathed as the guards cleared and the truck in front of us pitched forward once more.

It was our turn now. While our truck was filled, we scanned the yard for anything out of place, hoping Leo and Isaac had already both made it underneath the truck.

'Get ready,' Georg whispered as the loader turned away to manoeuvre the remaining debris into a pile easy to load onto the remaining trucks. I nodded, fear knotting my stomach. It was time. Together we opened the doors of the cabin and jumped down to the ground. I tried to ignore the tightness in my chest.

'What are you doing?' barked the guard.

'She doesn't have the skill to drive this fully loaded,' said Onkel Georg genially, walking around to us from behind the truck. 'I'll have to drive this back. We don't want any accidents on the road.'

'No, of course not,' said the guard hastily.

'Some are easier to train than others,' said Onkel Georg, capturing the guard's attention as I made my way around to the back of the truck. Everything moved in slow motion. The truck behind was still occupied with the guard checking their documents and the loader driver was still piling dirt. I ran my fingers lightly underneath, holding my breath. A single touch was all I needed, but I felt nothing, only the cold steel of the compartment.

We were out of time. My heart dropped and I wanted to scream and charge the guards, but there was Onkel Georg to think about and all those who had risked their lives in this attempt. We'd failed. I steeled myself to walk back to the cabin of the truck knowing we had to leave Isaac and Leo behind to an uncertain fate. I took a breath and arranged my face into a mask of blank indifference.

Then I felt it. Frozen fingers wrapped around mine for just a second, but it was enough. I didn't know whether they were both there, but I walked around the side of the truck without missing a beat and climbed back into the cab.

'Let's go,' I said, looking at Georg, who raised his eyebrows. I nodded quickly, and he started the engine.

The trip out of the camp was even more tense than the one in. I worried that at any moment we'd be stopped and our extra cargo discovered. My knuckles were white, my fingers digging into the seat.

'Breathe,' said Onkel Georg.

'Can't you go any faster?' I murmured.

'Not unless we want to be noticed.'

Finally we reached the gates, where we were stopped. I was sure my heart was about to stop as well. Freedom lay just beyond our reach.

'It's protocol,' said Onkel Georg. 'Nothing to worry about.' But I could see the tension around his mouth. He passed our papers to the guard through the window.

Other SS guards inspected the truck, walking slowly around the tray. Any moment the game could be up. I stared steadfastly ahead, willing the beads of sweat that were beginning to form all over me not to betray me. *Please let us pass,* I prayed, repeating it over and over again inside my head.

Finally the guard handed our papers back. 'You can go,' he said abruptly.

As the gates opened to let us through, the truck lurched forward and then we were free.

20

It was only when we got to the resistance safe house in Weimar that we would know whether we'd managed to get both Leo and Isaac out. As soon as Onkel Georg parked the truck, I jumped down from the cab and rushed to the rear. A pair of blue eyes stared back at me from the hidden compartment and my heart sank. I held out my hand to help Isaac down before he was mobbed by resistance members congratulating him on his escape. I peered into the gloom of the compartment, unable to breathe, and suddenly an arm shot forward. Stifling a sob, I pulled Leo from his hiding place and, finally, he was in my arms.

But there was no time for tearful reunions. Onkel Georg, although reluctant to leave Leo and me, went home in his own car while I took a car from the resistance and drove to Berlin, with Leo and Isaac hidden in the back. Their best chance of avoiding detection and capture was hiding in plain sight, disguised as Upper Silesian refugees fleeing before the

Red Army and arriving in Berlin, like thousands of others. The resistance had organised refuge for Leo in a safe house in Prenzlauer Berg in the north of the city, and in south-east Treptow for Isaac.

Leo and I were unable to speak until he'd been shown his bed down in the basement.

'You made it,' I said once we'd been left alone. It was hard to look at him. He was so thin, with sunken cheeks and exhaustion in his eyes. It made me want to cry for him, but I knew he wouldn't want that. Leo stared at me, tears sparkling in his eyes. He reached out and held my hand, beginning to tremble before he pulled me towards him and held me tight. I hugged him, savouring the moment. There was nothing of him except muscle and bone, but it was still Leo.

'I was worried we wouldn't get you out,' I whispered.

'I'm here now,' he said, his voice cracking.

'Don't you ever leave me again.'

'Thoughts of you and our last days together kept me going, especially while waiting for the truck. I wanted to see you again more than anything.'

I nodded, wiping my eyes and nose with the sleeve of my coat. 'Me too.'

'Stay with me tonight Nightingale. I don't want to be alone.' He kissed me softly on the lips. 'I don't think I can manage much just now, but I want to feel you next to me, know you're there and wake up to your face in the morning . . . to remind me I'm alive, that I'm with you, and that I have a future once again.'

'Of course I'll stay.' I took his hand and led him to the camp bed where we held each other fully clothed under the thin blankets, reacquainting ourselves with the feel of each other with only the comforting sound of our breath, until Leo fell into an exhausted sleep. It wasn't long before my own lids felt heavy and I slipped into a deep and dreamless slumber.

Leo was safe enough in the city, but it was too dangerous for me to see him. He was so close, but still so far. I went to see him once and had to go to elaborate lengths to keep his location secure, doubling back, changing trains, and going out of my way to get to the house in Prenzlauer Berg. Once there, my stomach lurched, hoping that Leo hadn't been discovered, that I hadn't led those that hunted him to his doorstep.

The SS had already visited Gut Birkenhof with the news of Leo's escape, questioning Onkel Georg and Tante Elya. They'd threatened her with deportation straight to Auschwitz and him with imprisonment, even with taking the estate, but had abruptly left again, presumably satisfied that they knew nothing of Leo's disappearance because they never returned. The SS had asked about me but Georg and Elya explained that I was living in the Zoo Tower and working at the military hospital and couldn't possibly know about his escape, let alone where he was. Nobody came to see me. It seemed that with the Allies closing in on Berlin there were more important things for the SS to concentrate on, like scrambling to finish underground headquarters for the Nazi elite and pushing production of the rumoured miracle weapons that were going to win the war. Not to mention the mass executions. One escaped *mischlinge* from a work camp made no difference to them, but I didn't think for a moment that we were out of danger.

Relief washed over me as I stepped safely and without incident into the basement and Leo took me in his arms.

'How have you been?' I asked, kissing him lightly on the lips.

'A little cooped up, but fine.' He smiled wryly. He was an outdoors man, especially after all those years working the estate.

I placed the dish of fortified stew I'd saved from the hospital on the table. 'Are you feeling better?'

'Much stronger now that I'm not digging holes in rock all day long.' He took my hand. 'Eat with me.'

'I already ate at the hospital. This is for you.' He nodded and sat at the tiny table while I sank onto the camp bed.

I watched him eat, slowly as though savouring every morsel. 'My stomach still can't take very much,' he said apologetically. 'I tried to eat more the other day, but I vomited it up. It was too much too soon, and so rich.'

'I should have brought you something lighter.'

He shook his head. 'No, this is perfect, full of the nutrition that I need. At the camp, we only got a little bread and watery soup with a few pieces of some kind of root vegetable floating in it. Not enough to sustain a working man. I just have to eat slowly. I'll keep some of it for dinner. Next time you come I'll be able to eat more.'

'How did you survive, Leo?' I whispered.

'I was lucky – many didn't ... because their bodies couldn't keep them going any longer. Those who could were constantly exhausted. Accidents were commonplace and beatings happened every day because we weren't fast enough, strong enough or efficient enough.' He stared into the distance, his eyes hooded with the difficult memories.

'I'm so sorry, Leo.' I could only imagine what he'd been through, although after driving through that construction site, I had a good idea.

He looked better than when he'd arrived. His dark hair was shiny and growing thicker and wavy once again and his cheeks had filled out. He was still thin, but not skeletal, and the hollow look in his eyes had all but disappeared except when he was remembering the camp.

'I feel so helpless. I don't know what to do.'

He left the table and sat beside me on the bed. 'You're already doing everything. I would've died if you hadn't rescued me, at terrible risk to yourself. How can I ever thank you?'

'You'd do the same for me. All I want is you. That's all I've ever wanted. I love you.'

'I love you, too, but I have nothing to offer you as a husband. I'm a fugitive now, and a man without property or means. I don't want to tie you down to a man with nothing.'

I wrapped my arms around him and buried my head in his bony chest. 'I don't care, Leo. I just want to share my life with you. I still have my inheritance, and in a couple of months when I'm twenty-one I'll have the estate and the money my parents left me. But, no matter what, we'll manage. We deserve some happiness.' I looked up into his face, alight with joy.

He bent his head to kiss me, with the passion of the old days behind it. 'Well, that's settled then.' I couldn't keep my eyes from his beloved face. He was beautiful to me in every way possible. 'It's not the way I imagined doing this, but I don't want to waste another minute.' His hands cupped my cheeks and all I saw was the love in his expressive brown eyes. Then I understood, and was overjoyed. 'I love you, Nightingale, with all my heart. Will you marry me?'

It was the end of February when the Allied bombs hit the south-east of the city, leaving thousands homeless. Marika and I had just finished the night shift.

'Kreuzberg's been hit,' I said, clutching her arm in alarm. 'Where's Johann?'

Everyone was on edge after the bombing of Dresden a couple of weeks earlier where the horrific firestorms had devastated the beautiful medieval city. The civilian casualty rate was astronomical and had come as a terrible shock to all of us, with medical staff from Berlin rushed to what had to be the worst disaster of the war for Germany.

'Home.' Her face paled. 'I need to go check. He would've gone to the public bunker but I want to make sure he's safe and that the house is still standing.' I knew Leo would be unscathed, north of the city.

I grasped her hands tightly. 'I'll come with you.'

We joined the emergency medical vans as they made their way tortuously through the city, back-tracking and ducking down side streets to avoid the worst of the damage to buildings, tram tracks and roads. Bombings were almost a daily occurrence by now and most civilians had made it to the air-raid shelters across the city, but it didn't stop either of us from worrying. And as we got closer to Kreuzberg, the destruction was worse than we'd realised. Houses were flattened, others burning. I held Marika's hand tight as we stared out the window, horrified.

When we were close enough to Marika's street, we leapt from the van and made our way on foot, climbing over debris and around burning homes. We stopped at the end of the road, a scene of devastation before us. Most of the houses had been hit, their roofs caved in, walls and floors collapsed. It was eerie, a thick layer of dust and dirt covering the street. Bricks, concrete, stone and twisted metal and smouldering timber were scattered across the road and the front yards of suburban blocks. Emergency crews were already on the scene, directing stunned residents away from the area.

Marika's house was a pile of rubble. We stared in disbelief at the ruins. There was very little to salvage.

'You'll be able to rebuild,' I whispered trying to console her. 'They're only things.'

'I have to find Johann and tell him,' she said, her voice trembling. 'I have to know he made it safely to the bunker.'

'I'm sure he did,' I said, gently putting my arm around her. 'But let's see if we can find him. Maybe he's already gone up to the hospital to tell you about the house.'

We turned to leave when we were stopped by a shout. 'In here,' yelled a man's voice. A group of emergency workers rushed towards Marika's house. 'There's somebody still in there.'

Marika's face paled, her eyes wide with horror. 'Johann? It can't be.'

We ran towards the house, following the men to the back, climbing carefully past exposed wires and broken pipes.

I suspected that the electricity was down, but I couldn't be sure. Four emergency workers were removing rubble from the collapsed wall and roof.

'Down here,' shouted one of the men. The other men hurried over, and Marika swayed on her feet.

The men began to move the rubble from what had been Marika and Johann's bedroom. 'When he's deep asleep he doesn't hear anything,' she said, her voice catching. 'He worked back to back shifts all week. He was exhausted.'

'He's alive, but he's trapped,' said one of the men. 'We have to get him out.'

Marika let out a sob of relief and grasped my hand, her eyes wild as she stared intently at the rescue.

'Is he hurt?' I asked. 'We're nurses, and this is his wife,' I said, gesturing to Marika.

'He's talking, so that's a good sign,' the man said. Marika nodded, unable to speak, and I squeezed her hand in encouragement. *Johann has to be all right. He and Marika are meant to be together – just like Leo and I.*

'Careful,' growled one of the others, gesturing to us to move away. 'It's unstable and the whole lot could go.'

Each obstacle to Johann was painstakingly removed by the men. Marika stood rooted to the spot and rigid as stone. It was only when we heard the sound of his muffled voice, directing the men to his position underneath the rubble, that she came out of her trance.

'That's him, that's Johann!' she said, clutching my arm, tears rolling down her cheeks.

'Thank God,' I murmured, surprised to find I was crying too.

Finally a dusty, scratched and bleeding arm appeared from between the bricks and concrete and the breath caught in my throat. The men lifted the last piece of concrete, allowing Johann to shuffle forward on his stomach. Marika rushed to him, grasping one hand while someone held the other and they pulled him free of the debris. The concrete collapsed behind him and the men lowered him to the ground away from the building.

'Are you hurt, Johann?' Marika looked into his face, blackened with dirt, and my heart clenched at the sight. A slow ooze of blood was seeping through his pyjamas and his face was pallid.

'A few soft tissue injuries to my legs where the wall fell on me and perhaps broken ribs, but I'll manage,' he said, coughing weakly while bracing his side with his hand. 'I woke to the sound of bombs and managed to get to the basement. The house collapsed on top of it, but the basement held. I crawled out but had a hard time getting through the rubble.'

'Do you know how lucky you are?' she murmured, holding his hand. 'You could've been killed.'

'I'd never leave you, *liebling*,' he whispered, trying to smile.

She kissed him lightly on the lips.

'We have to get him to the medics,' I said to the men urgently. 'He'll have to be checked over. Come on, Marika. Let's get him onto a stretcher and into good hands.' I could see his eyes beginning to glass over and knew it wasn't long before he'd lose consciousness.

Johann was rushed to hospital for surgery with Marika by his side. His injuries were substantial, but it was the internal bleeding that was the greatest cause for concern. He was in the care of Herr Bettingen, treating one of his own, and this gave her great strength.

But Johann never made it out of surgery. He bled out on the table.

Marika wouldn't leave his side, and I stayed with her as she wept uncontrollably until his parents arrived to say goodbye to their son. After the funeral, her parents took her home to Trebbin. In one day she'd lost everything: her home and the love of her life. I couldn't imagine the unendurable pain she was suffering. I thought about Leo hiding safely in Prenzlauer Berg. It could have been him.

After Johann's funeral, I had to see Leo. I needed the solid reassurance of his arms around me, the comfort to allow my own tears to fall for Marika and for Johann. We hadn't been able to tell anyone about our engagement because of the risk to Leo, not even his parents over the telephone, but I carried the guilt of my happiness when Marika had lost hers. Johann's death was a stark reminder of the fragility of life and how easily it could be taken away.

'I'm glad you're here,' said the resistance contact when I arrived at the safe house. 'Leo can't stay here. The bombs are getting closer every day. We've had information that the Allies are hitting the U-Bahn. Danziger Strasse station is only a few hundred metres away and if it's hit . . .' He shrugged his shoulders. 'None of us should be here.'

'What about one of the other safe houses?'

'Our network of safe houses has been all but destroyed and those that remain are either unsafe or crammed with others who have nowhere else to go. It's best you get him out of Berlin and back home.'

'But that's the first place anybody will be looking for him.'

'Then you'll have to hide him.' I gazed at him, aghast. 'I'm sorry. There's nothing more we can do.'

After everything we'd been through to free him, I couldn't lose Leo now to an arrest or another bombing. With thoughts of Marika and Johann still in my mind, I borrowed one of the men's cars, which was registered under a false identity. Nobody else need be implicated if we were stopped and caught along the road. Leo was hidden in the boot and, to all intents and purposes, I was simply travelling home to my family as I had many times before. It was a little hair-raising navigating the ruined roads through the bombed districts and I was redirected around damaged or unsafe streets a few times.

Just as we'd made it to the edge of Berlin some guards who were parked on the side of the road gestured for me to pull over.

'What seems to be the problem?' I asked, winding down my window.

'Just routine checks, Fräulein,' said the officer. He wore an SS uniform. My heart began to hammer in my chest. 'Papers, please.'

With a shaking hand I passed him my identification papers.

'Something wrong, Fräulein?' he asked, frowning.

I swallowed hard. 'No. I just want to get out of the city. These bombings are a little close for comfort.'

He glanced through the window at the back seat. 'Where are you going?'

'Home. My parents live in the country about an hour and a half away.' His face was unreadable. Sweat trickled down my back.

'Car registration.' I handed him the papers, keeping a steady hand this time. 'This is not your vehicle,' he said, after comparing the two documents.

'No. It belongs to a friend. I'm borrowing it for a couple of days, until I get back to Berlin.'

'Wait here.' He turned away abruptly and walked towards his companion. I couldn't hear what they said and I thought about hitting the accelerator and just going, but before I could think any more, an officer in uniform materialised and walked briskly towards my car. I drew back involuntarily as his intimidating bulk peered in through my window.

'Fräulein Göttmann? Susanna Göttmann?'

'Yes?' I said tentatively, looking up at the face in shadow.

'Ernst von Glaubrecht.' I stared blankly at him. 'I met you at the opera last year with Julius Siebenborn and we had to evacuate to the basement during the air raid.'

'Of course,' I said hastily. 'I'm sorry I didn't recognise you at first.'

'No matter. I don't think any of us can think clearly with all the air raids.' He smiled disarmingly. 'You're going home to visit your parents?'

'That's right. I just want to get out of the city and breathe some fresh air.' My thighs were slick with moisture.

'Understandable.' He nodded and turned to the SS man. 'She's fine. She's no risk.' He held his hand out for my papers.

'Good to see you, Susanna. Have a safe trip.' He passed me the documents.

'Thank you so much.' I smiled brightly. 'I can't wait to get home.' I edged the car back onto the road and waved at Ernst as I picked up speed and drove away, my knuckles white on the steering wheel.

It was only on the open road outside Berlin that I allowed myself to take a deep breath. I wanted more than anything to stop and make sure Leo was fine, but instead I put my foot down and made my way to the estate, glancing constantly behind me for cars. But nobody was following us, nobody was lying in wait, and we made it home in good time without further incident. I thanked God in a silent prayer for the gallant Ernst von Glaubrecht. My time among the Nazis had been useful in more ways than one.

I drove straight to the forester's cottage and helped Leo inside. Hans would be home for luncheon soon and he would help me hide him.

I hugged Leo tightly, my body trembling now that the danger was over.

'You did well,' said Leo. 'Kept your cool.'

'I don't know what I would have done if they'd opened the boot or refused to let me leave.'

He kissed my forehead. 'But they didn't.'

Hans was surprised to see us but took it in his stride. I didn't want to leave Leo, but we thought it best I return to Berlin immediately with the car and in time for my night shift so there were no questions asked at the hospital. Hans assured me he'd keep Leo safely hidden on the estate. Onkel Georg and Tante Elya would be over the moon to see him.

21

At the end of March, I came across my first corpse on the streets of Berlin.

The bombings had been relentless and the strain was evident on everyone around us. Even the most stoic and calm individuals were becoming short-tempered. With the constant influx of injured, there was no time to mourn and Marika had returned to the hospital, determined to help those she could. We were still sending boys and girls back to Onkel Georg at the estate where he and Hans also continued to manage the escapes of Russian officers from Sachsenhausen while Leo remained hidden.

Marika and I were walking to the Zoo Tower from the tram stop, engrossed in conversation about our famous patient, Colonel Hans-Ulrich Rudel. He was the most decorated pilot in the Luftwaffe and was the object of adulation by staff and patients alike.

Marika stopped on the path, gripping my arm. 'Look,' she said with horror. A silent crowd had gathered around a lamp post.

I glanced up and then couldn't look away from what I saw. It was a young woman hung by the neck. Her face was discoloured, her blackened tongue protruding from her mouth, and her pale hair had been shaved close to her scalp, which was bloody and raw. A sign with the words 'Slut' and 'Traitor' hung around her neck.

'Oh, Susie, we have to cut her down,' Marika whispered, her hand across her mouth.

'It's the work of the Gestapo and the SS,' said a woman in the crowd. 'I knew her. She was a good woman. She was just sleeping with a Polish worker.'

'She's not the first,' said a man. 'I've seen others, men and women strung up across the city. Who knows what crimes they've committed?' Vigilant Gestapo and SS units harshly punished any small or imagined misdemeanour to prove the might of the Reich and to rouse citizens to one final push to defeat the enemy.

'No crime deserves a punishment like this,' said the woman, indignant.

'Come on,' I said to Marika, pulling her away. 'We can't do anything for her now.'

The Americans and British had crossed the Rhine and were marching across Germany while the Soviets were drawing ever nearer to Berlin. It was only a matter of time before Germany would fall, and the Nazi regime was becoming more desperate. Bands of SS officers were rounding up anyone they believed could fight. Girls were armed and taught how to shoot and wield weapons such as hand grenades. And the SS were becoming more ruthless in their methods, executing their enemies without hesitation. We'd heard of mass executions within the concentration camps, and thousands of prisoners marched west from the camps in Poland in danger of liberation from the Russians, while thousands more were killed before their saviours' arrival. We assumed the worst about Onkel Tedi and his family since we'd received no further letters from him after his departure to Auschwitz. These things I knew, but I never expected the Nazis to turn on their own citizens.

But it wasn't just the Reich we needed to be wary of. Refugees from the east had brought reports of atrocities committed by Russian troops. Women and girls were gang-raped, often killed and their bodies desecrated; homes were being looted and villages burned. It was whispered that it was retribution for Germany's treatment of Russians earlier in the war. It was horrific to contemplate, and even more terrifying that the Russians were likely to reach us before the Americans. I couldn't believe that we could face a worse fate than the oppressive and unpredictable rule we now endured under the Nazis. It seemed especially ironic given my family and I had been responsible for the escape of Russian POWs, who had most likely re-joined the forces now moving towards us.

Boys from the Hitler Youth and girls from the BDM were on the street filling trams and carts with rubble and constructing barricades under instruction from the old men in the Volkssturm. Yet the feeling in the city was one of defiance. Berliners would defend the city until the end. Through the early days of April, placards in shop windows proclaimed that Berlin would never surrender and that it would always remain German. Nobody knew what to expect. Nobody knew what the future held.

Marika and I remained at our post. The flak tower was virtually impregnable and there were still men and women who required medical attention there. But Tante Elya begged me to come home for my twenty-first birthday. We were so close to liberation, but it was also the most dangerous time. We had to tread carefully to ensure we survived the end of the war.

Leo had been constantly on my mind. I wanted to feel him close to me, to stare into his eyes. Marika's parents had also pleaded for her to come home and she'd decided to go to Trebbin and wait for the end of the war. She had already lost so much. Together, we left Berlin.

Leo and I met at the forester's cottage on the evening of my birthday. We couldn't risk him being seen by anyone, and Tante Elya was adamant that we celebrate all together. Frau Kraus helped Hans and Leo cook rabbit stew with vegetables from her selection in the cellar. Onkel Georg brought the wine and cognac.

As we crowded around the table, Onkel Georg stood and raised his glass. 'This is a special night, not just because Susanna has come of age, but because we are all finally together again. We are family, brought together through love, loyalty and friendship, and Elya and I are grateful to be celebrating and enjoying the simple pleasures of life with the people we love most.' Hans nodded and Frau Kraus clasped his hand and blinked furiously at Onkel Georg's words, beaming with happiness. I wondered if they knew just how much we cherished them. 'To family, and happy twenty-first birthday, Susanna.'

I sipped the white wine slowly, savouring the rich creamy tones. It was one of Onkel Georg's good ones, an old sylvaner, more full-bodied than a riesling and with a wonderful herbal aroma. I glanced at Leo. There was a sparkle in his eyes that I hadn't seen for some time.

'I have something to announce,' said Leo, raising his glass and smiling at me. 'I want to propose a toast to my gorgeous Susie, who's agreed to marry me.' The looks of delight on everyone's faces made me pleased that we'd waited until we were all together to share our joy.

It was a memorable evening, filled with joy and happiness and heartfelt congratulations. Only Marika was missing. It was late when we finally said goodnight, Onkel Georg and Tante Elya going back to the house and Hans and Frau Kraus heading back home to the village. Leo and I were finally alone.

Fuelled by the wine and good food, and buoyed by the joyful response to our news, Leo took me by the hand and led me up the ladder to the attic where he slept on a mattress on the floor. 'I've been waiting for this moment all night,' he murmured in between kisses.

'Me too.' I sighed with happiness and relief, safe in his arms.

We undressed each other. I was mesmerised by his touch and the feel of his warm skin on mine, unable to look away from the magnetic pull in his dark eyes.

'Come to bed,' I said, breathless with desire.

'We've got all night,' he said, grinning. He took me in his arms and the feel of his naked body against me was glorious. 'Let's take it slow,' he whispered, nibbling on my ear. 'I want to draw it out.' He took his time reacquainting himself with my body, kissing and teasing ever lower, until the room dropped away and there was only he and I.

The next morning, Leo and I stayed in bed. Hans called in early and then left again, and the cottage was ours. We risked sitting downstairs in the kitchen, eating bread and jam for breakfast and drinking tea, constantly touching each other, to remind ourselves that we were together. We found ourselves back in the attic shortly after. We couldn't get enough of each other. Afterwards we talked about the future in our cosy haven.

'It's so frustrating not to be able to go out with Vati and Hans,' said Leo, scratching his tousled head, his hair now long enough for dark curls to fall across his eyes. He looked and seemed more like himself, the haunted look in his eyes beginning to fade. 'They need all the help they can get. The cows are calving and there's more timber to fell, cut and season. The crops need careful attention with weed control now it's growing season so we have a harvest to bring in during the summer months.'

I kissed him lightly on the mouth. 'I know it's what you love, but you'll get back to it soon.'

There was a knock at the front door.

'It'll be your mother or Frau Kraus with lunch,' I said, pulling my dress over my head. 'I'll go, just in case.'

Leo sighed, kissing the back of my neck. 'Looks like our morning's over.'

I climbed down the ladder in bare feet. The knocking came again, insistent this time. I walked quickly to the door, frowning. 'Tante Elya?' I said through the door.

'Open the door, Susanna, quickly now,' said Tante Elya urgently. I opened the door and she rushed in, panting, her face white. 'Lock the door. Where's Leopold?'

'In the attic.' Fear shot through me like sharp spikes of ice. 'What's wrong?'

'To the attic now,' she ordered. 'Quietly.'

I followed her up to the attic where Leo sat on the mattress, fully clothed.

'Mutti! What's the matter?' he said.

'Push the mattress against the wall, Susanna, and remove any traces of the two of you being here,' she said.

Leo grabbed his mother by the shoulders. 'Stop, Mutti. What's happened?'

'The Gestapo, they're here, at the house with your father.'

We stared at her, aghast.

'I have to go to him,' Leo said, starting for the ladder.

She grabbed him around the wrist. 'No, you have to hide. If they find you, it's over for all of us.'

'I have to do something to help,' he said desperately.

'It may just be routine questioning,' she said.

'But how will we know?' I asked, pulling the bed covers off.

'Frau Kraus is there. She'll come to us when they're gone. She saw them coming and got me out of the house.'

'Your mother's right, Leo,' I said. 'You have to wait in the bolthole. Both of you. It's not safe.'

Leo opened a wood panel in the timber A-frame of the roof, revealing a small space inside. I handed him the bedding. 'You might need this. I'll bring up some water and food.'

He nodded. 'Come on, Mutti.' He helped his mother into the tiny room and kissed me briefly before closing the panel.

There was no time to feel anything. I pushed the mattress against the wall, covering the bolt hole, and slid my feet into my shoes. I climbed back down the ladder and peered out from behind the curtain of the kitchen window. The lane was deserted in both directions – back towards the house and towards the mill. Nothing moved from the forest beyond. Everything looked normal. Taking a deep breath, I filled a jug with water and grabbed half a loaf of bread, a heel of cheese and the leftover stew, two cups and some cutlery. I took them up to the attic, along with some cushions.

'Sit tight, Susanna,' whispered Tante Elya, white faced, as she took the food. 'Hans or Frau Kraus will come and tell us what's happening soon.' Then she closed the panel once more.

It was some time later before Hans arrived, locking the door behind him.

'Susie, where's Leo?' His face was calm, but I could hear the urgency in his voice.

'The bolthole with Tante Elya.' He nodded, his shoulders sagging with relief. 'Good, make sure they stay there.'

'Do you know what's happening? Are they here for Leo or Tante Elya?' I felt paralysed with fear now that I could learn more about the situation. He sat abruptly.

'An SS patrol came across some Russian POWs making their way to the estate. One of my men was waiting in the forest for them and saw them being arrested. By the time he got back here to tell me, the Gestapo had arrived at the house.' He put his head in his hands. 'There was nothing I could do.'

'Are they still there?' I whispered, dropping to the chair next to him.

'The car's still out the front. I don't know anything more, but Adelina's there. I'm sure she'll let us know something when she can.'

'I want to go to the house to see her,' I said.

He shook his head. 'You can't! You'll look suspicious.'

'I can go through the back to the kitchen.'

He stared into space, thinking through the options and then nodded. 'Fine, but be careful.'

It was a ten-minute brisk walk back to the house and I kept to the tree line, all my senses strained for any sound of vehicles, voices or unfamiliar sights. I slipped into the kitchen without being seen, but nobody was there. I crept towards the stairs and heard shouting from above. I shuddered. Onkel Georg was being interrogated. I climbed the stairs one at a time until I reached the floor above, the yelling continuing in a long stream of abuse by one of the Gestapo men. Then I saw Frau Kraus, hiding behind the dining room door. Her eyes widened in fear when she saw me. She gestured to me wildly. I crossed the hallway and joined her in the dining room.

'What are you doing here?' she whispered, grasping my hand tightly. Her skin was clammy and I could see her brow beaded with sweat. 'Elya and Leo?'

'Safe.'

She sighed with evident relief.

'I had to know what was happening.'

'Come, we can talk in the kitchen.' Together we stole back downstairs.

'There are three of them in the study with Georg,' Frau Kraus whispered, closing the kitchen door quietly. 'I've been eavesdropping, although I could hear them down here, the amount of screaming they've been doing. Someone from the village betrayed us. They tipped off the SS patrol and the Gestapo were only waiting for confirmation.'

'Do the villagers hate us that much?'

'Some do.'

'What do you think they'll do to him?'

'I don't know . . . They've been in there for an hour now.'

A shot rang out from the floor above, making us jump.

Frau Kraus clutched my hands fearfully, her eyes wide with shock. 'Stay here.'

'Be careful,' I hissed as I followed her out the kitchen door and to the bottom of the stairs. My heart was pounding wildly and I was trembling with trepidation.

'If something happens to me, go straight to Hans,' she whispered.

I nodded, light-headed with fright.

Frau Kraus was gone for what seemed like forever. Pressed against the kitchen doorway, I strained to hear whatever I could, trying to make sense of the noises from above. The low sound of men talking urgently carried down, then I heard the sound of boots in the hallway and the front door slamming shut. The house was quiet. The stairs creaked suddenly in the silence and, stepping from the protection of the kitchen, I risked a glance at the figure on the stairs, ready to withdraw immediately.

I breathed a sigh of relief. It was Frau Kraus. I met her at the bottom of the stairs. She was pale and haggard, her eyes blank.

'What is it?' I whispered, the hairs rising on the back of my neck. 'Have they gone?'

She nodded, reaching out to me with trembling hands and pulled me tight to her body. 'Don't go up there.'

'Onkel Georg?' I struggled to break free, but she grabbed my shoulders, desperate to hold me still.

'They shot him,' I said, my voice dull, disembodied. 'He's dead, isn't he?'

She stared at me uncomprehending for a moment and then nodded. 'Executed . . . After everything he's done for the Nazi swine. He was such a good man.' She placed a shaking hand over her mouth, the terror of what she'd seen etched deep into her face. Panic bloomed inside me, but I swallowed it down. I had to see what they'd done for myself.

Pushing past her, I rushed up the stairs and ran to Onkel Georg's study.

Standing at the door, I screamed, unable to take my eyes away from the gruesome sight in front of me.

He was lying crumpled on the floor, his blue eyes wide with surprise, a single, neat bullet hole in his forehead. Blood trickled down his face and dripped onto the floor, and more pooled on the Persian rug beneath his head. Blood, tissue and brains splattered the wall and velvet curtains behind his body like some macabre childhood painting.

I was rigid with shock, unable to move. My whole world had contracted to this room, to this very moment, but I couldn't yet grasp what I was seeing.

Frau Kraus was with me in an instant. 'Come away. He's gone now.'

'No, it can't be,' I moaned. I'd seen death many times before, but never like this, the execution of someone I loved. The violence of it was the hardest part to comprehend. Frau Kraus pulled me to her again and held me tight as I began to shake.

'We have to tell them, Tante Elya and Leo,' I whispered, still staring at the bright blood on the carpet. There was a lot of blood for such a small hole. 'How can we ever tell them?'

We never imagined we'd have to safeguard Onkel Georg – betrayed by those who had benefited from his generosity and support for so long. I glanced up at the wall. 'We have to clean up. We can't let them see him like this.'

'No. They'd want to bear witness to what's happened,' she said. Tears were rolling down her cheeks unchecked. 'Their anger might be the only thing that gets them through these next weeks and months.'

I nodded slowly. She was right.

'Come now. Let's find Hans and bring Elya and Leo to see Georg before the Gestapo return,' she said urgently, pulling on my arm.

It was enough to jolt me from my shock. 'They're coming back?'

'They'll be back to confiscate the estate tomorrow. I heard them talking.'

'They'll lose everything,' I said, recoiling from the shock of that realisation. 'And Tante Elya won't have the protection of her marriage any longer.'

Onkel Georg had been our last line of defence.

'We have a lot to do before then,' she said, drawing me away.

We brought Tante Elya and Leo to the house under a tarpaulin on the back of Hans's truck. We didn't know who was watching. None of us could tell who to trust, outside the five of us.

We'd left Onkel Georg where he'd fallen. Hans stood in the doorway, his face implacable. Leo stared down at his father's body in disbelief while Tante Elya dropped to her knees and kissed her husband's lifeless hand, pressing it to her cheek while softly sobbing.

'Oh, my poor Georg. You didn't deserve this,' she whispered between sobs.

'The Gestapo will be on your doorstep come morning,' said Hans quietly. 'Inquisitive neighbours will be close behind.'

'We have to bury him,' said Leo, choking on his words. A spasm of grief crossed his features and I held his hand tightly.

'We can get him ready for burial,' said Frau Kraus slowly, looking desperately at Hans for help.

'You have to say your goodbyes to him before morning. Elya, I'm sorry, but it's not safe for you or Leo to attend his funeral. You'll both have to stay in hiding now, until Germany has fallen.'

'No,' she whispered, shaking her head. 'I have to be there.'

'You can't, Tante Elya,' I said gently, crouching next to her. 'Your protection from the Gestapo ended when Onkel Georg died. If they find you, they'll kill you.'

'No, no, no!' she wailed, clutching Onkel Georg's hand to her chest.

I wrapped my arms around her. 'We can't lose you, too.' My voice cracked and tears ran down my face.

Then Leo's arms were around us both, his wet cheeks against ours. 'He'd want us to live, Mutti.'

She nodded sadly.

'Today you'll have to take anything you want to keep before the Gestapo return,' said Frau Kraus. 'Hans and I will try to store whatever else we can . . . But that's not what I'm worried about. They'll come looking for you tomorrow, Elya.'

'But she'll be in hiding with Leo,' I said.

'It's not enough. Nobody knows that Leo is here, but they'll search high and low for you, and perhaps they'll discover you both in the forester's cottage.'

Leo's eyes met mine and I nodded. 'What about the cabin where we hide the Russians? They won't find them deep in the forest.'

'Yes, I think that'll work,' said Hans, his face pale. 'The Red Army's waiting on the Oder River only sixty kilometres outside Berlin. You only have to stay hidden for a short while. You'll have your home back in a matter of weeks.'

'Yes, a matter of weeks,' said Tante Elya bleakly. 'A few more weeks and Georg would still be alive.'

There was nothing any of us could say to that.

Tante Elya refused to leave Onkel Georg's side, but there was no time for the rest of us to mourn him. We moved through the house, packing essential objects in large hessian bags we used for grain on the farm. Photo albums, family documents, jewellery, a few sentimental gifts and a small bag of clothes – that was all we could keep at Frau Kraus and Hans's house. Anything more would have alerted the Gestapo to a planned escape and concealment. Even Tante Elya's family heirloom, the samovar, had to stay, and her Russian records, too.

Frau Kraus cooked biscuits and pastries with the remaining flour, eggs and butter: food that would keep well while

Tante Elya and Leo remained in hiding. The rest of the basic food stores she'd take home with her.

'No filthy thieves are going to take this good food,' she said defiantly. 'You might be in hiding, but you'll eat well for as long as you can.'

Finally it was time to prepare Onkel Georg. The blood had stopped oozing and had congealed on the floor and around his head like a thick, dark halo.

'Elya, we have to clean him up,' said Frau Kraus gently. Tante Elya remained motionless by his side.

'Come on, Mutti. The undertaker's coming at dawn and you and I have to be long gone.'

She nodded stiffly and Leo and I helped her to her feet.

We moved Onkel Georg onto the dining table and washed away the clotted blood from his face and combed back his thinning hair, bandaging his head as best we could. We dressed him carefully in his best suit and trimmed his moustache. Finally he looked presentable and Tante Elya was satisfied. With his eyes closed it looked like he was sleeping peacefully.

'There's nothing more you can do,' said Frau Kraus. 'You have to leave before someone sees you. Susie and I will clean up and wait for the undertaker. She can stay with me until the funeral.'

Tante Elya kissed Onkel Georg on the lips one last time. 'Goodbye, *lyubimyy moy* . . . He was the love of my life,' she whispered. 'How will I ever go on without him?'

Leo kissed his father's waxen cheek before turning away, tears glistening in his eyes. All I wanted was to comfort him and for him to comfort me, but my duty was to do what they no longer could do.

'Come, my children,' said Tante Elya with a tremulous voice. 'Let me hold the both of you.' Leo and I embraced her, feeling her quivering body fight for control over her ragged emotions. 'You know how much I love you both.' We nodded, both incapable of speech.

Love was all we had left.

22

Onkel Georg was buried in the village cemetery the following day. Friends, neighbours and curious onlookers came to the burial, under the fresh, green leaves of the linden trees. I heard the whispers, saw the satisfied glances and eager faces awaiting further gossip. This was truly the worst of humankind, but I couldn't blame them entirely. Nazi propaganda and the war had turned former friends and acquaintances into bitter, resentful and untrusting people afraid for their own survival. I understood that much. But there was kindness too, deep sorrow and regret for the passing of a good man, a friend and employer. It was enough for me to know that there were still those who loved him and would miss him. Most would never know what good he'd done, the astonishing things he'd achieved in his lifetime, the number of lives he'd saved. I wasn't born to this man, but he was my father and I was proud of him.

The Gestapo questioned Frau Kraus, Hans and others near the estate, but nobody had seen Tante Elya since before Onkel Georg's death. A cursory search of the property and the surrounding forest was made, but the Nazis had more important things to do – like take what they wanted for themselves. They took our tractor and truck along with any other portable farm equipment. They smashed and destroyed anything left, and then fled. The Russians were closing in.

I told everyone that I was returning to Berlin, but I didn't go back to the Zoo Tower. Berlin was surrounded by the Red Army and nothing could help the men, women and children in those towers now. Instead, I hid in Frau Kraus's basement until we were sure the Gestapo had stopped sniffing around. Chaos reigned even in the village as the Nazis scrambled to leave ahead of the Russians. Locals stocked up on water and food, locking themselves in their homes as they waited to see whether the Soviets would be liberators or brutal occupiers intent on gaining revenge for the Nazi atrocities meted out to the Russian people.

Two weeks after Onkel Georg's murder, the Red Army arrived. We'd heard the skirmishes not far from the village, the bursts of gunfire, the rumble of the tanks and the explosions of heavy artillery. Most people chose to stay in their homes and basements, and mothers armed their daughters with knives, ready to defend their virtue.

Tante Elya and Leo met Frau Kraus and I back at the house. We hugged each other tightly.

'We made it,' I said to Leo, kissing him so hard that I was sure I'd bruised his lips. It had been the longest two weeks, knowing Leo was so close, but not being able to see him.

'We did,' he said, smiling.

I glanced around the parlour. The Gestapo and their men had left a mess. The gramophone was gone, as were Tante Elya's records. Her precious samovar lay damaged and dented below a smashed mirror. The upholstery of the fabric lounge had been ripped and torn, and the Persian rug was gone.

'Nothing that can't be fixed,' said Tante Elya, cradling the samovar in her arms. She looked gaunt, with dark circles under her eyes.

'That's right,' said Frau Kraus brightly. 'We'll have this place cleaned up in no time.'

The parlour was tidied; we covered the slashes in the lounge with fresh sheets, washed the floors and windows, and placed flowers from the garden in a vase on the small table before the first Soviet officer knocked on our door.

'Are you the owner of this estate?' he asked curtly when Tante Elya came to greet him.

'Good afternoon,' she said in Russian, smiling broadly. 'Gut Birkenhof belongs to my son but we're very happy to see you.' She had no fear of the Russians: they were her countrymen and our liberators.

'Captain Vasily Petrovich Snopov,' he said, introducing himself. 'You're Russian?'

'Yes. We've been waiting for your arrival.'

'We may have need of your skills to translate.'

'Of course. My son and goddaughter also speak fluently. Anything to see the Nazis gone.' She smiled. 'Please join us for tea.' We had little to offer him, and even less to offer his men who waited in the truck outside, but Tante Elya insisted we serve him tea from the samovar and Frau Kraus brought the last of her biscuits.

'This is an unexpected pleasure,' said the captain, sipping the tea with a blissful expression on his face. 'And a compatriot so far from home.' He gestured to the samovar while casting his eye across the room. 'What happened here?'

'The Gestapo,' Tante Elya said. 'They killed my husband two weeks ago and confiscated the property.'

'Well, it's not theirs anymore,' he said grimly. 'Your husband's crime?'

'Aiding the escape of Soviet POWs,' said Leo.

Snopov raised an eyebrow in surprise. 'Russians?'

Leo nodded. 'From Sachsenhausen. We were part of the resistance, Free Germany.'

'How do *Junkers* such as you come to help the resistance?' the captain asked, intrigued.

'I'm Jewish,' said Tante Elya, 'and Russian. My husband was landed gentry. Before Leopold was incarcerated at Buchenwald, they helped many Russian officers escape from Sachsenhausen. Susanna was also involved in helping young flak helpers, only children, get home to their families before it was too late.'

'Is this true?' he asked.

I nodded. 'I worked as a nurse at the zoo flak tower.'

He shook his head in amazement. 'Well, I'm very pleased to meet you. We're moving on towards the city, but if ever you come to Berlin, please come and see me. I won't forget you and your hospitality.'

This was the Russian reception I'd desperately hoped for from any of the soldiers in the Red Army, courteous and friendly, but I wasn't sure that all Germans would be so happy when the Soviets arrived on their doorstep.

*

Life went back to normal, as normal as was possible after everything that had happened. Frau Kraus came each day with those who needed help from the surrounding district, requesting food, clothing or shelter and protection from the madness that surrounded the last days of the war. Gut Birkenhof was still the pillar of the community, the place villagers could turn to in times of trouble, despite the hurt many had caused Tante Elya. With them came stories from the villages that the Soviets swept through, decimating the last units of Wehrmacht resistance on their rapid march to the capital. Stories of girls being raped by Russian soldiers, mothers and daughters committing suicide to avoid the terror that they knew was coming.

'I know they're Mutti's compatriots, but we can't be responsible for what they do now. They suffered so much at the hands of Germans,' said Leo, placing another box of jars filled with preserves and sauerkraut on the kitchen table with a thump. 'We wanted them to bring down the Third Reich and they have. Now they're showing their dominance. Even liberation has its shadow side.'

'It doesn't mean it's right,' I flared hotly. 'Russian or German, both sides have conducted themselves atrociously.'

'Some men can be monsters,' said Frau Kraus, shaking her head as she took a box from Hans.

'Nothing can excuse what any of those soldiers have done but even good men will do bad things in the context of war, no matter what side they're on,' said Hans softly.

I understood what Hans was trying to say. There were those who journeyed past the limits of their morality, sometimes pushed by trauma and deprivation, other times nudged into the grey area over long periods through circumstance.

We all had that aptitude. Not just the Nazis, but also the Soviets, the villagers, Mueller or Julius. What mattered was whether we took responsibility for our actions and acknowledged the pain we caused. That was the difference between a monster and a good man.

But this wasn't the same thing. This was revenge. What these Soviet soldiers were doing was inexcusable. 'They're monsters,' I said vehemently.

'Let's hope common sense prevails in the days to come,' said Frau Kraus, smiling sadly at me.

I was thankful I wasn't still in Berlin. Nobody was safe there. I prayed that our other friends from the city had fled like many others into the arms of the Americans, where everyone knew it was safer.

News of the Führer's death was broadcast over the radio a few days later. It was a cruel joke really, his death right at the end of the war, at the point of Germany's defeat. But at least he was finally gone and could do no more damage. On the orders of the new President of Germany, Admiral Dönitz, Germany's unconditional surrender was declared on the eighth of May. Tante Elya, Frau Kraus, Hans, Leo and I sat around the radio in the parlour, expressions of relief and joy, mingled with sadness on our faces.

'Georg would have rejoiced to see this day,' said Tante Elya gazing at the chair he usually occupied. She had placed his pipe back on the small table next to his chair where it belonged after she'd found it mercifully intact. If only he'd survived two more weeks.

'To the end of the war,' said Hans, lifting his glass. The Gestapo's men had found Onkel Georg's wine and liquor stores so all that was left to celebrate with was the cognac he'd brought to the cottage the night before he died.

'And to all our fallen,' added Frau Kraus. I nodded, my elation warring with the sombre facts. Our loss was so fresh, but just about everyone had lost someone. Frau Kraus had lost her son and grandson to this war, with another son missing, and Hans had lost his nephew on the Eastern Front, and his sister and nieces in the Hamburg firestorm.

The fiery liquid was bracing as it slid down my throat. 'What happens now?' I asked.

'We live our lives,' said Frau Kraus. 'You two can bring us joy by being happy. Get married and have a family.' She smiled. 'I've waited so long to see this day. Your family no longer persecuted and you two lovebirds finally able to be together.'

'It's time to start living,' said Hans. 'No more hiding in attics, no more sneaking around.'

'We can breathe again,' I said, clasping Leo's hand. Excitement thrummed through me. The life I'd always dreamed of having with him was now a reality. Despite everything, hope burned bright within me.

'Yes,' said Leo. 'We can be who we are and live life on our own terms. I never thought Susie and I could have a future, but here we are.' He squeezed my hand.

'Yes,' said Tante Elya. 'A joyous occasion is what we need now. We can have a small affair here at home, a summer wedding . . . It's what your father would have wanted.'

'You're right,' said Leo, nodding. 'Let's set a date.' He gazed at me and smiled. 'What do you think, Susie?'

'The sooner the better,' I said, hardly able to believe that we were really finally going to get married.

Tante Elya took my hand. 'You need an engagement ring. It would make me smile to see you wear mine,' she said quietly. She twisted both rings off her finger and handed the diamond ring to me and the plain gold wedding band to Leo.

'You don't have to do this, Mutti,' said Leo, the ring small in the palm of his hand.

'But I want to. It's all I have left to give you both.' She closed Leo's fingers over the ring. 'Keep it safe until your wedding day. Now put the engagement ring on your bride's finger.'

Leo raised his eyebrow in question and I nodded silently. I was incapable of speech and on the verge of tears. I raised my hand and he carefully slipped the ring on my finger. Frau Kraus and Hans applauded.

'It's beautiful,' I whispered.

'It suits you.'

I stared at the diamond on my hand, watching it sparkle in the light. 'I remember playing with your ring when I was a child,' I told Tante Elya, 'hoping one day to wear one just like it, and to be as happy as you and Onkel Georg.'

'And now you have your heart's desire. A mother couldn't be any happier.'

I hugged her tightly. 'Thank you, Tante Elya. I'll never take it off.'

Tante Elya and Frau Kraus insisted on the most beautiful wedding they could plan and very soon I was swept into their vision of a June wedding in the village church where Tante Elya and Onkel Georg had been married, followed by a small reception at Gut Birkenhof. With a little good management we could still have a wedding meal using rations and Leo's black market associates. Tante Elya and Frau Kraus were determined to make me a wedding dress from an old gown of Ida's, adding small pieces of lace to edge the sleeves and neckline. The only thing missing was Marika, but it was impossible to get word to her in Trebbin due to the danger of continued skirmishes.

Finally the day arrived. I stood in front of the mirror in my room: the same place I'd stood with Tante Elya two years earlier on my nineteenth birthday – and the same place she'd stood on her wedding day twenty-five years ago with my mother by her side.

'You look beautiful ... I'm so happy that this day has come for you both, and that I'm here to see it,' whispered Tante Elya, brushing a loose strand of hair from my face. 'Your mother would be so proud of you; Georg too.' She gazed at the diamond ring on my hand sparkling in the sunlight.

'It means the world to me,' I said, blinking away the tears. They were mainly happy tears, but I wished my parents, my brother Friedrich and Onkel Georg could have been there too. 'You've been more mother to me than I could ever have hoped for.'

'You're the daughter I always wanted.' She kissed me on the cheek. 'Come, let's get you married. Leopold will be waiting.'

I stepped out in my blue wedding dress, holding a bouquet of wild cornflowers and poppies with Tante Elya on one arm, beaming with pride. Frau Kraus and Hans were our escort as we walked through the village to the little church on the hill where Leo was waiting for me. Many of the villagers had come out to watch, even those who had been so against us. Now that we were no longer a threat to their survival, they stood outside their homes to wish me well with a nod or a handshake, or even a kiss on the cheek and an embrace.

The breeze off the river caressed the loose hair at the nape of my neck and the dappled sunlight from the oak and beech trees fell across the delicate lacework Tante Elya and Frau Kraus had lovingly sewn onto my dress. There had been times when I thought I'd never see this day.

Leo was standing at the altar, proud and tall in his suit. He was the most beautiful sight I had ever seen, like a Greek god. The pews in the church were filled with curious villagers and friends, but my eyes were only for him. He was smiling, radiant with joy, and I couldn't have been any happier. Then I was by his side and he was holding my hands – solid, dependable and calming Leo. I sighed a little with relief. I was home.

'We've made it,' I whispered.

He nodded. 'You look beautiful,' he murmured. The tears glistened in his eyes. I knew that, in his darker moments, he'd also despaired of us ever reaching this day.

The words of the traditional Lutheran ceremony were almost a blur because we were lost in each other. Staring into his dark eyes I saw the love and passion, the commitment and devotion, the unspoken words of a rare love. We were meant to be together and, despite it all, we were here.

Then we kissed for the first time as husband and wife and, fingers intertwined, we walked from the church. Tante Elya was the first to embrace us outside the doors, tears of happiness sliding down her cheeks, while Frau Kraus looked on with a handkerchief to her eyes.

'I'm the happiest mother today,' Tante Elya said, holding us tight. 'Your father would be as happy as I am. I love you both so very much.'

'Vati's here and watching over us,' said Leo with conviction. Onkel Georg's loss was still so very raw and I'd noticed that Leo never took his father's signet ring off his hand.

'He'll always be with us,' said Tante Elya with a sad smile.

It was a small group of those dearest to us who came back to Gut Birkenhof for the wedding feast: Frau Kraus and Hans, Ida, Mina, Herr Wenck and his family, and the few villagers who had remained supportive of Tante Elya throughout the war. We sat around trestle tables under the cool green canopy of the cherry trees, eating and drinking as the sun cast its last golden glow across the garden and fields beyond. It was the most wonderful and magical day of my life, but the best was yet to come.

As night fell and the lanterns were lit, the enchanting strains of the balalaika filled the balmy evening air.

'Listen!' Tante Elya whispered, squeezing my hand and smiling, her face alight with anticipation.

I'd know Leo's masterful playing anywhere. He appeared at the table, sat beside me and took my hand.

'This is for you, my love,' he said. 'For my bride on our wedding day,' he declared to the table.

I was swept away by the lilting melody and his large, expressive eyes as he serenaded me with his love song. It was a moment to remember forever and when the last haunting strains faded away I reached across and kissed him.

'That was the most beautiful thing I've ever heard,' I said. 'Thank you, Leo.'

'I might give an encore performance in private tonight, Nightingale,' he whispered in my ear, grinning with a wolfish expression.

'I can't wait,' I whispered back, shivering with anticipation.

23

It was July and time to bring in the harvest, but the Gestapo had taken whatever equipment they could and we had nothing to help with the grain or to cut and bale the hay.

'Gut Birkenhof is the lifeblood of our community and I won't let Vati down,' said Leo. We were sitting in Onkel Georg's study going through the finances.

Hans nodded. 'No harvest, no income, no flour and no fodder for the cattle. We have to have some way of keeping milk production up. I think we're in for a hard year with few resources across the country and many mouths to feed and keep warm come winter.'

'Surely the Allies won't let people starve,' I said.

'Nobody knows what will happen,' said Leo. 'We're under Soviet occupation now, and we've already seen that they don't think too kindly of us after what our soldiers did to their people. We have to be prepared for difficult times ahead. The estate is all we have.' Germany, reduced to the spoils of war, was already being carved up like a roast chicken between the Allied occupiers into the Soviet zone in the east and American, British and French zones in the west. I didn't know how Germany would ever be the same again.

'We have to secure your future and Georg's legacy,' said Tante Elya. 'He did it all for you both. Gut Birkenhof is as much a part of you as it was for him and his ancestors before him. One day you'll pass the estate down to your children.'

But there was nobody we could borrow the necessary equipment from. The costs to lease it were exorbitant and we didn't have that kind of money. I couldn't even access my inheritance now that I was twenty-one due to the chaos of the post-war administration. In the end, we sold Tante Elya's jewellery for a fraction of what it was worth and managed to scrape enough together. We leased a tractor, a pull combine harvester to cut and thrash the grain – wheat, oats and rye – a sickle bar mower to cut the hay, and a baler to bale it when it had dried. But we couldn't do it on our own. With the hay alone, it took one person to drive the tractor and tow the baler, another to feed the hay into the baler and two more to tie the twine around each bale as it was released. Then the bales had to be carted into the barn using a truck we borrowed from Herr Wenck in the village, and stacked. Thankfully, we had enough to pay for a small team of farm workers and we still had enough friends in the village to help us get the harvest in as quickly as we could.

They were busy, long days through July and August, falling exhausted into bed at night, only to repeat the process the next day, but I was blissfully happy despite the desperation of trying to keep the estate afloat and our animals alive.

Hardship surrounded us, but though we were rake thin and constantly hungry like everyone else, we were happy, bronzed by the sun and surrounded by family. I was home and with the man I loved, and not even the uncertainty of Allied occupation, the splitting of Germany and Berlin between the four Allied powers, and what it meant for us now being in the Soviet Occupied Zone could deter us from doggedly working to get the farm back on its feet.

Leo took responsibility for managing the estate and much of the strain that went with it, but it did nothing to dampen his ardour at night. We spent many a night on top of the sheets, listening to the owls hoot, the whoosh of powerful wings and the rustle of small nocturnal creatures through the bushes beneath our open window. The soft breeze caressed our hot, damp bodies as we listened to the night and drifted off to sleep still in each other's arms.

But it was in the early hours of morning that I was faced with what the war had done to us. Leo often woke me, jerking in his sleep, crying out in despair as he tried desperately to claw his way out of his nightmares. Sometimes all I had to do was cup his cheek and put my head on his chest and he'd wrap his arms around me, his breathing deepening once again. Other times he woke, lathered in sweat and trembling violently. He wouldn't tell me what caused him such distress.

'It's nothing,' he'd mutter. 'Just a bad dream.' He'd kiss me on the cheek. 'Go back to sleep.' But then he would leave the room until just before dawn when he'd come back into bed. There I'd hold him, warming his cold body, and only then would he fall into an exhausted sleep.

I wondered how I could help him. What he'd witnessed at Ohrdruf and the terrible shock of his father's death had been traumatic events that would affect anyone. Onkel Georg's face came to me when I least expected it, dark blood against his pale and lifeless face flashing across my mind when I was on the edge of sleep, milking the cows, driving the tractor, baling the hay or washing the clothes. But it was at night, worrying about Leo, when I heard Tante Elya's heartbroken sobs. She was working as hard as the rest of us and presented a brave face through the day, but she had withdrawn into herself and I wondered if the farm was enough to lift her out of her misery. If only we could find Onkel Tedi or any other members of her family it would give her some joy, but our enquiries through Captain Snopov and the Soviet administration had come to nothing and we'd received no news from the Red Cross. With the chaos that had descended upon Germany it could be months before we'd know anything about their fate. I had to live in hope.

And then all of a sudden there it was: hope.

'It's so beautiful here,' I said to Leo. It was early September, in the final days of harvest, and we were arm in arm, looking out from the stand of ancient birch trees the estate was named after, down over the cropped and bare fields to the silver ribbon of the Dahme River beyond. It was peaceful, as though time had stopped still for just a few moments, the chattering of birds the only counterpoint to the soft breeze dancing with the delicate boughs of gold, sending a small procession of gilded leaves twirling around us to the ground.

He looked at me, his eyes soft. 'It is. And so are you.' He lifted my hand and kissed it, then held it to his chest.

I smiled, then moved his hand to my belly. 'Leo, I'm pregnant.'

He stared at me as he took in the news and then smiled and kissed me tenderly. 'I dreamed about this moment when I was in Ohrdruf . . . I can't tell you how happy I am.' He pulled me close. 'This is the life I always dreamed of with you, here on Gut Birkenhof, bringing up our children,' he whispered.

'Me too.'

'And Mutti will be beside herself,' he said, his hand still on my belly.

Life couldn't get any better.

The harvest was finally in. It was a relief and a profound sense of accomplishment. We'd had help from some in the village, friends and those who understood that, without our harvest, winter would be difficult for our community. But, despite this, there was still a slight air of resentment.

'I don't understand,' I said to Frau Kraus one afternoon a couple of weeks later. It was a rare moment of rest, still warm enough to sit outside in the garden and enjoy the sunshine. Although I felt well, everyone was protective of me, making sure I didn't overdo it. Tante Elya had already begun to knit booties from the unfinished jumper she'd been knitting before the Gestapo's visit, and had started suggesting baby names, Russian and German. 'You make me the happiest grandmother,' she told me time and time again.

'Can you blame them?' Frau Kraus asked. 'You sleep in a warm bed with wood to burn in your stove, flour, eggs and milk to cook with, your own meat to butcher and eat.'

'But we've given the Soviets all the rations they've demanded. Between what the district commander and local mayor's asked for, it's been difficult to fill the quotas. I know it's to be distributed to the local communes, so everyone can eat and stay warm, but we can't feed the entire Soviet Occupied Zone. And we help the villagers with whatever else we have. We need to keep enough to ensure we have milk and meat crops for next year.' I ran my hands through my hair in exasperation. 'It's not like anyone's going to give us what we need to begin again, not the village and not the Soviets.'

'I know,' she said, 'but many don't understand and don't want to understand. They just see what they've always seen: that you have what they don't. It's jealousy, plain and simple.'

I shouldn't have been surprised. In these desperate times, survival had become the prime instinct once again.

I nodded. 'Suffering and hardship can make people bitter.' I thought for a brief moment of Julius, and in my own bitterness hoped that he was incarcerated in a prisoner of war camp. 'I just hope that, with time, it can be like it used to be.'

The soft breeze rustled the leaves of the old oak tree above us. Before long, its limbs would be bare and we'd be turning our thoughts to managing the harsh winter ahead as well as the requests of the communal council.

'It will never be the same again,' she said softly. 'Those in the village who were committed to the Nazi way and followed Hitler blindly, those who vilified your aunt and turned against your family, are now self-professed communists.'

'I can think of two or three people with strong Nazi sympathies who are on the local committees,' I said, pouring cold mint tea into a long glass and handing it to her. 'And the

Soviets tell us that all Germans must bear the guilt and responsibility of what the Nazis have done. There were plenty of us who resisted and many more who disagreed.'

I turned to the sound of footsteps coming down the stone path and frowned. Leo looked furious and Tante Elya was pale. 'What's wrong?'

'We've received a letter from the local committee for land reform.' There were more and more committees being created every month. It was confusing to keep track of them all and the various rules and laws they were supposed to enforce. 'The land reform laws have been issued by the provisional government and now enacted by the local committee.' Leo handed me the letter.

I read the paper carefully. 'Expropriation of lands and agricultural assets belonging to active Nazi Party members and leaders, war criminals and those owning greater than one hundred hectares. These lands will be redistributed to landless farmers, agricultural workers and refugees.'

I was stunned by the words on the page. We owned more than one hundred hectares.

'They'll give it to anyone willing to work the land,' said Leo.

'What about us? We're working the land and providing the local and district communes with produce. We've just brought the harvest in.'

'It's too much,' whispered Frau Kraus, horrified. 'They can't do that to you.'

'We're considered *Junkers*,' said Tante Elya, her voice shaking. 'As if we haven't been through enough! My own countrymen treating us this way. We helped their officers escape during the war, but not even that seems to matter. I can't believe I'm saying this, but maybe we would've been better off with the Americans. They wouldn't treat us like this.'

'I'll be damned if a committee tries to take my ancestral home away from me. The Nazis already tried once,' growled Leo. 'We'll contest this decision,' he said, squeezing his mother's hand. 'Gut Birkenhof is the cornerstone of this district and provides for the community, ensuring the local economy is strong and bringing prosperity to the whole area. It's what you and Vati worked your whole life for. I'll present our case to the committee, as well as how we've actively resisted the Nazi regime and helped the Russians.'

'I only hope they listen,' muttered Frau Kraus.

After our conversation, I wasn't confident they would.

We were waiting in the kitchen when Leo returned from addressing the local committee of the Commission for Land Reform.

'The decision stands,' he said in disbelief. 'Because of the difficulties we suffered as Jewish people during the war, they're willing to extend the grace period from twenty-four hours and give us two weeks to vacate the property.'

'No,' moaned Tante Elya, slumping forward, putting her head in her hands. 'We've been betrayed by my own people.'

'I'm so sorry. I've failed you,' he whispered.

'This is our home.' I felt nothing but shock and incomprehension.

'Everything your father ever worked for ... gone.' The desolation on Tante Elya's face scared me out of my own stupor. I hugged her tight, as though I could stop the fine trembling that racked her slight frame.

'I still have Marienwerder,' I said hopefully. 'We can go there and start again.'

Leo shook his head. 'East Prussia's part of the Soviet zone too and subject to the same Soviet policy and rules. Marienwerder will be expropriated too.' He touched my cheek. 'I'm so sorry, Susie.'

'What will we do?' I whispered, stricken. We'd lost everything. After all we'd been through as opponents to the Nazis, and the support we'd given the Russians during the war. It meant nothing to the Soviet administrative machine.

'We'll go to Berlin,' said Leo, his jaw tight with suppressed emotion. 'They won't let us stay in the district.'

There was no time to think about what was ahead of us, no time to wallow in grief for what we had lost. If we were going to make a new life for the three of us, we had to do as much as we could before we were ripped from our home. Within the week, my letter informing me of the expropriation of the Marienwerder estate arrived and I knew then that Berlin was indeed our only option.

Numb with shock, with the help of Frau Kraus and Hans, we organised what we could take and what had to remain behind. But our lives were not the only ones being turned upside down. Frau Kraus and Hans no longer had their jobs. And the way our small community had functioned for generations had changed irrevocably – I wondered what would become of the village.

'What will you and Hans do?' I asked Frau Kraus, as we sorted through the kitchenware.

'I'll find something,' she said, helping me pull the pots and pans from the cupboard. 'Herr Wenck needs somebody in the shop. I could work there. The Soviets will probably realise that they need to keep Hans as forester. There's nobody as experienced as him.'

'That's a blessing at least. You've both been with us for so long . . . It doesn't seem right that you have to suffer too.'

She separated pots into two piles. 'You'll need a few to cook with. The rest I'll take back to our place and store until you're resettled.'

'Thank you, Frau Kraus. You and Hans have done so much for us and now we leave you with nothing.' Tears welled in my eyes.

'Stop it. You're family to us and we'll do whatever we can for you.' She pulled me to her, the smell of freshly baked bread on her apron, familiar and comforting, making the tears fall afresh. 'We have enough for ourselves. We'll be fine.'

'I'm going to miss you.'

'And I'll miss you too.' She kissed my head. 'Enough of that. We have work to do. The Soviets have taken enough and we don't want to leave anything useful behind for the looters to come in and take.'

It was the last night in our home. We'd spent the day planning and packing, but now as darkness filled the house, memories crept in like silent intruders.

'I can't leave,' said Tante Elya, gazing around the parlour. The shadows cast from the candles on the table made her and Leo's faces appear ghoulish, but they were only hollow with exhaustion. 'This is the last place Georg was, where he died. I still feel him here.'

I shivered, the hairs on my arms raised. I didn't believe in ghosts, but . . . the image of him slumped on the floor, blood staining the rug, and the feel of his skin as I'd dressed him for his burial had never left me.

'He'd want you to move on,' said Leo, frowning with worry. He glanced at me helplessly. 'We need you and now there's the baby . . .'

'This is where we had the happiest memories, watching the two of you grow up.' She picked up Onkel Georg's pipe and packed it carefully in the small box we were taking with us.

'We'll always have those memories,' I said, placing a suitcase near the doorway. In it I still carried the wooden horse Leo had carved for me as a child. It was the sentimental objects like Onkel Georg's pipe, the samovar, Leo's balalaika, my little horse and the rings on my hand that carried the most meaning, holding precious memories of the past. As long as we had them, we'd never forget.

'You and Leo must make new memories and start again with your baby. You're young enough, but me . . .' She stared off into the distance.

'We'll all find a way.' I crossed the room quickly to hug her, wondering how many times she'd comforted me over the years. This place had given me refuge as a child after the devastation of losing my own family, and the years since had been filled with warmth and love. But the future lay ahead and a new chapter of our lives was ready to begin. 'At least we're together.' It was all that mattered.

*

The following morning Tante Elya didn't come down for breakfast. She was still in bed asleep when I went to her room but something about the way she lay struck me as odd. Then I saw the sleeping powders that the doctor had prescribed her after Onkel Georg's death and I knew what she'd done. It was like a bad dream. I tried to rouse her, but her skin was cold. She was gone.

'Leo!' I screamed, as the sobs ripped from my throat.

He was there in an instant, standing in the doorway, rooted to the spot and staring at me in disbelief.

I shook my head in despair. 'She's gone,' I whispered, his pale face blurred by my tears. I reached out to him and, in a couple of strides, he was beside me, holding me tight, unable to tear his eyes from his mother's peaceful but lifeless face. With a shuddering breath he cupped her cheek with his hand, his eyes widening with the confirmation of his fears.

'She didn't want to leave Gut Birkenhof,' I said softly. 'She didn't want to leave your father.'

Leo nodded, kissing his mother's limp hand, before silent sobs racked his frame. We clung to each other.

A little while later I realised Frau Kraus stood trembling behind us.

'She's at peace now,' she said, her arms around us both, and I knew she was right. This was where Tante Elya belonged and nobody, not the Nazis or the Soviets, could force her to go.

We left the house as ordered, with Tante Elya, and buried her next to Georg in the village cemetery. She was reunited with her beloved husband once more, under the tiny white flowers of the linden tree. People who had celebrated our wedding only three months earlier filed past to pay their respects and I nodded, murmuring a few words of thanks, but I could barely believe we'd lost her. Their faces blended and merged with each other and all that kept me standing was Leo.

'I can't believe she's gone,' said Leo later, staring out the window of Frau Kraus's house towards the silent and empty estate. 'After everything she endured through the war . . . she was a survivor, and now . . .' He shrugged helplessly.

I wrapped my arms around him. 'You know the Nazis took away her reason to live when they took your father. All that kept her going afterwards was you and me, ensuring our happiness and rebuilding Gut Birkenhof for our future. Once she'd seen us married with a child on the way, I think her will to live began to fade. When the estate was taken from us, it was too much for her.' Even the strongest had their tipping point and Tante Elya had suffered so much heartbreak and loss over the course of her life, denting and weakening her until the pain had become unendurable.

'I can't stay here anymore,' he said, his voice catching.

'We leave for Berlin in the morning,' I said, kissing him.

'No, I didn't mean here, although I never want to set foot in this village ever again.' He shifted restlessly. 'I've failed you all. Mutti and Vati are gone before their time, and the estate too.'

I drew back to see the torment on his face. 'No, Leo. It's not your fault.' I touched his cheek. 'You couldn't have prevented any of this. Your mother made her choice, she did things her way and it was what she wanted in the end. She'd want us to stay strong, live life and find our peace with everything that's happened.'

He shook his head, brow creased. 'I've had enough of Berlin and Germany. Everything reminds me of what we've endured and what we've lost.'

'Where do you want to go?' I asked, shocked at this unexpected revelation.

'America. It's where my mother's family is, where my parents wanted to go. We'll be able to start again. I'll be able to give you and the baby a good life, a life you deserve ... What do you think?'

He leaned against the windowsill, his troubled brown eyes searching my face. I touched the diamond of my engagement ring, my link to Tante Elya. There was a kind of symmetry to the idea. Like her, we could do things our way rather than enduring a life that was dictated to us. We'd had enough of being told what we could and couldn't do and Tante Elya would be happy for us to be with the only family she had left, in a country that valued its freedom and civil liberties.

'We have to look to the future. Maybe it's time to start again, somewhere new and far away from this madness.' I reached out and took his hand. 'Yes, let's go to America.'

His shoulders sagged as the tension flowed out of him. He enfolded me in his arms, his body trembling, and I knew he was finally shedding all the tears he'd been holding back since the death of his father.

24

As soon as we arrived in Berlin, we visited Captain Snopov at the Soviet Military Administration headquarters in Karlshorst. Although the Soviets had liberated Berlin, it had been agreed that all four Allied liberation forces – Soviet, American, British and French – would govern the capital together, each through their own separate sectors.

Captain Snopov was part of the Soviet team of administrators sent in to create order in the eastern part of the devastated city that the Soviets now controlled, but from what I'd already seen on our journey in, it seemed that they were barely treading water. Little had changed since my nursing days – there were crumbling and blackened ruins everywhere we looked and the streets were filled with scurrying people with shocked or wary expressions. Berliners had always been resilient, but the city had descended into some kind of post-apocalyptic hell and it needed all the help it could get.

Snopov couldn't believe what had happened with the Commission for Land Reform, but was helpless to overturn its ruling. Instead he offered us work as translators.

'Just as well you weren't here any sooner.' He looked terribly tired with black smudges below his eyes. 'Berlin's still recovering from those last terrible days of the war,' he explained. 'At first there was no electricity, gas or fresh water. The sewage overflowed and made its way into the waterways and river. Then bodies piled up in the streets along with the uncollected rubbish.' He shook his head. 'It was a nightmare. It didn't take long for disease to spread across the city. Of course we arranged for local residents to be organised into teams to remove rubble from the streets and thoroughfares, and to find housing for those who were homeless. We worked around the clock to get services up and running as quickly as possible so that there was clean water and some power, not to mention organising ration cards, but we didn't account for the flood of people arriving every day.' He shrugged his shoulders in helplessness. 'People are living in bunkers, ruined buildings – even tunnels. Infectious diseases are on the rise again and the sanitation problems don't seem to be improving quickly enough. We can't stem the public health issues and now winter's here I don't know how many will die because of disease, or simple exposure.'

I was shocked at the state of the city. 'I have to go back to nursing,' I said. 'Even if for only a few months before the baby comes in March. You need all the medical help you can get.' Although we were now planning our emigration to America, and would likely be gone within six months to a year, Berlin needed the help of every one of its citizens to get back on its feet.

'Very good,' said Snopov, nodding. 'Try the Charité. It was damaged during the bombings, but it's still the most prestigious hospital in Berlin. They'll be grateful for someone like you.'

I went to see the senior sisters at the Charité. The German Red Cross had been dissolved, but many of the nurses I had worked with before were still in Berlin.

'We're desperate for nurses,' said one of the sisters I had worked with at Beelitz, as she pushed a trolley down the long corridor. 'The Soviets have dismissed all staff with Nazi membership or previous dealings with the party.'

'So you're recruiting?'

She nodded. 'We're lucky here at the Charité. The Soviets consider it an important hospital and some departments have been given new premises.'

'Aren't all hospitals important?'

'You would think so, but many of them have been dismantled, and equipment and supplies sent back to Moscow for reparations. Everything's remained intact here and department heads continue to run the hospital as they've always done.'

'That's a relief.'

'There's plenty of work. The most pressing problems are the infectious and venereal diseases. Soviet administrators are overseeing the new public health program and clinics have been set up all over the city. Anyone can go to them. We're still dealing with typhus, dysentery and typhoid fever outbreaks from the refugee camps, not to mention tuberculosis. Then there are the casualties from the building collapses and fires.

The majority of the city's residential areas have been bombed out, and with the flood of displaced Germans from the east, people will live in anything – anywhere – just to have a roof over their heads. We're short-staffed and the wards are overflowing. There's a shortage of beds, drugs and equipment and still patients keep coming, but you're lucky you weren't here a few months ago when it was hell on earth.'

I began at the Charité almost immediately. And I was quick to discover the true situation of the city when Leo and I began our search for accommodation.

'I can't believe it,' I whispered to Leo as we walked the suburban streets, navigating dangerous debris and ruined buildings wherever we went. Only a few years earlier Berlin was the most glamourous and vibrant city in Germany and now it was a wreck. It was so much worse than I had imagined – the artillery attacks of the last battles through the streets had been the final blow to the grand city. Now it was broken and scarred. 'It's like another planet.'

'Sewage pipe,' warned Leo in a strangled voice, guiding me around a gaping hole in the footpath. I gagged, putting my hand across my nose and mouth.

'How are we ever going to find something?' I cast my gaze around the dilapidated apartment buildings, noticing groups of people huddled in sheltered doorways and behind walls where there previously had been rooms intact. 'We can't even find a couple of rooms with running water and a functioning bathroom.' Although the Soviets were our liberators, the price for our freedom from the Third Reich was steep and so many had paid the ultimate price with their lives: dying in the weeks and months after the war finished from disease, sickness, exposure and starvation. Life for most was more difficult than it had been during the war.

'Don't worry. We'll find something,' said Leo, squeezing my hand in encouragement. We stayed with friends from the resistance until a few weeks later when we met up with one of the contacts who had hidden Leo after his breakout from Ohrdruf.

'I've been a communist all my life and looked up to the Soviets, but I never imagined anything like this occurring at their hands,' the contact said, shaking his head. 'They're as bad as the Nazis. We've gone from the frying pan into the fire. The sooner we set up our own German government, the sooner our Soviet occupiers will be gone.' He went on to tell us of the rapes and beatings the Soviets had committed with the fall of Berlin.

'I can't believe the state of the city,' Leo said. 'It's going to take some time to get Berlin back on its feet.'

'I don't know that it can ever be the same again,' the contact said with finality. 'Too much has happened here.'

But it seemed we were in luck, if luck was what we could call it. The contact showed us an apartment in one of the Wilhelmine buildings in Prenzlauer Berg surprisingly still standing. The area had had its fair share of air raids but had escaped the devastating damage of other districts. The apartment block next door had been bombed and was nothing more than blackened ruins and rubble. One side of our building was damaged, with the lower apartments exposed to the open, gutted by fire and filled with loose debris. Fire had destroyed the fifth-floor apartment and partially damaged the ceiling of the fourth-floor apartment we were looking at.

'I don't know,' whispered Leo, shaking his head as we surveyed the apartment. 'I don't want to bring you to a place that's unsafe.'

'Leo, we have to take it,' I said, grasping his arm. 'We've just about outstayed our welcome where we are and we might not get another chance to find something like this. We have running water, a working stove and, beside the ceiling damage and a few cracks in the walls, an intact apartment.'

'Haven't you heard of the building collapses across the city? I couldn't put you and the baby at risk.' I thought immediately of Johann trapped under the rubble of his house after the air raid. But I refused to live in fear of what might be any longer.

'All the apartments in this building are taken and everyone's been living in them for months without any problems. It can't be too bad. We've seen people live in much worse.' Leo's frown told me that I hadn't completely convinced him. 'Please, Leo. Let's give it a try.' I gazed up at him beseechingly. 'We won't be here for long and I want to be settled well before the baby comes.'

Despite all its problems, we knew how precious and sought after this apartment was and we soon moved in. Frau Kraus and Hans, who had been retained on the estate as forester, brought across the rest of our boxes and a few pieces of furniture.

'Now it feels like home,' said Frau Kraus, surveying the results of our day's work. We had three rooms: a kitchen, a bedroom and a sitting room. The toilet was off the stairwell and shared by four other apartments on the same floor. The small sofa and table were dressed with cushions and tablecloth. Candles sat in each room as the electricity was intermittent, often only on for a couple of hours in the morning and in the evening.

'Not for too long,' I said, glancing at the peeling wall plaster and the tar-paper-covered hole in the ceiling. 'We've submitted our emigration papers and we've been assured that we'll be granted priority for an American visa because we're both displaced persons and Leo's a Jew who survived Nazi persecution.'

'When will you go?' Frau Kraus asked as she poured tea at our tiny table.

'It could take some time to hear back. It has to do with quotas. I doubt it will be before the baby's born.' I placed my hand over my belly. I'd begun to feel little flutters. 'But I'll continue working for as long as I can. We have to save for the passage and to start again in New York.'

She squeezed my hand. 'You'll soon finally have what you've always wanted: your own family. That's what's most important. The rest will fall into place.'

I nodded. 'After everything that's happened, I don't care where we are, as long as Leo and I are together. And when our baby arrives, my world will be complete.'

I was working in one of the new clinics set up to treat girls and women. Venereal disease, including gonorrhoea and syphilis, had skyrocketed since the end of the war as a result of the many rapes perpetrated by Soviet soldiers.

One day a young girl of sixteen came in to the clinic. 'I can't tell my family I'm here,' she said desperately. She was thin like most Berliners, but not as bad as some girls whose ribs and pelvis were sharply defined under the worn fabric of their dresses.

'I'm not one of those girls,' she whispered, when I told her she'd contracted a venereal disease. 'I had no choice.' I helped her sit up on the cold hard surface of the gynaeco-logical table. 'Soviet soldiers came to our house when I was alone and raped me. I'd never been with a man before and I couldn't tell my mother when she got home,' she said, her voice breaking. 'When more soldiers came I begged their captain to let me become his girlfriend. It was the only way to protect my mother and me and ensure our survival. He's good to me and gives us gifts of corned meat, sugar and butter. It's a small price to pay, but he'll toss me aside if he finds out I'm infected with a disease.' She began to sob and all I could do was put my arm around her in comfort.

We all did surprising things when our survival and the survival of our loved ones depended on it. But it didn't erase the guilt and the shame. I knew that much. Thoughts of Julius and all that he'd done to me and to our family came rushing back. Although I had no idea what had happened to him after the war, I could only hope that there had been justice for his crimes. At the very least, it would be a cold day in hell before I would ever forgive him.

I was desperate to share my despair and deep sadness for these women and girls, and I missed Marika more than ever. There was only so much I could do to help their wretched situations and some part of me felt guilty for being happily married and pregnant, excited to be starting a family. I could have been one of those raped girls if I'd stayed in Berlin.

Thankfully I could speak to Leo.

'It's been a terrible week,' I said, one night in November as we huddled in bed under the eiderdown we'd brought with us from home. Coal for the stove was hard to come by and we could only buy enough to cook one meal and heat the room in the evening. It didn't help that the cold seeped through the cracks in the external wall of the kitchen, which I had to seal with wet newspaper every now and then. Overnight the temperature dropped and the water was frozen in the pipes by morning. 'It's bad enough seeing the desperate state of women and girls pregnant as a result of rape, or even those who've chosen to stay with a Russian soldier for protection, but when I see uterine infections and gynaecological problems after badly performed backyard abortions, it's too much. What's worse is that penicillin, the most effective drug of choice, is in short supply in the Soviet zone and there are such strict protocols about its dispensing that many aren't even treated properly.'

'After everything that's happened to them.' Leo shook his head and sighed. 'But people will do anything to make it through,' he whispered. 'I saw it at Ohrdruf many times.' I knew then that he understood what I'd come to learn. 'We're the fortunate ones.'

'We are.' I kissed him deeply. The bone-deep weariness I felt after a long shift at the clinic disappeared instantly. Even the gnawing ache in my belly from the constant hunger faded so it was barely noticeable. I sighed with pleasure as he kissed my neck and throat and I left the troubles of the day behind me as I surrendered to the joy of Leo's touch.

*

The next morning I was finishing writing up some notes at the clinic when our receptionist came in to see me.

'There's someone here to see you.'

'One of my patients?' I asked, looking up from the patient records.

She shook her head. 'A man, Herr Siebenborn. He said he knows you.' The room swam in and out of focus. It couldn't be.

'Susie, are you all right?' She put a hand on my arm.

I nodded and swallowed hard. 'Tell him I'm too busy,' I said curtly. 'And if he comes back, tell him I don't want to see him.'

She nodded. 'Of course. I understand.'

So Julius was alive and well. I was shaking with fury now that I was over the shock. He had no right to come back into my life. The sooner we left for America, the better.

I felt fortunate indeed when I was transferred to the maternity ward in early December. My work at the clinic gave me insight into the situation so many of the new mothers had found themselves in, giving birth to babies of unknown Soviet soldiers or their Russian lovers. Amidst the chaos of Berlin, and despite the often difficult circumstances they were born into, babies were still a joy, a new life to celebrate, and I couldn't help but look forward to my time as I cared for the new mothers and helped support them as they came to terms with their new life and responsibility. The wards were full and the work was relentless, but I was happy.

'I didn't expect to feel this way,' said a first-time mother. I was showing her how to swaddle her baby girl on the crisp white bed sheet and checking her over in the process. She hadn't lost much of her birth weight and was doing well.

She raised her little fist into the air like a defiant rebel and broke out into a loud cry before I had finished.

'What do you mean?' I brought the baby to her to breast-feed. Other babies' cries punctuated the soft murmur of new mothers across the ward.

'I didn't want her,' she confessed. 'I'm on my own. I was a flak helper and I went home at the end of the war, but our home was bombed out and I couldn't find my family. I decided to come back to Berlin, thinking they might be here, but they're not. I filed missing persons' reports with the Red Cross but I've heard nothing yet.'

We still hadn't heard about Onkel Tedi either.

I nodded. 'Don't give up hope yet. It'll take time.' The Red Cross were bringing in sick and injured people who'd been found to the hospital all the time. They were the good stories, but they couldn't cope with the numbers of enquiries about missing people, especially when those who were lost often had no official papers with them. Between the dislocation of families at the end of the war, missing soldiers, families fleeing before the Red Army, people returning home to find their homes destroyed and loved ones gone, and then the expulsion of Germans from the east making them displaced people, it was a logistical nightmare bringing families together. It was no wonder people were missing everywhere.

'I know,' she said sadly. 'I got pregnant then. The baby's father and I aren't married and I was worried he'd abandon us, but the minute I saw her, I knew that everything would be fine. I love her more than I've ever loved anybody and I'll do everything to make sure she's safe and looked after.' I readjusted the pillows around her so that the baby's head was at the right height, showing her how to place the baby's mouth around the nipple. Immediately the infant's crying stopped.

'What about the father?' I asked gently.

'He fell in love with her too, and he's asked me to marry him. We're going to be a family.' She'd lost her family and was desperate to create her own. I knew the feeling.

'I'm so happy for you,' I said, patting her arm. Babies brought hope and joy and we could all do with a little more in the world.

At the end of my shift, I looked up from the notes I was finishing to a familiar face. It was Marika. I couldn't believe my eyes, and it was only when I was hugging her tightly that I really believed she was there.

'What are you doing here?' I asked, tears sliding down my cheeks. 'I thought you were with your parents in Trebbin.'

It turned out she'd heard about Onkel Georg's death and had decided to join me at the Charité. 'It's been over a year since Johann died. I have to do something useful and Berlin needs us more than ever.' She leaned in towards me. 'I could have gone to the American zone where the facilities are better, but when I learnt how desperately people need us here, I had to come.' She smiled ruefully. 'So here I am, and the good news is that we're working together.'

'That's wonderful! I can't tell you how good it is to see you.'

'And you too but it seems we have a lot to catch up on.' She eyed my pregnant belly. 'We're a team. Let's look after these women in true Marika and Susie style until it's your turn to enjoy the expert care and attention,' she said, grinning.

*

It was already one of the coldest winters I'd ever experienced, but I was determined to make this Christmas special. Marika, Frau Kraus and Hans were joining us and I'd queued for hours since before dawn in the week prior to get the small rations of butter, eggs, sugar and meat that we were entitled to. Marika came home with me after work. As we alighted from the bus, pulling our coats tight against the bitter wind, I noticed a couple of men loitering outside one of the blocks of grey apartments.

'I don't like the look of them. Let's walk on the other side of the road,' I said in a low voice, guiding Marika onto the street. 'Leo's warned me to be careful of bandits.'

Even with the continued Soviet patrols, we'd heard reports of bands of disaffected, desperate, homeless and hungry souls, deserted soldiers or opportunistic criminals, looting homes and businesses and attacking innocent citizens. Petty crime, violent attacks and homicides flourished amid the chaos of the city and people often went missing, many of them among the unidentified dead from disease, violence, and the collapse of derelict buildings.

In the American sector, which encompassed the south-west of Berlin, resources had been brought into the city to aid its recovery. Food was more available, buildings were being made safe to live in and I knew that disease was better managed through stringent public health measures, properly trained staff and the availability of medicines and lifesaving equipment that hadn't been stripped from their hospitals. But I couldn't leave the Soviet sector when I knew how much we were needed here.

'It's not the Berlin I recognise,' Marika said as we walked down the other side, both of us keeping an eye on the men until we reached the door of my apartment building. And I had to agree. Berlin would never be the same again.

I was able to make a small batch of biscuits and served a tasty meat and turnip stew with potatoes. It was a far cry from the Gut Birkenhof Christmas feasts, but we were better off than many others in the city. The coal didn't last long and we had to wear our coats, but at least it was warmer than outside. A couple of the bigger cracks in the kitchen had widened and travelled down the wall and I had stuffed them with more newspaper to keep out the cold. Leo played Christmas carols and Russian folk tunes on the balalaika and we all sang along. It was difficult celebrating without Onkel Georg and Tante Elya, but we felt grateful for what we still had and for the people around us.

'This time next year, you'll have your little one,' said Frau Kraus as I shifted in my seat. I was six months pregnant and beginning to get a little uncomfortable.

'This time next year, they'll probably be in America,' said Marika, pouting.

'Then you'll have to come and visit us,' said Leo, smiling.

'Give me your hand,' I said to Marika, resting her hand on my protruding belly where the baby was kicking. 'See, the baby agrees. Maybe you should join us in New York.'

'Maybe I will,' she said, her eyes suddenly misty. It hit me that I didn't know how we would cope separated by an ocean from the three people dearest to us. My heart ached for Marika. I wanted her to be happy again, as Leo and I were.

Leo squeezed my hand reassuringly. 'Nineteen forty-six is a new year, the war is over and anything is possible. Let's toast to the future,' he said, raising his glass.

*

It was early February and I was trudging home through the snow, glad that I only had another week at work. I had intended to stop work around Christmas but the hospital was short-staffed and, as we needed to save for our new life in America and I was still feeling comfortable, I had stayed on for as long as I could. But now the long hours on my feet were taking their toll and Leo, Marika and the matron had persuaded me that it was time for me to rest and get ready for the baby. We already had a crib in the corner of our bedroom and a few baby blankets and tiny nightgowns, as well as the booties, jackets and pants that Tante Elya and Frau Kraus had knitted.

I shivered, as though someone was watching me, and glanced behind me, then down the street. But I saw nothing to fear, only a car driving by, women carrying the evening's groceries back home in string bags, children calling to each other as they played in the afternoon gloom.

I was so looking forward to putting my feet up, and to the hot meal that I knew Leo was preparing ... and one of his blissful foot massages before bed. It was in bed that I felt closest to him, when he'd whisper his heart's desires to me.

'I can't wait to hold our child in my arms,' he'd tell me as he'd wrap himself around me, his arms protectively around my belly, sharing his body warmth, until I'd melt into the mattress. If sleep was slow or I sighed and shifted with discomfort, he was attentive. 'There's nobody but you and me,' he'd whisper in our love nest. 'I want to spoil you, make you understand how much I adore you,' he'd murmur, nibbling my earlobe, kissing my shoulder and working his way down my body.

'I love you,' is all I could say, threading my fingers through his thick locks and surrendering to his touch.

A loud crack pulled me from my musings as I pushed open the door to our building. All the hairs on my arms were on end. Something was wrong. Confused, I stepped into the foyer to the eerie sound of the building groaning before the noise of smashing windows reached me and the cacophony of what sounded like terracotta and glass hitting the ground outside. I stepped back to the arched doorway in consternation. A sudden rumbling and vibration under my feet had me rooted to the spot in terror as dust rained on me from above. I looked up dumbly to find the ceiling of the vestibule shuddering as a roar erupted, growing into an almighty crescendo. I watched, as though in slow motion, as the ceiling bulged towards me like a distended belly and gave way. I realised in horror that the building was collapsing. Somewhere far away I could hear screaming as the internal walls disintegrated around me under the pressure of the imploding building, the impact throwing me to the floor. My last dazed thoughts were for Leo waiting for me upstairs before everything went black.

25

I woke on a soft feather bed, drowsy and limp. A corner lamp cast a subdued light across the darkened room and, from between the partially drawn curtains, I could see that it was night. I tried to move. A groan escaped my lips and excruciating pain rippled through my body. My hands immediately flew to my abdomen as I tried to remember what had happened. I wasn't dead, but I wasn't at home or in hospital either. I didn't recognise the place I was in.

'Leo,' I croaked, hoping that he was nearby. A face bobbed into view, blue eyes I knew.

'Julius?' I whispered, the past and present colliding in my head, making it spin out of control. I closed my eyes, thinking I was still in a dream, but when I opened them he was there, staring at me in concern. How could it be?

'You're awake,' he said. 'How are you feeling?'

'What happened to me? What are you doing here?'

He reached out to touch me, and I recoiled from him in alarm. I could barely move with the pain, but I tried to sit up, wincing at the pounding in my head. It felt like it would split in two and I closed my eyes briefly as I carefully rested back on the soft pillow.

'You were in a building collapse yesterday.'

The noise came back to me, the roar of what sounded like a freight train, and the memory of the ceiling bursting open like an overripe fruit. 'The baby? Is the baby all right?' Panic bloomed through me, my hands over my skin, feeling for movement, but there was nothing. I looked up at him, fearful of hearing the truth.

'The doctor said that he could hear the baby's heartbeat, but because of the trauma you suffered you need bedrest. He's worried that you could still haemorrhage and go into early labour.'

Dread swirled in my belly. 'Leo. He was waiting for me upstairs ... I have to tell him what's happened ... let him know where I am.' I tried to focus, feeling disoriented and confused and the thumping in my head preventing me from thinking clearly. 'Where am I?'

'Pankow, my apartment.' Julius sat on the edge of the bed and took my hand. 'There was nowhere else for you to go and I knew I could get you the best care here.'

'What?' I pulled my hand away, repulsed by his touch and wishing I could get out of bed and as far away from him as possible, but the throbbing in my head and my back was crippling. 'I don't understand.'

'You were pulled out and rushed to hospital after your apartment building collapsed,' he said. 'But with all the terrible casualties, there were no beds for those with less serious injuries. You were very lucky, the doorway protected you: no broken bones, no evidence of internal injuries, only cuts and bruises. After checking you over, the doctor prescribed you sedatives and told me to take you home and keep you on bedrest until the baby arrives.'

I frowned, trying to make sense of it. I remembered flashes then: coming home to Leo and opening the door to our building, the enormous crack and roar as the building came crashing down, the shouting as I lay on the ground, looking up at the leaden sky above me, the bright lights of the emergency department and the screaming and crying that made me retreat into my dark and silent world.

I clutched his arm. 'Leo? Has he been found?'

He shook his head. 'They're still digging and sifting through the debris. It's only been a day and it will take time to find everyone.'

I stilled for a moment as I took this in. Everything seemed hazy. I struggled to sit up, but a wave of dizziness forced me flat once more.

'You're not in any fit state to move. I had my own doctor check in on you this morning and he agreed with the hospital. Doctor Neis is one of the best in Berlin. You need bedrest – if not for you, then for your baby's sake.'

'But Leo,' I said in anguish. 'I have to find him.' Nothing was going to keep me away from him again.

'We'll have word as soon as he's found. You rest and recover. I'll continue to look for him.'

'Why would you do that?' I tried to glare at him, but it hurt my face. I felt trapped and the feelings of powerlessness and vulnerability I'd experienced with him before came rushing back.

'For you. He's your husband and you need him.'

As much as I didn't trust him, I had my baby to think of. I grabbed the front of his shirt in desperation. 'Promise me you won't stop until you find him,' I said with clenched teeth. I hated relying on him after everything that had happened between us.

'I promise.'

I collapsed back against the pillows. My head felt like it was going to explode and hot, sharp pokers of pain shot through my body. I didn't like it but he was right. I wasn't going anywhere. He was all I had.

Something brought me to the surface of sleep. It was light, even behind my closed lids.

'Leo?' I murmured, still fuzzy headed with sleep.

I slowly opened my eyes to find Julius placing a tray on the bedside table. I flinched, trying to sink further into the soft mattress. Then I remembered the events of the past few days.

'Have you found Leo?'

Julius shook his head regretfully. 'It's still early days.'

Tears filled my eyes and trickled down my cheeks, dripping onto the silk pyjamas.

'You have to stay calm for the baby,' he said, pouring water into a glass.

Doctor Neis had been to see me the morning before, checking on my condition and on the baby. He'd confirmed what Julius had told me, that the next few weeks were touch and go. I'd sustained soft-tissue trauma to my abdomen and pelvis and although the baby seemed fine, bedrest was the best precaution against possible bleeding and early labour. It was too soon for the baby to come. I'd been hysterical during his visit, desperate to find Leo but desperate to keep our child safe too. I couldn't risk it. This was Leo's child and he'd already lost so much.

Everything had been hazy since then, enveloped in a fog of drug-induced sleep that the doctor had insisted upon, but the frustration that my body wouldn't do what I wanted was more than I could stand. I struggled to sit up despite the pain. Julius tried to help me, propping pillows behind me.

'I can do it myself,' I snapped, forcing myself upright and lifting my heavily bandaged leg to get comfortable. The pain in my back was terrible after lying down for so long. The curtains had been opened to reveal parkland next to a small river below. Julius's luxurious apartment wasn't far from where Leo and I had been living.

My eyes narrowed, giving voice to the question that had plagued me since I'd arrived. 'What were you doing at our apartment building? How did you find me at the clinic?' I asked roughly. I couldn't believe that he'd imagined I'd want anything to do with him ever again.

Julius got up and paced the room, his face unreadable. 'I . . . regret what I did to you . . . and to Leo.' His face flushed at my outraged expression.

'You mean his service obligation letter and his transfer to Buchenwald?' I asked bluntly, wanting him to finally admit it.

His eyes slipped away guiltily from my face and he refused to answer, like the coward that he was. But his expression was enough for me to know the truth and I could barely contain the burst of rage that shot through me.

'I hate you,' I hissed. I only wished I could've risen from that bed to stab him through the heart before walking away forever.

Julius ignored my outburst and continued to pace. 'I saw him at Karlshorst, although he didn't see me, and I heard that you were married. It didn't take much to find out where you work. But when you wouldn't see me at the clinic, after weeks of deliberation I decided to visit you and Leo together, I . . . I owed you both that much. I was waiting near your apartment block that day, waiting for you to come home.' A look of horror crossed his face. 'I saw the building begin to collapse just as you went inside . . . I couldn't get there quickly enough. I tried to find you, and with the others who came, we dug you out.'

'You got me out?'

He nodded, raking a shaking hand through his greying hair. 'I helped. I just wanted to see you to tell you that I was sorry.'

'You're sorry.' I was shaking with rage. 'You put Leo and my family through hell.'

He dropped his head. 'I know. I've had plenty of time to think about it, but I'm in a position to help now.'

I stared at him a moment. 'Then find Leo.'

It was then that I glimpsed my reflection in the full-length mirror pushed to the corner of the room.

'Oh!' I gasped. I took a tentative hand to my head, lightly tracing the blood-encrusted bandages, one side of my face livid with blue and purple bruises.

'You were lucky. They're only minor injuries,' he said, hovering anxiously by the bed. 'But I remember how it felt after the Kaiserhof collapsed.'

I pushed the shirt back and gingerly touched the darkened areas across my shoulder before lifting it above my protruding belly, the taut skin bruised around a graze on the same side as my shoulder. The baby was still very quiet and hadn't moved since the accident, but I'd been told it was to be expected for a few days.

'What are you doing here?' I asked, exhausted, leaning back against the pillows. 'How did you get this apartment when the rest of Berlin lives in squalor?'

'I'm helping the Soviets restore the transportation system in their zone. They've given me this apartment and I have access to whatever I need: good food, good doctors.'

'I expected you to be helping the Americans, or to be long gone.'

He sat in the chair next to the bed. 'I *was* going to leave Germany. I had a plan . . . but I'd left it too late and I was captured by an advance Soviet patrol.'

'What happened to you?' I was curious in spite of myself. Although I hated being here, it was strange, disquieting even, being in the same room with him. I didn't know how to feel, how to reconcile what he'd done in the past with this act of pulling me from the building.

'I spent a couple of months in a makeshift camp until I was processed,' he said. 'The Soviets learnt of my connection to the resistance and my role in the assassination plot against Hitler.' I shut my eyes briefly and grimaced. Julius always knew what to say at the right time, embellishing the truth if he had to. 'The condition of my release was that I would assist them in bringing Berlin and the Soviet zone back to working order. They've been trying to exert their influence and power on Berlin ever since they arrived. If they control Berlin, they control the future of Germany and affect the rest of Europe.' He leaned in towards me. 'But I've heard that the Americans and British are going to merge their zones. The Western allies will do all they can to stop communism.'

I shook my head impatiently. I'd heard enough. Julius had landed on his feet, as he always did, while Leo and I had lost everything. I had to know about Leo. 'I want to see the building for myself.'

'I don't think that's a good idea.'

'Why not?' A wave of fury rose through me, pushing the cold, dark fear crawling in my veins aside. I swung my legs over the side of the bed and stood quickly, bolts of pain shooting through my back. Julius jumped to his feet in alarm as I swayed dangerously, the pendant light in the room a kaleidoscope.

'Please, Susie, don't. It's for your own good. Lie back down before you fall down.' The sight of tears in his eyes made me stop. 'I know you hate me, but I promise you I'm trying to protect you.'

The room was still spinning, but panic was building inside me too. 'What's going on, Julius?' I allowed him to support my weight as he guided me onto the bed.

He kneeled in front of me and took my hands. This time I didn't pull away. A chill came over me.

'Susie, very few have been brought out of the building alive and they were all in the first two days ... There was a fire, making some of the bodies unrecognisable. They don't expect to find any others alive now. Leo hasn't been found in the building, at the hospitals, or anywhere. The authorities assume that he's one of the dead.'

'Leo's dead?' I stared at him. But people went missing all the time – I knew that for a fact. It didn't mean they were dead. There was still a chance that Leo had been pulled out and was alive somewhere. I was right here, not far from our apartment, and alive.

'We can't know for sure, but the likelihood increases with each day.'

'You're wrong. He can't be dead. Our life is just beginning . . .' I pulled my hands free, unwilling to admit it could be true. But the horror was welling within me as a little voice of reason transported me back to that day and the weight of the building crashing towards the ground. Leo had been on the fourth floor and was likely dead upon impact. I swayed as the unthinkable hit me. If Leo was dead . . . how could I go on without him? I understood Tante Elya's desire to go with Onkel Georg now, but I couldn't give in to my overwhelming grief, even knowing I would never touch Leo's beloved face again. I had our child to think of.

Julius looked stricken. 'You have to accept it, Susie. I loved Leo, despite what you might think. We were family. I've lost them too – Georg, Elya and Leo. You're all I have left now. We have each other.'

'No!' I said, furious. 'You have no right to grieve for them. Go away and leave me alone.' I shoved him in the chest. I needed to be on my own. I wrapped my arms around the baby inside me as though I could protect it from all the harshness of the world.

In the small hours of the morning I went into labour early, my waters breaking on the parquetry floor as I rose from the bed. The contractions started hard and fast and, counting the interval between the contractions, I knew the baby was coming soon. All I could think about was Leo and how he wasn't here to welcome his child into the world.

'Julius,' I called out across the hallway. He was up in an instant and by my bedside. 'The baby's coming.' He looked at me, horrified. 'I have to get to the hospital.' The pain in my belly and back was excruciating, like hot knives stabbing me, and I'd begun to bleed profusely.

Julius took me to the municipal hospital in Pankow; there had been no time to go to the Charité. It was a quick birth but I didn't remember much of it. I was haemorrhaging, light-headed and ethereal one minute, screaming in agony with the sheer effort the next, until the baby was born tiny and blue.

'It's a girl,' said the midwife, before handing her to the doctor and nurses, who bent over her in concern. I lay back, exhausted but worried about how early the baby had arrived. If only Leo had been here.

'She's in respiratory distress,' I heard the nurse say before a gush of warmth flooded between my legs.

'I'm cold,' I said weakly, my body limp with fatigue.

'Doctor,' the midwife at my feet called urgently. My baby was whisked away and the doctor and two nurses rushed to my bedside. It was like watching a film in slow motion.

'*Scheisse!*' said the doctor from a distance. 'We have to stop the bleeding or we're going to lose her.'

'Leo, you have a baby girl,' I whispered into the air, as I closed my eyes and drifted off into peaceful oblivion.

26

The doctor placed the stethoscope on my chest, listening to my breathing.

'How long have I been here?' I asked. I was on a hospital ward – a place of familiarity – but feeling disjointed and alone.

'Weeks,' said the doctor bluntly. 'You suffered from separation of the placenta, sending you into premature labour. After you gave birth we couldn't stop the bleeding. You're lucky to be here. We didn't think you were going to make it.' He patted my hand. 'But you're strong.'

I didn't feel strong. I felt weak, almost transparent.

'My baby. How's my baby?' I couldn't lose her too.

'She was born very early, and very small. She couldn't breathe on her own and we don't have the facilities to look after babies so premature here.'

'So she's at the Charité?' I knew she'd need the incubator and oxygen tent we had there. It was a new, but expensive advance in neonatal medicine used in only a few hospitals across Europe. The Charité had been lucky to keep it when the Soviets began dismantling hospitals and taking valuable equipment back to Russia.

He shook his head. 'They didn't have the medications she needed for her condition, or the penicillin if she developed pneumonia. Your husband made the decision to send her across to the Martin Luther Hospital in the American sector. It has an excellent reputation and they have everything she needs there.'

My heart leapt. My husband! Leo was alive and well. 'He was here?'

'Of course. Herr Siebenborn has been by your bedside every day.' He stood and nodded at the nurse.

I closed my eyes briefly in disappointment and pain. Leo was dead. 'And she's still there?'

'She's doing well, I believe. Talk to your husband when he comes in. He'll be able to tell you more.' He picked up the notes at the end of my bed and flicked through the pages.

I nodded. 'When can I see her?'

He frowned. 'It's hard to say. We had trouble with your blood clotting, causing multiple organ problems. We need to make sure you're stable before you can be transferred to another hospital or released home.' He looked up and smiled at me. 'But you're both alive and well. It's a miracle really.'

'Thank you,' I said.

Julius was ushered in behind the closed curtain, dark rings under his eyes and his face haggard.

He kissed me gently on the cheek. 'How are you feeling?'

'Tired, but they tell me I'll be fine. How's my daughter?'

'She's beautiful . . . just like her mother. She's breathing on her own now, feeding, putting on weight. She's thriving.'

I nodded. 'I only wish Leo and his parents were here to see her.'

'I know, but you're not alone. I'm here.' He sat by the bed. 'I was worried I was going to lose you both.' His eyes were misty.

'I've named her Elena Christina, after both our mothers. She comes from a long line of strong women,' I answered instead, choosing to ignore his comment. Leo should have been by my side, not Julius. I blinked my tears away. 'Have they found Leo?'

'No, but they haven't been able to identify all the bodies yet.' He kissed my limp hand. 'I thank God every day for the miracle that you're still alive. You've had more than your fair share of tragedy. Let me look after you.'

I pulled my hand away. It was too much. 'I can't.'

'I know you don't love me, but let's put the past behind us. I know Leo would want me to do what I can for you. Let me give you what he would've wanted for you. If we can get to a place of mutual respect, and maybe one day even affection, I'll be a very happy man.'

Julius wanted to prove that he was a better man, and all he had done for me since the building collapse showed he still cared. But I knew what he was – a man who said and did whatever he needed to get what he wanted. He still wanted some connection to his childhood at Gut Birkenhof and he still wanted his own family. I was his golden ticket. But I had to think with my head. Survival for my baby came first and I had nowhere else to go. I couldn't stay with Marika in the nurses' quarters with a child, and Frau Kraus and Hans could never afford to support me and the baby. Julius was still a long way from paying his debt to me and Leo and, although I would never trust him fully again, supporting Elena and I was the least he could do. I would give her all the love I had while Julius would provide the financial security she needed. Maybe I needed to let him do this for us.

'Let me think about it,' I said. 'I know I have you to thank for sending Elena to the Martin Luther Hospital. You saved her life, just as you saved mine,' I admitted. 'But I want to go and see her before I make any decision.' My arms ached for the feel of her little body, the fresh baby smell of her skin and the bright, clear eyes that would gaze at me for the first time.

Julius's gaze slid away. 'You can't, Susie.'

'I know I have to wait until I'm better but it won't be too long,' I said, trying to sit up. Julius supported me while he placed pillows behind me, but I could see that wasn't what he meant.

'Julius?' I said sharply. 'What's happened to Elena?'

Julius pulled me to him and hugged me tight. 'She's safe and doing well. I wanted to bring her home with me but I couldn't; there was nothing I could do.' He shuddered against me.

'What? Where is she?' I pushed him away weakly.

He shook his head, dazed. 'Somewhere in the American sector. She's been adopted by a family who can look after her. She needs constant care and nursing.'

'What?' I stared at him, incredulous. 'She's my child. She can't be taken away from me without my consent.'

'Susie, you have to understand – you were dying ... I couldn't look after both of you.' His eyes were pleading with me. 'I was making sure everything was being done to save your life . . . I knew the baby was doing well. But the staff insisted that she'd require regular treatment and follow-up at the hospital because she was so premature. I couldn't bring her home when I was here with you all the time and I wanted her to have the treatment available at Martin Luther to ensure she'd grow and thrive. I was given papers to sign and I was so frantically worried about you that I signed without even realising what I'd done. Afterwards it was too late.' He was pale, beads of perspiration on his forehead.

The room began to spin and I shut my eyes, trying to force down the panic that threatened to overwhelm me. A roaring filled my ears, drowning out the familiar sounds of the ward as one thought consumed me. My baby was gone. I took a shuddering breath. But she still needed me and I was all she had left. I opened my eyes, ready to fight for her with everything I had. 'How could you just let it happen?' I snapped.

'I was fighting for you . . . She'll have everything she needs in the American zone, better than here.'

'Fighting for me means fighting for my child. But you didn't fight for her!' I was shaking so hard, I clenched my teeth to keep myself from exploding.

'I'm so sorry.' His voice was full of anguish, but I didn't care.

'You've never stood up for anything in your life,' I spat out. 'You didn't come home to face Onkel Georg when we got engaged, you didn't step up to the plot against the Führer, you didn't tell me the truth about Collette or your son until I found out, you didn't fight for the Jewish people on those transports and in the gas chambers, and you sent Leo, the son of your best friend, to what you knew would be his death!'

My voice had risen with every accusation and now I was screaming, unable to control myself.

I watched as his face fell briefly, unable to hide from the truth of what he'd done before it hardened once more. 'But I fought for you, Susie, always.'

'If you want me to believe that, bring my daughter home to me. I'm her mother and she needs me.' I was frantic now, sobs racking my body.

'I would if I could, but the red tape makes it impossible,' he said.

Something in me cracked and I screamed again, with the full force of my wrath. 'If you won't even try, get out! You're nothing but a coward and a liar, a manipulative, egocentric opportunist just like Mueller. I don't want to see you ever again. You're a monster!'

A nurse opened the curtain in consternation. 'I'm sorry, Herr Siebenborn. You can't upset my patient like this,' she said sternly. 'You'll have to leave.'

'Susie, please!'

'She was all I had left.' I turned away, my heart and body aching.

He threw me one last beseeching look before the nurse pulled him away and the curtain closed behind him. Nothing mattered anymore, nothing except finding Elena.

I asked the nurse looking after me to find Marika at the Charité. She was the only one I wanted by my side.

The following morning the nurse was smiling as she opened the curtain. 'She's here,' she said.

'Marika?' I whispered. Suddenly she was in my arms, trembling violently, our tears mingling as we clung to each other.

'It's really you,' she said, dumbstruck. 'You've been missing since the day your building collapsed. We all thought you were dead.'

I couldn't stop crying. 'I've never been happier to see you. Oh, Marika, I've lost everything. First Leo and now the baby.'

She stared at me, horrified. 'What are you talking about? Leo's been frantic to find you.'

'He's alive?' My heart felt like it stopped for a moment. A wave of dizziness came over me and Marika's voice seemed to come from far away.

'He was pulled out of the wreckage on the second day. He had cuts and bruises but refused to get treatment. He went from hospital to hospital, looking for you. We searched everywhere for you . . . for weeks.'

'I can't believe he's been out there all this time, looking for me,' I said, stunned.

'It's no surprise you didn't find each other. The rescue crews and hospitals here in the Soviet sector just can't cope with disasters like this. Leo would've disappeared too if he'd been disoriented or had amnesia. It's no wonder people go missing.' She shook her head. 'After a few weeks the authorities told us that you were most likely dead. There was a fire, and so many of the bodies were unidentifiable.'

I nodded. 'That's what Julius told me about Leo, too. Then I went into labour . . .'

'Julius?' she said aghast.

I told her everything that had happened, sobbing in her arms by the end of it. 'Where's Leo now? We have to get our daughter back.'

'He left Berlin,' she said quietly. 'He thought he'd lost you and the baby and just couldn't stay. He was so broken, Susie. He decided to emigrate to America like you planned, but Frau Kraus and I haven't heard from him since he came to say goodbye a couple of weeks ago.'

My elation warred with devastation. He was alive – it was more than I could ever have dreamed – but he had gone, unaware that I was still in Berlin and that his daughter and I needed him.

'Where would he have gone? We were still waiting on the visa.'

'Captain Snopov might know. Leo thought he might be able to help him . . . He might be able to help with Elena too,' she said. She paused, clutching my hand. 'How could Julius adopt her out?'

'Because he thought I was dying,' I said bitterly. 'It was too hard for him to fight for Elena or think about how he would look after a baby on his own.'

'He let it happen, just like the Jewish people who were transported east during the war. Once a Nazi, always a Nazi,' she said shaking with fury. 'After everything he's already put you through.' Marika went pale. 'How hard did he look for Leo? He's always wanted you all to himself. He would do anything to have you. It worked perfectly for Julius to separate you from him and then Elena.'

A cold and heavy weight settled in my belly. 'I went into labour only days after the collapse. But –' I stared at her. 'He allowed me to think Leo was dead and confirmed it again by offering to look after Elena and I when I woke up here in hospital.' Marika grasped my hand, the enormity of what

Julius had done hanging between us. 'He nearly did it again,' I whispered. 'He nearly manipulated me into doing what he wanted . . . How could I be so stupid?'

'If I ever lay eyes on him, I'll tear him limb from limb,' Marika said ferociously. She stopped at the look of desolation on my face. 'But first we have to find Elena.'

'Go to Captain Snopov,' I said, my eyes narrowing with determination. There was no time for weakness. I had to gather every bit of strength I had left for the greatest fight of my life – to find the ones I loved. 'He'll be able to tell us where to start looking.'

'We should tell him about Julius too.' Her expression was defiant. 'He has to pay.'

I nodded. 'It's time Julius gets what's coming to him.' With Marika by my side, and with the knowledge that Leo was alive, hope burned bright once more.

All my energy went into getting well for the sake of Elena and Leo. I was never more grateful for Marika. She was my rock, and she quickly found Captain Snopov.

'Vasily couldn't believe that you were alive and wants to come and see you when you're feeling better,' she said. 'He's so fond of you and Leo.'

'Vasily, is it?' I said with a raised eyebrow. I was sitting up in bed, feeling a little stronger, and I'd even managed some breakfast.

She grinned. 'We celebrated your survival and returning health with a bottle of vodka. I couldn't very well call him

Captain after that.' I clasped her hand and smiled. Friendship could spring up in the strangest of places.

'Has he found Elena?' I asked anxiously.

Marika's face fell and she shifted uncomfortably in her chair. 'No. Her adoption records are sealed. The way the law stands, there's nothing he can do.' The news hit me like a punch to the stomach and tears welled in my eyes. She squeezed my hand. 'But there *is* some confusion between the zones and he's going to speak to his legal team to see if there are any loopholes or precedence in the law. He agrees a travesty of justice has occurred and wants this righted as much for the reputation of his military government as for you.'

'I'll never give up.' I dashed the tears away.

She leaned forward. 'I know, and I'll help you any way I can.' I nodded and kissed her hand in gratitude. 'You would do the same for me,' she said and I nodded. She was right. We would always have each other's back.

'What about Leo?' I needed him now more than ever.

She shook her head. 'He'll send out enquires to the ports and border crossings. The visa hadn't arrived when Leo left Berlin, but he can't leave the country without it. Vasily's confident he'll find him.'

I squeezed my eyes shut for a moment to keep the rising panic at bay and leaned back into the pillows, feeling overwhelmed. We had to be reunited soon. Together we could find Elena and put an end to this nightmare. 'If he was here . . .'

'We'll find a way to bring Elena back to you . . .' Marika squeezed my hand before continuing. 'I told Vasily everything that Julius has done to you and Leo, and about the Nazi atrocities he was involved in,' she said grimly. I'd never have peace until I'd found Elena and Leo, but if Julius faced the punishment he deserved, not just for me but for the countless Jewish people he'd allowed to go to their deaths, the pain I carried would be a little easier to bear and maybe I could breathe again. 'He'll be passing on the information to the Ministry of Internal Affairs.'

I held my breath, taking in the implications, before letting it out slowly again. We both knew that it was Soviet policy to deal harshly with Nazi collaborators. 'He'll be interned?'

She nodded, her eyes bright with vengeance. 'Let's just say that he'll soon be enjoying the hospitality of an NKVD camp. He'll never be able to hurt you again,' she said with satisfaction.

An overwhelming rush of relief swept through me. Justice had finally been served. But it would never alter the destruction he had inflicted or the pain I felt at losing my daughter.

'Then I have my retribution,' I said, hugging her tight.

27

My daily walk took me along the river and up past the boundary of the old estate. It was 1995 and I was seventy-one, and although my body was stiffer and slower than it used to be, I was determined to stay active and maintain my fitness. Like the new Germany after reunification, the estate was whole again, part of the now expanding and dynamic town, the community it had supported for generations. Orderly rows of homes sat on neat plots along new streets and adjacent to grassy parkland dotted with community buildings. Much of the land was now privately owned and what remained of the state-owned land now belonged to the local municipality.

I remembered the deep sadness I'd felt when Gut Birkenhof was transferred to the Soil Fund by the Committee for Land Reform during the Soviet occupation. Just like our beloved Germany, it had been broken up. Small allotments of about five hectares each had been distributed to incoming refugees from the east and landless agricultural workers. The rest had been left as a central state-run property and cooperative where resources, farm machinery and equipment were pooled and shared among the small holdings. It was a new chapter for us all in the place I still called home.

When I was released from hospital all those years ago, Marika had taken me home to Frau Kraus. At first, my life revolved around finding Leo and Elena. My continuing requests to have access to information were denied and I was still no closer to knowing where she was. Captain Snopov tried but was unable to find a legal loophole regarding the adoption.

There was no trace of Leo. He had simply disappeared, and his relatives in America had not heard from him. I finally learnt that Onkel Tedi and his family had perished in Auschwitz. There was nobody left of Tante Elya's family in Europe. Snopov was recalled to Moscow in 1949 with the formation of the German Democratic Republic – the new state of East Germany governed by the Soviet-backed Socialist Unity Party. Germany had been split into the two new entities of East and West Germany, hostile to one another. I didn't know then how Germany could ever return to the proud and united nation it had been.

Climbing the incline to the top of the slope and puffing slightly, I glanced over to the hill where the stand of birch still stood. The manor house was gone now, along with all the buildings except the stables and the dairy, but I'd never forget seeing it uninhabited for the first time, left to lapse into a state of disrepair. Doors, windows and flooring were missing, the stone embellishments and facings pulled down and used for new dwellings or firewood, leaving the scars of their crude removal on the eroded lime-washed walls like the horrendous wounds I'd seen on the soldiers I'd nursed in the war. It was like disfiguring a beautiful face for no reason: a terrible violation. The house – the heart and soul of the district for generations – had become an empty shell.

I stood there a moment and sighed. I still mourned Gut Birkenhof, but it was gone forever: a sign of Germany's glorious past, a time that could never return after what the Nazis and Soviets had done to our nation. And yet life had gone on.

Although retired from nursing, I was still heavily involved in the community, running mothers' groups and mothercraft classes, cooking and providing care packages for those families who were struggling. Marika had decided to stay in the village with me and she'd married the new local doctor. Together we set up a clinic for new mothers and babies, working closely with doctors and midwives. There was great competition between East and West Germany, even in public health care where the East German government was determined to prove that we were leaders in lowering the rate of infant mortality.

Nursing had been my constant, the place where I felt at peace, invigorated by the joy of new life and bringing hope and practical experience to the expanding families in the village, just as Frau Kraus and Tante Elya had always done. Through my work and the support of those around me, my life returned to some semblance of normalcy.

A cool gust of wind pulled me from my musings and, although it was summer, I was pleased for the windcheater my children had given me. I was now living in Frau Kraus's cottage, which she'd left me when she died. Hans had passed away before her. Marika and her husband had retired to France where their grown children lived. In my moments of solitude, I'd begun writing letters to Elena, telling her about her birth, my life, and how I'd never stopped looking for her. The three beautiful children I'd had with my husband Gerhard lived in Berlin where there was work and I now had seven grand-children. I'd met and married Gerhard when he worked for the District Commission, managing the old estate. He'd passed away ten years earlier, but I was so grateful for the wonderful years we'd had together.

I smiled at the burst of colour, cornflowers and poppies in the small meadow next to the road. These days I tended to think about the good times. Now that the Berlin Wall had fallen and we were a united Germany once again, socialism was no longer a part of life, but the old dachas of the Socialist Unity Party officials from Berlin still stood along the river. It wasn't too long ago when limousines lined the streets of the town and guards surrounded the homes of powerful men from East Germany's politburo who liked to party on the weekends.

How things had changed, but there were still reminders of my childhood and youth. The outer wall of the old stables, now part of an apartment building, reminded me of the day Leo had given me the carved horse he'd made me, and of all the hours he'd spent teaching me to groom the horses. The few remaining cherry trees lining the village street took me back to my nineteenth birthday and the passion Leo and I had shared under their boughs, and to our wedding day, sitting under the green canopy, full of love and happiness.

Despite living a full life, I'd never forgotten Leo, thinking about our life together often and wondering how it might have been.

In the distance, a man leaning against the last remaining timber fence of the old estate caught my eye. He stared out across the new part of the town, where Gut Birkenhof had once stood. He wore a soft cap on his head and I couldn't see his face, but there was something about his posture, the way he stood, that seemed familiar. I made my way towards him.

The back of my neck began to prickle. 'It can't be,' I murmured to myself, and I shook my head with irritation. 'I must be daydreaming.' But the closer I got, the more my heart raced.

'Hello,' I said tentatively as I came near him. 'Are you looking for someone?'

'No,' he said, keeping his gaze over the land. 'Do you know what happened to the manor house that used to be here?'

I stopped, unable to believe what I'd heard. I knew that voice.

'It was pulled down shortly after the war,' I said tremulously. Although he stood tall, his hair was grey below his cap. 'How do you know the manor house?'

'I used to live there.'

I gazed at him, feeling faint, but I had to be sure. 'How could you?' I whispered, clutching the fence post next to him. 'Everyone who lived there is either dead or gone.'

'I'm the last one,' he said sadly, turning to look at me directly for the first time. His face was weathered and wrinkled, but his eyes were brown and alert, eyes I could never forget. I swayed on my feet.

'Are you okay?' He put out a hand to steady me and his touch made me gasp. He quickly withdrew his hand, frowning.

'Leo?'

He nodded warily then recognition dawned on his face.

'It's me, it's Susie,' I whispered.

'She's dead,' he whispered, with a haunted expression.

'I'm not dead, Leo. It's me, Nightingale.'

I grasped the rickety fence with two hands to steady myself, unsure if I was dreaming. He saw his mother's ring on my hand, now gnarled with age, and reached out to touch me, but dropped his hand by his side.

'How is it possible?' He took my hand gently then. 'Susie? You're alive.' His voice broke.

'Yes. You're finally here.' He pulled me into his embrace, both of us trembling. 'I searched for you for years, but you disappeared. I never thought I'd see you again.'

I brought him back to the cottage, holding onto his arm the whole time, afraid that if I let go, he'd disappear, or I'd wake up from a glorious dream.

'You live here?' he asked. He stood in the middle of the kitchen. It had been a big shock to see me and there was a lot for him to take in.

'Yes, I've been in the village for the last forty-nine years.'

He shook his head in amazement. 'All this time you were here, and I had no idea.'

'Come, sit down,' I said. 'I'll make you a cup of tea.' I filled the samovar with water and lit the bottom.

'You still have Mutti's samovar?'

I nodded, placing a plate of biscuits on the kitchen table. 'I don't use it as much as I'd like to anymore, but it still makes

410

the best cup of tea, and it always reminds me of you and your mother.' It was dented, and the enamel paint faded and chipped, but still a precious object that held our family story.

We drank tea and slowly I told him everything since the terrible day of the building collapse. 'I couldn't leave, Leo. This was always my home; it was the only way I could remain close to you and your parents.' I put a shaking hand to my mouth, the weight of that time coming back to me.

'Oh, Susie. I'm so sorry I didn't stay longer. We would've found each other, and Elena would be here with us too.' The burden of realisation and guilt seemed to age him further, bowing his back under the load.

I took his hand, blinking my tears away. 'They were chaotic days. People went missing all the time. You thought I was dead, just as I thought you were. I understand why you had to go. There were some days when I wished I could have left too.'

Leo brought my hand to his lips. 'I thought I'd lost everything. I had to leave my past behind altogether. I didn't care where I went or where I ended up.'

'We searched for you for so long. Even Captain Snopov couldn't find any trace of you.' I dashed the tears that threatened to fall with the back of my other hand.

'I went to Switzerland. I couldn't wait for the American visa any longer. I ended up in Australia and found work on big farms and stations across the country. I drowned my sorrows in my work and lost touch with the outside world for a very long time, but my memories never left me.' He paused as if in recollection, the tears bright in his eyes. 'I've been living in Sydney for the past five years on my own, but city life isn't for me,' he said softly. 'I had to come home.' I covered his hand with my own. I understood his pain.

'It was a long time ago,' I said, 'but you're right, the memories never leave and it still feels like yesterday . . .'

'I wish I'd been here for you, but I lost the estate, I failed my family, I lost you and our child . . . I was a broken man.' He shook his head. 'But now to find out that you're alive and our daughter's out there somewhere . . .' I could feel him shake as the tears fell. 'You have no idea where?'

'No,' I whispered. 'Since reunification, the laws regarding adoption have finally changed so that children have limited access to their files, but not birth parents. Maybe she was never told she was adopted, maybe she tried to find us when she was younger . . . Maybe she doesn't want to know.' I closed my eyes as all the anguish, all the pain I'd been carrying deep within me, rushed to the surface again. 'She'd be forty-nine years old now, and maybe a grandmother herself. I only hope that she has a good life.'

'We'll keep looking together. There has to be something we can find out.'

'You're staying?' I quivered with emotion: hope and fear.

He smiled. 'If you'll have me. I never want to be parted from you again.'

I kissed his hand. 'It was always you, Leo, and it always will be.'

Epilogue

Sydney

. . . Your father wound up his affairs in Sydney and we married again with the blessing of your brother and two sisters. The nineteen years we had together were a gift, more than I ever dreamed. It felt so good to be home with him once again. The estate had brought us together and it was what had brought Leo home and finally back to me.

Gut Birkenhof was always in our blood. It was part of who we were. The court battle to claim ownership of the estate lasted eighteen years: your father was never going to give up. The final judgement was delivered to us as he lay dying in hospital. Despite the odds, he was victorious, awarded the municipal land and compensation for the rest of the estate that's now part of the village and in private hands. He never wanted the money: it was always about having the property back in the family. He donated some to various Jewish foundations as well as charities for political persecution. There's more than enough money left for me to live on. And when I die the property goes to you. It's what your father wanted.

It's the last remnant of Gut Birkenhof, the home of your ancestors for generations, and a place where one day, if you choose, you can come, perhaps with your children and grand-children, to understand your roots. Just as with your father and I, you too may feel in your blood that you belong to this place as much as it belongs to you.

The love of my life died two weeks after the return of the estate. I buried him next to his parents under the linden trees and I know it won't be long before I join him there and go to my rest.

Natalie held the final letter in her hand. 'Susie and Leo finally found each other after all those years . . . and Gut Birkenhof is their legacy, part of our heritage too,' she said in wonder, wiping away the tear that trickled down her cheek.

'It was enough that she left us Elya's ring, but I never imagined anything like this.' Ingrid shook her head in amaze-ment, caressing the stack of letters bundled together.

'And she never stopped looking for you.'

'No, and my father was here in Australia all along.' Ingrid closed her eyes for a moment until she felt the sudden surge of anguish dissipate.

'Maybe we can visit them one day under the linden trees when the baby's old enough. Perhaps we can even meet your brother and sisters.' Natalie rubbed her distended belly absently as she shifted on the lounge to get comfortable.

'I'd like that ... I only wish that I'd tried again. Maybe I would have found both my parents and seen them – even once.'

'Nobody was to know, Mum. At least you know the truth.' She squeezed her mother's hand. 'You can find out everything about your adoption, now you know where to look. She would have wanted that.'

Ingrid nodded slowly. 'She would never have imagined I was across the other side of the world.'

'Oma and Opa wanted a better life for you away from the chaos of Germany. Susie would've been happy with the family you had,' said Natalie.

'And now she has a great-grandchild about to come into the world.' Ingrid smiled at her, tears in her eyes. 'I'm so very glad that I'm part of your life ... I can't imagine what she went through.'

'Me too, especially now. But I feel connected to her, as though she's with us.' Natalie's gaze rested on the pile of baby suits and tiny singlets Ingrid had given her. 'I always felt that a part of me was missing, a sense of identity and belonging to something beyond our immediate family.'

'Oh darling, I wish it had been different for you.' Ingrid kissed her daughter's cheek.

'It's okay. I understand about our family now. Susie's given us the greatest gift of all. We know where we come from.'

Ingrid picked up the diamond ring that had arrived with the package. 'Tante Elya's ring,' she whispered. 'My grandmother's and my mother's engagement ring.' It was dented and scratched, worn thin with age and wear, but still intact and strong.

The perfect symbol not just of never-ending love, but of all their family had endured to remain together.

Author's note

Dear Reader,

    While researching my very first book, *The Girl from Munich*, and sifting through the treasure trove of documents, photos and memorabilia that my German grandmother left behind after she died, I discovered a single letter from her cousin that began the journey to *Letters from Berlin*.

The letter was sent to my grandmother in her twilight years by newly connected relatives in Germany trying to find other branches of the family that had dispersed after the war. They had found my grandmother's cousin, recently returned to Germany after spending nearly sixty years living in South America where his mother's family had migrated in the early 1900s and he had written them a short letter in response to their enquiry about his family.

He wrote that he remembered meeting my grandmother's brothers, who visited his family on their way to the war and learnt that both had perished on the Eastern Front, but he'd lost contact after his father's death at the end of the war. It was wonderful to discover a part of my grandmother's family that I knew nothing about, but frustrating too, as there was little more detail. However, accompanying the letter was a copy of a German newspaper article and, intrigued to know what it was about, I set about translating it. I was blown away as it contained everything I wanted to know and so much more! What I learned was explosive detail about his family during the war years in Germany and into the Soviet occupation, information I subsequently found in multiple German newspaper articles that had reported his story and even in a British tabloid.

This story was so sensational because he was involved in a landmark legal case in Germany involving his family estate. After the reunification of Germany it was possible to lodge claims for property lost as a result of the war. However, properties expropriated by the Soviets were precluded as part of the terms of reunification. The question then became whether the estate lost at the end of the war was confiscated by the Gestapo, as a result of persecution or acts of resistance against the Third Reich, or expropriated during the Soviet land reform after the war. Archives from Moscow had eventually been accessed, documenting aid given by the family to Soviet soldiers in escaping from Sachsenhausen. One Soviet captain had returned in 1947 to find the family gone and the estate expropriated in the Soviet land reform. He was able to obtain an order from Moscow to restore the estate to the family, making the expropriation null and void. But by this time, my grandmother's cousin, the only surviving family member in Germany, was unable to be found, having begun his journey across Europe to Genoa in Italy where he boarded the ship for South America.

The case took over 20 years to be settled, moving through various courts in the land, until it reached the Supreme Court. The final verdict, a resounding victory, was handed down when my grandmother's cousin was lying in hospital. His courage, determination and persistence had finally paid off. He died two weeks later.

Besides being an incredible story, the amazing thing for me was to learn more about my family. I discovered through the newspaper reports that my grandmother's uncle was married to a Russian Jew who received her Jewish registration papers, officially marking her as a Jewish person in January 1943, after years of her husband dealing with Nazi officials to keep her off the list. He owned a large estate outside of Berlin and was predominantly a timber merchant. His son, my grandmother's cousin, wanted to follow his father into agriculture but was prevented from attending university. Government contracts with the Reichspost and Reichsbahn were cancelled, as were orders for seed and fuel. The family was denied emigration to South America twice, once just before the war and again after her registration. I was so proud to find that my grandmother's uncle had joined the Free Germany resistance movement and took part in aiding the escape of Soviet POWs from the Sachsenhausen concentration camp near Berlin and later helping the escape and hiding of deserted child flack helpers from the Luftwaffe.

My grandmother's cousin was sent to a work camp in November 1944 as part of the wave of labour recruitment of 'mischlinge' or 'half-breeds' and was further sent to a satellite camp of Buchenwald in late 1944 where he was told by the guards that his days were numbered. His father orchestrated his escape and he hid in Berlin as a Silesian refugee where the safe house he was in collapsed in an air raid. He came home to the estate, hiding in a forester's cottage with his mother when the Gestapo visited their home in the final days of the war, where they remained until Soviet liberation. His father was betrayed to the Gestapo when deserter flak helpers he'd been helping hide were seen, with the devastating consequences described in the book.

After the war, the Soviets expropriated the estate in the land reforms, even after an appeal had been submitted with information regarding the family's connection to the resistance and aid given to Red Army POWs. They were evicted with twenty-four hours to leave the district and subsequently moved to Berlin. There, my grandmother's aunt met her tragic end by jumping from a bridge into the Spree River. She just couldn't take any more.

My grandmother's cousin left Germany in 1947, making his way through the different zones of Germany to Lake Constance in the French zone where he was detained for a time before being allowed to travel on to Switzerland. There he obtained the paperwork he needed to board a boat in Genoa bound for South America where his sister and family members and friends were living. The estate remained part of the land reform, subdivided into smaller allotments and the manor house was demolished, pulled down piece by piece until all that remained were the stables.

I couldn't believe everything this family, my relatives, had endured. Their story made me immensely proud and I knew that I had to tell it – not just because it's such an incredible story full of heartbreak, survival and human endurance, but also because it's about family. What a family will do to stay together, what a family will do to protect its own. The particulars contained in the reporting of this legal case were the only details I had to begin with but I soon realised that the shortage of information also gave me the freedom to tell a story of family and war from a unique but fictional female perspective. Susie, an upper class German girl from Georg's world with the understanding of what's happening to the Heckers and the Jewish people as a whole, is in the perfect position to complement the heroic actions of my grandmother's uncle to protect his family, actions which I attributed to Georg and Leo. We see the war through her eyes and as experienced by a rarely mentioned group of people, those Jewish people married to Germans and their children who were considered 'half-breeds', like my grandmother's cousin.

Once I began researching, I was fascinated to learn that even with the Nuremberg Laws of 1935, German law still protected Jewish people in mixed marriages, especially Jewish women not practising their faith married to German men, like Elya and Georg, who were considered to be in 'privileged marriages' with the status and privileges of German citizens. Despite these privileges, children like Leo, with a German father, were forbidden to join the military, attend university, have a relationship or marry a German, among other restrictions. Although not in immediate threat of deportation to the eastern ghettos and concentration camps of Poland, the lives of those in 'privileged families' were still tenuous. This was made increasingly difficult with the 'Final Solution' and as the war continued and the closer Germany came to defeat, the threat to their very survival rose exponentially.

As I began writing, I realised that I was writing about family and legacy. Weaving through the fictional storyline of Susie and Julius has added layers to the story of war, building on the picture and the extent people were prepared to go to protect the ones they loved. I found that this was a reoccurring theme running through the war years – ordinary people doing extraordinary things in extraordinary times.

In the process of learning about this branch of my family and what their lives were like, it seemed fitting that the prologue and epilogue are told by Ingrid and Natalie, Susie and Leo's descendants in Australia, mirroring my own breathtaking journey of discovery of my family on the other side of the world.

I hope you enjoyed reading their story as much as I enjoyed writing it.

Tania

Reading group questions

1. In the novel, Ingrid and Natalie discover their roots and family they never knew they had. How do you think this discovery would have affected them? How would their perspective of family have changed?

2. Many families were fragmented and dispersed, often across the world, as a result of World War II. Generations later, how do you think this separation has affected families? How has it impacted those who remained in their homelands? How has it influenced the cultural identity of those who left, and their descendants?

3. How do you think Elya's childhood experiences, fleeing the pogroms of Kiev, shaped her as a woman and affected her choices in life?

4. How do you think the idea of family is represented throughout the novel? What does family mean to you?

5. Susie and Marika are best friends throughout the novel, helping each other through highs and lows over many years. Why is Susie's friendship with Marika so important to her? What do you think makes an enduring friendship?

6. Susie and Julius both suffered the loss of their family and home at a young age and were taken in by the Hecker family. How did their responses to their childhood trauma change as they grew from children into adulthood? What are the similarities and differences in the ways they handled it?

7. How have the events in Susie's life shaped her identity? What are the events that have shaped your identity?

8. What do you think drove Georg to take such risks in joining the Resistance and helping Russian POWs and child flak helpers escape from the Nazis? His marriage to Elya was the primary source of protection for his family. What kind of man do you think he was?

9. Leo has mixed heritage: Jewish, Russian and German. What do you think Leo's sense of identity would have been in his childhood, and how would it have changed through the Nazi era of the 1930s, during the war, and after the war with the Soviet occupation? How may this have changed again as he spent decades living away from his homeland? How do you think he felt when he returned to Germany as an old man?

10. How would the events in Leo's life, especially the perse-
    cution he suffered as a result of his Jewish heritage and
    the loss of his family estate have changed him as a person
    and have shaped his attitudes?

11. What do you think is the legacy left behind by Leo
    and Susie?

Acknowledgements

The letter which began my journey of discovery that became *Letters from Berlin*, was found among my German grandmother's family documents after she passed away at ninety-one. Because of her meticulous keeping of documents and letters such as this, I have learnt about a part of my family I didn't know I had. This story is because of her.

Thank you to everyone at Simon & Schuster Australia for their support and belief in me, especially Dan Ruffino, Fiona Henderson, Michelle Swainson, Anna O'Grady and the amazing sales and marketing department. And to my publisher Cassandra di Bello, for her endless behind-the-scenes work, ensuring everything runs smoothly and I can focus on writing at my best. Thanks also to my fabulous editor Roberta Ivers for her guidance, support and friendship. Her insights and expertise helped me sculpt and fine-tune my story to make it sing. I would be lost without her. I am blessed with a wonderful team who have helped make *Letters from Berlin* the beautiful, eye catching book you now hold in your hands.

This book has been a legacy to family, and nowhere is this sense of family more evident than through the love and support of my own family. I was most fortunate to have my mother Giselle Brame beside me in this journey and who shared my fascination as we discovered this branch of our family. A big thank you to her, my father Domenic Martino, my wonderful in-laws Christine and Terry Blanchard and my sister-in-law Trish Casey, for their interest in my story and for the gift of their thoughtfulness. It's wonderful to know that my family is always behind me.

I'm so grateful to my friends, who have coaxed me away from the writing desk for fresh air, cups of coffee and conversation, particularly when I'm too brain dead to think straight! They have helped keep me sane. My special thanks to Diana Schamschula for her support and generous gifting of background information on the European Jewish community during the war, and to all those who have helped with research and support while writing this story.

A massive thank you to all my readers, especially those who have reached out to me to share your kind thoughts, insights and your own stories after reading *The Girl from Munich* and *Suitcase of Dreams*. As a writer, there's nothing better than to know that the story has connected and resonated with a reader. I've been so touched by the stories you've shared, many so very similar to my own family story. I'm so grateful for your support which drives me forward to bring you the very best and most authentic story that I can.

Uncovering such a sensational but heart-wrenching story has been a rollercoaster of emotions. I thank my own immediate family for their support and patience as I spent hours upon hours hidden away, delving deeper into the background of this story, as I tried to craft a story that wove together fact and fiction and bring the characters to life on the page. Their small acts of love touched my heart; bringing me cups of hot, strong coffee and tea, putting freshly picked flowers on my desk and listening with interested expressions as I explained excitedly how the latest bit of research fit into my story. They are my number one fan club, sharing my stories and updating my progress with friends, teachers, associates and peers, and are with me each step of the way, celebrating the little successes and encouraging me whenever I hit a wall. I'm thankful for the support of my daughter Hollie and her insightful ideas on how to make the story flow, even in the midst of studying for her HSC. It's been a great joy to share my historical findings with her as she is a history buff just like me. I love the discussions we have about historical events and the course of history. Thank you to my beautiful boys Nathan and Benjamin, for their excitement and pride in what I do. To my wonderful husband Chris, your unflappable calm and vast knowledge of all things to do with construction and agriculture, and not to mention practical solutions to technical problems within my story, helped me past so many challenges and allowed me to breathe.

My family is my rock and they make it all worthwhile. This handing down of family stories through my novels is my legacy to them.

About the author

Tania Blanchard was inspired to write by the fascinating stories her German grandmother told her as a child. Coming from a family with a rich cultural heritage, stories have always been in her blood. Her first novel published by Simon & Schuster Australia, *The Girl from Munich*, was a runaway bestseller, as was the sequel, *Suitcase of Dreams*. Tania lives in Sydney with her husband and three children.

To find out more, sign up to Tania's newsletter at www.taniablanchard.com.au or follow her at Facebook.com/TaniaBlanchardAuthor

Read on for a sneak peek of *Echoes of War,*
the next novel from Tania Blanchard.

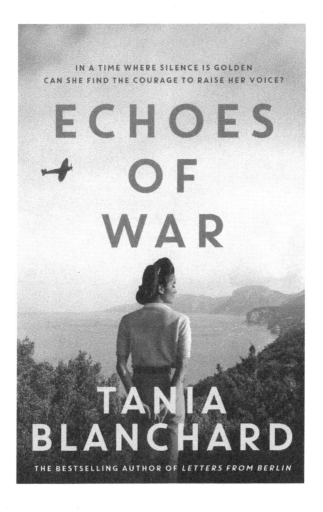

Available from October 2021.

1

February, 1936
Calabria, Southern Italy

I followed the nun in a haze of exhaustion. I had been trying to memorise the turns along the corridors of the monastery, but when we finally stopped, I realised that I was utterly lost.

'Here we are,' said the nun, opening the door to my cell. 'You'll find it has everything you need.' She smiled encouragingly. 'It will feel like home before you know it.'

'Grazie, sorella,' I said in a small voice.

'One of the sisters will take you to see Mother Superior in the morning. Buona notte,' she said, before turning back down the long corridor.

I raised my lantern and surveyed the tiny room. A wave of loneliness overcame me and I burst into tears. I'd never been away from home before and I already missed my family.

The single bed against the whitewashed wall was covered with a sheepskin spread, with another sheepskin on the stone floor under the narrow window. The plain cell was more than I was used to. I'd never had the luxury of privacy or the freedom of my own space before – but it wasn't home. How would I ever sleep without the comfort of my sister Paola's warm body next to me and the soft sleepy noises of my eldest sister Teresa in the bed beside us?

I sat heavily on the bed. I was so far from everyone I loved and it was my own fault. My family would be celebrating the last night before Teresa's wedding, enjoying a specially cooked meal. I could picture them laughing, singing and dancing to the music of fiddles and accordions, as our neighbours and friends joined in. The view of the village from our hillside farm, about a fifteen-minute walk from our home, flashed through my mind: the tumble of red terracotta roofs and white lime-washed walls on the river flats. Bruzzano was a small village situated on the very tip of the toe of Italy, just a stone's throw from the island of Sicily. The Bruzzano River ran right alongside the town, moving slowly towards the east coast, while the Aspromonte Mountains towered around it, stretching to the very edges of Calabria's coastline like guardians. A wave of fresh tears turned into gasping sobs as I collapsed into the comfort of the sheepskin.

Two days earlier, Papà had summoned me to the dining table, his face like thunder. At forty-two, he was fit and strong from all his work on the land and, despite the long hours and constant worry that we wouldn't have enough food to keep us going for another year, he didn't look his age; his hair was still thick with only a few strands of grey that glinted against his black curls. He often told us that his grey hairs had sprouted because he had to provide for five children, and when I looked at Mama, who did the most for us, three years younger than Papà but her hair already streaked with grey, I thought maybe he was right. Vincenzo was the oldest of us at twenty-one, then Teresa a year younger. Paola, eighteen, was nearly two years older than me and then there was Antonio, who was fourteen. But I was the one who gave him the most grief.

'Did you look after the sheep yesterday for Vincenzo?' he asked as he finished off his caffè latte.

'No, Papà,' I whispered, standing before him in bare feet on the tiles. But I *had* covered for Vincenzo, who was supposed to look after the sheep on our thirty-acre farm. As shepherd it was his job to keep them safe from wild animals, especially wolves, but he'd wanted to visit a girl, his latest amore, in the village before he left for Africa with the army. He had taken his best friends, Stefano and Angelo Modaferi, cousins who lived in the next village, with him to act as look out. Although the cousins were just like brothers to us, spending as much time at our home while we were growing up as Vincenzo did at theirs, sometimes I wasn't sure I liked them, despite their jokes and clowning around. They could be dismissive, arrogant and annoying: pulling our hair, taking our biscotti and refusing to let us play football because we were girls.

But I didn't mind helping Vincenzo because, when I did, I felt like I was a part of a world that was carefree and wild. I longed for the freedoms the boys had.

Papà stared at me, his dark eyes, usually filled with kindness for his daughters, hard as obsidian. 'Don't lie to me, Giulia.'

'I'm not.' I knew how much trouble Vincenzo would be in if Papà found out he was sneaking away rather than doing his work. Papà had caught me telling lies more than a few times, but there was no way he could know the truth this time. I'd been so careful and even though one of the boys from the adjoining farm had come across to play cards and offered me my first cigarette, I'd only taken one puff before giving it back.

'Mamma mia!' He slammed the table. 'Then who did? Because he was seen in the village when he was supposed to be with the sheep. If anything had happened to even one of them . . .'

I flinched and swallowed hard. 'Whoever thinks they saw him must be mistaken,' I lied. I was in too deep now to come clean.

'Testa dura!' Papà rumbled, his hands pressed together as if asking for God's help. 'You told your mother you were going to help Zia Francesca at the trattoria but I was talking to Signora Lipari at the post office this morning and she said she saw you walking in the opposite direction, towards the farm and, worse still, that her nephew saw you in the field.' He shook his head. 'I don't know where to begin. It's bad enough that you were smoking cigarettes but you were alone with a boy and you're still lying to me? You know how much I hate lying! I'm so very disappointed in you.' My heart fell.

'But Papà—'

He put his hand up to stop me. 'Basta! Enough, Giulia! You will go nowhere until I'm satisfied that you've learnt your lesson. For a girl your age, you should know better. I thought you'd learnt after the incident with the bicycle.'

I dropped my gaze. I'd taken the bicycle without asking, to borrow a white blouse I was supposed to wear as part of my uniform for the weekly Fascist parade. I'd hidden my own blouse, which had a large mud stain and a tear from chasing my brothers after the last parade. The only problem was that I got a flat tyre on the way home. Mamma found out about the blouse and the tyre cost a lot for Papà to have fixed.

'I've indulged you and tolerated your impetuous ways for far too long. You have to learn obedience and your place in this village, because this is where you belong.'

I saw red. 'I'll never belong here!' I shouted. 'And why do I have to do what I'm told when the boys do whatever they want?'

'Because it's the way things are done. If you don't learn some respect and you keep on like this, nobody will want you.'

'I don't care! Damn the way things are done. Why would I want to be stuck here in a dead-end village with people who can't see beyond their own noses?'

Papà got up so quickly his chair crashed to the ground. 'I've a good mind to find you a husband who'll tame your wild ways and teach you respect.'

'I'd rather die than marry anyone you want me to.' We were nose to nose.

'Go to your room!' bellowed Papà. 'And don't come out until you're ready to see sense.'

'Well, that would be never!' I'd screamed, turning on my heel and rushing to my bedroom, slamming the door behind me.

*

The memory of that fight still made my blood boil. Sobbing, I buried my face in the sheepskin and pounded my pillow with fury until I was spent.

I took a shuddering breath and stared at the shadows the lantern made on the cell wall. I was here now and had to make the best of it. Somehow, the Madonna had heard my prayers and given me an opportunity to do what I'd always dreamed of.

I'd finished school nearly two years earlier, at the age of fourteen. At first, I helped Papà on the farm with Paola. As well as tending our flock of sheep, we planted wheat and had an olive grove, a small orchard of citrus trees and some grape vines for wine. We raised pigs, chickens and goats, and had our milking cow Bella and our donkey Benito, named after Il Duce, Prime Minister Mussolini. I helped milk the sheep and prepared the milk for cheesemaking, threshed wheat at harvest time to separate the grain to be milled into bread and pasta flour, and picked olives to be crushed for oil, grapes for wine, and the citrus fruits. I never seemed to do my chores as well as Paola and I usually disappeared as soon as I could to spend time with my Nonna Mariana, Mamma's mother, who was a maga, a traditional folk healer.

I'd always been interested in healing and I loved walking with her as she picked wild herbs from the surrounding hills and explained how to find them and what they were good for. I enjoyed watching her in her busy clinic, which she ran from the front room of her house, choosing herbs to treat someone's illness. But spending time with Nonna was another thing that Papà had forbidden, after his younger sister had died after treatment from a woman who called herself a maga but was really a strega, who practiced witchcraft. He never went as far as stopping Nonna from visiting us at home because he knew it would break Mamma's heart. He reluctantly accepted her place in our family, on the condition that she never treat any of us.

Even though Papà yelled at me time after time and punished me for disobeying him, I continued to sneak away to Nonna's whenever I could. Finally, he'd decided that I'd be better off working in his sister's trattoria, where I could be kept busy helping Zia Francesca prepare and cook meals. Whenever I wasn't needed at the restaurant, I was helping Paola on the farm.

Papà didn't realise Zia Francesca gave me freedoms he would never allow. After her customers were gone, she often let me look through glamourous magazines that came from the big cities of the north, like Milano. The women in these magazines were dressed so differently from me, in clothes that looked like they were designed for lives of purpose and independence. There had even been an advertisement for women to join the Red Cross as volunteer nurses. Could women become more than wives and mothers, forever controlled by their husbands and fathers, despite the Catholic Church's rules and the Fascist teachings we had drummed into us at school? If the women in these magazines could choose how they lived, perhaps I could find a way to do the same. I wasn't going to live my life like a prisoner.

*

After my fight with Papà, I decided to run away. I would join the Red Cross in Reggio and become a nurse rather than marry the husband Papà would choose for me, trapping me in the village. Reggio, the biggest city in Calabria and the capital of our province, was over forty miles away on the opposite, west coast.

I'd packed my few belongings and was walking the road to the coast, where I'd meet the bus to Reggio, when Zia Francesca caught up with me. She begged me to come back before anyone saw me, telling me she had an idea to get me what I wanted.

Back at the trattoria, I waited in the kitchen making the sugo for the evening's menu while Zia Francesca, Mamma and Nonna Mariana talked in hushed whispers.

'What are we going to do?' Mamma whispered in a panic. 'Mannaggia! I know she's strong willed but I never thought she'd do something like this. If Andrea finds out . . .'

'She's safe now, Gabriella,' said Nonna soothingly.

'But she can't stay here and I'm worried that if she comes home, she'll do something stupid or try to run away again the next time she and Andrea fight. '

Hearing Mamma's deep sigh, I hunched over the pot, ashamed I'd disappointed her. She was right, I couldn't go back home. If Papà found out I'd tried to run away, my life was as good as over. Family honour meant everything and my actions would only bring shame on my family. And even if he didn't, I couldn't forgive him for what he'd said. The memory of that morning flared my anger, hot and explosive, once more. I took a breath to calm myself.

'Allora, so, I have an idea,' said Zia Francesca. 'Maybe we can solve this problem and at the same time get Giulia the education she needs to fulfil her desire to become the type of healer that Andrea would approve of.'

'Basta!' said Mamma abruptly. 'We've been through this before. Andrea won't hear of it.'

I crept to the door to hear better and peered at the three women, their dark and grey heads together. It was reassuring to see Nonna Mariana, her long hair plaited into braids and twisted onto the back of her head. She was always a steadfast and calming presence.

'Mariana, didn't you once tell me that you know the renowned herbalist Fra Fortunato?' asked Zia Francesca. She was immaculate as always in a tailored skirt and blouse that Teresa had no doubt made for her from fabric sourced from Milan. Her long hair was parted in the middle and swept up in a fashionable knot at the back of her head, no strand out of place. I touched my own hair briefly. Like hers, it was thick and black, but unruly and hastily tied into a braid, loose pieces snaking down my back and around my face.

'Si,' said Nonna, her eyebrows raised in surprise.

'And that he now resides at the Monastery of the Madonna where you know the abbess?' Zia continued. 'With your connections, Giulia could go and study herbalism under the tutelage of the monks.'

I was taken aback by this new revelation. Perhaps there was more to Nonna than I knew.

'What do you think?' Zia asked, looking from my grand-mother to my mother. I felt sure she was holding her breath, just as I was.

Mamma shook her head. 'Do you really think it's possible?' she asked. Her curly brown hair spread around her head like a halo. At least I knew where I got my unmanageable locks from.

Nonna squeezed Mamma's hand, her luminous green eyes beseeching. I had inherited Nonna's eyes, less common in this part of Calabria. 'Giulia has a gift from God and it would be an affront to Jesus and the Madonna if she was not allowed to develop her talents.' She shrugged an apology. 'Fra Fortunato's knowledge of herbal medicine is second to none, not just of our local plants, but of other Italian and European remedies too. And if Giulia's half as good as I think she'll be, she'll make a decent living. People will come from all over the region to see her once her reputation spreads.'

Butterflies fluttered in my stomach at her words. I'd often wondered about the strong connection I had with her and how we just knew what was wrong with somebody when they weren't feeling well.

Calabria was an ancient place and its history of healing dated back thousands of years. Many rituals and traditions were passed down generation to generation, mother to daughter, and most maga used 'the old ways', a combination of herbal treatments, common sense remedies, superstition and the power of faith in God, Jesus, the Madonna and all of the saints of the Catholic Church, to help people to feel better. Nonna carried on the traditions that many locals expected her to use. As she had explained to me, there were many ways to treat illness, but if a patient didn't believe in what you were doing, it was much harder – if not impossible – to heal them.

'But what about Andrea?' said Mamma, pulling her hand away in frustration. 'He'll never allow it.' Mamma had happily given up any thought of being a healer to marry Papà; her passion didn't run as deep as mine and Nonna's even though she had talent. Nonna's world was the realm of women and magic, unfathomable and uncontrollable, something Papà didn't understand. But what upset Papà the most was Nonna's treatment of people affected by il malocchio, the evil eye. He believed she resorted to witchcraft to treat such cases.

Zia Francesca nodded. 'I've thought about that . . .' She put her head close to Mamma and Nonna, even though they were alone. 'Andrea doesn't have to know that she's studying, only that she's learning how to behave from the nuns.'

Mamma shook her head, eyes wide with alarm.

'Think about it, Gabriella,' said Nonna firmly. 'This could be a good opportunity to give Giulia and Andrea time apart, give them a chance to calm down, and for Giulia to think about her future with a level head without the worry that she'll run away again. Andrea gets what he wants too – a disciplined daughter.'

I wasn't sure how I felt about the idea of going to the monastery. It was an isolated place high in the mountains not too far from here. The thought of joining the Red Cross had been filled with adventure; spending my days with monks and nuns sounded dull in comparison. But I knew I'd go anywhere to learn any form of healing. And if it took me away from Papà and his anger, even better.

'But what happens when she comes home?' Mamma said.

'Since she's not yet ready for marriage, once she's gained skills in a reputable manner, she can bring in a proper income for the family. Surely Andrea can't object to that?' If Nonna thought this was a good idea, then maybe it was a way to get what I wanted: a purpose for my life besides marriage and children.

'I want Giulia to be happy, just like you, but it's just not possible,' said Mamma, her voice rising in desperation. She dropped her head into her hands and my heart dropped too. Of course it was too good to be true.

'This is the perfect opportunity to help her do the work she was born to do,' Zia Francesca said. 'If somebody saw her on the road and my brother finds out, especially after he caught her lying again, the monastery's far enough away to keep her safe and they'll both have time to come to their senses.' She hesitated. 'I know that it means deceiving Andrea, but this is Giulia's future. All that matters to my brother is taming Giulia's wild ways and if she learns a craft in the process, then surely he'll be happy she's bringing in an income, just like Teresa.' Zia looked pleased with herself and I had to admit that I couldn't see a single hole in her argument. My sister Teresa always did what was expected of her and Papà had supported her wish to become a dressmaker. I wasn't sure about being tamed by the nuns but if it meant Papà would let me work as a healer . . .

Mamma sighed. 'I want Giulia to have a chance. But we'd have to make a plan to convince him.'

'Then it's settled,' said Nonna Mariana, smiling broadly and sagging back into her chair with relief. 'We'll arrange for her to go as soon as possible, otherwise who knows what she might do next.'

'What about Giulia?' asked Mamma. 'We should make sure she's happy about this.'

'Oh, she knows,' said Zia Francesca with a smirk. 'She's been listening at the door this whole time and hasn't been stirring my sugo.'

Papà agreed to send me to the monastery after Mamma and Zia Francesca spoke to him about an opportunity to work there that had become available. Hard work and discipline were all I needed, they reminded him, not the threat of a husband.

The night air seeping through the stone walls of the cell was enough to force me from my stupor. I changed out of my dress and into my nightgown, slipping between the coarse sheets on the small bed, desperate to get warm. If only I was still in the kitchen at the trattoria, surrounded by the rich aromas, talking and laughing with Zia Francesca, warm, happy and content. My stomach grumbled loudly. I knew I should be grateful for being here but I was finding it hard to be thankful. I missed my mother, brothers and sisters, Nonna, and Zia Francesca's cheerful disposition and optimism. I still couldn't believe I wasn't going to be at Teresa's wedding. Had it been only this morning that Zia drove me to the village at the bottom of the mountain pass where Fra Giacomo, a monk from the monastery, waited for me with his cart loaded with supplies?

'Forza! Take this opportunity with both hands,' Mamma had said as we parted. 'Make us proud. Study hard and do what the nuns and monks ask of you. When you come home, what happened between you and your father will be forgotten.'

Papà had barely looked at me as he'd muttered a gruff goodbye before he'd left for the farm that morning, which made me even more angry.

'He might forget, but I won't.'

Mamma touched my cheek. 'He loves you and wants the best for you but he doesn't understand what it's like to be a young woman with her life just beginning. You're passionate and stubborn like he is. Just remember: if we're smart, we can get what we want, even in a man's world. But you have to be sensible. We rarely get second chances.'

My father might have thought that this was a way to subdue my wild ways, to remind me of my responsibilities as a young woman, but I saw this as an opportunity to improve my life.

However, it was only with my first sight of the monastery as the sun began to fall behind the mountain peaks that the enormity of what I'd done hit me.

'Home – there's no better sight,' Fra Giacomo had said with a sigh.

Home . . . I had never been so far from my home before. How was I going to manage among strangers without the love and support of my family for seven months?

Tears fell down my cheeks as I huddled under the covers. Tomorrow I would meet Mother Superior and I needed to make a good impression to prove that I deserved to be here. Without her support, I'd never last long enough to learn all I needed to become a herbalist – and change my path.